# HAVENWOOD FALLS SIN & SILK VOLUME THREE

## A HAVENWOOD FALLS SIN & SILK COLLECTION

MICHELE G. MILLER    R.K. RYALS    JD NELSON
E.J. FECHENDA

# HAVENWOOD FALLS SIN & SILK BOOKS

*Taming the Beast* by Nadirah Foxx

*Plans Laid Bare* by J.D. Nelson

*Shift of Fate* by Victoria Escobar

*Stolen Wishes* by Victoria Flynn

*Damned Allure* by Justine Winter

*Savage Salvation* by Kristie Cook

*Dark Seduction* by Michele G. Miller & R.K. Ryals

*Soul Laid Bare* by J.D. Nelson

*Stray With Me* by E.J. Fechenda

*Chase the Flames* by Desiree Lafawn

*Flirting With Death* by Nadirah Foxx

Also try the signature line, Havenwood Falls, the historical paranormal line, Legends of Havenwood Falls, and stories from the local supernatural college in Sun & Moon Academy.

Stay up to date at www.HavenwoodFalls.com

# ABOUT THIS BOOK

Three steamy paranormal romance novellas in this multi-author series showcasing the darker, edgier, and sexier side of Havenwood Falls.

*Dark Seduction* **by Michele G. Miller & R.K. Ryals**
Tied since birth to a darkness that longs to break free, spiritual psychic Harper Sinclair fights a never-ending battle with demonic spirits. Her only relief comes from the fallen angel for whom she's long ignored deep feelings. Elias Jamison lost his place in Heaven when he chose his friends over his creator. He fell, but he is not lost. For centuries, Elias maintained his innate goodness, fought against evil, and protected those in need—except for one. Grief-stricken, Elias pushed his loss aside for over a hundred years, but the deeper his feelings grow for Harper Sinclair, the deeper old guilt digs in.

*Soul Laid Bare* **by JD Nelson**
**The story of Mavis and Cameron's romance and fight to be together continues in this sequel to *Plans Laid Bare***
Mavis LeGrand is content in the mountains of Colorado with her incubus fiancé, Cameron, and things seem to be going well, but she knows behind the picturesque town and smiling faces, an evil lurks. She throws herself into finding a way to get Cameron's soul back from her soon-to-be father-in-law. But with a strong feeling of malice lingering over the town like a dense fog, Mavis can sense that she'll soon be in for a fight. Evil has no place in Havenwood Falls, and she'll be damned if she lets anyone or anything hurt the town or the ones she loves.

*Stray With Me* **by E.J. Fechenda**
As a descendant of a founding family of Havenwood Falls and

granddaughter of their coven's high priestess, Harlow Augustine's been raised to adhere to certain expectations. Dating a biker is the exact opposite of those. At first, it's an act of rebellion. Ryker Pride is like a forbidden fruit. Where she has deep roots in town and a big family, Ryker is an orphan lion shifter who grew up on the streets. His family is the SIN MC—"thugs and outlaws," according to her grandmother. When tragedy strikes, Harlow makes a rash decision and quickly learns that her magic has deadly consequences.

# DARK SEDUCTION

## MICHELE G. MILLER & R.K. RYALS

~ A Havenwood Falls Sin & Silk Novella ~

# Havenwood Falls
### sin & silk

## Dark Seduction

## MICHELE G. MILLER
## R.K. RYALS

# ALSO BY MICHELE G. MILLER

*From the Wreckage Series - Coming of Age Drama*

From the Wreckage

Out of Ruins

All That Remains

West: A POV Novel

After the Fall - Austin's story (New Adult)

Into the Fire - Dani's story

*The Prophecy of Tyalbrook Trilogy - YA Fantasy Romance*

Never Let You Fall

Never Let You Go

Never Without You - Coming 2018

*Havenwood Falls Novellas*

Awaken the Soul, A Havenwood Falls High novella Bk 1 (YA Fantasy)

Avenge the Heart, A Havenwood Falls High novella Bk 2 (YA Fantasy)

*Individual titles*

Last Call - New Adult Romance

**Co-written with Mindy Hayes (as Mindy Michele)**

*Paper Planes Series - Sweet Contemporary Romances*

Paper Planes and Other Things We Lost (YA)

Subway Stops and the Places We Meet (Adult)

Chasing Cars and the Lessons We Learned (NA)

# ALSO BY R.K. RYALS

## PARANORMAL ROMANCE BOOKS:

The Redemption Series

Redemption

Ransom

Retribution

Revelation

The Acropolis Series

The Acropolis

The Labyrinth

Deliverance

The Thorne Trilogy

Cursed

Possessed

Dancing with the Devil

In the Land of Tea and Ravens (Standalone book)

Havenwood Falls

Ink & Fire

Curse the Night

The Collector: Awakening

Dark Seduction

## FANTASY BOOKS:

The Scribes of Medeisia Series

Mark of the Mage

Tempest

Fist of the Furor

City in Ruins

The Standalone Embrace Yourself Series

The Story of Awkward

An Introvert's Tale

## CONTEMPORARY ROMANCE READS:

The Singing River

Hawthorne & Heathcliff

The Best I Could

Sex & Such

Capture the World

*To lovers of darkness*

# CHAPTER 1

## HARPER

"Oscar Wilde," I whispered, the author's name rolling off my tongue, merely a breath in the middle of the night. The name was an odd thing to think aloud, but I'd been listening to an audiobook recently and, after the dream I'd just had, it was a Wilde quote I thought of as I locked gazes with myself in the mirror.

*A dreamer is one who can only find his way by moonlight, and his punishment is that he sees the dawn before the rest of the world,* I mouthed.

I thrived during the night, but I felt lost after the dawn. The darkness was my friend, the day my punishment for paying too much attention to the night. Hell, the darkness was my family, in the form of shadow demons and spirits. My constant companions.

My face was pale, my long brown hair a chaotic nest around my head, my eyes home to dark circles put there by too little sleep.

The bathroom mirror was too honest, telling me things I didn't want to know about myself.

As a spiritual writer who'd been brought into this world after my pregnant mother was stabbed by a necromancer's athame, I'd always been tied to darkness in one form or another. It was this gift that introduced me to the fallen angel who helped me understand myself and subsequently, the other fallen angel who became my closest friend.

It was Elias Jamison—my best friend—I thought of now, my gaze on my reflection. My breathing was too rapid, my heart pounding, beads of sweat clinging to my brow. All because I'd had a scorching hot, completely inappropriate dream about the man who'd slowly worked his way past my wall of defenses over the last year. I trusted him more than I did anyone else.

He'd helped save my life twice.

I wasn't an easy person to befriend. I was reclusive, but Elias didn't seem to mind. The way he checked in with me—the texts he often sent—was important to me. Which was why when he left recently, his absence affected me more than I thought it would.

*Because you're angry*, the spirits around me said bluntly.

"No," I argued. "It was good he left."

When Elias had disappeared on angel business, I honestly thought the distance would be good. I'd become too dependent on having him near. I needed to be more open with the friends I'd made recently, but while I'd become closer to the others in town the last year, especially after our recent alliance to battle against the one known as the Collector, it was still Elias I felt most comfortable with.

Until now. Until this dream. This was why I shouldn't sleep.

"Is this going to become a habit?" a snide voice asked. The bronze-barbed mace—he was basically a baseball bat on steroids—who lived with me bounced near the doorway, impatient and agitated. Desi—short for Destroyer—was a sentient weapon that shape-shifted into a huge lion with wings. He'd been a gift from the first and only lover I'd ever had. I didn't quite know what finally losing my virginity to a high-ranking fallen angel at twenty-three and being rewarded with a weapon said about me, but I was all about collecting odd experiences and memories.

Desi was annoying as hell, but I couldn't live without him. Some people spoiled their cats and dogs. I spoiled my ancient shape-shifting pet weapon. Go figure. He needed lots of love, attention, and validation.

"What woke you up this time?" Desi asked.

It wasn't a nightmare that had me this restless.

A red blush bloomed across my skin, and I turned on the sink to splash cold water on my face. Images of flesh on flesh, Elias's hands and lips in places I'd never imagined his hands and lips being before, burned into my subconscious. Elias was a big man, brawny and broad, a beard covering a handsomely rugged face. His voice was raspy, deep, and sexy in a rock star kind of way.

He'd called my name in the dream. Over and over again.

I stared at the running water, watching as it circled the drain and disappeared, the dream replaying in my head.

*"Harper."*

*Elias breathed my name into my ear, surprising me, because I'd been asleep when he slid into bed behind me. His voice and the warm feel of his body woke me. I should have pushed him away, the shock of him being there bringing me to my senses, but all I felt was excitement and contentment.*

*"Finally," I whispered, because I wanted this.* Really *wanted this.*

*"Harper," he repeated, his arms pulling me into his embrace.*

*He was naked and hard. As was I—the naked part anyway—which was strange, because I didn't sleep naked. Tonight, however, there was only desire and need between us, his hand sweeping over the smooth contours of my stomach before slipping between my legs to caress me.*

*"You're wet," Elias said, satisfied.*

*His fingers slid through the moist heat to my clit, the sensation he caused with his touch so painfully pleasant that I almost lost it. My whimpers filled the room.*

*What was I doing? What were we doing?*

*"Elias—"*

*He stopped me with a kiss, rolling me over so quickly, I had no time to think before his lips crashed down onto mine, his tongue invading my mouth. His hand gripped my ass, our bodies pressed so closely together there was no space between us, the hard length of him hot against my belly.*

*"Tell me you're ready for me," he told me, pulling back to rest his forehead against mine, his breath fanning my lips.*

*"I'm ready."*

*He had me on my back in seconds, entering me quickly, as if he were afraid I'd change my mind. He filled me up completely.*

*"So tight," he growled.*

*His hips moved, and I lost the ability to think.*

*"Eli—"*

I had woken on the verge of saying his name. My hand drifted to my stomach, the sudden tickle in my gut new and fresh and different.

"I want Elias," I heard myself say, my voice huskier and sexier than usual.

My eyes shot to the mirror, to the gaze staring back at me.

"What'd you say?" I asked myself. My free hand found my lips, my fingers tracing my mouth.

Desi snorted from his spot by the door. "Look what you've done to her. She's finally gone crazy," he said, his words directed at the dark spirits.

Shadow figures ducked in and out of the bathroom, ghostly images that played with my shower curtains and hissed at Desi.

Despite the chaos and their presence, the hand I had on my stomach drifted lower, and I jerked, forcing it up and away from my body.

"Out!" I yelled suddenly, my voice too rough. "All of you!" Embarrassment turned my skin hot, and I shooed the mace and ghostly shadows out the door before slamming it shut and turning to slide down to the floor. "Holy shit!"

I wasn't sure what bothered me more. The fact that I had been about to pleasure myself in front of a group of demonic spirits and a sentient weapon or the fact that I was about to masturbate while thinking about my best friend.

"What's going on with you, Harper?" I asked aloud.

The freaky thing wasn't me talking to myself or having sexy dreams about Elias. It's not like dreams could be controlled, and I talked to myself all the time.

It was the fact that I *answered* myself, my voice seductive when I said, "Being horny isn't bad. Not doing something about it is completely terrible for a person's health."

I knew what this was. This was me fighting with myself because part of me wanted what another part of me wasn't sure of, but fear and confusion shot down my spine nonetheless, immobilizing me. The last time I'd fought with myself like this, the last time I'd been this conflicted, was when I was taken captive by an evil doll—long story—and held in a creepy dollhouse for weeks in a nightmare that had ended with me physically wounded and emotionally bruised.

*"No one understands you, Harper."* The shadows returned, thick, dark, and seductive, their voices strong and powerful in my head. Their voices didn't sound like mine. I was used to their voices.

*"But we understand you. We understand you like no one else ever will. We understand your desire and your needs."*

Trembling, I slid back up the door and turned cautiously toward my mirror.

It was just me. The same plain Jane I'd always been—messy brown hair, scared green eyes, and a plaid pajama set that was two sizes too big.

*This* was the Harper I knew. Only there were dark forms crowded behind me, shadow people, their wispy, sinister arms outstretched as if to hug me.

*"We are everything you will ever need and more."*

Desi pounded on the bathroom door. "At least use the air freshener when you're done."

His light joke broke the tension, and the shadows scattered. A small, nervous laugh escaped me, my wide eyes dropping to my hands where they gripped the bathroom sink so tightly, the knuckles were white.

I felt like I was torn in two, completely divided between who I used to be and who I was tempted to be. I'd even started talking to myself in my sleep, getting up at night to leave written messages I found later. I'd once written a message in red lipstick on my mirror. It was hell to clean off.

Releasing the sink, I walked on unsteady, light feet from the bathroom, into the bedroom, and out into the kitchen. My hands were swifter than my brain, quick to make a cup of hot cocoa that I cradled in my palms, the warmth comforting.

Desi followed, quieter than he'd been before. It was hard reading him in weapon form. He didn't have eyes or lips. When he communicated, words were just *heard*. I didn't question how it worked. I was just glad he could speak, sarcasm and all, because he kept me from feeling lonely.

My mouth was full of hot chocolate when Desi murmured, "You feel different, and I don't think it's because you had a sex dream."

*Holy hell!*

Cocoa spewed everywhere. "You didn't just say that!"

"What did I say then?" he asked sweetly. "It's—"

"There are certain pet privileges you don't have."

"I'm not a pet," he spat.

Arguing was normal for Desi and me, but tonight it cloaked an entirely different problem. And it had nothing to do with dreams. I felt different. Antsy and impatient. As if my body was telling me I needed to *do* something.

My phone, which I rarely used because the signal tended to be bad in Havenwood Falls, lay on the kitchen counter, and I touched it lightly.

The urge to text Elias was strong, but I'd promised myself I wouldn't reach out to him until he returned. Elias had an entire life and problems of his own outside of me. Besides, it would be a little weird to text him after having an erotic dream about him, right? More so since it was the middle of the night.

I tapped the phone's screen and touched the messenger icon to scroll through our old texts. I was one of those people who never deleted anything.

Sweet memories surfaced, the messages a reminder of the first time I'd met Elias outside Coffee Haven. The day I realized he was open to befriending a naïve, shy girl who'd just experienced her first heartbreak and learned exactly how deep her ties to Hell and the spirit world went. Christmas in Havenwood Falls a year ago. Back when all I'd cared about was tackling a list of firsts.

A lot had happened in a year.

"You've got too much drama for being a loner. You need a fuck buddy." The moment the words left my mouth, my hands flew to my lips, my eyes widening.

Desi bounced up onto the counter, leaving scratches on the surface. He was going to ruin my house.

"Was that you?" he asked, incredulous.

It *was* me, but I was behaving differently than usual.

Me and *not* me.

*"Because you have different needs now,"* the shadows revealed. *"Let go, Harper. Let go and be everything you were born to be. Listen to yourself."*

"Your eyes," Desi breathed.

Grabbing my phone, I clicked the camera icon and put it on selfie mode. My eyes were dilated, the black pupils completely overtaking the green.

"I'm pretty, aren't I?" I asked myself, a small smile lifting the corner of my lips.

Me and *not* me.

This me liked the way she looked in oversized plaid pajamas. She oozed a confidence about her messy hair and startled eyes that I lacked.

This me had a thing for fallen angel Elias Jamison, and she wasn't the kind to sit back and let him slide through her fingers.

"We know each other so well," I said aloud, my gaze on the camera. My finger pressed the picture key, my brows arched as it captured my image. "I should send this to him. I look good."

Was I possessed? All because of a sex dream? Did demons possess you if you had dreams about sex? Because if they did, the entire population was a walking exorcism project.

"Wow." Desi whistled. "You've officially lost your mind."

I didn't answer him because I was sending a picture text I wasn't sure I wanted to send.

# CHAPTER 2

## ELIAS

*I* flipped through my stack of mail and stomped up the stairs leading from the Ski-Ventures hangar to my residence, my boots bleeding slush and snow with each step, my hand stilling when I spotted familiar writing.

*Miss us yet? Enjoy the snow!*

Breckin and Viv. My smile was automatic. I flipped the postcard and was greeted by the cerulean water, golden sand, and lush foliage of the Maldives.

"Assholes."

Thanks to the Court, which had made a special exception to the rules on the memory wards that protected the town, the damn teens could traipse about the world without fear of forgetting home, while I was stuck in the frigid hell of Havenwood Falls, Colorado, in January.

*But they're safe.* That's what mattered.

I slapped my keys onto the hook by the door, then opened the drawer of the table sitting at the entrance to my place and dropped the postcard in with the rest. A postcard sent as they left each destination. Albania, Bhuton, Sri Lanka, now the Maldives. They hit destinations average eighteen-year-olds wouldn't consider, because unexpected meant harder to find.

Mentally exhausted from my own unexpected trip, I left the lights off and did a sweep of the place. I'd finished walking the rooms and was headed for the couch when my cell phone vibrated with an incoming call. *Hamon.*

Falling into the deep cushions, I answered the call on an exhale. "Yeah?"

"Everything secure?" Breckin's father asked with little emotion. He may have stepped away from leadership last spring, but Hamon would always be a commander.

"Everything's fine here. I stopped by the Medical Center and let Rachel know we were back."

"*You're* back," Hamon corrected. "I'm already on my way to Bintan."

"Bintan?" Bintan, an island in the South China Sea, was Hamon's base of operations when he played the role of dirty angel. After what happened with him, Breckin, and Viv down in Amartía —a playground, of sorts, for fallen and damned angels—I'd assumed he'd stay clean for a while. Apparently, I was mistaken.

"Do you think Andras and his crew were the only fallen after them, Elias? Did you think our trip to Latvia would be the last of its kind? While threats to Breckin and Vivienne remain, I can't walk away."

There would be more trouble, of course there would be. Hamon had amassed a long list of powerful enemies through the centuries. As a Nephilim, his son was a target. And Viv? Her bloodline and special connection with Breckin made her a larger target. That's the only reason the Court agreed to change the memory wards. Allowing Breckin and Viv to leave town, and still retain their memories, not only kept them safe from our enemies, but kept Havenwood Falls safe as well. No one wanted a bunch of fallen angels and demons with vendettas roaming this town. At least not the kind who had no qualms about shredding our peaceful community. I'd raised Breckin as my own, and I'd watched over Viv since birth, and her mother, Rachel, before her, and Rachel's mother before that. For more than a hundred years, I kept the Freeman women safe. All but one, and her loss had fueled Hamon's rebellion from the Divine—and my guilt—ever since.

"There are other ways. Ways that won't risk your redemption."

"Always worried about my redemption," Hamon said with a low laugh. "She would be proud."

"She'd call us idiots for all the shit we've done wrong through the years, that's what she'd do," I corrected as the dagger of her loss twisted. "Go to Bintan, gather intel, boss a few lowlifes around, then get your ass back here without inciting a war we don't need." I'd promised Breckin I would try my best to keep his father around.

"Take a break, Elias. Keep your eyes and ears open, maybe stay at the house with Rachel, but take a break. Give that cute little psychic of yours a call."

"She's a friend," I replied as evenly as possible. "And how in the hell would you know if she's cute?" All I needed was Hamon and his damn movie star face sniffing around Harper Sinclair.

Hamon chuckled. "Mm-hmm, sure she is. I'll keep in touch." He ended the call without giving me the opportunity to reply. Frustrated, I flipped my phone onto the coffee table.

*Harper.* Closing my eyes, I combed my fingers through my too-long beard as a vision of her face the last time I'd seen her played behind my eyelids. She was a mess after the ordeal with the Collector, her green eyes haunted, her brow permanently wrinkled, like her mind fought back a barrage of demons. She'd looked like hell, been through hell—and I'd left.

*"You left her alone, like you left Phaedra alone,"* a voice skittered across my mind. My eyes snapped open. The living room was dark, but I could see everything clearly with my angel vision. There was no one here. I turned on the lamp anyway. A shadow seemed to move away as the feeling of something scraping against my brain shocked me. *"Alone and weakened,"* the voice teased.

"Fuck." Panic seized control. I jumped up from my couch and steered myself toward the bedroom, peeling off the filth-covered clothing I'd worn for days as I went. The shower door bounced off the wall as I flung it open and yanked on the hot water knob. While waiting for steam to appear, I grabbed fresh clothes, brushed my teeth, and laughed at the man reflected back at me over the sink. "It's fucking three in the morning. What's your plan here?"

"I'll drive by, make sure things are quiet. No big deal." I answered myself like a lunatic.

*That's why you're taking a shower and putting on clean clothes? Because you're just driving by?* My internal voice made a nuisance of itself.

Clearly, the man in the mirror believed my motives about as much as I believed in shaving. I glared at my reflection and turned toward the shower, in dire need of the hot water and a good head clearing.

While I lathered, shampooed, and rinsed, I shook my head at the crazy ride my thoughts took. Harper was fine. The fallen wouldn't hunt her as they had Phaedra. They couldn't connect me to her. We'd been friendly, social. There was no reason to worry. Not yet, anyway.

She was fine, but that didn't stop me from throwing on my clothes, grabbing the keys to my truck, and hauling my ass across town fifteen minutes later.

Just in case.

The first flakes fell before I hit Main Street. Fantastic. It was three in the morning, snowing, and I was driving to Harper's unannounced after weeks with no communication. *Checking things out, that's all*, I reminded myself.

Harper lived north of town in a secluded little mountain cabin she'd bought over a year ago. It was her first step toward finding herself after years of seclusion, thanks to her gifts. She loved the place. As her friend, and an overprotective one at that, I'd prefer it if she lived closer to town. Or other humans. Though the whispers that had toyed with my mind less than thirty minutes ago had not returned, the closer I came to Harper's, the tighter my grip on my steering wheel became.

Nerves maybe? I'd missed her more than I'd expected. Even after tracking four fallen ones across the Baltic states for weeks and ending them, the first thing I'd thought about when it was over was returning to Havenwood Falls and finally dealing with Harper and whatever was between us.

I frowned, bothered by my desire to see her, and slowed as the narrow drive to the cabin curved left, the path covered with thick snow. Hidden and untouched by tracks of any sort. By the looks of it, Harper hadn't left home in days.

As the trees thinned and the silhouette of her small cabin came into view, I cut my headlights and rolled to a stop on the edge of her property. The glow of the winter moon reflected off the white powder covering everything, giving me plenty of visibility along with my enhanced vision. I rolled down my window, then sat back and listened.

I stiffened and sniffed at the cold air, the vague scent of Hell making the hair on the back of my neck raise. Harper oozed darkness—it was sexy as hell—but tonight it was different. Stronger. I shoved back my angelic gifts as they rose to destroy the evil I sensed beyond her door. *She's not evil,* I reminded them. *Her darkness is beautiful. She's chosen goodness.*

*And you think you can keep her that way, angel?* The voice of doubt shouted in my ear.

My cell phone vibrated twice in the console, indicating a text. "So help me, if this is another picture of paradise from Breck . . ."

*Harper,* my screen read, with no message in the text field. I looked at the cabin, then back at my phone. Could she see me sitting out here, like the creeper I was? There was no message, but there was an attachment. My finger tapped the screen, almost reluctantly, as though it were afraid of what might pop up.

What greeted me was a picture so damn alluring, my jeans became uncomfortable. Her normally green eyes appeared nearly black as she stared at me with flirtatiously arched brows, a gently crooked smile, and the sexiest bedhead I'd seen in a long while.

I peered through the falling snow and searched for the telltale sign of her face peeking through a crack in the curtains. The rumbling of my truck must have woken her. I looked back at the phone again. *Shit.* There was something in that smile, something so not like the shy woman I'd come to know. I should have left, but I wasn't an idiot.

**Elias: Can't sleep?**

**Harper: Not alone I can't. Not when I've been thinking about you. When are you coming back to town?**

Not alone? Thinking about me? *Go home, Elias. This woman deserves better than a middle-of-the-night booty call.* And that's exactly what my body begged for. I typed a reply.

**Elias: I walked through my door about an hour ago.**

The three little dots that showed she was replying moved. Then stopped. Then moved again.

**Harper: What are you doing?**

My fingers touched the keys dangling from the ignition. *Go. The. Fuck. Home.*

**Elias: I'm sitting outside your door.**

# CHAPTER 3

## HARPER

*W*hat the hell was Elias Jamison doing outside my house?

"Yes!" I cried, triumphant, the flirtatious side of me happy to see he'd responded to the text while the rest of me revolted. I'd flirted with the man I considered my best friend, whether or not he considered me that in return.

I'd just changed the game. With a text. With words. It was always words that changed my life—first with a spiritual message from a demon a year ago, and now this.

I clutched my stomach, afraid to text back. Afraid to look outside my window. This new antsy feeling—not to mention the sudden lustful thoughts I was having—was not something I wanted to invite Elias into.

"I swear I'm not crazy!" I hissed.

"Is it you telling me that or this new psycho side of yourself?" Desi asked. He was enjoying this. "Life with you is never dull. Not recently."

I was not amused.

"And when did you start being rude to guests?" Desi asked, headed for the door. I knew exactly what he planned to do.

"Don't you dare!" I warned, horrified.

The door flew open, blowing in frigid air, the wind hitting me from across the room. A truck door slammed, and I pressed against my kitchen counter. Something about Elias, even with the trust I had in him, made me uncomfortable. In a good way.

The minute he stomped onto my porch, his burly frame filling my door, I knew I was in trouble.

*"He'll bring nothing but misery,"* the shadows warned.

"Come in," Desi invited cheerfully.

Elias perused me, his sharp gaze searching my face. "Hey." His voice sent shivers down my spine. It always did. Even before the dream. He took a hesitant step into the room, his brows furrowing. "Feels like it's been longer than what it has."

My silence was loud, but I was scared to speak, scared of what might pop out of my mouth.

My front door closed behind Elias.

"Little late to be out, isn't it?" Desi asked the angel, amused. We were making his night.

Unlike with me, the mace never bothered Elias. Angels knew who and what the Destroyer was—an ancient weapon created by gods to fight alongside heroes and heroines. From the days when immortals walked the earth freely and legends were born until now, the mace existed to defeat and triumph.

"How have you been?" Elias asked me, ignoring Desi.

"G-good," I answered finally, tucking my messy hair behind my ears.

Elias's lips twitched, affection evident in his gaze, and for a moment I saw him the way I should see him. A good friend.

Until he moved.

Sauntering over to my kitchen counter, he propped his hip against it and leaned forward, bringing him a little too close despite the barrier between us. "Quite the text you sent, Harper?"

And there it was. The reason for our awkwardness.

He made it sound like a question, as if he was trying to figure me out.

I was trying to figure me out, too. Right along with why the hell my belly was a mess of fluttering butterflies.

"Quite the response I got," I replied, bolder than was usual for me.

"Response?"

"You showing up here."

Elias fidgeted. "I was checking in after being gone. I missed you."

Warmth and unease bloomed in my belly. Warmth because he'd been worried about me. Unease because his absence—because of the timing— was another reason for our awkwardness. I'd been healing from a physical and mental injury when he left.

"I'm okay," I whispered.

Elias's eyes narrowed. "Are you?" He leaned closer, his height enough to eliminate the space between us even with the counter. "The text, Harper."

He wasn't going to let that go.

I shrugged. "I was feeling photogenic."

"You are a terrible liar."

Truth was, I had no idea how to answer him.

"Maybe I wanted  . . ." My words trailed off as Elias's eyes darted off to the side.

"They're still here," he said.

I knew he was talking about the shadows, the demons and dark spirits attracted to my kind of power.

*"He hates us."*

A sense of foreboding settled over me, my heart filling with dread. "They never left," I told him.

The shadows kept a healthy distance from Elias, their dark forms a smoky blackness against the walls near the bedroom.

Guilt flashed across Elias's face. He'd left right after our battle with the Collector, missing everything that had transpired since.

Time healed many wounds, but there hadn't been enough time for mine to scab over. Since my captivity, I'd been a mess of night terrors and prophetic dreams. My need for the shadows and their presence as well as their need for me had also grown.

*Don't mock me!* I told myself.

I wanted to hit my head against a wall.

"Have they bothered you?" Elias asked finally, his gaze tracking the shadow forms.

I could breathe around Elias in a way I couldn't breathe around anyone else. He calmed the darkness in me. Now, though, he was bringing out something just as terrifying.

"Lust," I answered myself aloud, the word a husky sigh I knew came from deep within me.

Elias turned back to me. "What?"

Desi laughed. "I should probably go away for a few days."

"Don't you dare!" Elias and I both commanded simultaneously.

It was obvious neither of us was comfortable with the way things were going between us at the moment. This was uncharted territory.

"They aren't bothering me," I replied, finally answering his question the way I'd meant to answer it, while backing farther into my kitchen. "As a matter of fact, I'm doing great."

My body was on fire, my cheeks heated, my hands wanting desperately to get rid of my clothes and his.

"You s-should really go." My words came out ruder than I meant them to. "*Be angry at him!*" the shadows yelled within my mind.

Elias rounded the counter.

I grabbed at a kitchen towel hanging from the handle of my oven to hold it up like a shield. "Don't."

"What's up with you, Harper?" he asked, genuinely concerned.

If he came any closer, I was going to do something I wasn't sure I'd regret, but I wasn't sure he'd be open to.

"You know, I'm actually not feeling all that well. Could be contagious. Maybe—"

"I don't get sick."

"Elias," I whispered.

He leaned down, and I did the one thing I knew would change our relationship forever. For better or for worse.

# CHAPTER 4

## ELIAS

*H*arper's tongue shoved its way into my mouth with the aggression of a sex-starved teenager, and I shifted back, off balance at the unexpectedness of her move. The small step drew our lips apart just enough that Harper gasped and looked up, her eyes clouded with confusion. Her pupils were completely dilated, the shadows infiltrating her home coming closer.

"You stopped. Why did you stop?" Her face collapsed, her small fists suddenly pounding my chest. "You're not supposed to stop."

Her words were thick with desire, but there was also anger.

"Whoa." More worried for her safety than mine, I caught one of Harper's wrists and twisted, pinning her arm to her side. "What the hell, Harper?"

Her shadows pushed closer still—crowding around her feet and spitting obscenities. Their hatred for me—an intruder—was evident in every vile comment they hissed my way.

"Make me forget," she begged, her eyes welling with tears. "Why won't you make me forget? You owe me that much."

*Fuck. Me.* My hand shoved into the mass of hair at her nape.

"Owe you for what?" I asked, my gaze holding hers.

Harper's emotions were at war. Desire curved her body invitingly into mine even as torment clouded her eyes. Why bother

28

asking? I'd left when she'd needed me. I was an asshole. And this confusing woman—who was both light and dark, powerful in ways I wasn't sure she yet knew—had me tangled up in emotions I couldn't process. I knew sex. I knew pleasure. But this? This was something entirely different.

*This* was Harper. She was unlike any woman I'd ever met.

"Elias?" My name was a petition whispered in the breath between us.

I licked at my bottom lip, and Harper lifted on her toes with a whimper. Fueled by guilt, and a good dose of lust, my right hand slid over her ass and gripped the curve of her thigh. "I didn't drive over here to seduce you."

She stiffened, desire becoming rage, before pushing at me. "Why not seduce me? Seduction is better than abandonment." She laughed coldly. "It seems I'm much better at being seduced than making people stay."

*Lucas.* Damn him! I ached at Harper's vulnerability. It radiated from her being the way Lucas's mark colored her aura. It was that mark, that iridescent blue hue of another fallen angel, that made me keep my distance, romantically, for more than a year. Lucas didn't own her. He never claimed he did. But loyalty to a long-ago comrade had tied my hands. I'd thought he might return to her. I should have known better. Very few angels settled down. We were warriors, protectors, the ones with Divine knowledge of what had been and what will come—we weren't created to play house with humans. We were merely biding our time, and choosing sides, until the end.

Lucas had hurt her more than I'd realized. I was happy she'd allowed herself to be angry, but . . .

I leaned against the counter and crossed my arms. "Who is talking to me right now, Harper? I'll take the anger if that's what makes *you* feel better, but I'll be damned if I let those little shits—"

"Are you attacking them, Elias?" She waved her hands at the room, at the spitting shadows flanking us. "They've been there for me."

Fury filled my chest like a child's balloon as I glared at our audience. "Oh, to hell with that. *I'm* here for you," I countered, my fingers snagging her oversized top to tug her against my chest. "I won't abandon you. I'm not him, Harper."

She pushed at me again, ducking out of my embrace to move away from me. Her fist hit the countertop and dishes rattled in the cabinets below. The sound seemed to set her off, and she spun. Jerking open another cabinet above her head, she grabbed a glass tumbler and threw it. It flew across the room to shatter against her wall.

I started, shock momentarily paralyzing me. No matter what emotions Harper was feeling, this wasn't entirely Harper.

Yanking her toward me, I gripped her chin. "Do you want my kisses?" I ground out, my fingers digging into her skin. Harper fought my grip. I won.

Grinning at her submission, as minuscule as it was, I dropped my forehead to hers and slipped my free hand beneath her top. "You want me to touch you, Harper?" Twin flashes of red colored her cheeks when my fingertips brushed the underside of her bare breast. She leaned into my touch, her desire evident in her scent, her coloring, the way her throat moved as she swallowed. Her eyes said yes, when her voice didn't. Anger hardened my features. "Then get rid of the damn shadows."

We held our positions, deadlocked in this battle. Then her defiance disappeared. I tensed at the change.

"You want us gone?" she asked, smiling sweetly. "Are you that afraid of the darkness, angel?"

Rage blinded me at her use of *us*, sending my arms around her waist and back, as I kicked Harper's leg and swept her off her feet. We hit the wooden floor and Harper growled and bucked, her hands pushing at my shoulders while I straddled her hips.

"Get the fuck out," I said through a growl of my own, my hands catching hers and pinning them over her head. "You do not control her."

I released the damper on my powers, sending a flood of light across the kitchen.

"You can't have her," I said as I dropped my elbows on either side of her face. My hands still gripped her wrists above her head. The shadows screeched as my power hit them in pulsing waves. My eyes studied hers, watching for their change. "She's mine." The truth of the sentiment burned my throat like a brand.

On a heavy exhale, Harper went from fighting me to lying still, her dilated pupils returning to normal. "Elias . . ." Her words trailed off, guilt leeching the color from her face. She inhaled, as if bracing herself. "I-I . . ."

I maintained my position—my hands locked around her wrists, my body hovering over hers. I should have released her, but I couldn't. I didn't want to. "How often have they done that since I left?"

"Often enough." It was obvious by her pained expression that Harper may have been consumed by shadows, but she'd been coherent the entire time. "I want to tell you I'm sorry, but I can't. I won't." Tears leaked from her eyes.

I bent lower, bringing our chests flush, and released her arms. My hands went straight to her jaw, cupping it. "Don't." I swiped at her damp cheeks. "You don't owe me, or anyone else, apologies, Harper. You're allowed to be angry. Though I'd prefer for you to tap into those emotions without the help of your little friends. Think we can work on that?"

She hesitated. "What if part of me doesn't want to do it without them?"

"I'll be here to help, regardless." I kissed her forehead and moved to stand over her. "But I know you have the strength to do it on your own." I offered her my hand.

Harper stared at my palm. "I'm not sure you know what you're getting yourself into." Her fingers slipped into mine. "I-I think I prefer forgetting," she stuttered, almost shyly, as I brought her to her feet.

"Forgetting, huh?" I asked with a wink and, once again, my

hand found its way around the curve of her ass. "I could help with that. If you want me to?" I drew her leg up toward my waist.

Her unease cleared at my question, her earlier brazen confidence returning with it.

"Are you finally seducing me, Elias Jamison?" she asked as she walked her fingers up my chest until she cupped my neck. We'd crossed a line tonight, and neither one of us wanted to go back.

"If I were seducing you, Harper Sinclair, I'd be buried between your legs and you'd be screaming my name already."

Her fingernails sank into my skin. "Show me."

My mouth collided with hers, my tongue sweeping from one side to the other, with as much grace as a drunk sailor after nine months at sea. Harper moaned, then bit my tongue gently. Before she released her bite, I had her propped on the edge of her countertop, both legs wrapped firmly around my backside, my fingers unbuttoning her plaid pajama top.

I'd liberated three buttons when a muttered "It's about time" came from somewhere in the cabin. *Desi.*

Harper wrenched back with a gasp, and my gut tightened. I stole a glimpse of the flesh beneath her top before my hands went to her knees to unwrap myself from her legs. Leaving my palms resting gently on the tops of her thighs, I stared down at her flushed face and perplexed expression.

My knuckles brushed over Harper's beard-rashed chin. "He's a pain in the ass, isn't he?"

"It's not my fault you two turned me into a voyeur," Desi said from wherever he hid. "I offered to go."

He poked out from around the bottom cabinet, and I pinned him with a glare. "You're not allowed to leave her side, *Destroyer.*"

My hands settled on Harper's hips, and I picked her up and lowered her to the floor as Desi snorted. "I never pegged you for an exhibitionist, angel."

Harper leaned her shoulder into my chest as she turned toward the mouthy mace, a comical look of exasperation on her tired face. "Go away."

For a weapon with no actual facial features, he came off as rather disgruntled when he huffed and bounced out of the kitchen. "Tell me to stay, tell me to go," he mumbled as he passed by my foot.

"Go cuddle one of Harper's pillows, if you're lacking companionship."

Laughing softly from my arms, Harper poked my side. "You're antagonizing him."

"I'm sure he'll return the favor."

"You know I will," Desi shouted before a door slammed shut.

I lifted a brow and caught Harper's gaze. Her hands clasped in front of her chest as we parted awkwardly. Now that the ardor had cooled, and Desi had left, our aborted kiss hung between us.

I covered her wringing hands with mine. "Let's get you to bed. You have to be exhausted."

"Stay with me?"

At Harper's urging I lay—fully clothed (my requirement; I knew my limits)—on my back as she snuggled into my side, her face resting in the dip between my arm and chest. She fell asleep quickly, her arm heavy across my waist. I spent the hours counting her breaths and watching the way her shadows lingered in her bedroom. They kept their distance, a very good thing for them, because I was in the mood to kick some demon ass for what they'd done to her.

She'd come to rely on them while I was away. I should have considered that possibility before I'd left. I would not let the darkness consume her. I would show Harper how to live life. A life she controlled.

# CHAPTER 5

## ELIAS

*H*arper rushed out her door as I pulled up in front of her cabin just after noon the next day, a smile on her face. She waved for me to stay in the truck as she locked up, and I took the moment to appreciate the view. Her tiny frame was bundled up against the cold in layers of clothing. She looked like a colorful snow woman. *A hell of a sexy snow woman*, I thought when she turned my way, her ever-present backpack, also known as Desi's ride, swinging from her hand as she crossed the yard, then climbed into my truck.

She looked more Harper-like today. It wasn't fair of me to assess her that way, but it was true. Her demon shadows lingered in the cab and around the truck as we drove, gently sweeping her shoulders when they got the chance, as if caressing her. But her eyes were a twinkling bright green—happy, excited—which meant she was keeping them at bay. I reached across the cab and snagged the thick braid pulled to the side of her head beneath her red knit hat. "Thank you for coming today."

Harper's lips pursed as I tugged her hair. "Thank you for asking me out."

I'd woken her early this morning, telling her I needed to run some errands before asking her to join me for the day at the town's

34

annual Winterfest celebration—our first official date. A badly needed date, after a year of tiptoeing around our feelings, my weeks away, and last night's battle. She'd eagerly agreed.

We parked two streets over from the square, and I rounded the back of my truck to grab the large duffel I'd packed earlier as Harper jumped down from the passenger side. Her brows lifted when she caught sight of the heavy bag on my shoulder.

"So I did something." I held out my hand and her gloved fingers slipped around mine. A shadow hissed at my side, then disappeared.

"You did something?" Harper prompted. We moved with the rest of the pedestrian traffic and walked toward the square. "Do I want to know what you're carrying in that bag?"

"I figured it was time I got to see just how talented you are with those hands of yours." My words caused Harper to stumble, her mouth parting slightly as she looked up at me. I grinned wickedly. "With art, my little *umbra amans*. Your mind is terribly dirty these days."

Harper inhaled sharply, her shadows nearing at my words. It was an endearment, *umbra amans*—shadow lover. They circled Harper like lovers, constantly weaving inky paths in her presence. And the way she embraced them . . .

*"You play with fire, angel,"* hissed the little guilt demon who'd suddenly appeared at my side. Walking on, I pretended he didn't exist. If Harper heard the shadow's comment, she ignored it as well. She threw me a thoughtful side-eye through her dark lashes as we entered the square, and I steered her toward a table with sign-in sheets.

Nodding to the teen volunteer, I took a plastic numbered snowflake stake and turned to Harper. "In case you hadn't guessed, I signed us up for the snow sculpture contest."

Winterfest was a celebration of all things ice and snow. Like every Havenwood Falls festival, this one had food, live performances, and booths selling themed items, but the main attractions were the competitions: one for ice castles, the other for snow sculptures. The residents in this town came out of the woodwork for competitions, even on below-freezing days. When it came down to it, Havenwood Falls was a bunch of supernatural beings trying to prove whose species was best in the only way the Court would allow—random contests. There were plenty of humans here, too. Competitiveness wasn't owned by the supes. Hell, the humans carried feuds as spitefully as the shifters and vamps did.

"Does it bother you?" Harper asked suddenly.

Stepping out of the line forming at the table, I closed the gap between us. "Does what bother me?"

"You called me a shadow lover. I—"

"*My* shadow lover," I corrected, my arm slipping between Harper and Desi's backpack to draw her closer. "I called you my shadow lover. There are things that bother me about you, Harper Sinclair, but that is not one of them." What her shadows intended for her bothered me. What bothered me even more were the emotions she brought out in me. Breckin was right—love was such a human sentiment. A feeling angels shouldn't have. But this human had sparked the forbidden inside of me.

Her concerned gaze searched the area. She didn't like drawing attention.

I cleared my throat. "Hey, don't worry about everyone else. Look at me."

Darkened green eyes found mine. They weren't completely dark; she was still there. "They hate you."

I spied one of her shadows ducking toward me. My face lowered, my lips brushing hers. "They can kiss my ass."

I gave her no chance to reply or address the public kiss I'd just given her in front of half the town. Instead, I applied pressure to her back, leading her toward the other end of the town square.

When we found our assigned spot—number nine—I dropped my bag of tools at the base of a mound of snow shoveled in by the event organizers for each contestant and circled the area.

Scratching at my beard, I cursed myself. How in the hell did I end up here?

A shriek followed by a masculine peal of laughter drew my attention over my shoulder in time to see Graysin Ravenal shove Weston Everett into their mound of half-sculpted snow.

"This is a family event, Everett!" She kicked at the pile. "I can't take you anywhere." Behind them, Callie Montgomery and Ronan Bishop stood watching as Graysin's tantrum continued, "I can't believe I was sitting here stroking the shaft, trying to get it nice and smooth . . ."

"Stroking it, huh?" Everett chuckled from the snow bank. Graysin dropped her head with a self-deprecating groan and slapped at his leg.

Ronan snickered at whatever Weston had sculpted, and Callie pinched his side, as her whispered "Don't you dare laugh" carried my way.

"For once, I can't fault the guy. I'd have revolted, too, if you'd forced me into that."

Callie fought back her own laughter. "You would have formed a massive hard-on?"

Leaning into her side, his cool blue eyes held hers. An intimate look passed between them, and I averted my gaze, but I couldn't help but catch his words. "I always form massive hard-ons when I'm with you."

I snorted, and Ronan's attention jerked my way. My hands rose in apology for eavesdropping. It's not like I could help my angelic hearing.

Ronan nodded. "The shit we do for our women, huh?"

Glancing up, Callie's face turned bright red when she caught my stare, before her gaze landed on Harper behind me. Or so I assumed, from the curious grin forming on her lips as she moved to help Graysin.

I turned to Harper, ready to tease her about Ronan's comments, but she wasn't there. I looked over the snow mound to find her outside our little roped-off work area, hugging herself, her hands rubbing at her arms as she glanced about the festival. Her shadows gathered around her, as if they wanted to keep her warm but she wasn't letting them. It was odd seeing dark spirits acting chivalrous. Most of them lingered at her feet and legs, like stray cats seeking attention, but one loitered near her shoulders, floating from one ear to the other.

*"You don't belong with him, Harper,"* it whispered. *"This will only hurt you in the end, not him."*

The little bastard.

"Harper?" I scooped a handful of snow from our pile and walked toward her carefully, like one would approach a frightened child, my actions agitating the shadows. "Stepping out, remember? Remember that first-time-for-everything list you were so adamant about a year ago?"

Harper blinked once, then twice, her nearly black eyes coming into focus as I drew closer. There was something so exposed about Harper since her abduction and captivity last month.

"I thought we could sculpt Desi in his winged lion form," I suggested, reaching for her. All but the shadow at her shoulder slinked away.

Her backpack shook. "I like that idea," the mace with the giant ego sang.

Harper looked at me, her wrinkled brow smoothing. I kept speaking. "Though I thought we could improve on him some. Maybe give him a hump?"

Desi hissed. "I am a lion with majestic wings the likes of which you've never had, angel."

He had me there. "A horn, then? Desi, the uni-lion?"

A strangled laugh burst from Harper's mouth. "You're egging him on," she managed as Desi grumbled. The black slowly leaked from her eyes.

"I am," I admitted, drawing her into our work space. "But only to get a smile out of you. You okay?"

She nodded. "Sorry. I don't think I've gotten over it . . .

everything that happened with the Collector. I feel . . . exposed somehow, being out here."

I released the damper on my power, allowing my energy to scare her demons away. After last night, I'd withdrawn the force I used over them, out of respect for her relationship with the darkness. But seeing her like this shattered my willingness to allow them to siphon away her strength. The last shadow hissed and floated back.

I tilted her chin and cupped her face. "Harper, nothing is going to hurt you here. Look around."

Her eyes danced around the square to study the people enjoying this sunny, but cold, Saturday in January.

"Whatever you're worried about isn't going to happen on a day like today. And, if it did, I'm here." I drew her gaze back to mine. "Desi and I won't let anything hurt you again."

It wasn't my fault she'd been hurt. I wasn't in her life then, or not in any way that counted. I wasn't officially in her life now either, but that was fast changing. As complicated as things would be between us—a semi-fallen angel and a psychic tied to demons— I wanted it to happen.

Harper lifted to her toes and kissed the side of my mouth, her hand on my shoulder for balance. "A winged lion with a horn?" she asked playfully. "I like it."

We spent the next several hours carving a winged Desi, sans horn, out of snow. Harper's hands were artistically talented, as I knew they would be. She was drawn to art and photography, and had a good eye.

I admired the wings she'd built up, her hands deftly wielding the metal tools I'd brought to individually carve out each feather. "It's a shame you weren't able to draw growing up."

Biting her lip, she leaned back and studied her work. "I wanted to, but when all you see is death and fear every time you touch pen or paper, you lose interest. A beautiful hobby becomes a very scary undertaking."

"Hey, Harper," a high school guy who'd worked with his friends and flirted with Harper all afternoon from our left side suddenly called, his eyes full of hope. "We're going to get some hot cider. Would you like some?"

Harper threw me an embarrassed glance. "Um, I'm good, but thank you for offering."

The teen's face fell, but he nodded and turned back to his smiling friends. The boys were amused by their buddy's rejection. His *no big deal* face reminded me of Breckin's during his teenage years when he'd been let down. Feeling embarrassingly parental, I jumped to my feet under the pretense of needing to examine our work from another vantage point.

As Harper lowered her head and went back to making wings, I stopped the guy. "She's too old for you and spoken for, but if you buy her a hot chocolate, she'll think you're a hero."

Handing him five bucks, I watched him and his buddies take off, pushing and shoving each other as they went.

The clock on the competition ticked toward the finish time—thirty minutes. I knelt by Harper's side, my knuckles brushing the joint Harper had expertly carved in Desi's wings. "If I didn't know any better, I would think you had wings of your own."

"Why is that?" she asked while using her fingernail to fuss with a curved line she'd created in a feather. Her fingertips were bright red.

When did she take off her gloves?

Sighing, I took her hands in mine. They were icicles. "Because you've formed those like someone who has studied wings. It wouldn't be hard to believe they were real. The details . . ." I trailed off as I drew her fingers to my lips and blew on them.

Harper leaned in. "What were yours like?"

I felt, rather than saw, the return of her shadows as I considered her question. Their chittering laughter was louder than usual, mocking me and the painful loss of my wings.

Demons danced around us, and Everett Weston's frame came into view over Desi's ice wings, his brows furrowed in silent question. Most of the supes in Havenwood Falls wouldn't sense or notice the shadows, but as a gargoyle, Everett did. As much as I'd love to watch the gargoyle dropkick the sons of a bitches into next week, I cocked my head back, letting him know things were fine. Harper needed to figure out her shadow demons on her own without my interference.

My silence hung between us.

Harper attempted to tug her hands free from mine. "You don't have to talk about it if you're not comfortable discussing it."

"No." I tugged back, maintaining my hold, before I lowered our intertwined hands between us. "You can ask me anything, Harper. The only way this works is if we're willing to discuss the ugly stuff along with the good."

Her reply was cut off by her high school suitor's reappearance, a large cup of steaming liquid cradled in his hands.

"Um, I know you said you didn't need anything, but I brought you some hot chocolate." He circled our Desi sculpture, remaining far enough away to ensure Harper would have to leave my side if she wanted the drink.

She stood, her awed thank you filling the air as she hugged the boy. Her icicle-cold fingers eagerly wrapped around the cup, a sigh escaping as she took her first sip. "Oh, you're my hero!"

"I figured you could use the warmth considering all the work you did." His brown eyes flicked from Harper's euphoric face to mine. I gained my feet. "This lion is awesome, by the way."

His friends chimed their agreement. I had to concur that we made a good team. Our Desi looked just like the real one.

I glanced at the backpack the mace had spent the day hidden away in. What would he think of our project?

"Thanks, you guys did great, too. I like your . . . um, car?" Harper said.

Stepping behind her, I placed a hand on her waist. "That's not a car, Harper. That's an Audi R8."

The teenagers nodded appreciatively just as the bell signaling the end of the competition blared through the square.

"There's a difference?" Harper whispered.

"Between a car and an Audi? Yeah."

41

Releasing a little harrumph, Harper took a long sip of her drink before bumping her hip into my side. "By the way, don't think I didn't notice the little collar and tag you carved around his neck."

Grinning, I looked at my handiwork hanging from snow Desi's neck. "You do treat him like a pet."

By the time we'd cleaned up our tools and the judging had concluded—we came in second to a group of girls who'd sculpted mice in a winter scene I didn't bother checking out—the sun was gone and the square was aglow with lights.

"A lion losing to mice." I chuckled, speaking loud enough for Desi to hear. "Must be demoralizing."

Harper's backpack shook. I swiped the bag from the ground and threw it over my shoulder. "Just messing with you, Des. We absolutely should have won."

With Harper's agreement, we wandered through the booths. While we ate and browsed, I told her about my wings. "They were black, an inky black, like a fresh oil slick—you know the way the colors shimmer upon the oil? A sheen of blues and greens?" She nodded. "Dominion wings are quite large, rising above our heads and draping to the ground when resting. They were a symbol of pride, as they are for all angels."

"And you lost them in a battle."

"Yes. I was ambushed. I would have run and avoided the fight, but they used Phaedra to draw me in. By the time I realized I was too late to save her, it was too late to save myself, too."

She didn't bother telling me she was sorry for my loss, and I was glad. Instead, she weaved her arm through mine, touching her head to my shoulder as we walked.

"This public display of affection is bound to have the coffee shop talking in the morning."

Harper laughed. "I'll have to call Aunt Eloise, and tell her about our date right away, then. She'll be ecstatic. She thinks I'm a prude, but then this *is* the same woman who decided to reclaim her virginity in her forties just because she thought it would make the experience feel new . . ."

I chuckled at her eccentric aunt. There was likely no need for Harper to call her. The way this town worked, her aunt already knew we'd spent the day together.

We had conquered a Havenwood Falls town event together. She looked content and unguarded, and it made me smile to see her that way.

"Okay, Harper Sinclair, you've won second place in the ice sculpture competition, stuffed your face with traditional festival food, and gone on a date with a hot angel. What's next on your list of firsts?" I asked as we headed back to my truck. It was almost eleven o'clock, and we'd shut down the festival before moving to the bookstore to find a quiet corner to enjoy more hot chocolate and chat.

Harper chuckled. "Is that what today was? You trying to help me check off my bucket list of things I've never had the courage to do?"

I lifted a shoulder. "It was about finding out if we were as compatible as I thought we were, despite our differences."

Snatching her hand, I pushed her against a building and lowered my mouth to her jaw. I licked at her skin. Her shadows whined. *Screw them.*

# CHAPTER 6

## HARPER

$\mathcal{M}$y eyelids fluttered closed as Elias's lips found mine. We'd held hands, he'd hugged me, but his lips hadn't touched mine today, until this moment. I sank into his embrace. Savored his taste.

Elias groaned, my name falling from his lips in a low, gravelly tone.

The memory of him calling out to me as he plunged into my body hit me. My dream . . .

Lust ignited within as Elias pressed me against the wall, jagged bricks digging into my shoulders. The pain felt good.

"Elias," I said, the word strangled against his lips. He pulled back. Tears choked the back of my throat, and I coughed them away.

"Harper?" he asked gently.

*"Find relief, Harper. What you want isn't something the angel can give. We can help you find it."*

Their promises stirred my restlessness. Yes, I needed relief. Their dark laughter caressed my ear, and my body jerked, like it wanted to move toward them.

No! My gaze slid up to Elias's face. I wanted him. I wanted to let go and be with someone else, skin to skin and breath to breath. I wanted to share everything I felt, both good and bad, with someone. The shadows understood that. They just didn't approve of the person I was with now.

"Do you want to go back to your place?" Elias asked.

*Just do it, Harper*, I told myself. I'd prepared myself for this moment. Hoped for it, even.

His eyes narrowed when I didn't respond right away. "This isn't about sex, Harper. I want more from you."

Shadowy fingers stroked me, the spirits' whispers urgent and needy in my head. *"Sex is a good thing. He makes it sound like a sin. Show the angel who you are."*

My body itched, my skin crawling with desire and power. I knew this feeling. I cleared my throat. "I have an idea."

Elias smiled, curiosity burning in his gaze. "I don't know whether to be excited or wary of the look in your eyes."

"Be both," I replied. "You should definitely be both."

Tonight I was going to do the least Harper thing I'd ever done, and I wasn't going to feel bad or guilty about it.

Offering Elias my hand, I wrapped my fingers around his and tugged him toward his truck. "Let's go."

Elias was quiet when I directed him back to my place and told him to use his angelic magic to change his clothes, while I hurried to my bedroom and changed my own. He was even quieter when I stepped out of my bedroom in a skintight black shirt and miniskirt with heels. However, he did visually devour me from head to toe before he used his angel gifts to match my attire with his own— snug black slacks and an obscenely fitted dress shirt that molded to his muscular torso so completely my panties were damp before we left my cabin.

Though his eyes flicked to my face throughout the drive that followed, he remained quiet as we drove back through town, past darkened houses, and finally to a secluded parking lot down a hidden road off County Road 13.

Located in a network of caves accessible only by a gondola lift, the establishment I took Elias to now was not publicly acknowledged by many people in Havenwood Falls, though most, if not all, residents of age knew it existed.

My pulse accelerated as I stared out the windshield at the gondola lifts before I climbed out of the truck, took a deep breath, and rubbed my gloved hands together.

Surprise marred Elias's features when he slid out of the vehicle, but he still didn't speak. It was as if he was afraid of breaking the spell I'd created by coming here at all. Even my shadows were subdued, hanging back in a pack as though they were watching and waiting for what came next.

Hand in hand, we walked toward the bouncers who checked IDs just outside the lift. I stole a glance at the angel beside me, curious about his thoughts, as he nodded solemnly at the men, then placed his hand on my hip. His eyes remained straight ahead, but the edge of his mouth twitched as we stepped into one of the gondolas and started up the side of Miles Mountain. A nameless emotion built in my gut the higher we went. Elias rubbed my back.

Once we paid the high cover charge and entered the establishment, Elias finally found his voice. "Somehow this was not what I was expecting from you."

I laughed. "Remember that list of firsts?"

"I remember that girl who listed 'making friends' as one of her firsts." He shook his head, a smirk on his lips. "I think she matured."

A shadow brushed past my calf, and I shivered as the look in Elias's eyes turned me bolder. "Maybe I have a different kind of list now."

Elias's hand crept up and gently gripped the back of my neck as he lowered his lips to the shell of my ear, his breath hot. "Well then, show me what you've got."

"Dance with me." Music pulsated throughout the entire room,

the beat a sultry *thump, thump* that felt like an external heartbeat. My body reveled in it, my hips swaying along with the other patrons in the cavern. My clothes felt too hot against my skin, my hands pulling at the fabric to fan myself.

This was lust, one of the many emotions I'd cut myself off from. One of the many sensations I wanted to explore without worrying about regrets.

Silk was just the place for that.

An upscale nightclub in Havenwood Falls, Silk was an establishment where the very rich and those specially invited could fulfill their fantasies or get their kink on, all in a safe environment closely monitored and controlled by the female hellhound who owned it, Melaina Savage.

The main area had bars, tables with stools, lounge areas, a VIP area, and a dance floor. Off the main room was a secure area that was a little edgier for supes only, a place where they could drop all pretenses and be themselves while partaking in exotic drinks and exotic fun.

After my recent involvement with the Court, and the new additional powers I'd discovered, I'd earned my right to the club and the supes area. The shadows tailing me were as excited as I was the farther we moved into the club, their dark forms weaving in and out of the patrons' undulating bodies. Something about the way the spirits glided along the skin, causing those who couldn't see them to shiver from a sudden chill, turned me on.

Reaching back, I grabbed Elias by the hand, my eyes wide and bright when I glanced up into his face. "Can you feel it?"

Energy. This place was bursting with energy. As if, at any moment, the building would explode. It hummed through me, followed by a barrage of voices in my head, and I found myself laughing—a joyful, wicked sound that poured out of me.

"There are so many of them here," I gasped. The shadows were everywhere, the usual group of spirits that followed me having doubled. They were always there in the darkness, waiting, the need in me having called them forth from Hell.

Elias pulled me close, the hand he had on me possessive, his gaze focused on the room.

"So many people," I breathed. "And spirits."

I'd never felt so close to life and death simultaneously. Psychics bridged a gap between the living and the dead, but most of the time there was a firm line between the two. Even if a psychic was strong enough to see the dead, he lived in the world of the living and merely *channeled* the beyond. Lately, I felt like I *lived* in both worlds, with one foot out of the grave and one foot in it. It was an odd sensation that made me feel like the rope in a game of tug of war, but it wasn't a terrible feeling. It was exhilarating.

"Harper?" Elias called. I'd pulled away from him, my body making its way through the throngs of people until I was at the edge of the room, near the stage.

My body was on fire, the lust building up in me ready to explode. This was part of who I was now. Demons fed off greed, lust, power, and gluttony. Amongst other things. And I was feeding off it, too. Partly because of the shadows' influence. It wasn't sex and lust the shadows had a problem with. Because of the shadows, and the power I was gaining from them, I wanted to do naughty things I wouldn't have dared before. It was the power that made me antsy, the power that had turned me into this new impatient and seductive person. I needed to quit ignoring it.

*"Feed the need, Harper. There are men here who want you. Can't you feel that?"* The shadows pressed up against me. *"Pick one. Any of them. Except the angel."*

"Harper," Elias called again.

I was lost to sensation, want, and need. I felt like I was free-falling, as if I'd bungee jumped from a cliff, cushioned by air and adrenaline. By power.

A hand wrapped around my upper arm. "Harper," Elias breathed.

There was a low whistle, the sound sultry and pleased. "Well, this is new. I've had necromancers in my club and never felt the presence of the dead like I do today." Melaina Savage appeared through the crowd, her dark hair swept up, the style accentuating the plunging neckline of her tight dress. Her stiletto heels drew the eyes to drool-worthy legs, but it was the satisfied look on her face that garnered the most attention.

"And not just any kind of dead," she continued, her gaze flicking to the shadows hovering near us. "Hello, Harper." Her eyes shone, a pair of special contacts keeping her stare from being deadly. If a human looked into a hellhound's eyes three times, he would die. Some supernaturals were immune to the glare—Elias for example—but even with my tie to the Infernum, I wasn't sure if I was.

"Melaina," I greeted her, my voice shaky but confident. My shadows spoke for me and with me. Tonight, we were one.

She winked, her breath pushing against my ear when she whispered, "Your shadows are hungry, darling. They're good for my business, the lusty need you are drawing off of each other being fed to the crowd. But if you lose control of them . . ." Her warning trailed off, a sudden red glint sparkling in her eyes.

Spirits often influenced the living without the living even being aware of it. A cold spot in a room. A sudden angry outburst by a normally calm person. A sudden sense of sadness when there was no reason to be sad.

My spirits and I were bleeding lust.

"You don't need to worry," Elias said fiercely, his broad frame dwarfing my thinner, smaller one.

"Don't I?" Melaina asked, arching her brows at the angel. "They say it's the quiet ones."

I giggled, and then rushed to cover my mouth. My head was spinning. Shadows danced close and then edged away, keeping a healthy distance from the angel at my side. The hellhound, they approached, but didn't mess with.

Melaina shook her head. "For that kind of power, you should have been trained a long time ago, psychic. It's a shame they didn't figure out what you were until recently."

I'd gotten to know the hellhounds well after our ordeal with the

Collector, though my powers were also enough on their own to put me on their radar.

Melaina's gaze slid to Elias. "She's shadow drunk. Not an unusual occurrence for someone drawing too much energy at one time from the Infernum, but it is unusual for someone her age."

I giggled again, completely unable to control the urge to laugh. There was no way she was calling me old. I was only twenty-four.

"I know what shadow drunk is," Elias responded, petulant.

"Then you know—"

"I get it, hellhound," Elias cut her off.

Melaina shrugged, her face smug. "Just keep it contained, angel."

I was no longer listening to them, my body swaying to the music, my vision blurring. Shadows drew toward me like magnets. I found myself calling to them the same way I had when I was taken captive by the Collector. Then, while standing in a pitch-black room afraid for my life, the one holding me prisoner had told me not to be afraid, to use the spirits. I hadn't completely understood then, and I didn't completely understand now.

"Holy shit! It smells like the Infernum in here," a biker near me said, awed. By the insignia on the back of his leather vest, I knew he was a member of the local chapter of SIN, Swords of the Infernal Night. It was an outlaw motorcycle club that operated within town but kept its illegal business outside of it. The only reason I even knew about the club's dealings in the first place was because I'd been drawn into quite a bit of dark town business lately.

Harper Sinclair, now the girl everyone went to for help when things went wrong. Loyal. Dependable. Trustworthy. Safe.

*"Don't be safe,"* the shadows told me. *"Be anything except safe."*

Inhaling deeply, I breathed in the smell of Hell, the smell of death and freedom. The golden light from the club around me transformed into a halo of blurred glitter, the world a beautiful kaleidoscope of sounds and bright colors.

There was a stage in front of me, a pole rising up from the floor, any dancers absent. Elias called my name, but I was too far gone to care. I just wanted to strip myself bare, literally, in front of the world.

*"No more hiding,"* the shadows prompted.

I was so very, very tired of hiding.

I'd climbed the stairs, my hands yanking on my clothes, my body swaying against the pole, when the first whistles broke through. Yells of encouragement rose up from the crowd. I wasn't a splendid dancer, but I wasn't a terrible one either. It was the *removing the clothes* bit that was awkward.

The shirt went first, my clumsy fingers pulling the tight top I wore over my head. The bra beneath was red and lacy, and I toyed with the straps, my eyes closed as I made love to the music.

Using the body to express oneself was a splendid way to tell a story. I told stories every day with my fingers. I translated for the dead, writing words and beseeching requests, and snapped shots of other people's stories with my camera. My fingers were windows into other people's worlds.

Tonight, my body was the window into mine, my hands gliding down my flesh, enjoying the sensation. The shadows danced with me, and I didn't care who saw us. Right now, I was a queen of darkness, and I was enjoying the power. There was no room for embarrassment, no room for regret or doubt.

"More!" someone shouted. "Give us more."

I moved closer to a group of men sitting nearby, cash and drinks littering their table. One in particular, a blond with a cigarette hanging from his lips, crooked his finger. I obeyed the silent command. My eyes flicked to Elias, catching the way his jaw worked, before they went back to the unknown man who'd stepped to the edge of the stage.

The dark desire in the blond's gaze had me enraptured. My pulse pounded in my ears as I shimmied my way over—his head nearly even with my core as he looked up at me.

"Remove it," he said, a crisp Benjamin between his fingers, his eyes on my chest. The bra I wore snapped at the front between the breasts. Power surged through me. Not lust, not desire for this stranger, but power, because I could control this man with my body. I smiled, and a pale hand reached up and touched my thigh.

Somewhere from the back of the room I heard a growl I knew. *Elias.* My gyrations slowed, then dark whispers rose above everything else. "*Show him. Control him.*"

My attention returned to the man. He raised his brows and tapped the one-hundred-dollar bill against his chin as he waited. *Easy money.* I undid the clasp, letting my bra fall open.

"I think that's good," Elias's voice said suddenly from behind me, a large jacket enveloping me, the thick material covering the nakedness I'd bared.

A tear streaked down my cheek, the feel of it unexpected. Why was I crying?

"It's not nearly enough," I whispered. My head swung back to the blond. He was covered in shadows, and his face had turned hard.

Elias picked me up, using his body to shield me as he carried me off the stage and through the room, his breathing fast and hard, his voice husky when he said, "No, it's not nearly enough. It's damn well not nearly enough."

# CHAPTER 7

## ELIAS

*W*ith my jacket around her shoulders, I carried her toward the exit. I'd let her carry on for too long. She needed to have the freedom to find herself. I wanted that for her. Or, I had wanted that for her until her clothing became optional. *Holy fuck.* Her body radiated need. The spirits and demons had worked her into a frenzy, and though I hated the malevolent bastards, I wasn't immune to desire. Hell, the bulge in my pants had me limping as I pushed my way through the crowd.

"The lady didn't pick up her tip," a voice drawled from behind.

*What the actual . . .* I stilled, but didn't turn around. "Go back to the stage. Another dancer will be along to entertain you shortly."

The man grunted. "What if I don't want another dancer?"

Harper's flushed face lifted to mine, her eyes wide. I shifted her to my side, keeping one arm tightly around her back as I finally gave the man my full attention. "I don't give a rat's ass what you want."

His brown eyes flashed. Just my luck. This douchebag would have the balls to challenge me. Harper had worked her magic on this one. I could smell his need. He was two minutes from climax; all he needed was a willing body—or his hand.

Melaina caught my eye from near the bar, her face tight with irritation at the crowd building around us. One touch and I could have the man drooling over the biker sitting in the corner, if I wanted. I jerked my chin. It was time to leave.

Ignoring the cocky tourist who had no clue the shit he'd put himself in, I spun for the door and murmured to Harper, "Let's go."

I took one step, then everything happened in slow motion as Harper gasped and stumbled away from my side.

"Stay with me, darling," the man said. "I'll make those tears disappear."

His words didn't register half as much as the sight of his fingers wrapped around Harper's slender wrist. I lost my shit.

We flew across the space and slammed into a wall, his head bouncing at the impact. "You don't fucking touch her," I hissed, my face in his as my forearm locked across his neck. "I could crush you—"

"Elias?" Harper's small hands pulled at my hips, her body against my back. "Don't," she begged.

The blond turned red, his mouth moving like a fish out of water as he groped for words he wouldn't find, thanks to me.

A commotion broke out behind us, and Harper yanked at me again. "We need to leave. Now." Her voice was stronger this time, an order instead of a plea, and my anger tempered.

Shoving my weight against the blond once more, I released him. "Don't let me see you near her again. Got that?"

He nodded, rubbing at his neck. Bending down, I swiped the bill he'd dropped when I rushed him. Without looking for Melaina or her bouncers, I grabbed Harper's hand and hurried for the door.

I flicked the hundred toward the bouncer at the entrance. "For the trouble. Tell Melaina I'm sorry," I said as we stepped out into the cold night and toward an awaiting gondola.

"Out," I ordered the couple who had stepped into the lift right as Harper and I arrived. The man balked, and I released a low growl that had him pulling his companion back outside without another glance.

Fixing my gaze on the bouncer, I reached for the door handle myself. "Just us."

He gave me a nod as the door slammed shut. A moment later, the whir of the motors sounded, and we pushed away from the cliff.

I had ten minutes.

*Shit.* The sulfur scent of Hell had temporarily paralyzed me. I may be locked out of Heaven, but Hell was certainly no friend of mine. My very existence rebelled against everything Harper was so drawn to—she embraced the seduction of the darkness, and I longed to destroy it. By the time I talked myself down from the urge to dispatch the club of its less savory occupants—those species being the reason I didn't visit this place to begin with—Harper was sans shirt and tits flying. Then that asshole had touched her. Not once, but twice.

I spun Harper around and fisted her hair, pulling her head back until she met my gaze. "Tell me you want this."

Tears fell from her demon-fed black eyes as she blinked. She nodded.

I took a step forward, and she moved back.

"Tell me." I hated the anger in my voice, but siphoning off the massive amounts of darkness her demons had filled her with had me punchy. Somehow, one of the gifts I'd received upon my creation was the one thing a girl like Harper needed—everything she absorbed, I could pull away. It had taken a few coffee meetups with her before I'd noticed the way my power worked around her. I was like an antidote to her brand of poison. And her poison had just infected me. I'd almost killed a human . . .

I released Harper and shoved my hands through my hair. "Fuck!"

I'd attacked a man for touching her. *Not good.*

Harper's hiccupped sniffle settled me as she breathlessly admitted, "I want this."

Green returned to her eyes, and I released the lingering anxiousness in my tense limbs. I had been prepared to fight up there; my muscles had begged for it. In the eighteen years since

Breckin was born and I'd taken over raising him, I'd somehow came to believe I'd become more human. More accepting to those species in this town who weren't on my side of the battle. To the stupidity of humans.

*"You have, angel. You didn't want to fight because there were damned in there. You wanted to fight because they looked at her."* Never had her shadows been so right. *"She fuels your rebellion from Heaven."*

My breaths came in shallow pants as I took another step forward. "Do you want me?"

"I do. I want you." Harper nodded and moved back again. Her retreat caused me to drop my hands. *She wants me, but she cowers?* I studied her tear-streaked face. It was a flushed, beautiful mess. "I need you, Elias."

She clutched the edges of my black jacket closed over her naked chest. I smiled and slipped my hand in, my fingers brushing her side. "Do *you* need me? Or is that the shadows speaking?"

"They don't—"

"Don't insult me by telling me they don't speak to you like that, Harper." My other arm wound around her backside and jerked her hips into contact with mine. "You let them control you. Yes, they are part of you, but you let them become you."

My palm skimmed up her ribcage and settled beneath her breast. Harper whimpered. "Tell me you want me to touch you." I stole a look out the window. "We have seven minutes."

She released her grip on my jacket and touched my jaw. "I want you to touch me."

With my gaze holding hers, my thumb slid over the soft curve of the underside of her breast and circled her nipple twice. Her eyes shifted left at my touch, and I palmed her. "Look at me."

She did. Our eyes held while I massaged her left breast, then dragged my hand across her breastbone and gave the right the same attention. The pad of my thumb flicking at her raised nipple coaxed another whimper from her lips. My jacket slipped from her shoulders, exposing her nakedness, as I leaned forward and used my hand against her chest to bend her backward over my arm at the base of her spine.

"Do you want my lips on you?" I murmured against the hollow of her neck.

She grabbed at my bicep with one hand and weaved her fingers into the hair at the base of my neck with the other. "I want everything, Elias. Your lips, your tongue, your—"

My tongue stopped her list.

I drew one puckered nipple into my mouth and pulled, my teeth nipping at her soft skin as the flat of my tongue suckled. Harper's nails drew across my scalp, holding me to her breast. The slight tang of her salty skin on my lips had me thrusting my dick closer to the heat between her legs. The air smelled like sex.

She was so fucking perfect. "You're beautiful," I said as I righted her. "I want you, Harper Sinclair."

Our mouths collided in a battle of dueling tongues. We were starved.

My larger body pushed until her back was against the glass of the gondola, her hand grabbing the rail as I removed my arm from behind her. Her pheromones were wildly alluring, her scent driving my hands up her thighs and under her skirt. My fingers rounded the curve of her ass and grazed the edge of lacy panties as Harper sucked in a sharp breath and caught my bottom lip with her teeth.

I pulled my head back in silent question. Her hips jerked forward in silent answer.

My middle finger found her heat first. "Fuck me," I mumbled.

Harper giggled. "Isn't that the point?"

Cupping her breast with one hand and toying with her folds with the other, I smiled and licked her lips once. "That is absolutely the point."

The lift slowed its descent. "Damn." I pulled my damp fingers from her panties.

"You've got five minutes to change your mind, if you want to," I said as I brushed one fingertip across her bottom lip. She surprised me by shifting forward and drawing it into her mouth, sucking her own taste from my hand.

I groaned when she let go. "Stingy girl, I'd planned on doing that."

"You can get down on your knees and taste me all you want, angel."

"In five minutes, I will." I sealed that promise with a kiss.

Harper giggled, still a little shadow drunk, as we pulled down my gravel drive, not a mile from Silk's parking lot. Before we'd initially passed my place on the way to the nightclub, I'd assumed she was directing me back to my house. Since my place was over the hangar that housed my helicopter and business, I lived in a relatively secluded area on the outskirts of town off County Road 13.

"Don't move," I warned, jumping out of the truck and going around to open her door.

She laughed for a second time as she slid to the ground, one hand still holding my jacket closed over her chest. "You weren't kidding about the five minutes."

I stood entirely too close as I stared at her upturned face. "It's only been three. I have two minutes left to get you inside and on my bed."

Her hand found mine at our sides. "Lead the way."

Harper Sinclair being assertive was not something the people of this town would expect. Then again—after her aborted striptease—their feelings about her were bound to change. I didn't bother giving her the grand tour of the place as we entered. It was simple enough. A stairway in the office of Ski-Ventures led upstairs to a spacious, yet cozy, open living space which consisted of one living room, dining room, and kitchen, along with two bedrooms, each with an en suite bath.

I closed the door and leaned against it, removing my shoes as Harper eyed the place. What did she think of it? It was a bachelor pad, but it was warm and lived in. Vivienne had even bought me a bunch of throw pillows for the couch, because she and Breckin had liked to visit me here when they needed to get away from Hamon and Rachel at the house.

I crouched down and touched Harper's calf.

"Foot?" I asked as she glanced over her shoulder. She lifted her leg from the floor, and I removed the shoe from her left foot, then her right, before standing and taking her hand. "Do you want a drink or anything?"

"Just directions to your bedroom." She glanced at her wrist, like she wore a watch. "You're down to one minute."

Her flirtatious grin had me laughing as I swiped a bottle of water from the counter and pulled her through my living room and down the small hallway to the master bedroom. When we stepped inside, I twisted the lid from the water bottle and took my time downing half the contents as I studied Harper standing in my bedroom. The hard-on that had barely deflated on the drive from Silk perked right back up. As if by design, she stood in the shaft of moonlight coming in from the uncovered windows that flanked my bed. Her fingers had gone to her hair, combing it up and out of her face, which left my jacket gaping open.

Everything about the way she looked, and what she had been through, sparked the protective nature in me. Her shadows worried me. They allowed her to be more direct and aggressive, but they also posed a danger to her. The man at the strip club was a perfect example. If I hadn't been there . . . It was danger like that I wasn't willing to risk. A danger I wanted to protect her from.

I held the water bottle out for her. After a pause, she took it.

"Now, what am I going to do with you?" My index finger drew a line down the naked skin peeking out from the open zipper. Harper shivered and took a sip of water. "I believe we were right about . . . here," I said as I touched the top of her skirt. I curved my fingers into the waistband and jerked her against my body. "I want to taste that sweet scent lingering on my fingers."

The water bottle fell to the floor as I shoved my jacket over her shoulders. Dropping to my knees, I pulled it down her arms. I trailed a circle of kisses around the silky skin of her stomach while I reached up and cupped one breast, then the other. Harper slipped back and fell to sit on the bed with a low laugh.

"How did you feel in that club, Harper?" I asked as I inched between her knees and took her face in my hands. "What did the shadow demons make you feel?"

"Freedom." Her hands worked at the buttons of my shirt. "Powerful." Her words turned me on even as they warned me away. She had the kind of power that could go very, very wrong if the shadows controlled her or if my enemies discovered what she was capable of.

I spread my arms until she freed me of my button-down and undershirt, then returned to exploring her exposed skin. My fingers traced her collarbone, over the peaks of her breasts, through the valley between them, and down along the ridges of her ribcage. Her skin was a maze, and I was following every path available down to the promised land.

"You *are* powerful." My thumbs slid into her waistband. "Just look at me. You put an angel on his knees. *I'm* on *my* knees for the privilege of worshiping you, my little *umbra amans*."

A rush of air expelled from her parted lips, but no words came. Instead she grabbed my face and kissed me deeply. Her nipples grazed my chest, our position awkward enough that we touched, but weren't skin to skin. I inched as close to her body as I could get. It wasn't enough.

"You make me feel freedom, too," she said between kisses. "You accepted me when I had no one. You weren't scared of what I am—"

I broke our kiss. I wasn't scared of what she was; I feared what that meant for her.

"Don't." Wrapping my arms around her waist, I pressed my face against the swells of her chest. "You are a beautiful soul, Harper Sinclair. You are powerful, and complicated, and . . . and you are not something to fear. Okay?" The words burned my throat and clutched at my heart, because I was working to convince myself as much as I was to convince her.

"Okay," she agreed softly, her mouth pressing to the top of my head.

Feeling weak and helpless in a way I had never known, I turned in to her skin and rained kisses across her chest. Harper's head rolled back, her eyes closing as I lavished each breast with all my attention before I gently pressed her backwards onto the bed. My hands made quick work of peeling her skirt and red panties down her legs. My mouth followed their trail, leaving wet kisses on the inside of her thigh, knee, calf, and ankle as I tossed the unneeded clothing across the room. When I stood to remove my own pants, my hands stilled at the waistband as I took in the temptress on my bed. My cock protested the holdup.

I unhooked my button and shoved the slacks to my knees. Harper rose to her elbows with a twinkle in her eyes. She licked at her lips, and the image of a starving animal ready to pounce upon its next meal came to mind. Harper looked famished. Or maybe that was me?

"Leaving on your boxers?" she asked.

I kicked my pants away and settled a knee on the bed. "For now." I tapped at her leg, nodding for her to move, and she crawled backward as I climbed over her, then settled between her knees. "I have a little business to attend to first."

"A little busin—" Her words cut off as I moved between her thighs.

The first swipe of my tongue—from her damp center to her clit —brought Harper's hand down on the covers beside me. Her nails scratched the fabric as she fisted my comforter. The second— executed with the flat of my tongue at a lazy pace—brought curse words.

"Elias?" My name was a plea on her lips.

I gripped her ass, and she clenched her thighs around my head as I lapped at her juices. "You taste like freedom to me."

Harper pulled my hair with a low "yes" when my tongue plunged deeper. A finger followed. Then two.

"Yes. Oh, God . . . shit."

I kissed her left thigh and lifted my head just enough to see her face. "You like that, huh?"

Her eyes were clenched tight, her head moving restlessly from side to side as my fingers pumped. I shifted my thumb to press against her clit, and Harper jerked at the touch. Her teeth bit into her bottom lip.

"Yeah, you like that, baby?" My voice was thick with desire. The woman was killing me.

Harper hissed, "Fuck me."

Smiling, I lowered my face and nipped at her thigh to keep my satisfaction with her response at bay. My temptress wasn't having that.

She yanked at my hair, pulling up my head and settling a wild and wickedly wanton look on me. "I want you to fuck me, Elias. Now."

I'd barely moved to my knees before Harper sat up and tugged my boxer briefs over my ass, her hand diving in to wrap around my very hard and very ready cock.

It was my turn to groan as she gripped me tightly, her thumb swiping at the bead of moisture on the head. "Shit," I said through gritted teeth.

She ran her hand from tip to shaft, alternating her hold from tender to death grip. My balls tightened with the urge for release. "Harper"—I sank my hand into her hair— "if you keep doing that . . ."

I didn't need to finish my sentence. She shook her head with a smile. "No way. I want to feel you deep within me when you get off."

My forehead dropped to hers. "Holy hell, how did we fight this for so long?"

"I honestly don't know."

Removing her hand from my member, I kicked off my boxers. I reached for the condom box I'd tossed in my bedside table this afternoon. Harper's brows knitted together as she watched me tear the package open.

"I bought these this morning. I don't sleep around, Harper. In fact, I've never slept with a woman in this bed. I just figured after last night . . ." I shrugged.

"I wasn't worried about that. I just . . . you're an angel, it's not like you have to worry about disease." If it were possible, I would have sworn her face had turned a brighter shade of red.

"No, but I can father Nephilim," I reminded her. "I raised one, remember? I might not be human, but I am a responsible guy."

Her thumbs pressed into my hips as she drew me forward and arched her hips. "I don't want responsible right now, I want—"

Lifting her ass higher, I slipped inside her in one smooth motion.

"Sex," Harper exhaled. I joined her husky moan with one of my own.

Her body clenched around mine—holding me tightly—as I withdrew, then sank back in. I dropped to the bed and covered her body with mine. My hands held her face still as I lowered my mouth to hers and kissed her slowly, my tongue moving at the same languid speed as our bodies. I wanted to take my time, to savor the feeling of friction building between us. I wanted to allow her body to suck every drop of life from mine. I could give that to her, I could give myself to her. Love her. Honor and protect her . . .

"Oh, fuck," I groaned as Harper shifted her hips and met me thrust for thrust. Her nails scratched at my back and pressed into my ass. Her whimpers shifted from gasps to exaltations.

I rose to my knees and increased my rhythm, my thumb rubbing circles around her clit as her breaths caught in her throat. She was close, her walls clenching and unclenching my length with each thrust. Her eyes had closed a while ago, and I joined her in that bliss. Letting our bodies form the pictures. Letting our ears take in the slapping sound of desire meeting desire. I inhaled the proof of our passion with every ragged breath—heat, salt, sex. It coated my lungs.

"Yes. Yes. Yes." Harper came with her fingers gripping my right knee. Her other hand had clutched the pillow she'd pushed out of her way at some point. Her body trembled as she sighed. A few thrusts later my release came, and I fell to her chest with a growl.

I sucked the salty sweat from her neck as I came down from the high. "I'm not done with you, Harper Sinclair. Not even close."

She stretched her limbs out beneath me, and I rolled to my side to give her room to breathe. After a moment, she propped her head up. "I would hope not."

My lips brushed hers before I shifted toward the edge of the bed. "Let me get rid of this and wipe off. I'll bring you something." A little of the vixen within had vacated in our post-sex haze. She offered me a small smile and looked a bit lost, her eyes failing to meet mine for more than a moment. "Crawl under the covers. I'll be right back."

"Under the covers?" Her eyes went wide as she pulled at my blankets. "I'm staying here?"

I couldn't help but notice the hopeful note in her tone. The condom and mess could wait. Angling myself away from the bed, I perched on the edge and touched her arm. "Harper?" She stopped her flurry of movement. "Of course you're staying here. Or, if you prefer, we could go to your place, but I see no reason to leave here when we're already dressed for bed. Either way, I planned on sleeping with you. This isn't a one night stand."

With a smile, Harper scooted the distance between us on her knees and kissed me.

"Why *did* we wait so long to act on this?" She asked the same question I'd asked right before I lost all concept of thinking when her hand touched my dick.

I gave her the same answer she had given. "I honestly don't know."

I brushed my knuckles over her cheek and went to the bathroom. When I returned with a washcloth for her, she was fast asleep. I stared at her, concern etching my brow.

Tonight, I'd seen her let loose for the first time, but I'd also seen what she was capable of, what her shadows were capable of doing to her. And what they might do to me.

"You can't have her," I told them fiercely. I'd spent the last year watching over Harper Sinclair. I'd spent the last year seeing her tackle a list of firsts she'd been too afraid to tackle when she was growing up because she feared hurting people. I didn't want the shadow demons to ruin what she'd accomplished.

But she'd also mentioned needing the shadows, as if their power was hers.

"I won't let you have her," I repeated.

*"You don't have much choice,"* the shadows replied. *"We are a part of her, angel. This has to be up to her."*

# CHAPTER 8

## HARPER

"*Why did you do this to us, Harper? Why did you do this to yourself?*" the shadows screamed at me, the sound jerking me from sleep. My body was tangled in white sheets, the smell of popping bacon strong in the air.

My limbs were pleasantly sore, and I stretched, my hand falling on the empty space beside me. *Elias.*

His name had barely crossed my mind when the shadows appeared above me, larger and scarier than they had been in the past month. Like looming, hooded grim reapers ready to swallow me whole. They were pissed.

"*You betrayed us,*" they accused. "*Do you want us gone? Do you hate us that much?*"

My heart clenched, memories of the glorious night before suddenly tainted by the shadows' hurt feelings.

"Don't do this," I whispered.

My words were barely audible, but Elias heard them anyway.

"Are you hungry?" he asked from his kitchen.

I rolled from the bed, my gaze on the ghostly forms hovering near me. Their anger was a scary thing, dark and foreboding. It felt like being trapped beneath murky water, unable to breathe.

Elias's white button-down shirt from last night was laid out on the edge of his dresser, and I picked it up, his delicious scent comfortable and safe against my nose as I wrapped it around me. Pushing my arms into the sleeves, I buttoned it over my bra-less chest and lifted the collar to sniff the fabric.

*Elias.*

*"Why, Harper?"* the shadows asked, insistent. *"Why the angel?"*

I wanted to clasp my head in my hands to drown out their voices, but it wouldn't do any good. I loved the shadows, but I also cared about Elias in a way I'd never cared about anyone else before. *"Please,"* I mouthed, being careful not to speak aloud.

"You didn't have to cook," I said, exiting the bedroom.

Elias Jamison stood at the stove, shirtless, his jeans riding low on his hips. He was magnificent, the sight of him sending a renewed rush of desire straight to my core.

"There's hot cocoa on the bar," Elias informed me, his voice bright.

My gaze fell to a plain, sturdy brown mug, steam rising from the top. The shadows' sadness, anger, and betrayal stole my appetite.

*"After everything we've done for you?"* the shadows asked.

When I didn't say anything, Elias turned, his gaze finding my face. I knew by the way his muscles tensed that he sensed and heard the darkness.

He abandoned what he was doing, setting the breakfast he'd cooked aside. It seemed like such a waste sitting there untouched, but I couldn't make myself offer to eat the food or drink the cocoa.

"Let's sit," Elias suggested.

I followed him to his couch.

Curled into the cushions of his deep sofa, I reclined against the armrest.

He pulled a folded blanket off the footrest and draped it over my legs. "If only you knew how delicious you look right now . . ." He smiled. "This blanket is for your safety, not mine."

My grin answered his. "And if I don't want to be safe?"

*"We could have kept you safe,"* the shadows wailed, invading the sweet moment. *"You're hurting us all."*

My smile fell. I'd chosen to sit in a way that kept me from getting too close because I'd already upset the shadows enough. Even so, I felt like I was suffocating.

Elias took the middle spot on the couch, lifting my feet to place them in his lap.

Chewing the side of my lip, I tucked my legs in closer, removing my feet from him.

He sighed. "What's going on in that head of yours, Harper?"

I encircled my legs with my arms and settled my chin on my knees. Hesitant. How did you tell the person you were falling in love with that your head was full of hate? The shadows wanted nothing more than to separate us. Which meant they'd constantly be attacking him.

Elias threw his head against the back cushion and looked up at the ceiling. "Do you want to know why I drove to your house Friday night at three a.m.? Why I couldn't even wait until morning to see or call you?"

Relief and curiosity overwhelmed me. Relief, because I had time to gather my thoughts. Curiosity, because I sensed this was something that had been plaguing his mind.

"There are things you don't know about me."

"You've been around for an eternity. I imagine there are a lot of things I don't know." He turned his head at my light tone.

"True." His hand snuck under the blanket and settled against the back of my calf. Warm. Comfortable. "But there are things you should know, if we're going to . . ." He trailed off.

What? Continue this relationship? Remain friends?

"I'm pretty sure I understand all about being complicated, Elias." The shadows gathered along the walls, and even though they didn't have defined facial features, I knew they were sneering at me.

He gave my leg a squeeze. "I've lived an unconventional life, for an angel, for a really long time. I wasn't meant for Earth, but I chose my path, forsaking my place in Heaven because a friend needed me.

"I've cared for very few things during my existence. Angels were made to worship only one, but He gave us free will and, because of that, I formed bonds that would never break. Not even in death."

Leaning further back into the corner of the couch, I relaxed. A little too much. Drawing so much on the shadows' energy the night before and allowing them to draw on mine had sapped me of strength. Even after sleeping a few hours, I was tired. "Breckin's father?"

"Hamon is one, then Breckin. There were two other angels: one who betrayed us all and one who forfeited her angelic existence out of guilt, because she couldn't help him—they are both gone now. Our bonds made his betrayal harsher and her loss unbearable."

"What happened?"

His jaw tightened and I longed to touch it, to soothe the pain there. "Our history is a mess of wars and betrayals, some we won and others we lost. Revenge was had, but peace is not something we've found."

I listened intently. Listening was something I'd always been good at. *Too* good. Being a good listener kept people from asking questions.

"I stepped away from my duties long ago. After Phaedra was stripped of her angelic being, she was basically rendered human. I dedicated my time to protecting her. Hamon sacrificed himself, pretending to be something he isn't, so that we might stay safe and hidden away. It worked for a time, but our demons always find us, don't they?"

He shook his head and drew my feet into his lap again, tucking the blanket around them. I didn't withdraw this time.

"The betrayals of our past haven't gone away. When Breckin found Vivienne, it opened a whole new problem. That's why Hamon and I left so quickly after the incident with the Collector. We tracked some fallen who'd been hunting Breckin and Viv. We ended them, but there will be more." Sitting forward, he angled his body toward me. "There's always more. Giving in to my feelings for you, giving in to my desires, could make you a target."

"I don't understand. Why—"

"You live in a town full of the supernatural, Harper. You yourself are unique. Hamon and I are angels. This isn't a fight between two shifter species, or for magic, or power. Demons and angels, Heaven and Hell . . . our fight is for the world. For eternity."

"But you're not a part of that life. You don't have duties—"

"I have an allegiance to my creator, to Heaven. If I were called upon, I would return, and I would fight."

I inhaled deeply, my worries momentarily forgotten. "Why are you telling me this? Are you leaving again?"

"I'm not going anywhere." He massaged my feet, his thumbs applying deep pressure to the arches. "I told you because the last time I cared about someone, she was taken from us."

I flinched.

"Phaedra was like a sister to me; we were not romantic," he added, as if he sensed my jealousy. "Harper"—his serious gaze caught mine—"something nagged at me the other night. No . . . not something. It was one of your shadows. It was waiting for me when I arrived home. It reminded me of my mistakes. The way I left you here, alone. My failure to protect Phaedra. That's why I drove to your door, through a snowfall, at three a.m. I'd had a horrible feeling. I have this fear of losing you," he confessed.

I stared at Elias, his words squeezing my chest, my heart fluttering. He, like all the angels I'd met, was complicated. To live an eternity meant seeing and hearing things no one else ever had. I couldn't help but wonder why the men I'd let closest to me in life were angels. Maybe it was because, deep down, I knew they were the kind of beings I may never fully understand. The kind of beings part of me may never accept.

Maybe that was the fascination. Maybe *my* complicated being introduced to an even *bigger* complicated was my fate in life. If I was going to go with a complicated relationship status, Elias was definitely the way to go. No matter how fierce he looked or what kind of dangers knowing him might bring, he was a genuinely nice guy, the kind of guy a girl could trust with her heart.

Behind him, my shadows loitered near the ceiling at the back of the room, watching.

I stared back at them, my heart hurting. Why did seeing the dark spirits keep their distance make me feel sad and lonely? As if I was trying to end my friendship with them in favor of a relationship with Elias. A friendship I had to admit I didn't want to give up. Something about the shadows made me feel whole.

"You look thoughtful," Elias murmured. "It's hard to read you sometimes."

My gaze edged back to his, the curiosity burning in his eyes making me shiver.

Under the blanket I'd pulled over myself, I touched my side. There was a small scar there, a reminder of how deep my connection to the shadows went. I'd let the spirits inhabit me once, similar to a possession, so that I could use their power, only to have them rip free of my skin when I couldn't control them. Elias had worshiped that scar last night, kissing circles around it.

*The shadows understand you*, I told myself.

"I'm sorry," I said suddenly, the apology flowing thickly off of my tongue. I'd had too little sleep last night. Even as important as this moment was, I couldn't seem to hold on to it. Sleep was a villain waiting to steal me away. "What I did Friday night. Attacking you . . ."

"No apologies," Elias said, a gentle smile on his face. "I think it's safe to say we have some things we need to work out."

Exhaustion, deep and intense, invaded my body, dragging down my eyelids and weighing down my limbs.

"I obviously wore you out," Elias whispered as his hands continued massaging my feet. "Nap, Harper."

He watched me, his gaze passing from me to the walls beyond. I think, on a deeper level, he may have sensed my warring thoughts, even if he didn't understand them.

Elias leaned toward me. "What are the shadows to you now, Harper?"

Sleep made my tongue drunk and loose. "Family," I answered.

I wanted to take it back as soon as I said it. Maybe it was better to tell him now before things got too twisted.

"I'm a demon," I whispered.

Elias frowned, but I saw the knowledge in his gaze, the truth he wanted to ignore. "You're a psychic with a link to the Infernum, not a demon."

"It's much deeper than that. Because of the circumstances of my birth, I'm a demonic human."

There. I'd said it.

"Most importantly, your parents were *human*," he insisted. "Demon connection or not, you can choose to ignore the dark side."

Sleep, and the way it weakened my defenses, was not my friend. I blinked it back.

"Harper?" Elias prodded. "Why do they hate me so much? Your shadows?"

The vulnerability in his voice tugged at my heart. "Because they're scared of you. They're afraid that me being with you will make me push them away."

"Is that such a bad thing?" he asked, genuinely curious.

I looked at the shadows. "You know what they are. They were terrible people when they were alive. The ones who were human, anyway. They sold their souls to the Infernum, and none of them expected to find redemption or affection in the afterlife. Until they found me. I care about them, and they don't want to give that up. *I* don't want to give that up. Th . . ." My words trailed off, and I narrowed my eyes, frustrated at my weariness.

"Th . . ." I tried again, but exhaustion finally got the better of me, carrying me away, sending me reeling into a dark world I was more than comfortable in lately.

My words hung in the air, bridging reality and dreams. *I don't want to give that up.*

Strange how the truth a person doesn't want to admit to themselves comes out when he or she least expects it to.

I didn't want to ignore the darkness. I liked how comfortable it was. Like a warm fire on a cold winter night. Or a grilled cheese sandwich and a cup of hot chocolate.

~

I awoke back in Elias's bed, the early afternoon sun filtering in through a picture window, a carpet of blinding white snow sparkling in the mountainous world beyond.

The house was too quiet, the shadows too calm, and I knew by their behavior that Elias was gone.

My head rolled to the side, my gaze landing on a note left behind on Elias's pillow.

*Harper,*

*I'm sorry. There was an emergency on the mountain with some skiers. I'll be home as soon as possible. My truck keys are on the counter if you need to leave. Help yourself to anything you need.*

*Love, Elias*

Relief washed over me, not because there was something going on in the mountains, but because Elias hadn't abandoned me because of the confession I'd made.

# CHAPTER 9

## ELIAS

*I*t was late afternoon by the time I returned to Havenwood Falls after flying a rescue mission out on Mount Sousa. *Damn tourists.* As secluded as our little town was, due in large part to the Court and magical wards used to keep the town safe, we still allowed a good number of high rollers to vacation here —especially during ski season—to keep the local economy pumping. This morning's rescue was just that: big-city daredevils who didn't pay attention to the mountain conditions. The fact that those egocentric pricks pulled me away from Harper chapped my ass. Walking out my door after our revelations this morning was tough. And now here I was, enduring the Winterfest crowds in search of her, because she'd left my house.

*"Did you think she'd stay? Did you think she'd choose you over us?"* The warning scraped across my forehead, and I looked over my shoulder at the little shadow friend I'd picked up, thanks to Harper. His smoky form flitted about, encircling tree trunks and slinking along the slush-and-snow-covered sidewalks, as he followed me. He'd lingered in my presence all day.

In that vulnerable moment between wakefulness and sleep earlier, she'd called the shadows her family. Why had she made that connection? Yes, she was tied to demons because of the circumstances surrounding her birth, but *she* wasn't a demon.

*"Or is she?"* The shadow's question tickled my skull.

"No," I said aloud, then ducked my head as a group of high schoolers stopped and stared. I lifted a wave and kept walking. *I would know if she were a demon. I would sense it*, I justified in my head. Then I cursed, because I'd felt the need to reply at all. *Damn creature.*

I considered crossing the street and heading into the Haven Saloon for the sole purpose of getting drunk—if only angels could get drunk—when a small, tightly bundled-up figure appeared from around the gazebo. The dark hair spilling out from beneath her red knit hat and over her puffy white jacket gave her identity away as much as the camera plastered to her face. Harper rotated in a slow circle, her index finger snapping away at the festivalgoers enjoying day two of Winterfest.

I shoved my hands into my pockets and watched, mesmerized by her focus as she pointed and clicked over and over. The joy on her face was undeniable, giving her a youthful quality that was enchanting. I was thirty yards away, but the click of each shot she took reached my angel ears. My gaze followed her lens, curious as to what had caught her attention.

When peals of laughter tore through the air, Harper lowered the camera, then crouched and began snapping again. Three young girls had entered the square hand in hand, their faces bright red from the cold, their bodies skipping and dancing in circles as they kicked at the thick snow on the ground and sang songs I didn't know. I envied their carefree exuberance. Their safe human existence.

Somewhat uncomfortable at the unusual jealousy blooming in my chest, I shifted and looked for Harper once more—only to find her camera lens pointed at me.

I drew a short breath.

The camera lowered an inch, and dark brows arched above sparkling green eyes.

*"She could cost you your redemption, angel. Stay away,"* the shadow whispered.

"I can't," I murmured. My legs brought me toward the bewitching woman who'd stolen my affection. I knew this was a dangerous game. I'd stayed alone for a reason, but it was like I had no control where Harper Sinclair was concerned.

Memories assaulted me, images of the past year spent with her. The conversations we'd had over coffee and hot chocolate, the texts we'd shared, and the fights we'd survived.

And now I understood. I knew why Phaedra had risked her salvation to save Andras. I knew why Hamon lived with such hatred after her loss. Why I followed my best friends and left our birthplace. Why Breckin and Vivienne sacrificed their lives to be together.

Love. This was love.

Let this woman ruin me. Let her darkness do its best at breaking me down. I would fight for her. I was already fighting for her against an enemy I was afraid to lose to—herself.

Harper stood as I neared, a sweet smile on her lips, and lowered her camera to hang around her neck by the strap she wore. "Hey."

I didn't answer, my mind preoccupied by the sound of her heartbeats accelerating, the awareness that shot through me at the sight of her, and the warnings I was receiving from her shadow demon.

Her boot-covered feet shuffled back as I bore down on her, a man on a mission. "Elias?"

At the sound of my name, Desi's handle popped up out of the backpack Harper carried him around in.

I stopped just short of knocking her down and wrapped my arm around her back, my hand drawing her against my body. Leaning down, I touched my lips to her temple.

"Hey," I said, my mouth lingering on her chilled skin.

Her face turned into my touch, as though seeking the warmth my angelic skin provided.

"I'm sorry I left without saying goodbye." I kissed her cheek—

right at the edge of her lips—worried anything more would lead to an embarrassing make-out session, then relinquished her.

Harper shook her head. "There was trouble on the mountain?"

"Skiers stranded—no injuries—but it took a while to find them."

Her gaze volleyed as she shifted in the space between my arm, still around her back, and my chest.

A light breeze blew her hair across her face, and I reached up to brush away a piece that stuck to her cheek. "I see you went home. You didn't feel like looking sexy and lounging in my dress shirt all day?"

"I needed to get out and get some fresh air."

There were too many unspoken sentiments in that statement. "We need to discuss the shadows." Harper's grip tightened on her camera strap, and I ran a finger over her white knuckles. "Can we go back to my place? I'll make you dinner," I teased.

"Grilled cheese?"

Her simple request brought a smile to my face. "Damn, how'd I get so lucky? I just happen to have all those ingredients in my kitchen." I held out my hand. "C'mon, gorgeous. I'll throw in all the hot chocolate you can drink, giant marshmallows included." Things I kept on hand these days, thanks to Vivienne.

The sun had set over the mountains by the time I'd fed Harper, and we moved outside, where I stoked up a large fire in the pit beyond my hangar door. Unease grew between us. The longer I put off talking about the shadows, the thicker the tension became.

I couldn't sit across the fire from her and admire her pretty profile as she stared off into the mountains all night. I had to speak.

"Last night at Silk," I began, "what happened with me and that guy . . . that can't happen again. That's not me."

Harper glanced at the fire, the flames dancing in her eyes. It suited her. "I know." Her gaze flicked to me. "What set you off like that?"

I scoffed. "Besides a stranger lusting after you?"

A smile tugged at her lips. "Besides that."

How did I explain this? Leaning forward in my seat, I rested my elbows on my knees. "Have you never noticed how my powers work when I'm around you? How I take your edge off? From the first time we met, I sensed the darkness surrounding you. It was like your energy had its own frequency, and it called directly to my abilities. You came around, and my angel senses lit up. I was created to draw all that iniquity burdening your soul away.

"The problem is, the more of your shadows I fight off, the more consumed I become." I tugged at the hair on my cheeks and stared into the flames.

It seemed symbolic somehow that we were separated by fire.

Harper's expression grew pained. "I feel less heavy when you're around." A sad laugh escaped. "You take my edge off, and I cause you trouble."

I closed my eyes at the defeat in her voice. "I can rid you of them. You know I have that ability. It would be simple." More than simple.

I reopened my eyes, curious for her reaction. It was what I'd expected. Shock, pain, maybe even a little revulsion. Unsurprisingly, she was surrounded by inky silhouettes, their murmurs low as they kept their distance.

"I haven't done that," I reminded her, lest she forget. "I've only used my gifts to banish them when they were a danger to you. I know you feel as though you need them. I don't understand it, but I know where you stand. I care about you enough to respect your wishes."

Harper's gaze was guarded, a look she'd worn her entire life.

"What I'm asking is that you understand my place here. I'm an angel in . . . who's falling for a summoner. I don't care. I'll deal with the bastards all day, every day if it means I get you. But if you don't rein them in and control them, they will turn dangerous. To everyone." I stood and circled the firepit slowly, giving her time to argue if she chose. "You don't have to get rid of them. You just need to control them."

Harper looked at me, her green eyes huge. "Now understand my position. I haven't lived a lifetime, and I admit I don't have the type of control I should, but when the only thing you've ever had to depend on is darkness, it makes the light harder to look at. When people have spent so long being afraid of you that you even start fearing yourself."

"I'm not afraid of you, Harper Sinclair." I squatted down in front of her chair. "Depend on me."

"I don't want to hurt you."

I rocked forward, my palms running up her jeans-clad thighs until the tips of my fingers were close enough to tease her center. "Does it look like I'm being hurt here?" I gripped her hips and tugged her forward in her chair. "Babe, if this is your definition of hurt, please, hurt me."

Harper's mouth parted in a silent *O* and white puffs of air mingled between us for one . . . two . . . three breaths before she fisted the collar of my shirt and fell forward from her seat. With her mouth on mine, I landed back first on the cold concrete with my little shadow lover straddling my lap.

Last night we'd made love, our pace slow, exploring. This was the opposite. This was hands tearing at buttons, teeth clashing, arms wrestling. This was Harper grinding into my rock hard erection until I dug my fingers into her hip flexors to pause the torture.

Harper lifted all of five inches from my mouth, a frown on hers. I bucked up and sucked her pouting bottom lip into my mouth, pulling a lusty groan from her throat.

"I'll fuck you out here all spring, summer, and fall, but your ass will be numb and your tits will freeze off in this weather. Since I happen to be extremely fond of these"—my hands tweaked her breasts—"could we move this inside?"

Harper giggled and agreed.

The reprieve didn't last long. She stripped as she led me up the stairs and into my bedroom, looking over her shoulder the entire way to verify that each piece of her abandoned clothing was matched with something of mine.

She took my dick in her palm the moment we reached my bed. "You want me to exercise control?" she asked, a hint of aggression flashing over her features.

I raised my arms in surrender. "I'm all yours."

It was a good thing I was immortal because this woman could kill me.

Harper wasted no time, rolling a condom on me before she slid her wet folds down my shaft with a relieved sigh.

I bit my lip and swallowed every curse known to man at the absolutely exquisite feeling of her body riding mine. Her head dropped forward as she pressed up on her knees, then sank down on my dick.

I fisted her long hair with one hand and circled her clit with the other.

Harper cursed, then twisted her hips. I nearly blacked out.

"Look at me," I ordered as I pulled at her hair again.

Her flushed face met mine, but she didn't stop moving over me.

"Do you see me?" I asked. Her eyes widened in answer. "Not good enough. Do you see me, Harper?"

My thumb applied a little more pressure to her clit, circling. "Yes," she gasped.

"Am I hard to look at?"

Her head shook. Not in answer, but in confusion.

I growled and yanked her arms, which were anchored on my chest for leverage, out from beneath her. Her chest fell forward, and I wrapped my arms around her back before flipping us over without losing our intimate connection.

"Am I hard to look at?" I asked again. I lifted her hips and sunk into her body as deeply as I could. "Does my light bother you?"

Recognition at her own words being thrown back at her hit, and she dug her nails into my ass, holding me still when all my body wanted to do was withdraw and slam its way back in. "I see you, Elias."

Her hold released, and I slipped my palm beneath her knee and shifted it toward her chest. The move changed my angle. Harper's head tossed from side to side on my pillow, her hand clenching my bicep as I quickened my thrusts.

"I want you to trust me," I told her. "I need you to know I won't desert you. I'm not afraid of you."

I believed in her innate goodness, but I also knew how strong the darkness was within her. *Even the devil was an angel once.* The sentiment had never failed to remind me of how precarious the battle between Heaven and Hell was. And I wouldn't forget how close she was to both sides—her beautiful soul and her hellbound fierceness.

I sunk forward and hid my face in the crook of her neck as my balls grew tight and release found me. Harper murmured and gasped, her hips riding out the waves of my orgasm, then following up with one of her own not a minute later.

It was only after I'd collapsed on my side and Harper had fallen asleep that I allowed myself to acknowledge that the aggression in our coupling—on both our sides—as mind-blowing as it was, had been fueled by her darkness.

# CHAPTER 10

## HARPER

Sleep was a double-edged sword for me. It gave me the chance to rest, but it also thinned the veil between reality and my subconscious. It made me more vulnerable to the darkness within, and to the temptation it wrought.

This was the reason I'd begun sleepwalking. Not the kind of sleepwalking that caused problems or put me in danger. So far, I'd never left my house. On some level, I wasn't even fully asleep. I knew what I was doing, but I couldn't stop it. Or maybe it was that I didn't *want* to stop it. It was more like my brain's free time to leave me messages to myself, making me aware of the things I fought to ignore when I was awake. And because I was a spiritual writer by birth, those messages usually came in words. Such as a red lipstick message on a mirror or a dry erase marker on the refrigerator.

I knew the moment I woke up that my world was about to come crashing down.

The last few days had been a high for me, a shadow-drugged binge that let me experience more emotions than I'd experienced in my entire life. All at once.

And the person who had been there to carry me, the one who'd seen me through the chaos, was Elias Jamison.

He was sitting next to the bed when I opened my eyes, his hard gaze on my face. There was no softness to his expression, but there was a softness to his eyes. It was his eyes I was trusting my heart with.

"I think we need to talk," Elias said, reaching out to push my hair off of my face.

My heart broke, and somehow I knew it was my fault.

"What did I do?" I asked.

*"You told the truth,"* the shadows said, satisfied.

Rather than wait for Elias's response, I sprang from his bed, making a beeline for his bedroom door. My body knew just where to take me. Which meant one thing.

I'd left him a message.

Pausing in his kitchen, I let my mouth fall open. *Oh, Harper! What have you done?*

There, written in marker, were the words, "Go to hell. The darkness is my sanctuary. Release me to it."

The message was cold, cruel, and completely unlike me. It was my handwriting, but the words were rougher, the strokes I'd made with the marker bolder than usual.

But, deep down, I knew they were my words. I knew what I had written was even how I felt to some extent.

I'd said to him what I'd been wanting to say to the world. But to Elias, because of what he was and because of what we'd shared, it had to feel like a knife stab through the heart. The way he'd begged me to trust him, to look at him . . .

A tear slipped down my cheek.

*"You did nothing wrong,"* the shadows whispered, their dark forms creeping into the space. *"Walk away from him, Harper."*

"Get out of my house!" Elias roared from behind me, having obviously followed me to his kitchen. "You aren't welcome here."

He had every right to be angry, every right to send them away. This was his house, his space. Not mine. But the shadows were part of me now. In a way, I was part of them. Images of the two of us making love, the wild way I'd let go of myself, ran through my head, and I placed a fist against my mouth. I'd never felt like this before. Not with anyone except Elias.

That was part of the problem.

*"Get away from him!"* Whatever warmth I received from the spirits was gone. Their anger, their hatred, was palpable.

I touched the scar on my side, the place where the shadows had once ripped out of my skin. "I-I . . ."

The shadows weren't weak. They were fierce, completely capable of controlling me as much as I was capable of controlling them. Only the way they acted now around Elias—agitated and inconsolable—made it hard for me to get a handle on them.

Words wouldn't come. Sobs tore out of me instead, the racking tears completely shaking my body. I had never been cruel before.

"I don't know whether to be pissed or sad," Elias said. "Did you mean that?"

I didn't turn around to see if he was looking at the words. Because if I looked at him, what I had to say next would be harder.

"Yes." But not the way he thought. "I'm not good for you."

"Bullshit. They're lying to you, Harper. They hate me. They want you all to themselves."

*"We're not the ones trying to change who she is, angel."*

My shoulders slumped. The shadows weren't lying, as much as I hated to admit it. Elias wasn't trying to change me, but when I was around him, I kept trying to change myself anyway. For him. Even if he wasn't asking it of me. And that, in itself, was exhausting. "I'm tired of holding it back. It hurts me to pretend I'm not part demon. It hurts me to pretend I'm not a summoner. It makes me act worse and raises the chance of me hurting someone if I hold it back, because then it just builds up."

"Dammit," Elias gripped the back of his head. "I'm not asking you to cover up who you are! I love who you are, but you can't let them control you, Harper." His words were a repeat of the night before.

"No." Inhaling, I choked back my tears. "I have to quit

pretending the shadows aren't my responsibility. I've tied them to me, and I am responsible for them."

I turned toward him. "You make me feel good, Elias. You make me feel better about what I am, but you also make me feel guilty." There it was. The honest truth. "You make me feel guilty for wanting to invite the darkness in."

Elias stood before me, magnificent in only a pair of low-slung blue jeans. "That's not my intention. That's . . . I can help you."

The shadows screamed, the sound of their wails so loud, I fell to my knees, my hands gripping my head. "Stop."

This wasn't helping. The shadows' reaction to Elias was hurting me. "They're hurting me because of you," I said.

*"You'll be stronger if you walk away,"* the shadows assured me. *"We can keep you safe. You need us, not him."*

Elias fell to his knees and grabbed my arms. "I'm trying to understand this. I've seen creatures, good and evil of every kind, but you have changed the rules of what you are. These spirits and demons do not belong to you; they belong to the Infernum. How can you trust them?"

I ignored Elias and concentrated on the shadows' arguments. "They're going about it all wrong."

Elias frowned. "What are you talking about? Going about what wrong?"

"Protecting me."

Elias inched forward. "Demons don't protect people, Harper."

"These do. They protect me." I didn't mean to sound argumentative, but my words came out defensive and hard. These demons had stayed with me even after my ordeal with the Collector. They'd been there when I screamed in my sleep and woke up covered in sweat, my heart a beating drum in my chest. I owed them a certain amount of loyalty.

Elias's gaze darkened, his voice lowering as he fell back to sit on the floor. "Is that what it feels like?" He paused, studying me. "I'd know if you were possessed."

"Then you know I'm not." I wasn't possessed. The shadows

weren't here to use me. Were they? They wanted me to use them. I just hadn't quite figured out how to do it safely.

"You're not a bad person," Elias told me, his tone certain, as if he needed to convince himself.

*"Say it!"* the shadows yelled. *"Admit it!"*

The words poured out of me before I had the chance to hold them back. Deep down, I didn't want to admit what I knew I needed to face. I *liked* what I was becoming. "You don't have to be a bad person to want bad things."

I expected Elias to jerk back, to use this moment to completely break away from me, but he surprised me by staying firmly in place. He dipped his head and locked his gaze on mine. "What kind of bad things are we talking about?"

"Depends on if we're talking about the bedroom or in general." I'd gone from defensive to suggestive. And it felt *good*.

"Don't try to distract me, Harper. Not now," Elias said firmly. "Speaking of, I'd like to make love to you, Harper, not your shadows. Is that unreasonable?"

"You haven't made love to the shadows. I haven't let them in enough for that. Would you like to see what it's like when I really let them in?" There'd only been one time when I'd allowed the shadows complete entry into my body. I'd been a prisoner of the Collector and afraid of losing the people I loved.

*"Do it!"* the shadows cried gleefully. They lived for this.

"Don't," Elias warned.

*"Let us in, Harper. We'll take care of him."*

I pounded the floor with my fists. There were too many voices in my head. Too many things both the shadows and Elias wanted from me. It was all too much. "I can't learn to control them when you're around."

Elias stared at me. "I can—"

"No, you can't. Not with the way they feel about you." I wasn't choosing the shadows over Elias. I was choosing to control this on my own so that I could invite Elias into my chaos.

I was tired of being a risk. Some demons did have hearts. At least this demonic human did, because I could feel it breaking.

I'd never felt this way about anyone, not even the fallen angel who'd swept into my life more than a year ago. Lucas Fox had been exciting, different, and new. Wise in ways I would never understand.

But it was Elias who had called to my soul. Even then. The moment he'd locked eyes with me on the sidewalk outside Coffee Haven a year ago, right before my first demonic experience since childhood, I'd known he was different.

Elias was the one who stayed. Elias was the one who helped me accomplish my list of firsts. Elias was the one who sent me texts of encouragement when I needed to be a hero. Elias was the friend who never pushed. He simply offered.

I'd depended on him too much.

"I need to help myself." My words were shaky, but honest.

What I really wanted to say was, "I love you, Elias. I love you so much I need to figure myself out so I can love you the way you deserve." But I didn't say that, because I was afraid he wouldn't let me leave.

Elias dropped his head, his hands working their way into his pockets. The way we were now was nothing like we'd been the night before. I saw the worry on his face. He was having doubts, too, but his need to protect me was stronger than his misgivings. Which meant I needed to be the one to push away.

I'd never felt so vulnerable and yet so true to myself. I was letting Elias see a part of me no one else had ever seen. Even my Aunt Eloise.

"Take me home?" I asked quietly.

Elias nodded.

Leaving me, he entered his bedroom and returned fully clothed, my clothes in his fist. He pulled my shirt over my head, then handed me my jeans. "I'll take you home."

He walked toward the door and stopped. His spine stiffened as he looked at his ruined wall.

"Hey, Harper?" His voice broke, and he cleared his throat. I couldn't make a sound, and Elias looked over his shoulder. "Just so we're clear, you're the one doing the abandoning here. I was willing to stay."

He opened the door and disappeared down the stairs.

I had never felt so broken.

# CHAPTER 11

## ELIAS

*G*o to hell. *The darkness is my sanctuary. Release me to it.*

Two days later, Harper's words remained scrawled across my kitchen wall in bold black marker. And, as if that wasn't enough of a kick to the groin, she'd also left a friend behind.

*"An angel and a demon."* The shadow demon taunted me day and night. *"Tell me your real fear, angel?"*

"That I'll never have another moment of peace." I sank lower on my couch. "Would you get the hell out of here?"

I'd angled the couch toward the wall so I could see Harper's truths on display whenever I needed reminding. Instead of strengthening my resolve, it served to weaken it. I refused to believe that she thought we weren't good together. I refused to believe that two nights of passion was all we would ever have.

The demon floated toward the wall with a sort of snickering laugh. *"She wasn't wrong. I know your truest fears, angel. You cannot hide them from my kind."*

"Yeah? What's that?"

*"You killed her."*

For a moment, I was confused. Then the *her* he meant came into focus. He wasn't speaking of Harper. No, he was tearing at the bandages of my past. Ripping the hastily sewn seams loose.

Phaedra—she was my one true weakness. Or she had been, before Harper.

Sitting forward, I dropped my forearms to my knees and grabbed my head. "Clever little bastard, aren't you?"

*"They will want to use her powers for their purpose. She is strong, but she is alone."*

His warning was clear. He didn't mean the shadow demons that haunted her, although they were problematic. He meant others. The fallen ones, higher-class demons, even some residents of our town—the ones you wouldn't trust with your worst enemy—would be interested in the girl with the power to channel spirits and demons. And they would especially be interested in using her ability to possibly find a way to open a portal to the Infernum. Harper's skill set, even when she was at her weakest, was dangerous. The more self-aware she became, the scarier she was.

"What do you care? You and your damned friends wanted me out of her life . . ." I shut my mouth. Why in the hell did I continue to argue with these contradictory creatures?

*"You could join us, angel. Feed the darkness of the world,"* the shadow hissed.

In this moment, with my heart shattered and strewn about the floor, the offer was more appealing than I cared to admit. I took the glass sitting on the floor at my feet and threw it across the room. The shadow disappeared.

I picked up my phone again and again over the next few days, wanting to text Harper. Her shadow demon had not returned to my place since I threw an empty scotch glass at its inky little body. I almost missed the guy. One thing he'd said replayed in my mind: *"She is strong, but she is alone."*

It was like these creatures truly *did* care about her. His comment wasn't a warning to goad me into anger or pain; it felt more like his own thoughts. Like he knew that Harper couldn't handle herself alone forever. She was so much more capable than she knew, but even the strongest beings needed someone at their side. Wasn't that what I'd tried to convince Hamon of for years after he set his vendetta into action, alone? He survived, but at what price? What was the price for my mistakes? Andras and Phaedra were gone. Breckin and Vivienne were hunted.

I wanted to protect her. That was all. The shadows wanted to protect her, too. I could finally admit that, as hard as it was. They didn't want her to be alone. They just didn't want *me* with her. Unless I gave in to the darkness.

And that I would not do. I was made of light. But I could embrace her darkness. If she'd let me.

# CHAPTER 12

## HARPER

*I* was perched on the side of a snow-covered cliff holding a camera, my gaze on the mountains before me, when the pain of the last few days hit me. The wind ran its cold fingers through my hair, the lightly falling snow stinging my cheeks. Winter in Havenwood Falls was as brutal as it was beautiful.

The shadows that trailed me swept up into the air, hovering. They were euphoric because they thought they'd won.

Staring up at them, I breathed the frigid air into my lungs and braced myself.

*"You're angry,"* they said. It wasn't a question. They stated it because they knew they were right.

"You did the same thing that everyone else has done to me," I told them. "You think you know so much about what's right for me that it's clouding what is *actually* right for me."

My voice rose on the word *actually*, and it echoed off of the mountains.

Desi lay in the snow in the distance watching. He was only there to observe unless something went wrong. Today, I was working on controlling the shadows, even if it meant I was hurt in the process. Because I needed to get control of them before I saw

Elias again, before I confessed how I really felt about him. Otherwise, I wouldn't feel right about being a part of his life.

I'd taken a long journey over the last year. It had started with me discovering what made me different and ended here, with me gaining control. A complete circle.

"He who is not courageous enough to take risks will accomplish nothing in life," Desi called.

Pulling my camera from my neck, I placed it in my camera bag and set it in the snow. "Wow. When did you become a philosopher?"

"I didn't," he replied. "But Muhammad Ali's words sure sounded good coming from me, right?"

I snorted. "I should have known."

Desi scooted closer, and then backed away again. "In all seriousness, Harper. Sometimes it takes risking yourself to realize yourself. And those *are* my words."

Risk. It was a four-letter word that held a big punch. Like *love* and *fear*. Actually, there were a lot of scary four-letter words. I made a list of them in my head: like, love, fear, lose, and fail.

Desi studied me. "The way I see it, the only way you're going to find out whether or not you can exist the way you want to in this world, despite your powers, is to fully put yourself out there. Why do you think things happened the way they did with Elias? You've held yourself back from feeling a full range of human emotions for so long that you intentionally separated your thoughts, turning them into an internal battle between the angel on one shoulder and the demon on the other. When really, your demon and angel are the same person."

It was more than I'd ever heard Desi say at one time. In that moment, I realized just how old and observant he really was.

My gaze returned to the shadows. "Come to me," I told them. They obeyed, lowering until they were eye level. "You belong to me. Not the other way around."

*"We belong to each other,"* the shadows argued.

"I think you've gotten confused. You lived, you broke the rules, and you died to become a part of a terrible place full of terrible energy. You're not here to be redeemed. You're here to be controlled." My voice was confident. Most of the dark spirits who followed me had been people once, people who'd lived a life of crime and cruelty or who had sold their souls to darkness. In death, they had gone where all dark souls go.

It was the same for the lower-caste demons who also followed me. They were too weak where they came from to rise in rank, too weak to become the demons they really wanted to be.

I pitied them, but I wasn't their redemption. No matter how much they wanted me to be.

I'd drawn them in, my power a beacon of light. Which was ironic, since I brought darkness to the ones I loved the most.

My hand fell to my side, my fingers lifting the hem of my shirt to feel the skin beneath, to the raised scar that would always remind me of what had happened between me and the shadows. I'd been weak and injured then. I wasn't weak or injured now.

"We need boundaries, if this is going to work," I told them. "You either listen to me or I find a way to send you back to where you came from. Understood? Seriously, I'm the lesser of the evils here."

The spirits circled me, growing in density until they became a vortex of darkness. I was standing inside a funnel cloud, the center of a hurricane of hell.

They were testing me.

I thought back on my time in captivity, when I'd been trapped inside of a pitch-black room with nothing except the Collector's advice. Then, I'd been trying to escape the darkness and the shadows that liked to trail me.

"*You were never meant to escape it. Embrace it,*" the Collector had said. "*Use them.*"

I closed my eyes, then reopened them. The shadows were glowing, having transformed from the dark forms I was used to into black masses full of sparkling glitter. It was as if someone had poured jewels onto the night sky, and then turned the world upside down so that I was walking in space among the stars.

My mouth fell open, my eyes widening. This was the moment of truth.

I let myself be sad because my power fed off lesser-used emotions, tears spilling down my cheeks. My heart hurt, thoughts of Elias fresh, his love an open festering wound.

The frustration I felt, the ineptness, and the regret all gathered within me, and I fed off it, inhaling sharply.

The shadows were sucked toward me, as if they were liquid inside of a straw. Each time I inhaled, they drew closer until they were right in front of my face, a whisper on my lips before I swallowed them.

I felt like the wolf in *Little Red Riding Hood*.

When I was growing up, my aunt Eloise had either read me stories or played books on audio because I'd been unable to read. Since spirits came to me in words, and I'd once predicted a man's death by accident as a child through a written message, I hadn't been allowed to read or write. I'd been guarded and kept in check.

So much of my life had been regulated. All because I was innately evil.

Maybe this was why I'd related the most to the villains in fairy tales. The heroines had always been too perfect, their perfection part of what led to their victory. I'd felt sorry for the villains. Like the stepmother who'd been afraid of losing her beauty in *Snow White*, or the stepmother who'd been afraid of losing her position in *Cinderella*. They'd had real fears, real concerns. Things most of us fear, but are too afraid to admit. And they'd lashed out at the people they could have loved, had they faced their demons.

Fear. It's a mighty four-letter word.

The shadows' warmth pressed into my skin, chasing away the winter chill, as they seeped into my body through my pores, mouth, and nose.

I choked them down, my skin glowing, my vision sharpening.

There was no doubt in my mind I looked like an ice queen at the moment, my skin luminous, my eyes chunks of coal.

Power filled me, and I reveled in it.

*Control it, Harper,* I told myself. *Don't let them control you.*

I was treading a fine line between giving in and taking over.

My skin hurt, and my heart pounded.

"*Harper,*" the shadows pleaded. "*Use us.*"

Greedy little bastards.

I may have related to the villains in the stories I'd heard growing up, but there was one way I differed.

I loved someone more than I loved power. I loved someone more than I feared failure. And I needed to show him I was worthy of him.

Love. It's a scary four-letter word. It's also a triumphant four-letter word.

"My way," I said. "This is going to be done my way."

The dark funnel cloud that had churned around me before now churned inside of me, growing in power, making my stomach hurt and my head throb.

I gritted my teeth. "My way!"

Swallowing hard, I focused on the ground before me, my hand reaching for the snow.

"Please," I whispered. Even though I felt confident, a little *please* to the universe couldn't hurt.

"Heat," I breathed. Energy rolled off me.

The snow melted before my eyes, turning the ice into slush around my boot-covered feet.

I laughed, and the shadows used the vulnerable moment to rocket out of me, desperate to escape.

"Holy wow!" Desi exclaimed.

My laughter continued, the sound relieved and gleeful all at once. All I'd done was melt a little snow, but it was a start. I'd controlled the shadows rather than letting them control me, even though it had hurt like hell.

Today, I had succeeded. Tomorrow, I might fail. But with each success I'd get stronger. With each failure, I'd learn something new.

This was the Harper I wanted and needed to be.

This was the Harper I was going to quit fighting. This was the Harper that was going to return to Elias.

~

For more than a week, I couldn't quit thinking about Elias and the way I felt around him.

Deep down, I knew the way we'd separated after making love had not been a bad thing. Even if it had been emotional and painful. I think, in retrospect, I'd gained strength from Elias, the kind of strength I needed to fight for myself on my own for the first time in my life. I'd needed this time to find a way to rein in my shadow demons enough that they wouldn't constantly torment him. That seriously wasn't healthy for a relationship.

Even so, I missed him so much it hurt. A week had passed, each day spent in different locations around Havenwood Falls while I practiced using the shadows. It helped me gain a confidence I'd been lacking, even though I failed as much as I succeeded.

The Court was watching me. I caught glimpses of Court members, their gazes tracking me, when I was around town, and I knew part of that was because of the striptease I'd done at Silk. There had been a lot of supernaturals present when I lost control, and the way I'd pulled magic from the Infernum had filled the space with a dark frenzy I knew people would talk about for weeks to come. The supernaturals, anyway.

The humans were, fortunately, completely oblivious.

For the first time in my life, I'd caused a true scandal. I kind of enjoyed being looked at in a different light. Even if it was embarrassing. The worst part was Aunt Eloise. Because she raised me, I thought of her more as my mother than my aunt, and she'd been giving me the side-eye ever since she overheard Irene Beckett telling one of the other busybodies in town that I had nice firm breasts. How Irene discovered things like that even when she wasn't present blew my mind.

*Only Irene Beckett.* The woman was incorrigible, her age and human status making her gossip all the more impressive. For some reason, the Court members respected her enough to leave her be, completely overlooking the fact that she knew too much about the supes when she wasn't a supe herself.

"Hmm," Aunt Eloise murmured when I entered her shop, her head down, her lips pursed. It was a few days away from Valentine's Day, which was one of the busiest times of year for Eloise's Into the Mystic New Age shop. People got sentimental around Valentine's, especially those whose loved ones had passed on. Widows wanted to reconnect with their deceased spouses, and lovers wanted to talk with their deceased loves one final time.

I felt their anguish, and the angel I'd shared a bed with wasn't even dead. As a matter of fact, I was pretty sure he was close to impossible to kill.

"Would you quit *hmm*ing me already?" I requested, frowning. "So I did a thing, and it's over now."

The shop was a colorful mess of mismatched furniture, purple fabric, crystals, candles, books, and magical objects. As for where everything was located . . . well, that changed quite a bit. Aunt Eloise had a penchant for rearranging things. She also had an affinity for herbal teas and Van Morrison. As a matter of fact, she had a Morrison record playing on her turntable even now, the sound of it filling the space.

"Hmm," Aunt Eloise repeated, throwing me a look.

"What?" I asked.

"So it's over now?" she asked. "The whole stripping thing or Elias?"

My cheeks burned from embarrassment. "Elias isn't over. He's far from over."

Eloise sauntered toward me, as bright as ever in a pair of hot-pink leggings and a long-sleeved tunic covered in pink, puckered lips. Silver hoop earrings dangled from the bottom holes in her ears, a line of heart earrings fastened in the holes above them. Her white-streaked auburn hair was pulled up into a ponytail, held back by two pink scrunchies.

My aunt had always been this way, as loud in the way she dressed and looked as she was kind and compassionate in nature.

"So"—she leaned on the store's counter and placed her chin in her hands—"so what you're saying is that you—"

"Love him," I finished. It was easier to say out loud than I thought it would be, the words feeling warm and beautiful on my tongue.

Van Morrison crooned "Someone Like You" in the background, and Eloise sighed. "To be young again." Her gaze met mine. "Have you told him?"

I shook my head.

She glared. "Does he read minds, Harper? Because the last time I checked, angels had a hard time reading your thoughts because of the Infernum. Which means he needs to hear you say it."

"I needed to get control of something first," I said quietly.

There were things Aunt Eloise didn't know. Or maybe she did, and she pretended not to for my privacy's sake. She was a psychic, after all, which meant she could sense the darkness that followed me. Either way, I'd never spoken aloud to her about the shadows. Only those closest to me and the Court members actually knew about the spirits that trailed me. Eloise had kept her distance when the Court questioned me after the incident with the Collector. I hadn't wanted to burden her with my fears. She'd done enough raising me.

"And now?" Eloise asked.

I'd been working on my powers for more than a week while Desi guarded me. While I'd had trouble and even slipped up a few times, I'd gotten better and better at pulling the spirits into me and using their energy. It no longer hurt to open myself up to them, and they no longer fought to control me. I had a long way to go, possibly many years ahead, but I had enough control over them to keep them from bothering the man I loved. Which meant I could move forward.

I think the shadows were afraid I'd send them back into the Infernum forever, but they were wrong. Then I'd be at a disadvantage. I may not be a bad person, but I liked being able to express myself more. I liked knowing that if the time came that I needed to protect myself, I had the power to do just that. I had the power to control a shadow army.

The shadows no longer crowded me; their inky forms wavered in the distance until I called them forward.

I liked the way they made me feel wicked without me actually being wicked. I wanted to save the wicked for the one person I knew I could share it with, the one man I knew could handle that side of me.

My kind of wicked was perfect for the bedroom.

Visions of me and Elias, our limbs tangled together, popped into my head, and I fisted my hand into my shirt.

*Please let him accept the darkness in me,* I thought. I knew he didn't mind the demonic side of me, but I also knew by the look I'd seen in his eyes that he worried about it. Even if he pretended he didn't.

Valentine's Day was coming, and I wanted to prove to him—and to myself—that I was capable of being the strong woman he needed in his life.

"Are you going to the Cupids and Cuties party at Whisper Falls Inn this year?" Eloise asked suddenly. "Because I think maybe you should."

I'd never attended before. A masked formal affair, Cupids and Cuties was an annual Havenwood Falls event held on Valentine's Day for guests eighteen and older, where attendees could supposedly find their true love. My aunt had been on my case to attend since my eighteenth birthday.

Honestly, there was no reason for me to go.

"I'll be there." My response surprised both of us, my wide gaze meeting my aunt's equally wide stare.

"You're going?" she asked. "Really?"

I started to shake my head, but the word "yes" escaped my lips in the gesture's place.

Eloise whistled. "Well, I'll be damned, Harper. I thought it would be harder to convince you."

"You said I should go," I defended.

My aunt straightened, stepping away from the counter she'd been leaning on to check her appointment book. "Just don't strip."

"Aunt Eloise!"

She shrugged. "What? Did you think I was going to avoid saying that out loud forever?" Her eyes fell to my chest. "Luckily you took after your mother's side of the family."

"Aunt Eloise!" I protested again.

She tapped her appointment book. "I don't suppose you feel up to talking with the Juniper widower, huh? Poor guy comes every year, and I don't have the heart to inform him that his wife keeps saying 'That damn bastard nagged me enough in life. Tell him to give me a break in death while I have the chance.'"

A snort escaped me. "Now that's romance."

The sarcastic joke automatically left my lips, but my thoughts weren't on the Junipers. They were on Elias.

My heart needed him.

# CHAPTER 13

## ELIAS

*T*he embossed invitation had arrived three days ago with no return address.

Cupids & Cuties
Valentine's Day, Twilight
Whisper Falls Inn

*Black tie affair.*

I'd laughed my ass off first. Then, after I'd sat on my couch, staring at Harper's words still covering my kitchen wall, it hit me. The invitation had to be from her. Who else would send one to me? No one, that's who. No one in their right mind would invite me to some fancy party where, per the invite, "Cupid's aim strikes at the heart—that's how you know it's true love."

What the hell kind of shit was this?

With great reluctance, I dressed in formal black and headed toward the town square and Whisper Falls Inn. I shuffled my way inside behind the long line of arrivals as Michaela Petran greeted us at the door. In her hand were two items, both of which I was forced to take. The first was a white face mask.

"Seriously?" I cocked a brow.

"Love goes beyond what we can see on the outside," Michaela explained. "Cupid's aim strikes at the heart—that's how you know it's true love."

"Okay, and what's the arrow for?" I asked with a resigned shrug, looking at the white arrow with gold trim.

This time Michaela smirked at my tone. Surely she'd dealt with her fair share of men arriving under duress tonight. "When their aim is true, they'll light up for you. Follow the arrow's tip to your special lover's lips."

"Follow the arrow's tip?" I looked at the people behind me and leaned in. "You know what I am, Michaela. Can you please explain exactly how these little paper arrows work?"

Her lips pursed. "And ruin the fun?"

My blank face told her exactly what I thought of her fun. This type of party wasn't my idea of a good time to begin with, but add my stress, and the fact that I hadn't spoken to or seen Harper in nearly three weeks, and I was about ready to tell Michaela where she could stick her arrow.

"The magic doesn't lie." She winked.

I shook my head in disbelief and followed the flow of guests toward the ballroom on the first floor. Everything about this event shouted at me to turn around and run. The possibility of seeing Harper kept me rooted in place. The room wasn't packed, but there was a good turnout. More than I would have thought, considering a private date and a nice meal out seemed like the better option for tonight. Never underestimate a person's desire to know if their one true love is truly their one true love.

I tied on the mask and skimmed the crowd, looking for long brown locks and bright green eyes. It was the faded hue of an angel she wore that I spotted first—a mark of protection—only it was no longer Lucas's blue. It was a pale red. *My* mark alerted others she was watched over by angels. To most, that was deterrent enough to stay clear. I wished the mark gave her angelic gifts, because then she'd have that to help her with her own powers, but it was only a warning for those who might try to harm her.

My heart rate accelerated as I watched her speaking with her aunt Eloise, who stood by her side. Even though masks covered half their faces, I could spot the Sinclair women anywhere. *Angelic perks.*

It took twenty seconds of watching Harper's backside in the slim red column dress she wore before I walked her way. Thoughts and phrases tumbled over themselves to be the first to be said.

"I'm sorry."

"I miss you."

"I think I'm in love with you."

Something that proved I knew her demons and accepted them, and whatever came with them. Words failed when she turned around and I found her green eyes staring back at me.

~

## HARPER

The arrow in my hand lit up, and I just knew it was him. I didn't need an event or even the arrow itself to tell me whom I was in love with. I knew. Heart, body, and soul, I simply *knew.*

The moment I looked up to find Elias Jamison gazing down at me, I wanted to soothe away the worry I saw in his eyes. His lips were slightly parted, as if there were words he wanted to say trapped by indecision. I'd done that to him.

He was magnificent in a black suit and tie, his broad frame filling it out in a way most men couldn't. Even with the mask he had pulled over his face, I would have known it was him. Well, with the beard, it was also kind of obvious.

Elias had always been there for me, even when he'd had his doubts. It was time for me to be there for him. I wasn't the same Harper I'd been a year ago. I was stronger, more confident, and brave. In large part because of him.

"Thank God, you got my invitation," Aunt Eloise exclaimed from behind me.

I should have been surprised by her declaration, but I wasn't. I'd wondered why she'd pushed me to attend, even after hearing about my declaration of love for the fallen angel. I think that's why I accepted her push to come without a fight. Because, somehow, I knew my aunt would get Elias here.

Startled, Elias's gaze shot up and away from me, but I placed my free hand against his arm to draw his attention back to me. This wasn't his kind of event, but he'd come, and I knew it was because of me. This was *my* Elias, and I loved him more than words could say.

Raising my glowing arrow, I pointed it at him and nodded at the lit up arrow in his own hand. "I think this is where we're supposed to kiss."

"Harper—" he began.

I didn't give him the chance to speak. Lifting onto my toes, I planted my lips against his in a gentle kiss that didn't demand anything. It simply said words I didn't think I could say here inside a crowded room.

"Can we do this somewhere else?" I asked, pulling away just enough to glance up into his face.

Elias yanked the mask off, his gaze fierce. "If you leave here with me, Harper, so help me—"

"I'm yours," I whispered. The shadows that followed me appeared behind him, hovering, and I shooed them away. The darkness didn't control me. I controlled it. "I'm yours."

Elias saw what I did, an impressed glint lighting up his eyes as his hand dropped down to mine, his fingers entwining with mine before tugging me toward the entrance.

Michaela tried to stop us at the door. "But you just got here," she protested.

We kept moving forward, dropping the arrows into her hands as we passed by. Elias and I were both reclusive people. It was one of the things that had drawn us together. We were wounded souls with too many stories to tell. Especially him.

I didn't ask where he was taking us, and I didn't care. Honestly, I barely remembered getting into his truck or the ride to our destination.

It hardly even registered that we were at his house before we were suddenly through his front door.

We shed our clothes before we even made it to the bedroom, leaving a trail of fabric from his front door to the side of his bed.

The words I'd scrawled on his kitchen wall were a blur as we passed by, sending a jolt through my soul. He'd kept the message. Maybe as a reminder? I knew, for me, it was imprinted in my brain and on my heart as the moment I took charge of my life, all in the name of love.

With Elias, I wanted what we had together to be forever, no matter the obstacles. No matter the dangers.

"Harper."

Coming up behind me, Elias whispered my name into my ear, the feel of his breath sending shivers down my spine. His voice and the warm feel of his body sent wet heat pooling between my legs.

"Harper." He embraced me, his naked frame a wall of steel against my softer flesh. Elias did things to me and for me that no one else had ever been able to do. I was open with him in a way I never could be before. He made me want to spend every day just being with him, and every night sleeping next to him naked. I never slept naked. I slept so overdressed it would make other people uncomfortable. At times, it made *me* uncomfortable, but clothes— even sleep clothes—had always been like a shield to me, a fabric barrier against the world. So many things had changed. For the better.

Tonight, right now, there was no shield, no barrier between my skin and Elias's.

"What—?" I began.

"Shhh." He didn't let me speak, his hand coming up to cover my eyes. "Don't look," he said. "Don't speak. Don't think. Just feel."

I didn't question him. I simply let myself get lost in the sensation, in this beautiful moment when the one person I never suspected would end up my lover was here with me now. Warm. Hard. Safe. In love.

Rather than turn me around, he kept my back to him, my backside pressed into his hard erection while his hand dropped away from my face. I didn't reopen my eyes, leaving them closed, because in truth I liked trusting him like this.

His lips found the sensitive spot just below my ear, his tongue teasing my skin, the feel of his beard adding even more friction, increasing my need. His hand moved over and down my chest, his fingers circling my nipple, gently tugging on it before continuing his journey south. The moment he touched my wet folds, I arched, a cry escaping my lips.

"That's it. Come for me, Harper. Let go." His whispered breath sounded strained yet controlled, his fingers working their magic against my clit.

I lost all strength in my legs. He guided me toward the bed, and my knees sank into his mattress, his large frame bent over mine.

"Please," I begged him.

I'd never made love this way before. I'd lost my virginity at twenty-three, but because I'd only ever had sex with two people, my second time with Elias, my knowledge was limited.

"God, Harper," Elias swore, his fingers bringing me to the edge of oblivion as he entered me from behind, his hips pumping hard and fast.

His fingers applied just the right amount of pressure on my clit, and I came, my muscles clenching around his cock. I screamed his name as his hand left the dampness between my thighs to grip my hips, his thrusts coming quicker and quicker until he stiffened, my name joining his in the still bedroom.

"Shit," Elias breathed, his arm circling my waist to guide me farther onto the bed before rolling us to the side. He slipped out of me, but he didn't let go, his limbs tangling with mine as he embraced me. His chin found my shoulder, and I tugged at his beard.

My emotions were everywhere, the feelings inside me a churning mess.

"I love you." The words slipped out of me unchecked, and I was suddenly glad my back was to him, my gaze on the room's opposite wall.

Elias grew still, our panted breaths the only response to my confession, before his hand suddenly found my chin.

He turned my head gently, leaning up just enough he could look down into my face. "Say that again." The way he looked at me was beautiful, an almost desperate plea in his eyes.

A smile played on my lips. "I love you." The words came easy, the emotion behind them strong. "L-O-V-E. Love, four letters."

Elias grinned. "Last time I checked, I could spell."

"You sure about that? Cause I've got a new hobby. Remember that list of firsts I used to have?"

"Yeah."

"Well, now I'm collecting four-letter words."

Elias laughed, and then sobered. "Please, for the love of God, tell me fuck is one of them."

"I don't know. I think I forgot how to spell. Care to show me instead?"

Elias didn't need any further invitation. This time, he rolled me over, taking me more gently, his lips next to my ear when I came for him. On an exhale, he breathed, "I love you, Harper Sinclair."

I'd never felt so darkly seductive in my life, and yet so full of light and life.

Instead of finding his own release, Elias surprised me by slowing his thrusts, his body stroking mine with a deliberate laziness that extended my pleasure with little aftershocks.

"I think I have another four-letter word for you," he muttered as he teased my neck with his beard.

I clutched at his hip, unsure if I wanted him to stop or if I wanted to go again. "Yeah?"

Jerking his hips, he buried himself deeply. "Mine." He lifted his head and brushed my hair away from my face. "You're mine, Ms. Sinclair. You, Desi, and every one of your shadows—I accept you all."

Lifting my hips to draw him deeper, I touched his cheek. "And we accept you."

The angel born of light and the human born from darkness. The odds were against us, but with love and acceptance on our side we could overcome any obstacles.

# EPILOGUE

## ELIAS

My fingers traced a lazy path along Harper's inner thigh as she slept soundly beside me. Two months together, and I couldn't stop touching her. I doubted if I would ever get enough of her. She'd teased me again and again about watching her sleep.

"Why don't you watch a movie, or read a book, instead of lying here staring at me?" she'd ask. "Don't you get bored?"

Not a chance in hell. My new favorite pastime was studying her. I loved how her flesh faded from passion-tinted pink after we made love to its normal creamy tone. How she slept curled into her side with her hand shoved under her cheek, as she was right now. I spent many nights studying her facial expressions, always watching for that change that told me her shadows were taking hold. I never tried to wake her from her demon-possessed sleepwalking. But I did keep a notepad and pen on nearly every surface of my place and hers. No more writing on the walls for my little *umbra amans*.

I was deeply in love with this woman. Inching closer, I kissed her shoulder gently. In Harper I had found the purpose I'd lost when I'd come to earth.

My hand moved closer to the heat between Harper's thighs, and she sighed, her bare ass shifting backward to grind against me. "This is why I tell you to watch movies."

I chuckled at her sleepy, disgruntled tone. "Am I bothering you?" I teased, my middle finger skimming close enough to know her body was more than ready for me.

"Not in the least." She arched her back and turned, looking over her shoulder.

I cupped her sex and leaned forward to meet her kiss when a ripping pain tore down my spine.

"What the—" I lurched to my knees with a gasp.

"Elias?" Harper's voice shook, panic making it sharp.

"I'm okay. I—" A brilliant light filled my vision, blinding me, as my back erupted with white-hot burning. "Shit."

Harper screamed.

"Harper?" I reached out, searching for her hand.

"I'm right here." Her shaking fingers clutched mine. "What's happening?" Her voice joined the chattering coming from her shadows.

As though my back was tied to bungee cords, twin joints punched through my shoulder blades and threw me off balance, sending me into Harper.

I righted myself, my hands gripping at her arms as my vision cleared. "Are you all right?"

Harper nodded, her green eyes wide. "You . . . um, you've got . . ." Her trembling hand waved toward something over my shoulder.

Black shadows fluttered in my peripheral vision. I twisted around, expecting to see Harper's demons lingering, and was met with inky black and blue feathers. My stomach dropped, and I leapt from our bed.

*Wings.* Heat rushed through me as my emotions went crazy. *I have wings.*

My gaze went skyward. "Is this a joke?"

Rolling my shoulders, I pulled the limbs forward, wrapping

them around my body. I'd lost my wings a century ago. The silky touch of feathers against my skin stole the air from my lungs. *Why?*

"Elias?" Harper whispered. Parting the curtain of my wings, I thrust my hand out and pulled her into my arms. I hid my face in the crook of her neck and shoulder, holding her naked body to mine. "You have wings. They're amazing."

*Why the hell do I have wings?* Leaning back, I brushed a tear from Harper's cheek. I stretched my newly acquired wings to their full span. It was like they'd never been torn from my body. The feathers twitched, as though they'd heard my thoughts. Our bond had already formed. "What is this?"

The telltale scrape of Desi's barbs screeched across the floor, and I knew by the way he entered the space that he knew something.

"This is fate, angel," Desi said as he stopped in the middle of the bedroom. Harper and I shared a glance. Fate. Another four-letter word. The sentient weapon paused before adding, "You will need every advantage you can get for what's to come. You must protect her. You must protect this town."

Harper stiffened in my arms, her eyes fixed on Desi. "How do you know?"

With a knowing sigh, I laced my fingers with Harper's. "The Destroyer would know. His connections run deep."

My wings were back because I was a Dominion angel who'd just been granted a guardianship.

We hope you enjoyed this story in the Havenwood Falls world featuring a variety of supernatural creatures. If you want to read more about Harper, her story begins with *Ink & Fire* by R.K. Ryals and continues with *The Collector: Awakening*, both in the main Havenwood Falls series. You can also see more of Elias in *Awaken the Soul* and *Avenge the Heart* both by Michele G. Miller, in the Havenwood Falls High series.

# ABOUT THE AUTHOR

Writing-obsessed since childhood, Michele once failed seventh-grade math in pursuit of the perfect teen drama (anything for her craft!). These days she fails at housework, cooking, and getting to the school pickup line on time in pursuit of the perfect plot.

Michele writes novels with fairytale love for everyday life. Romance is central to her plots where the genres range from Coming of Age Fantasy and Realistic Fiction to New Adult Romantic Suspense. Among other titles, she is the author of the bestselling From the Wreckage series, a Havenwood Falls author, and co-writes the Paper Planes series with author Mindy Hayes. Mindy and Michele also write clean contemporary titles under the pen name Mindy Michele.

Michele is represented by Italia Gandolfo of Gandolfo Helin & Fountain Literary Management.

Spoiler Alert: Michele still fails at math.

Website: http://www.michelegmillerbooks.com/
Facebook: https://www.facebook.com/AuthorMicheleGMiller
Twitter: https://twitter.com/chelemybelles
Pinterest: http://pinterest.com/chelemybelles/
Instagram: https://instagram.com/chelemybelles/

# ABOUT THE AUTHOR

R.K. Ryals is the author of emotional and gripping young adult and new adult paranormal romance, contemporary romance, and fantasy. With a strong passion for charity and literacy, she works as a full-time writer encouraging people to "share the love of reading one book at a time." An avid animal lover and self-proclaimed coffee-holic, R.K. Ryals was born in Jackson, Mississippi, and makes her home in the Southern U.S. with her husband, her three daughters, two playful cats named Delphi and Paris, and a coffeepot she honestly couldn't live without. Should she ever become the owner of a fire-breathing dragon (tame of course), her life would be complete. Visit her at www.authorrkryals.com.

# ACKNOWLEDGMENTS

Michele:

"I'm so grateful to the people who support me through the book process and life:

My husband and kids deal with me forgetting laundry, dinner, carpool, emails, and the list goes on. How they put up with me I'll never know!

My amazing crew of readers, bloggers, and friends—on Facebook and in real life— keep me sane. You make this solitary writer life a little less solitary, and a lot more lifelike.

My core reader groups on Facebook, Chele's Belles and Mindy and Michele's M&M's: Thanks for being a sounding board when needed, book pimps when needed, and friends always.

To Jo Pettibone: Thank you for walking with me from day one with Viv, Breck, and Elias. And for being the best alpha a writer could have. I'm so lucky to have you. Oh! And for the cookies and brownies you send me. When's the next shipment? (wink)

To the Havenwood Falls family: This group continues to grow, but their generosity, creativity, and enthusiasm for this project astounds me. I'm so lucky to be able to write and collaborate with these amazing creatives. Many of the characters and places I mention in my Havenwood Falls books were created by others in this amazing group.

More specifically, thanks to these ladies for creating and sharing your characters with us in *Dark Seduction*: Randi Cooley Wilson and Kristie Cook. Liz Ferry for your editing genius, and Regina Wamba for your kick-butt cover design.

I can't forget a shout-out to R.K. Ryals for agreeing to co-write #Harlias with me. You have been a dream to work with, my friend.

And of course, a final HUGE thank you to Kristie Cook for creating Havenwood Falls and making this all possible. I will forever be in awe of your business savvy and ingenuity. I'm honored to be a part of this world and blessed to have you as a friend.

R. K.:

I am so thankful to be a part of the Havenwood Falls journey. Writing this story was an adventure I will never forget.

This story would not have been possible without our fearless leader, Kristie Cook. Thank you so much for creating a town that brings authors and characters together in a unique and amazing way. I am so grateful that you are a part of my life.

I am always blown away by the amount of people it takes to bring a story together. There are so many that I want to thank.

First, I have to thank my husband, whose patience and diligence is always such a support for me. To my daughters, who inspire me on a daily basis. I am truly blessed with amazing children. They have passion, determination, and resilience. Raising them to be the strong women I am watching them become humbles me.

A heartfelt thank you to my personal assistant, Christina Silcox. Not only does Christina assist me so much in life, she is a beacon of strength. I am amazed by everything she does.

To Melissa Wright, Jessica Johnson, and Amanda Engelkes, who are always letting me use them for a sounding board. Your input and your suggestions always mean so much to me.

A special thank you to a group of loyal women who have followed me since the beginning of my career. To my Archive girls and my Scribes group. The dedication you have shown me is not taken for granted.

There are no words big enough to express how grateful I am to be a part of the Havenwood Falls family. Huge thanks and crushing hugs to the Havenwood Falls authors who let me borrow the wonderful characters that make this story so strong. To the rest of the Havenwood Falls authors for the characters they've created. This town is possible because of all of you.

A massive shout out to Regina Wamba for the beautiful cover art. You are seriously incredible.

To Liz Ferry and Kristie Cook for your amazing editing. You make these books so much stronger.

A very special thank you to my co-author, Michele G. Miller, for being such an amazing writing partner.

Finally, to my readers, you take my breath away. It means the world that you read my words. I am extremely grateful for your support on this insane journey full of crazy twists and turns. My love to you always.

# SOUL LAID BARE

## JD NELSON

~ A Havenwood Falls Sin & Silk Novella ~

# HAVENWOOD FALLS

sin & silk

*Soul Laid Bare*

## J.D. NELSON

# ALSO BY J.D. NELSON

Wicked Ways Series

*A Night of Wickedness*

*All I Want For Christmas Are My Two Front Fangs: A Wicked Ways Companion Novel*

*Wolves Will Be Wolves*

*Too Cute To Spook: A Wicked Ways Companion Novel*

Night Aberrations Series

*Night Aberrations*

*The Fire within the Night*

Stand Alone Novels

*Control: A Tale of Desire*

*To Nels, always Nels*

# CHAPTER 1

$\mathcal{A}$s I filled out my billionth online job application for the month, I lamented the fact that I couldn't add *demon-killing badass* to my list of job skills. I mean, what's the use of having a kick-ass power like that if you couldn't use it to pad a skimpy résumé? Sure, accounting had fascinated me in my pre–Exitium Daemonium days, but now, it bored me to tears. These days, I needed a job that had a bit of excitement and room to be promoted, not a dull stay-at-home position where my best coworker friend was a calculator.

"Ugh," I said, sighing as I stood up from Cameron's desk and stretched. "I'm officially sick of the job hunt. I think I'm going to take a page out of your book and become an escort."

"What was that, darling?" asked a deep voice gruff with sleep.

"Nothing," I told my fiancé, ogling his muscled chest and the erection lifting the sheet as I climbed onto our king-sized bed to join him. "Well, nothing unless you like dull employment that makes you want to tear your hair out by the roots."

He flashed the devilish grin he knew made me weak in the knees and stroked my hair back from my forehead. "How could I like anything that changes one strand of your beautiful blond hair?"

"So," I said, straddling his hips and leaning in for a kiss. "You think my hair is beautiful?"

Cameron tugged me tight against his erection, a smoldering look of desire in his honey-brown eyes. "I think every part of you is beautiful, Mavis, no matter what color your hair."

I closed my eyes and let my body gradually change from a blond-haired, blue-eyed young woman to the pale demon with white-blond hair and silver eyes he preferred. "Better?"

He grinned and lifted my shirt over my head, taking care not to catch it on the tiny twin horns above my hairline. "As soon as I get you naked, it will be."

"I think I can make that happen," I told him, giggling as he shivered from the chill of my partially ice-covered skin.

A loud bang sounded against the wall we shared with our neighbor, making us both jump. Cam groaned and glared at the wall. "For the love of everything holy."

I suppressed another giggle. "I guess Penelope is awake . . . and still in her sex drought."

"I'm willing to ignore her if you are," he said, thumbing my hardened nipples through my bra.

I rocked against him, lost in the sensation, and gasped out, "You know she won't stop," when he fell into rhythm with me.

He sighed and flopped back onto his pillow, giving up. "Fine, but if she doesn't let us have some very enthusiastic sex in my own bed soon, we're moving to Tibet."

I laughed at his cynicism, but on this one, I was in perfect agreement with him. She had interrupted us so many times in the last week, I was thinking about talking to the management about permanent soundproofing or maybe even eviction.

But to be entirely fair, our mutual bestie wasn't exactly keeping us completely celibate. Because of Cam's nearly insatiable incubus appetite, we were still having sex two or three times a day. We just weren't allowed to have sex within earshot of our not-by-choice-chaste neighbor.

To be honest, I didn't care where we had it as long as we had it.

Cam's father might have taken his humanity when he'd taken his soul, but he was still the same tall, dark, and inappropriate guy I'd met on the side of the road five months ago while I was on the run from my own crazed family member. In almost every single way, he hadn't changed one bit. He still made me laugh with his charming, sarcastic wit, and, of course, he was still the sexed-up asshole I wanted to smack upside the back of his head on occasion.

All in all, I couldn't complain too much. Things were pretty close to perfect in the little life we'd carved out in Havenwood Falls —apart from Cam's stolen soul; the looming threat of my future father-in-law, Severin DeSalle, trying to kidnap me to use my demon-killing power for his own evil purposes; my jobless state; and a neighbor actively trying to keep me from getting laid, that is.

Okay, so maybe things weren't that great. But we had to play the hand we were dealt, right?

Penelope knocked on my front door mere seconds after she heard Cam reluctantly leave to meet his latest client. Brunette and bubbly, the brown-eyed beauty usually had a happy expression pasted on her face, but what stood in front of me on this day was a downtrodden, hopeless wreck.

"What's wrong?" I asked, pulling her inside to keep the heat from escaping. Ice demon or not, I wasn't immune to Colorado's frigid temperatures, and Penelope was an expert at complaining about my cold apartment . . . or really anything that was pissing her off.

"It's Ray," she said, sighing as she shed her bright red coat.

"Nooooo," I whined. "No more demon problems, Penny. I have enough demon problems of my own, you know."

She frowned. "That six-month deadline Severin implemented is coming up pretty quickly, isn't it?"

"Very," I muttered, taking the coat from her and hanging it on a hook near the door. "But it's not as if I'm actually going to let him use me or my powers for his plot for world domination or whatever he's up to."

Brows raised, she asked, "Oh, have you and Cam finally come up with a plan to stop him?"

"No. Well, sort of. Do you think sticking my size sixes up his ass will work?"

"I don't know," she said, smirking. "He's an incubus. He might actually like that."

I glared at her. "I'm telling Cam you said that."

She glared back. "Fine."

"And then I'm telling Ray you want to have his demon baby," I added for good measure.

Penelope looked off into the distance and shrugged.

"Penny, no."

She threw her hands up, exasperated. "Well, what do you expect? The constant innuendo is slowly wearing me down. Realistically, I don't know how much longer I can resist him."

My jaw dropped. "He's actually wearing you down with those terrible sex jokes and thinly veiled come-ons?" I shook my head. "You know, I think that might say more about you than him."

"Yes! And screw you!" she exclaimed, throwing herself into the corner chair. "Do you know how hard it is to turn down sex from a hot demon like Ray?"

I stared at her. "Are you seriously asking me that question right now?"

She laughed, remembering her interference in my super-sexy-happy-fun-time this morning. "Oh, yeah. I guess you do."

"Of course I do! You won't let me have mind-blowing sex with my freakin' fiancé in my own bed, you jealous cow!"

Penelope threw her hands up. "Do you think I want to stop you?"

I raised an eyebrow.

"Okay, maybe I do, but fuck, Mavis, I can't take hearing the constant banging anymore. I'm about to start humping the furniture over there!"

I wrinkled my nose. "Gross. Stay away from the couch. We just managed to get that spot of disintegrated evil henchman out of it."

"Ew."

"No more 'ew' than you lusting after Rayonus," I said.

"He's Ray," she deadpanned.

She had a point there. Rayonus Rixa, or Ray as we called him in secret, was smoking hot. He was tall and dark-haired with a creepy bright blue and solid black eye combo that would give any normal woman nightmares, but he was also every bit the devious, troublemaking demon your mother warned you about. He had a knack for always being there with a bad idea or to influence you into doing something you'd normally never do. For Penelope, he was her sexual kryptonite. For me, he was a good demon friend of Cam's that had been squatting in our guest bedroom for the past four months.

Penelope sighed. "I don't know how much more sexual tension I can take before I crack, Mavis. Every time he stares me down with that black demon eye of his, I need a fresh pair of panties. Why is that so fucking hot?"

"What's this about needing new panties?" Ray asked, opening the front door and stomping the snow off his boots.

"You could knock, you know," I griped.

A smile spread across his disturbingly handsome face as he said, "I could, indeed, Miss LeGrand, but then I wouldn't hear half of the dirty things that come out of Penny's mouth." Then he hung his coat next to Penelope's and traipsed into the kitchen like he didn't have a care in the world.

I rolled my eyes. If anything, Ray was consistent with the effortless charm and bullshit.

When he was out of hearing distance, I sat on the arm of Penelope's chair and leaned over to ask, "Have you considered just getting it over with? It's clear both of you want to fuck each other's brains out."

"He's a demon," she said, as if that settled it.

"Um, I'm a demon," I countered.

131

"Yeah, but you're a good demon, and you're not trying to fuck me."

"True, but you don't know that Ray isn't decent deep, deep, deep down."

She lifted an eyebrow. "I don't?"

"Okay, he's probably not," I conceded. "But a little demon dick won't kill you, Penelope. Ray can't take your soul like Cam can."

"I don't need a little demon dick!" Penelope hissed.

"That's good to hear," Ray said, coming out of the kitchen with a glass of water. "Because I've got more than you can handle, Penny."

"Stop calling me Penny!" she snapped at him.

He inclined his head, a small smile playing on his lips. "As you wish, Miss Osbourne."

Penelope and I rolled our eyes and went back to ignoring him.

"I was thinking about going to Callie's," I said, changing the subject. "Do you want to tag along after work tomorrow? I remember you saying you needed a skirt to go with that white eyelet top."

Before Penelope could answer, Ray said, "A skirt is a fantastic idea, Penny. I do love easy access."

"Don't you have somewhere to be?" I asked, annoyed. "And before you answer, remember that I can destroy you where you stand."

The sarcastic smile he wore fell from his lips. "You know, I do think I have an appointment elsewhere. I believe I'll bid you beautiful ladies adieu for the afternoon."

Penelope watched him quickly retreat with a wistful expression. "He's going to my apartment, isn't he?"

"You're the one who showed him where you keep the spare key," I pointed out, shaking my head. "Honestly, I don't know why you're putting off the inevitable. Fuck him or don't fuck him—I don't care —but you have to do something soon. This can't go on forever. Cameron is starting to get really pissed with the blue-ball situation you're forcing on him."

She groaned and buried her face in a beaded throw pillow. "I'm doomed."

"Doomed is better than damned around here these days," I reminded her, shrugging.

She lifted her head and narrowed her eyes at me. "I think Cam and Ray are starting to be a really shitty influence on you."

# CHAPTER 2

*T*he next day, I met a peeved but much calmer Penelope outside of Callie's Consignments. The clothing and accessory store was usually bristling with activity, but today, it only had a handful of shoppers, a rarity to be sure. I, for one, was overjoyed. My bestie was a lot of things, but she wasn't quiet. She didn't seem to have a volume button when it came to conversing about my love life, or really any topic, in public.

And today would be no different. I could tell she was already in a fine froth when she stomped toward the store, looking cuter than anyone should be allowed to look in her restaurant uniform and fur-lined parka. Something had set her off—something big.

"People are schmucky jerkwads," she informed me, kissing my cheek.

"Agreed," I said. "Want to talk about it?"

"No, let's just spend Cam's money."

I laughed. "Oh, is Cam floating this little outing?"

"Fuck yeah, he is. He promised he would do anything to repay me for the awkwardness of last month's failed soul stealing, remember? I've decided that's going to be with actual money."

I winced as I remembered the unbearably long six seconds it took Cam to remember that his incubus seduction skills didn't work on Penelope (or anyone in Havenwood Falls) and the resulting mortification of him (a) doing it only one day after him proposing and putting a diamond the size of a brick on my finger and (b) trying to come on to his longtime best friend. He still didn't want to talk about what he'd dubbed "the incident," even in private.

Shuddering, I opened the door and said, "Rock on, sister. We are all ready to put that weirdness behind us."

She held her hands out as if Cam was still standing in front of her. "Yeah, but his face when he realized what he was doing will forever be etched into my memories. Shit, it's easily going to stay in the top ten. It. Was. Hilarious."

"I still can't think about it without laughing," I said, making the horrified yet disgusted face he'd made when he came out of whatever sex-seeking trance he was in that night.

We both burst into raucous laughter, then immediately stifled it when we got reproachful glares from the other patrons.

"Don't do that, Mavis! You're going to get us kicked out of here," Penelope reprimanded. "I still need to see if they have that aqua skirt from the window in my size."

"Fine," I said brightly. "We can talk about your date last night."

She shook her head, not looking me in the eye. "No. We really can't."

I turned to her with a pouty face. "Come on, Penny!"

"No. And it wasn't a date," she added glumly. "It was Ray, sitting on my couch, doing his best to get in my panties without actually touching them."

I stopped, unwilling to go farther down the aisle until she gave me something. "What do you mean it wasn't a date? It took us an hour to tame your crazy long Rapunzel hair and make you presentable before you went home." I lowered my voice. "Do you think he has erectile dysfunction or something?"

She huffed and made her way to the other side of the rack of jackets we were flipping through. "If he does, I wouldn't know anything about it. He'd have to actually try to put his dick in me for that."

"So, nothing happened?"

"Yeah, that's what I said," she nearly snarled. "Absolutely nothing happened."

"Look, Snappy McSnapperson, forgive me, but it is Rayonus we're talking about. Something had to have happened. I think it's illegal for him not to do something untoward. It's against his demonic code of douchebaggery or something."

Ignoring me, she handed me a black leather jacket that wasn't my style at all. "Try this on. I want to borrow it tomorrow night."

I raised a brow. "A few additions to your wardrobe, huh?"

"Hey, the demon owes me. Who am I not to take advantage of that?"

"Will you hush?" I hissed, grabbing her arm and rushing her away from a bewildered Harlow Augustine who was flipping through a rack of shirts next to us. "I think she might've heard you! You know her grandmother is a Court member!"

"Oh, please!" Penelope said, waving away my panic. "Anyone that knows me probably thinks I'm talking about Ray. If anyone is really a demon in this town, I think we're all in agreement that it's him."

I tilted my head, thinking about the way Ray looked, acted, and skulked around town like he was casing the joint, and shrugged. "You know, I think you may have a point."

Loaded down with shopping bags full of skirts, tops, and whatever else we thought we could get away with, Penelope and I walked out of Callie's Consignments feeling slightly guilty over the amount of Cam's money we'd spent but excited to replenish our stock of shared clothes.

I'd broken down mid-shopping trip and called Cam to confess our shopping sins; after feigning anger for half a second, he'd told me to have a good time, but not that good of a time. Since becoming a full incubus and gaining the power to steal an entire soul from a human instead of just a part, I'd asked him to scale back the number of clients he took, so money was tighter than it had been at the beginning of our relationship.

He didn't have to tell us twice. After all the stress of dealing with Cam's demon shit, my demon shit, and Ray's lovable yet aggravating demon shit, we needed to relax, and shopping was a good start. We'd see how sideways the day would go from there.

"So, I'm thinking wine and a girly movie night," I said, pointing Penelope to the snow-covered blue SUV Cam had insisted I buy for the times he was out of town.

She shrugged. "That sounds good. But you know what sounds better?"

"What?" I asked tentatively. With Penelope, you never knew what crazy plan she'd come up with. "Will prison stripes be involved?"

She continued as if I hadn't spoken. "Picture it, Mavis. Me and you, *Supernatural*—"

"Naturally," I interrupted.

She glared at me and hissed, "I'm working on a theme here!"

"Oh, pardon me," I said, unlocking the doors and popping the back hatch open with the key fob. "Do go on."

She met my eyes over the top of the car and squinted. "Next time, I'll just lead with the tequila, *Supernatural* hater."

"Hey!" I retorted, following her into the car to defend myself. "I am not a *Supernatural* hater. I just don't get all freaky about it like you do."

"Freaky?" she asked, laughing as she buckled her seatbelt.

"Frea-kay," I assured her. "You can love *Supernatural*, but you shouldn't LOVE *Supernatural*."

She put on her sunglasses and refused to look at me. "Everything you just said is wrong, and I hate you."

I chuckled and pulled away from the curb. "So, tequila, you say?"

∿

Three hours later, we were back at the apartment, pleasantly buzzed and starting season fourteen of *Supernatural* with Rayonus. Like clockwork, he had shown up as soon as we came home. I was beginning to think he was tracking Penelope with GPS. He was rarely here when she wasn't.

"Who wants another shot?" I asked, clumsily getting to my feet and stumbling over to the side table.

Ray stood up and quickly wrested control of the bottle before I could spill it everywhere—again. "Penelope?" he asked. "Fancy one?"

"Shhh," she said, too engrossed in Castiel's ambush by demons to be bothered.

"That's a yes," I told him.

He grinned, his straight teeth glinting in the light of the television. "You guys need some food to soak up all this alcohol." He checked his watch. "And I've got the perfect thing. I'll be right back."

Penelope unexpectedly turned her attention away from the TV. "If you bring me tacos, Ray, I will reward you with unspeakable acts using only my tongue."

Rayonus let out a nervous little laugh and ran a hand through his dark hair. "Yeah, you guys need food."

When the door closed behind a weirdly skittish Ray, I whirled on Penelope. "Unspeakable things with your tongue? What the actual fuck?"

"I know!" she exclaimed, groaning in humiliation and flopping down onto the floor. "I don't know what is wrong with me."

"Alexa, pause," I said, stopping the show on the streaming device and joining Penny on the floor. "Penny—"

She grimaced. "You know I hate it when you call me that."

"No, you don't. You hate it when Rayonus calls you that. Just like he hates it when you call him Ray."

"What's your point?"

"My point is that you guys are one hundred percent hot for each other. Look at how he's acting around you tonight. This choir boy routine is disturbingly abnormal for him. I honestly think you guys need more alone time together so you can figure out the next step in this weird love affair thing you have going on." I snapped my fingers when inspiration suddenly hit. "We can go camping! The temperature is supposed to be a balmy thirty-two degrees over the weekend. That's nearly unheard of for March. And I know you're off from Sakura those days. It's perfect!"

She scrunched up her pretty face and sat up. "There is nothing perfect about camping."

"You can't tell me that you don't want to cozy up in a two-person sleeping bag with a certain sexy demon to keep warm."

Penelope chewed her lip. "Yeah, but I don't have a two-person sleeping bag."

I waved away her excuse. "Backwoods Sport & Ski will likely have one in stock. You're just coming up with excuses, and you know it."

"Are you sure this sudden need for outdoorsy fun doesn't have anything to do with the fact that the six months Severin gave you in exchange for Cam's soul are nearly up? And that he's going to come looking to collect you soon, and you don't have a clue how to get rid of the protection amulet that keeps you from shanking his sorry ass?" she asked.

"Yes . . . no." I frowned. "Okay, maybe, but it also has everything to do with you and Rayonus finally putting the nail in this coffin, so to speak."

"What about wild animals?"

I sat up and selected a lime slice for a chaser. "Besides the one that could potentially be in your panties this weekend?"

"You know what I mean, weirdo."

"And you know what I mean. What are you afraid of?"

She feigned thought. "Getting hurt by a demon with a deliciously huge cock?"

I choked and sputtered on the shot of tequila I'd just taken. "How do you know Rayonus has a huge cock?"

"I might have seen the outline of it in his sweats the other morning when he slept on my couch. Oh, and he's mentioned it a couple hundred times this week."

"Here," I said, handing her a refilled shot glass. "Drink a few more of these, and you won't care how big that demon cock is. You'll climb on that thing like it's Mount Everest."

"Who's climbing onto a Mount Everest demon cock?" Cam asked, shaking snow out of his short hair as he closed the front door behind him.

"Me. Now that you're home," I said, staggering into his arms and reveling in his clean, manly scent for a moment before I grinned up at him.

He shook his head as he took in Penelope laying on the floor and my drunken state. "I see you ladies started the party without me."

"If someone would've told me he was coming home, we would've waited," I said, lifting onto my toes to give him a kiss.

Cam groaned and ran his hands down to cup my ass, then hitched me up to let me wrap my legs around him. He deepened the kiss, thrusting his tongue into my mouth in a hypnotic, teasing way that made me do a little groaning myself. When he broke the kiss, he leaned his forehead to mine, breathing heavily. "I missed you, Mavis."

I stroked the side of his face. "I missed you, too, baby. Now, kick Penny out, so you can take me in the back and fuck me until I scream."

Cam grinned wickedly and pulled me tight against his erection, making me whimper. "Tell me what you want," he growled. "And I'll give it to you."

"Hey!" Penelope exclaimed. "You guys are just being rude! Some of us aren't getting any, you know!"

"What's rude is not letting your best friends have an orgasm in their own bed," Cam spat back. "So help me, Penelope, if you don't let me fuck my bride-to-be tonight, I'm putting a deposit down on a house in Havenwood Heights."

"Fine," she snapped. "Have your unnatural monkey sex, Cam,

but don't say I didn't warn you when Ray wants to join you for a threesome."

We all turned around as a throat cleared and the front door closed. Ray grinned in delight at the spectacle in front of him and held up two bags from the Tacos for Daze truck. "Who's hungry?"

"Me!" I said, unlocking my legs and sliding down to the carpet, leaving Cam scrambling to cover his erection.

Ray smirked and handed over the bags, sitting on the couch next to where Penelope sat on the floor. Smiling down at her, he asked, "What's this about a threesome?"

# CHAPTER 3

*a*fter a little pouting, a lot of begging, and a whole fuckload of shots, Penelope and I finally got Cam and Rayonus to agree to go camping over the weekend.

Well, to be precise, I got Rayonus to agree after I cornered him to mention the potential of happy naked fun time he could have while alone with Penelope, and once I told Cam I'd be chaperoning them whether he came with us or not, he knew he really didn't have a choice in the matter. Longtime friend or not, there was no way he'd send an untrustworthy demon like Ray out into the woods with the two of us, especially with his father's deadline coming up in the next few weeks.

To say Cam wasn't happy about the camping trip would be an understatement. He sighed every time we mentioned it. He only grunted when I asked him if he wanted me to pack for him. He downright refused to go to the store with us for provisions. He basically just sucked the fun out of the whole thing and made me a cranky mess.

"This camping trip was supposed to be fun," I griped for the hundredth time since we'd arrived at Backwoods Sport & Ski.

Penelope, not wanting to deal with me, made a beeline to the lanterns to avoid my whining, leaving Rayonus to talk me down from the tree this time.

"Whatever you're worried about, it's nothing, Mavis," he said, wrapping a companionable arm around my shoulders. "Cam's irritation has little to do with you. It's Severin who's causing his stress. How can he relax on a nice camping trip when the last time you trekked out into the woods together, you had to kill your grandfather, and he had to stand up to his father, which ultimately cost him his soul? Not to mention, his father or his underlings are sure to be lurking out there somewhere to keep an eye on you. Can you see why he might be more than a little uncomfortable with the idea?"

"Yes," I grumbled. "But can you please stop making sense?"

He ruffled my hair. "Come on, Mavis. Cheer up. You know he'd do anything for you and Penelope. Give him a little credit."

"I'll try," I muttered.

"You should." He smiled, but it didn't reach his eyes. "Not all of us demons have the capacity for good that he does."

I squinted at him, not quite understanding him, but I asked, "When did you get all insightful about this kind of stuff?"

"I didn't," he said, shrugging. "I just want you two to pull your shit together, so I can get some alone time with Penelope. After that panty comment the other day, I think she's starting to cave on her sex-with-demons embargo."

We set out for our hike up Mount Mae late on Saturday morning. Though Penelope and I made a show of pouting and glancing forlornly at the ski resort and its promise of hot chocolate and warmth as we drove past, an unmoved Cam reminded me that this was my idea, continued on, and parked at Danzan Park to start our trek up the long snowy trail he said would take us to several good places that he'd camped before. It was cold, and the wind was brisk, but it was nothing we weren't accustomed to, living in the high altitudes of Colorado. Not that that kept Penelope from complaining about it—and then complaining about how many times Rayonus offered to "warm her up." Cam and I didn't speak much on the climb up the mountain, opting to stay out of reach of Penelope's bad mood, but we were making our own conversation with rolled eyes, commiserating glances, and shrugs as we listened to our two besties bicker like an old married couple.

We'd only been hiking through the calf-deep snow for an hour or so when Rayonus spotted what I thought was the perfect camping spot. The meadow he found was surrounded by trees and brush that had obviously been cleared since the last snowfall, and there was even a stone fire pit ready for us to use for our requisite marshmallow and hot dog roast. It was perfect.

"I don't think we're going to find a better place than this," I told the group, letting my backpack slide to the ground beside me. "Nice going, Rayonus."

He bowed. "My pleasure, Mavis."

Penelope rolled her eyes, still irritated. "Next time, find a spot with spa services."

"If you're interested in a facial, I think I can . . ."

Cam stepped between them before the situation could get any uglier than it already was, turning his back on Ray. "Penelope, can you help Mavis find some firewood while Rayonus and I set up the tents?

"I think foraging in the woods should be the guy's job," she said through clenched teeth. "Mavis and I can set up the tents."

I shot a significant look at Cam. Clearly, Penelope was on edge. When she got like this, it was best to let her have her way until she was done venting.

He held up his hands in defeat, slapped Rayonus on the shoulder, and they made their way toward the path just up the hill without another word.

"Why do I like him?" Penelope asked. "He's disgusting."

"No, he's not," I told her, handing her the tent parts as I took them out of the bag. "He's inappropriate in public, but I've never heard him say anything that Cam doesn't say to me in private. Honestly, I think Cam is way nastier than Ray is. He has a lot more practice."

"Ew."

"Oh, you love that dirty talk. Don't act like you don't. You'll be thinking about Ray coming on your face for the rest of the day."

She looked stricken. "Fuck me," she groaned.

I chuckled. "I think Ray has that particular activity covered."

"Oh, ha ha," she said, shaking her head.

"Listen, Penny, I'm going to be brutally honest with you. I'm worried that you really are going to end up that crusty old waitress with the twelve cats that everyone talks about in town. I'm also worried that Rayonus is going to become boring without his charm and blatant sexual come-ons if you keep snapping his head off. So, lighten the fuck up, okay? Flirt a little, for goodness' sake. Don't forget we need Ray around for comedic relief. We sure as hell won't be getting it from Cameron this weekend."

"You're right. I'll lighten up."

"And?"

She sighed. "And I'll try to flirt without hyperventilating or punching him in the dick."

"That's all I ask," I said, laughing as I looked at what we'd unpacked. "Do you know what the fuck any of this is?"

She picked up a short metal rod and shrugged. "I have no idea. I just didn't want to go into the woods. There are wild animals in there, remember?"

I wriggled my eyebrows. "You mean besides Ray?"

She smacked me on the shoulder. "Shut up and tell me how we're supposed to put up these tents."

I stood and brushed the fresh snow off my knees. "I don't have the first clue, but I do have an idea I've been working on that might work even better than these flimsy tents."

"What kind of an idea?" she asked warily. "I've seen this look on

145

your face before. This could either go really right or really, really wrong."

"I'm thinking about making an igloo."

She stared at me in amazement. "Like, from the Arctic Circle place in Finland?"

"Like that, yeah. But without the amenities. You'll have to get your facial the old-fashioned way," I said, laughing and jumping back when she tried to smack me again.

"And you'll be doing this with your magic, I suppose?" she asked.

I shrugged. "Why not? Ever since the throttle holding back my magic broke open, I'm practically Queen Elsa over here."

"You're going be a hit at all of the parties in the summer," she joked. "We'll never have to send someone on an emergency trip for ice."

"Funny," I told her, my tone frosty.

She grinned. "Well, it's true!"

"And still not funny," I said, squinting at her.

"Fine, fine. Let's build an igloo. How can I help?"

I pointed toward the path Cam and Ray had taken. "Go stand over there."

"That's it?"

"Pretty much. There's not much to it. The basic principle is easy. I just need to use my magic to dig out a circle in the snow, make ice blocks that angle slightly at the top, stack the ice blocks, leaving a way for the smoke to get out, and strengthen it with ice and snow. I think I've got this. I've tried things like this before, just on a way, way smaller scale."

"Well, give it a go," she said, glancing warily at the woods behind her. "It sounds a hell of a lot safer than a tent out here in the open."

"It is," I told her, walking around until I found the flattest spot. "It's warmer, too, because it'll retain our body heat."

"You had me at 'warmer,'" she said, her teeth chattering as the wind kicked up. "Fuck, it's cold up here now that we've stopped hiking."

"Give me a sec," I said, closing my eyes and raising my arms to push my magic forward.

Freeing myself of the control I'd worked so hard to master over the past five months, I started out slow, going through the steps with more concentration than I'd ever given anything in my life. I was careful that every detail was taken into consideration before I finally opened my eyes to see what Penelope had been softly gasping at since I'd started.

And when I opened my eyes—holy shit. It had worked. Before us stood a gigantic igloo, wrapped heavily in snow and looking as sturdy as the mountain itself.

"You did it!" Penelope crowed, dancing around the igloo like she didn't have a care in the world before falling backward to make snow angels. "That was the most amazing thing I've ever seen!"

"I leave you for ten minutes, and I come back to a delirious human and a giant-sized igloo," Cam admonished, walking out of the woods with Ray, a huge load of branches in each of their arms. "What am I going to do with you, little ice demon?"

I grinned and skipped over to him. "If you're thinking punishment, you could save one of these switches for later."

"You can bet your sweet sore ass that I will," he growled, swatting me with his free hand.

"Maybe I should set up our tent inside the igloo," Ray said to Penelope, offering her a hand up from the snow. "We may need it, so we don't see something that scars us for life."

"Maybe we'll be the ones to scar them for life," Penelope retorted. "I did promise to perform unspeakable things on you the other night."

Ray swallowed hard and seemed unable to speak for a few seconds while all the blood from his brain rushed to his dick. "Trust me, Penny. I haven't forgotten."

"No one is going to scar anyone," I told them, laughing at Ray's shell-shocked appearance. "The igloo is divided into thirds. We're on the left. You guys are on the right. We can put the fire pit in the middle, toward the front. We won't even have to see each other after we go to bed."

"Why did 'go to bed' seem like it was in special sexy quotations?" Cam asked quietly.

"I'm seriously disappointed that you have to ask," I teased, nipping him on the lips before sashaying toward the igloo.

# CHAPTER 4

*B*y three o'clock in the afternoon, we had unpacked what we could and were settled around the fire to cook a well-deserved late lunch of hot dogs and coffee from our thermoses. Everyone was in high spirits, especially Penelope. I think the prospect of staying in a tent on a mountainside was stressing her out more than being in one with an actual demon who was trying to get in her pants. With the relative safety of the igloo, she seemed much happier, which meant there was a good chance of Ray feeling much happier later on when they were alone.

We had been chatting good-naturedly about the weather, the ridiculous depth of the snow on the mountain, and how superior igloos were to tents for only a few minutes when Penelope suddenly blurted out, "Guys! We should play Three Questions!"

I raised my brows. "Three Questions?" I asked. "With this group?"

"Well, why not? I played it all the time when I was a kid. It's a good icebreaker."

When no one in the group showed the proper enthusiasm for her suggestion, she huffed and snapped, "It'll distract me from the lack of TV in front of me, okay? So make with the questions, demons."

"What is Three Questions?" asked a confused Ray.

"It's a children's getting-to-know-you game," Cam answered.

"When it's your turn, each of the other players gets to ask you a question," I added. "It's pretty simple and definitely better with booze involved."

"What do I win?"

Penelope's eyes twinkled with humor. "You win knowledge about the human and demons you've been living and hanging around with for the past few months, oh man of mystery."

Ray made a sour face. "This does sound like it'd be better with booze."

"Well, it just so happens, I brought booze," Cam said, getting up to rummage through his backpack. "Fireball or vodka, take your pick."

I clapped my hands together in excitement and joined him where he'd temporarily stowed our things. "Have I told you that I love you lately, Cameron?"

"Yes, but I think that's something better shown than told," he said, leaning down to plant a soft kiss on my lips that spoke volumes about what was to come.

Penelope shuddered. "You guys are so gross!"

"Yeah," Ray agreed. "At least wait until we get a few shots in us before you start the sexy talk."

"This ancient wisdom is coming from you, the innuendo king?" I shot back, hands on hips. "Do my ears deceive me?"

Rayonus rolled his eyes and grabbed the bottle from a preoccupied Cam. "Penelope, hand me your mug. If we drink this really fast, we may not remember all the sordid details."

She shook her head. "I've tried, Ray. It never works."

"It's Rayonus," he reminded her.

"It's whatever I want it to be," she insisted. "Ray."

He smirked as he poured a healthy shot of Fireball, clearly up to something. "Fine, but just remember, I've seen your mail. I know your middle name. I can and will start using it if you keep this up. Penny."

"Fine," she conceded, accepting her filled mug from him. "But you just wait until it's my turn to ask you questions, buddy. I'm going to make you sweat."

"As hot as that sounds, you'd have to separate the two lovebirds first," he told her, grimacing at us as our cuddling took on a more sexual tone than we'd initially intended it to.

"You know we can hear and see you, right?" I asked, breaking away from Cam and his deliciously wicked mouth. "We're literally standing right across the igloo from you."

"Then you know you're holding up the game," Penelope griped. "Get back over here so we can get started."

Cam walked me back to the fire pit and handed me down into my little folding camp chair before sitting in his own next to me.

"Do you have any questions for me, Mavis?" he asked, his voice barely above a whisper.

The way he said my name sent a shiver of excitement through my body, and he smiled at the sight, his wolfish grin telling me that he'd seen my reaction and couldn't wait to make me do that again, preferably when we were both naked.

Penelope demanded that Rayonus answer two questions as soon as he chose the short stick. He grimaced at her, but we all knew he'd cave to her wishes. He was as close as he'd ever been to getting something he'd wanted since the day they met. Right now, he was putty in her hands.

As predicted, he gave up right away. "Fine, love," he said. "What do you want to know?"

She tapped her chin. "What's your favorite color and food?"

Rayonus's brows raised at the basic questions. "Is that all you want to know?"

Before she could answer, I said, "Don't get comfortable. I want to know what kind of demony stuff you do when you're not in Havenwood Falls."

Ray laughed and waved my interest in his secret personal life away with a careless hand. "You don't want me to bore you with tales from my mundane life. It's not as exciting as you'd think."

I wasn't about to give up on learning more about him so quickly. His open-ended stay at our apartment had been shrouded in mystery since he arrived. "Come on, Rayonus," I urged. "You've been living with us for months now. I know less than nothing about you. Tell us a little about yourself."

"Really, there's not much to tell," he hedged, looking to Cam for help with the tiniest amount of desperation in his expression.

Cam ignored his silent plea, apparently not interested in saving his friend from our interrogation. Instead, he handed me a stick with a hot dog pushed onto the end.

I promptly took the hot dog off and brandished the sharpened stick like a weapon. "Tell us your life story, Rayonus Rixa, or I'll poke you with a hot dog stick."

"Have you had her checked for rabies?" Ray asked Cam, while he leaned as far away from me as possible.

"I think you'd better answer her," Cam said, pushing a hot dog onto another stick without glancing up. "She can get a little stabby when she hasn't eaten."

"Stop being a little bitch, Rayonus," Penelope said, exasperated. "We're not asking for government secrets here."

Ray sighed. "Fine, but only because you used my name. He smirked and added, "And asked me so nicely."

She regally inclined her head.

"My favorite color is the beautiful brown shade of Penelope's eyes, my favorite food is potatoes, and . . ."

"What kind of potatoes?" Penelope interrupted. "You can't just say potatoes."

"Most women would have been flattered by my compliment. You're asking me whether I like mashed or fried?"

"Heck yeah," she said. "This may be deal breaker stuff."

"Deal breaker stuff?" he asked her. "I think I need some clarification."

Cam and I watched their conversational volleying, trying to contain our laughter. Seeing Penelope, a human, fluster a demon who was used to women fawning all over him was better than TV.

"Just answer her," Cam said finally. "Mashed or fried?"

"Fried with onions, actually."

Penelope scrunched up her face in disgust. "Ew. Why?"

He shrugged. "It's what I've eaten the most of. I've lived through some very lean times."

"What about the demon shit while you're out of town?" I asked, not wanting Penelope to delve deeper into the subject. It wasn't my finest conversational segue, but damn it, I wanted an answer.

Rayonus fidgeted with the mug in his hands, hesitating a moment before he answered, "I have . . . uh, business dealings that I tend to from time to time outside of town."

"What kind of 'business dealings'?" Penelope asked, making quotation marks with her fingers.

"The kind a nice human woman like you doesn't need to worry about," he answered.

She harrumphed. "So, it's something shady. What. A. Shocker."

He glowered at Penelope. "When is it your turn in the hot seat, young miss?"

"Right after Cameron asks you his question," I said, passing Ray a hot dog to roast. "Go ahead, Cam."

Cam studied his best demon friend for a moment, then he asked a question none of us expected. "Are you here to hurt any of us, Rayonus?"

Startled, Penelope and I stared at Ray, waiting impatiently for his answer. I think in the back of our minds, we always wondered if Ray was in Havenwood Falls for some flagitious reason, but we were always too afraid to ask. Some questions you just didn't want an answer to.

"I have no desire to hurt anyone in Havenwood Falls, least of all you three," he answered, nonplussed. "No matter what you think of me now, or in the future, that has never been, and will never be, my intention."

"Good," Penelope said. "Because I didn't want to have to kick your ass, Ray."

Rayonus smirked at his tipsy love interest. "That is a relief, love."

"Okay!" I exclaimed, rubbing my hands with excited glee. "Now that that awkwardness is behind us, Penelope, you're up."

She sighed. "Just get it over with."

Cam snickered. "Is someone regretting suggesting this game?"

She held up her fingers to indicate *just a little* and asked, "Who's first?"

"I am," Ray said, rubbing his hands with glee. "Tell us, Penelope. Why aren't you dating anyone?"

She blushed and shifted her gaze from him to the fire. "I sort of am dating someone," she admitted.

Surprised at her honest answer, we all stared at her, waiting for her to continue.

"What?" she asked. "Can't I like a guy?"

"Who is he?" Rayonus inquired. His voice was soft and barely above a whisper. He was obviously hurt by her confession.

I sighed. "You, dumbass. You haven't noticed that you two are in a relationship?"

"Shouldn't both parties know that they are in the relationship?" he asked Penelope, who looked like she'd rather be out in the cold than getting pleasantly buzzed around a fire with her best friends.

She threw her hands up. "You keep asking me out. You spend ninety percent of your downtime with me. Not to mention, you treat trying to get into my pants like it's an Olympic sport and you're going for the gold medal. You don't call that dating?"

Rayonus didn't say anything as he pondered over his past actions. He knew she was right. It was clear as day that they both liked each other and wanted more.

"You're right," he said finally. "I do like you. I just wasn't sure if you were okay with a casual fling. You're not the type of girl that sleeps around with no strings attached."

"Is that all you want?" she asked.

"No," he said truthfully. "But right now, that's all I can give you." When he saw the hurt look on her face, he quickly added, "It's not as if I don't want more. You're a very welcome surprise that I didn't expect to find when I came to visit my old friend."

Slightly mollified, she nodded and turned her attention back to the fire. "Fair enough."

"Well, that was fucking painfully awkward," I said. "Next question, Cam?"

Cameron tapped his chin for a moment, then asked, "What's it like to have demons for friends instead of regular humans?"

"There's nothing 'regular' about most of the people in this town," Penelope replied.

"What do you mean?" Ray asked.

"I mean, there are a shit ton of not-so-human folks running around Havenwood Falls. Haven't you noticed?"

"Why would I? I don't have the soul-detecting magic Cameron does." He stopped talking and stared at her. "Wait. How do you know?"

"Then what is your demon power?" I asked, distracting him so that Penelope could keep her little secret if she so desired. "You've never said anything about it."

Ray took a deep breath and pursed his lips, looking away from us.

"Is it that bad?" Penelope asked.

"I guess that depends on your perspective. My magic isn't as cut and dried as Cameron's. I cause discord, havoc, destruction. One touch of my hand on a person, or really, any being, and I could destroy every hope, every dream you've ever had." He held up his hands and stared at them. "I may not be able to kill demons with these, as Mavis can, but for every other object, my hands were made to destroy them, either emotionally or physically."

My mouth fell open. "How do you keep it under control? Cam has women falling all over themselves when he's out in public."

"My Court-issued tattoo keeps the people in Havenwood Falls safe, but outside of the town, I have to keep a constant vigil over my magic. If I let any part of it slip out, there's no telling what will be unleashed."

With a note of fear in her voice, Penelope asked, "So, you don't sleep? You're constantly keeping it suppressed."

Rayonus pulled a delicate ebony charm attached to a brown leather string out of his collar. "When I'm around you, this allows me to sleep. I don't dare trust the coven's magic alone. You are too important to me."

I rolled my eyes. "And you thought you weren't in a relationship. Pu-lease."

Cam laughed. "Oh, he's definitely smitten. He hasn't told a female about his affliction in the eighty years I've known him."

"It's been much longer than eighty years since I've shared this part of myself with a woman," Ray told his friend. "Much, much longer."

Penelope's eyes bugged at that little piece of information. "*How* long have you guys known each other?"

"Since Cameron was a young man. I worked for his father before he went over to the dark side."

"So, that makes you how old?" she pressed.

He reached out and stroked Penelope's cheek. "Promise you won't run screaming from the room?"

She barked out a sharp laugh. "No way."

"Just tell her," Cam said. "You've put it off too long as it is."

Rayonus sighed and reached for the bottle of cinnamon-flavored whiskey I offered. "I turned six hundred and three years old last Thursday." He took a swig from the uncapped bottle and handed it to Penny. "Freaked out yet?"

She accepted the bottle, then stood, motioning for me to join her. "Mavis? A word, please?"

I scrambled out of my chair and followed her outside the igloo, confused. She'd known that Cameron was over a century old and that Rayonus was likely just as old, if not older. Could his revelation be that shocking to her, or was it something else?

"What's going on?" I asked, giving her my jacket when her teeth immediately started chattering. With my ice magic, it felt like it was seventy-two degrees on the mountain.

"I can't fuck a demon that's nearly a thousand years old, Mavis."

Intrigued, I asked, "And why is that?"

"What do you mean, 'why is that'? What if he thinks I'm some inexperienced virgin?"

I laughed and took the whiskey from her hand, taking a swig of it. "What? Has your hymen grown back? Did you forget what goes where? How long has it been, Penny?"

She glared at me. "You know what I mean, asshole. I'm an infant compared to him. He's probably invented sex positions."

"Or he's just as nervous about it as you are. Don't you remember his reaction to your tongue comment earlier? He looked like he was going to sink through the ground. Where was Mr. Confident Lovemaker then?"

She wrinkled her nose and took the whiskey back. "Can you never use that name again? It skeeves me out. It sounds like something my foster mom would say."

"Well, stop acting like a mousy introvert, and I won't have to use mom words. This isn't you. Where's the loudmouth, sarcastic bitch we all know and tolerate?"

"Point taken," she said, sighing heavily. "Do you think he's going to think I'm ridiculous now?"

"No, I think he's going to take you up on your tongue offer if you'll get in there and stop worrying about nothing. You've got this."

"What about you?" she asked. "Are you and Cam cool? He seems a lot less keyed up."

I bit my lip and twisted my engagement ring on my finger. "I hope so. He hasn't seemed antsy or weird since we arrived, but I know he's still worried."

Penelope wrapped me in a hug. "We'll get the old Cam back, Mavis. And we'll kick Severin's ass back to whatever part of hell he's from for good. Stop worrying."

"I wish I could, Penny. I really wish I could."

# CHAPTER 5

*W*e stayed up late, sitting around the fire and talking about nothing until the many desirous looks a quiet Cam was shooting in my direction from the other side of the fire became impossible to ignore. Making our excuses, we bid our friends good night and were out of sight in a flash. Cam hadn't been able to slake his lust since the night before, and I knew that, by now, he'd be hardcore jonesing for sex, especially since alcohol only fueled his hunger.

As expected, Cam pounced on me as soon as we were alone, his eyes soulless and black as he pressed me to the icy wall and kissed me hard. I shivered, though I couldn't feel the cold. When Cam was channeling his incubus lust like this, he unnerved me as much as he tempted me. I wanted him, but I couldn't help but be a little intimidated.

In my heart, I knew Cam was a good, decent man, but the past five months without a soul had made him almost cold at times. I knew tonight would be no different. The pure animal need on his beautifully cruel face told me I would be in for one hell of a ride . . . or ten.

Gripping my hips, he dragged me closer, his erection

unforgiving as it dug into my stomach. "Do you want my cock, ice demon?"

"Shhh," I whispered. "They'll hear us."

"Let them hear," he said, ripping my jeans open with the superhuman strength he rarely displayed. I gasped as he yanked them down my thighs and spun me to face away from him.

Snaking a hand between my legs, he bit down on the tender spot where my neck and shoulder joined hard enough to make me yelp. "I asked you a question."

"Yes," I moaned, now fully into whatever hurried, dirty sex he wanted.

His voice was harsh as he hissed, "Take your demon shape."

I complied, willingly morphing to the form I knew he preferred, and arched my back, wanting him to claim me, to ravage me until I couldn't think about all the problems waiting for us at home.

"Cam, please," I begged.

"On your knees," he demanded.

I obeyed, dropping down to the sleeping bag we'd set out earlier, nearly shaking with the anticipation of feeling the fullness of his massive cock inside of me.

The slow slide of his zipper and the thump of his belt buckle hitting the floor sounded loud in my ears as I waited. I'd thought he'd take me quickly, but he seemed to be weighing his options as if he was having a hard time choosing what would bring him the most pleasure.

That was when I felt the first stinging strike of the switch across both cheeks. The pain was sharp but exquisite, making my breath catch and my center dampen with want. "Please," I cried out, needing more.

A breath I didn't know I'd been holding escaped in a quick whoosh as he brought the switch down twice in quick succession. I squirmed involuntarily to move away from the pain, and Cam chuckled as he sank to his knees beside me, running a soft hand over the burning welts before slapping my ass so hard, it brought tears to my eyes.

"Have you had enough?" he asked, his voice little more than a growl.

"Never," I told him defiantly.

"Be careful what you ask for, beauty," he warned, pressing his hard cock against my hip as he trailed the scratchy wood across the same path his fingers had taken. "I like hearing you scream."

"Then make me scream," I said, bracing myself.

He brushed over my clit with the thumb of his free hand, teasing me with the pleasure that was to come. "I can make you scream in other ways," he said, whipping the switch across my ass again.

"Fuck me!" I cried out. "Please."

Cam chuckled darkly and thrummed his thumb against my clit again. "You are so beautiful when you beg, Mavis. I almost want to give you what you want."

I glanced behind me and gave him a sultry smile. "Then why don't you, big boy?"

He sucked in a deep breath through his teeth as he looked at my reddened ass. "Do you think you can handle this while I'm in my demon form?" he asked, stroking his cock. "It's a little bigger than you're used to."

I froze. He'd only ever shown me what he looked like as an incubus once. Though I knew he could transform his appearance to any humanoid thing, since he'd gained the ability, he'd always maintained the form he was born in while he was with me.

"Mavis?"

"Show me," I said, turning over to sit, then hissing in pain.

"How's that ass feeling?" Cam asked, a devilish grin spreading across his handsome face.

I kicked off my boots and shimmied out of my jeans. "You tell me."

"Pretty fucking good, darling."

"Damn right it does," I said sassily. "Now make with the demon form and give me my well-deserved orgasm before I go get it elsewhere."

He narrowed his eyes. "You wouldn't."

"Wouldn't I?"

He shook his head. "You are a bad, bad girl. You deserved every lick of that switch and then some."

I leaned up to kiss him. "I loved every lick of that switch. I'm thinking of taking it home with us."

"You do that, and I'm using it every chance I get," he promised, pushing me to my back and settling between my legs.

I smirked. "Can't wait."

He rocked against my wetness, groaning with restraint. "Are you sure about this?"

"More than sure," I said. "I'm a demon. You're a demon. We should be having lots of demon sex by now."

"What do you call all the sex we had before?"

"Foreplay?"

He laughed, showing sharp fangs. "So, this is our first time?"

"You could say that," I said, watching as his skin and hair changed to a darker hue and his cheekbones became more pronounced. Even with the black eyes, he was so beautiful as a demon, I could scarcely believe he was real.

"Well?" he asked lifting himself to show me the complete transformation.

My eyes widened as I took in his body. He was taller, much more muscular, and his cock was . . . well, huge. "Fuck, Cameron. I don't know whether to run screaming or to tell you to do your worst with that thing."

"I can make it smaller."

"Don't you fucking dare. I'm going to ride you like a horse."

He laughed. "I'm glad you approve."

"Oh, this is more than approval. This is your ten-second warning to get that dick in me before I take matters into my own hands."

Eyes flared, he dove for me, driving into me in one quick, crazed movement that had me crying out into his mouth as I became accustomed to the increased size.

"So. Fucking. Tight," he whispered, withdrawing then snapping his hips to sink back into me. "I could come right now."

I moaned and dug my fingers into his ass as the first twinges of my own orgasm shot through my body. "Come with me, Cam."

I didn't have to ask him twice. Roaring, he hitched my legs up and pounded into me faster and harder than he ever had before. I closed my eyes tight, reveling in the new feel of him, the sound of his breath, harsh and shallow in my ears, and the sweet taste of cinnamon on his tongue as he kissed me carefully through his fangs. Soon, my quiet whimpers of pleasured pain became all-out screams as I writhed and shuddered under him, and we barreled over the edge.

When our breathing had calmed, Cam lifted his head from the crook of my neck and looked at me with an expression I'd never seen before.

"What is it?" I asked, stroking his hair back and then groaning as he flexed his hips to drive his semi-hard length deeper into me.

"I love you," he said, through clenched teeth.

I laughed. "I sure hope so. I mean, you have your penis in me, and more important than that, you've asked me to marry you."

Cam smiled, but it didn't reach his eyes. "No, I mean . . . I don't know what I mean. I guess I just thought it was the man in me that loved you, that couldn't live without you, but it's not. Even without a soul, I love you, Mavis. You're everything to me."

I looked deep into the black eyes that, until now, had been devoid of any emotion. "And I love you, Cameron DeSalle. But this really shouldn't be a surprise. I've loved you all these months, and I've never had a soul. Love is love. It's a feeling, not something tied to humanity."

He pursed his lips. "You seem pretty sure of that."

"Of course I do." I glanced down to where we were joined and smirked. "But honestly, I'd probably say anything to keep this big demon dick in me right now. Holy shit, babe. You've been holding out on me for the last five months."

Cam grinned and buried himself as deep as he could go. "Trust me. I won't be holding out on you from here on out. You'll be lucky if I let you out of bed."

"You have to let her out of bed," Penelope called. "It's illegal to keep a sex slave in the state of Colorado."

"Yeah," Rayonus agreed. "I'm not bailing your ass out of jail. I don't think Sheriff Kasun likes me very much."

Stricken, Cam and I stared at each other in horror.

"Do you think they heard everything?" I asked, mortified.

"Every single bit of it," Ray said. "Nice work with that switch. It sounded like she really enjoyed it."

Penelope made a gagging sound. "I'm pretty sure I'm going to need therapy for PTSD after this."

# CHAPTER 6

*J*jerked awake sometime before daybreak and sat up. Something was wrong—really wrong. An odd feeling of foreboding wound through my entire body.

"Mavis!" Penelope hissed, running into our part of the igloo. "Wake up! Something is out there!"

Cam jumped up and turned on the camp light, only to realize he was still in his demon form and still as naked as the day he was born.

"What the fuck?" Penelope yelled, covering her eyes, then smacking into the icy wall when she couldn't see. "You're both naked. And demoned out! And are those wings, Cam?"

"Sorry, Penny!" Cam said, jamming his legs into his jeans as he morphed back into his human shape.

Ray snickered as he came around the wall to see what was going on. "Nice tits, Mavis."

"Get out, Ray!" I yelled, pulling the sleeping bag up to cover myself while frantically looking for the shirt Cam had quietly torn off my body after our sarcastic friends stopped giggling about our sex life and went to bed.

"What's going on?" Cam asked Penelope.

"I went outside to pee and heard loud rustling and something tromping through the snow. It's something huge, by the sound of it. What if it's a bear?"

"Do you think it's a shifter or a regular animal?"

"How the fuck would I know?" Penelope asked.

"You always know," Cam deadpanned. "It's literally your gift."

"Yeah, but I'm not going out there and getting close enough to check! I'm not an idiot!"

Now fully dressed, I wrapped an arm around a thoroughly worked up Penelope and led her back to the fire to sit with Ray. "Everyone needs to calm down. I'll seal off the igloo, okay? Whatever it is, it won't be able to get in here."

"But I still have to pee," she whined.

"Okay, why don't you take Ray with you?"

"Me?" Ray asked. "Why not Cameron?"

"What is he going to do if that thing attacks? Fuck it to death? Take off your little talisman and go destroy whatever's out there."

"That's pretty risky, Mavis," Rayonus admitted. "I could destroy something else without meaning to. And what if it's a demon? Wouldn't she be safer with you?"

"And put her at risk of Severin grabbing them both?" Cam asked incredulously. "No fucking way."

"Well, someone has to go with her," I told them. "She's not going out there alone."

Penelope stood up, a determined glint in her chocolate-brown eyes. "We'll all go."

Cam sat down in his camping chair. "I'm not going out there to watch you pee."

"Yes, the hell, you are," she retorted. "Get up. Now."

Grumbling under his breath, Cam stood and zipped up his jacket. "Why are we friends again?"

She scoffed. "My awesome personality. Obviously."

Ray grinned as he wrapped a scarf around his neck. "This may be the weirdest thing I've done in three centuries."

I shrugged, thinking this was just par for the course in our strange little friendship with Penelope. "Seems like a regular Sunday to me."

~

Around ten o'clock, we packed up the igloo to leave. After the anticlimactic outcome of the bear situation the night before, we were all tired and ready to go home. The only problem was, I didn't know what to do with the igloo now that we were done with it. I could produce and manipulate ice, but I couldn't change it once it was made or make it melt.

"Maybe we could just leave it," Penelope suggested.

I shook my head. "What if someone's in there when it starts to melt? It could collapse on top of them."

"I can do it," Ray offered. "But I'll need you guys to be at least fifty yards away when I do it. The talisman is going to have to come off."

Brows raised, I asked, "What's going to happen?"

"In a perfect scenario, it will crumble where it stands."

"And in a not perfect scenario?" Cam asked.

"The mountain crumbles."

Penelope slipped her backpack onto her shoulders and started down the trail. "And that's my cue to get the hell out of Dodge. See you guys."

Cam watched her hightail it down the mountain with a surprised expression on his handsome face. "She's really going to go by herself?"

I blew out an undignified raspberry. "No. The second she remembers that there are wild animals out here, she'll be back."

"I don't know," he said. "She's already gotten pretty far."

"I'll bet you twenty bucks."

"You're on," Cam said, spitting into his hand to shake.

I stared at his hand in disgust. "Yeah, that's not happening."

"I'll take that bet," Ray said, spitting in his hand.

The two demons shook on it, and Cam said, "You're on."

Ray smirked. "I think you're going to regret this one, Cameron."

"You sound sure of yourself, but you forget, I've known Penelope Osbourne for many, many years."

"I don't have to know her for years," Ray told him. "I spent last night with her after she thought she heard a bear in the woods. I know she's not going down this mountain by herself."

As if it were planned, almost as soon as he finished speaking, Penelope came back into sight. "Are you guys coming?" she asked, her voice testy and impatient.

Giddy because of the win, Ray smiled at his would-be paramour and said, "Penny, I'd love to come with you . . . or on you. Really, I'll come anywhere you want me to. All you have to do is ask."

I laughed and patted Ray on the shoulder as I walked past him to meet a thoroughly irritated Penelope. "All right! The old Rayonus is back! I was hoping to hear some tasteless come-ons today."

Ray laughed and bowed. "Happy to oblige, ice demon."

"Hurry up," Cam grumbled, slapping a twenty-dollar bill into Ray's hand. "I'm fucking starving from all the sex I had last night that you didn't."

"Dick!" Ray called after him, pocketing the money.

"Yeah, that'd be what I gave Mavis nearly all night," Cam retorted without turning around. "I know it's been a while since you've used yours, but I didn't think you'd forgotten what it was used for altogether."

Ray huffed at his retreating form and yelled, "Fuck you, sex demon!"

"No, thanks," Cam said, throwing an arm around Penelope and me. "Mavis took care of that last night—and again this morning."

Ray was still shaking his head in exasperation when we stopped at the bottom of a small hill to wait on him but only hesitated a moment before he reached into his shirt to take off the talisman. As soon as it was over his head, he touched a finger to the igloo, and it fell like sand being dumped onto a beach. It just fell where it stood. I couldn't even tell where it had been seconds before.

"Wow," Penelope whispered, watching Rayonus put the talisman back over his neck.

I nodded in disbelief. "You took the word right out of my mouth."

Cam rolled his eyes, obviously jealous of Ray's superior power. "If you two ladies are done gawking, I can hear pizza calling my name."

Ray joined us, smiling at his handiwork. "They can't help but stare, Cameron. I'm fucking amazing."

"Yeah," Cam agreed. "An amazing asshole."

"Jealous?" he asked his friend.

Cam gritted his teeth before admitting, "Maybe just a little."

After another hour of insulting banter and ridiculous wagers, we dropped our gear off at the apartment and walked down Eighth Street to Napoli's. I could have wept when the glorious scent of cheese and garlicky goodness hit my nostrils. Spotting a big booth near the back of the surprisingly empty restaurant, we sat down, eager for Cokes and pizza all around.

"Dude, I would perform sexual favors for some of whatever that smell is," Penelope said, shooting a longing look toward the kitchen.

"I don't think that's a valid form of payment," Ray teased. "But if you want to perform sexual favors for me, I'd be happy to spring for your lunch."

Penelope laughed. "Don't tempt me, demon."

"Penelope, you have to stop offering sex for food," Cam admonished, frowning at her. "It's starting to be a thing with you."

"Until I get either food or sex, I'll do whatever the hell I want," she shot back, much to Ray's delight.

I smiled at my group's typically quarrelsome behavior, but as entertaining as they were, I couldn't shake the niggling feeling of menace that had plagued me since we sat down. The feel of it was so strong, it was almost making me nauseous. Breathing in deep through my nose, I exhaled through my mouth and said, "Guys, I feel like something is wrong."

Ray nodded in agreement. "Yeah, the waitress is taking forever."

I shook my head. "That's not what I mean. I feel something . . . something inherently evil."

"Cue the danger music," Penelope said, rolling her eyes.

"I'm being serious, Penny," I said, rubbing at the weird vibration in the center of my chest. "I felt this way last night when you woke me up for a few minutes, but it seems way stronger now."

"Could you still be worked up about the nonexistent bear?" Ray suggested.

I pursed my lips. "I'm not so sure it was a bear."

Cam furrowed his brow, looking concerned as he threaded his fingers with mine. "Why didn't you say anything last night, Mavis?"

"It was only a weird vibe then. I thought it was a fluke. But now, I think it may be something more—a warning, maybe. You don't think Severin could be back in town, do you?"

"Wouldn't someone warn you if dear old dad was back?" Penelope asked. "Isn't there some kind of tracking system that monitors who goes in and out of Havenwood Falls?"

Cam shrugged. "My father, yes. The coven would contact me at once. But any of his lackeys, probably not. I can imagine they would question them as soon as they sensed their arrival, but I doubt they could tell if a visitor was planning some kind of demon kidnapping unless they tell them they're going to do it. And I really don't think that's likely to happen, do you?"

"No," I muttered. "But wouldn't it be nice if one thing went our way for a change?"

# CHAPTER 7

$\mathcal{E}$arly the next morning, Cam and I visited Sheriff Kasun to see if he knew something we didn't. It was, of course, a bust. We knew it would be before we even arrived. Ric was good at his job. He would have immediately contacted us if there was something we needed to worry about, but to appease us, he did promise to be on high alert on our behalf. After the mess with the Collector this winter, no one in the town was taking any chances.

We went home after a quick breakfast at Eggstravaganza to talk about what we were going to do on the days he had to go out of town. We both knew Severin would make his move soon. There was no way he'd wait out the entire six months he'd promised. That was out of the question. He knew he'd have a fight on his hands.

After talking most of the day about contingency plans, safety, and options, we realized, as much as we wanted it, the one option we couldn't afford was Cameron staying at home with me for an extended time. He had to see his clients to pay the rent. That was non-negotiable, no matter how much he didn't want to leave me alone.

What was negotiable was how far I was willing to go to help Cam take his mind off the impending doom while simultaneously making the most of his incubus abilities. Since our romp in the igloo in our demon forms, Cam was keen on testing out the limits of his shapeshifting ability and the limits of what I could take in terms of size, stamina, and kink level. He'd shapeshift into one my favorite actors and surprise me in the living room, or shower, or bedroom . . . basically anywhere I was when the urge struck him.

I wasn't about to complain. You haven't lived until you've had countertop kitchen sex with massive-cocked Chris Hemsworth and Misha Collins lookalikes back to back. Penelope would lose her mind if she knew how many orgasms I'd had with her favorite, Castiel.

Unfortunately, the ridiculous amount of torrid sex we had didn't seem to lessen the annoying sense of danger I'd been feeling since our return. I just couldn't shake it. It was there when I woke and didn't go away until I went to sleep at night.

And, of course, Cam, being the martyr he was, blamed himself for it. Somehow, he had convinced himself that he was the cause, though I tried to explain over and over that it couldn't be him. Whoever I was feeling, they planned to do us harm. Cam would never hurt me. He loved me too much.

That explanation seemed to appease him for a while, but after forty-eight hours of watching his fiancée pace, worry, and rub her chest, he finally asked, "Mavis, really, darling. Don't you think it could be me?"

"No," I told him, stopping my pacing to curl up on the couch in his arms. "I've already told you. This just started while we were on the mountain, and it amplifies at weird intervals. If it were you, wouldn't it be stronger when I'm near you?"

"Maybe," he said, stroking the side of my face. "But you can't deny that all of this started the night I showed you my demon form. That seems like too much of a coincidence."

I shook my head. "That may be true, but you have to remember, it started after Penelope woke me. You'd been in your demon form for hours before I first felt it. It can't be you." I bit my lip, going over the events of that night. "I'm starting to think it might have been someone working for your father," I admitted.

Cameron frowned and hugged me tighter to his body. "That is not what I want to hear six hours before I leave town, Mavis."

"Trust me. I don't want it to be true either, but what else could it be?"

"Could the throttle Severin had placed around your heart be completely broken now? Maybe you're just feeling this because of all of the other demons in town?"

I sighed. "I do feel like this has something to do with my Exitium Daemonium thing, but I don't think this feeling would wax and wane like it's doing if it wasn't a specific demon doing something nefarious. It's almost as if I'm sensing their evil intent or something. Sometimes it's strong. Sometimes it's not."

"So, you think your Exitium Daemonium magic is sort of like a douche radar?"

I lifted my head from his chest and met his eyes. "That's exactly what I'm thinking."

"And you're sure it's not me?"

"Are you doing something douchey or evil?" I asked, smirking at him.

Cam grimaced and stared out the window at the snowfall before answering. "Sometimes my control over my urges slips and the need to steal souls is overwhelming. I'm trying to figure out a way to conquer those feelings, but I can't seem to do it without a sexual release."

"Is that why we've been having so much sex lately?"

Cam slid his hands down to cup my ass and said, "No, we have so much sex because you're the hottest demon I've ever had my dick in."

I narrowed my eyes at him. "How many demon chicks have you had your dick in?"

He pursed his full lips, looking like he wished he'd never said anything. "No comment."

"That many, huh?" I asked, laughing at his expression.

"Let's just say it's more than a handful and leave it at that, okay?"

"Oh, it's definitely more than a handful," I said, trying to take his mind off his worry by tracing the outline of his growing erection through his pajama pants. "Way more than a handful."

"I think that's just hearsay unless you prove it," he said, his voice thick with lust.

"Is that right?" I asked, tugging down the waistband of his pajamas to expose the hard length of him.

"Yeah, it's science or something."

I smiled and wrapped both hands around his cock, using them both to stroke him. "I was right. You do have more than a handful."

He groaned, letting his head fall back. "What do you intend on doing with this knowledge?"

"I don't really know," I told him, sliding down to my knees in front of him. "I think we might have to do a little more research. Maybe see if it's more than a mouthful. You know, for science's sake."

He lifted his head and ran a thumb over my bottom lip. "I guess you better find out. I wouldn't want to stand in the way of your pursuit of knowledge."

"How magnanimous of you," I said, running my tongue from base to tip.

Cam leaned forward to rid me of my short nightgown, leaving me in only a pair of black lace panties. "I do what I can, little demon."

I gave him a sensual smile and said, "Let's see what I can do," before enveloping his cock with my mouth as far as it would go.

"Fuck!" he barked out, bucking his hips.

Letting him slide almost all the way out, I swirled my tongue around the head, then fully took him in my mouth again. He moaned and wrapped my ponytail around his hand, yanking me away so he could stand. I stared up at him hungrily. "Fuck my mouth, Cam."

He didn't waste a second complying with my wishes. Forcing

his way past my lips, he held my head still as he pumped his cock into my mouth, hard and fast. My jaw ached, and my scalp hurt from his firm grip on my hair, but I didn't care. I wanted to please him. I wanted his cum down my throat. I wanted him to use me however he wanted, come wherever he wanted, then I wanted him to fuck me until I couldn't take it anymore.

"Fuck, you're beautiful," Cam growled. "I love the way you look with my cock sliding in and out of that perfect little pouty mouth."

Unable to respond, I wrapped a hand around the base of him and cupped his balls with the other, all while staring up at him with ravenous eyes. I wanted him to know how much I liked this, how wet it made me just to taste him.

He groaned loudly as his body transformed into his demon shape, and his cock grew bigger, stretching my aching jaw to a painful level. I knew he would come soon, and I wanted it, craved it.

Panting for breath, he roared as he slipped from my lips, covering my face and breasts with his cum before shoving himself back into my mouth to finish himself off.

I whimpered, desperate for him to give me the same release, the same extreme pleasure.

He didn't disappoint. Without missing a beat, he pulled his slick cock out of my mouth and gingerly guided me by the hair until I was positioned over the arm of the couch. "Beg me to come inside of you," he said, sliding two long fingers into my wetness. "Beg me to fill you up."

"Please," I pleaded, chasing the pleasure he was giving me with my hips. "Shove that big fucking cock into my pussy. Make me your whore. I want to feel your cum dripping down my thighs."

I knew he'd be shocked. I'd never said anything like that before, but I couldn't bring myself to care. I wanted everything I'd asked for and more.

His voice was dark, dangerous as he asked, "You want to be my whore, Mavis?"

"Yes," I replied, moaning as he removed his fingers and forced them into my mouth, so I could taste myself.

"You want this big dick in that tight little pussy?" he asked, guiding his massive cock to my opening and teasing me by only pushing the head in.

"Yes!" I cried out. "Give me more. I want all of you inside me."

He chuckled and cupped my breasts, pinching the nipples cruelly. "You like being my little slut, don't you?"

"Yes. Please, Cameron. Fuck me," I begged, unable to wait any longer. I felt like I would go out of my mind if he didn't let me come soon.

Finally relenting, he slid in to the hilt, making me cry out in pleasured pain. Moving his right hand from my breast to my clit, he asked, "Is this dick what you wanted?"

"Yes," I said, nearly sobbing with relief. "Fuck, I love the feel of you filling me up."

"Do I make you want to come on this big cock?" he asked, working my clit at the same fast rhythm he was fucking me.

"Harder!" I screamed, rocking my body against him as the orgasm I'd so desperately wanted hit me all at once.

"That's it," he hissed into my ear. "Milk my cock, Mavis. Make me come in that tight little pussy."

"Come in me," I growled out, already close to another orgasm. "Make me take it all."

Yanking my head back by my ponytail, he pulled me flush against his chest and pinned me there as he pounded into me over and over. "Come," he ordered. "Make that pussy come again."

He didn't have to ask me twice. I howled out my release loudly, riding out wave after wave of pain mixed with throbbing, exquisite pleasure.

He followed right after, yelling, "Fuck!" as he pumped harder and harder into me, finally collapsing, spent, breathless, and satisfied, on top of my sweat-covered body.

We stayed that way for a few minutes, catching our breaths,

before I sighed and asked, "Are you sure you have to go out of town tonight?"

"I'm not sure I can move," he said, chuckling in my ear. "I was going to make you dinner before I left, but now I'm thinking you should call Penny and ask her to bring you Chinese on her way home from work."

"Deal," I agreed. "And I will . . . as soon as I can walk."

# CHAPTER 8

*P*enelope got home from her shift at Sakura Buffet in record time. As soon as she came in the door, she threw the little paper containers of food she'd brought home on the coffee table and ran to plop down onto the carpet in front of the TV, eager to catch every second of the *Supernatural* episode starting in two minutes.

"Hey, stranger. It's nice to see you, too," I said, laughing at her theatrics from the couch.

"Yeah, yeah," she said, not looking away from the screen. "Less talky. More watchy."

"Oh no," I told her, grabbing the remote. "We will be talking about the fact that I haven't seen you or Ray in more than forty-eight hours."

She frowned at me. "Ray hasn't been home for two days?"

I shook my head. "Nope. I figured you guys might be finishing the little tête-à-tête you started on the mountain."

She snorted. "Tête-à-tête? No. I worked back-to-back double shifts just to keep myself from taking him up on the facial he offered. I haven't seen him since we all had lunch at Napoli's."

I sat up, alarmed. "So he's missing? Why does this stuff always happen when Cam is out of town?"

177

"What stuff?" Ray asked, coming out of his room with a fluffy blue towel wrapped around his hips and nothing else.

"What the fuck, Ray?" I asked, pinching the bridge of my nose. "I thought you were gone, or, at the very least, clothed."

He shrugged. "I got home this morning while you and Cam were getting it on in the shower. I didn't think you'd want me to interrupt your multiple orgasms to tell you I was here, so I just went to bed."

I glared at him. "I have told you that you can knock, right?"

"Yes, you have," he said, grinning. "Now be quiet so Penny and I can watch Castiel get his ass kicked by the thing from the Empty."

"Really? You're going to sit on my couch in a towel and watch *Supernatural*?"

Penelope huffed. "Mavis, you're missing this touching moment with Jack and his mom. Either shut it, or I'm shoving an egg roll down your throat."

"*Supernatural* makes you violent," I complained, getting up to go to the kitchen.

"Sticks and stones, babe," she retorted, turning back to the TV.

"She doesn't get it," Ray said, bending down to kiss her on the cheek. "She's too caught up in her own supernatural drama."

"Says the demon who's wearing a towel instead of pants," I said, coming out of the kitchen with plates and forks.

He flashed a grin in my direction and said, "Mavis, if I don't do things like this, how else am I going to show Penny what she's missing?"

"I've seen what I'm missing," Penelope said, not taking her eyes off the TV. "I don't suppose you can make it whatever size you want like Cam, can you?"

Clearly insulted, he said, "No, but I promise you that I've never had any complaints about my size before."

"Yeah, well, I don't want to have to go get a designer vagina because you've massacred it with your giant dick."

I stopped spooning the fragrant Kung Pao chicken onto the plates and had to brace myself on the coffee table to keep from laughing at Ray's dumbstruck face. "Penelope, I think you broke him."

Clearing his throat, he stood up, careful to keep said dick out of our eyesight. "I think I'm going to take that shower now."

"Don't you want to eat first?" I asked, holding up his plate.

"Later, Mavis," he said, rushing down the hall to the guest bathroom. "I've got to . . ."

"Masturbate in the shower while you think about massacring Penelope's vagina?" I suggested.

"Something like that, yeah," he admitted. "Sorry, ladies."

"It's not your fault you were born with a massive cock," Penelope called after him.

She looked at me with mischief twinkling in her eyes and laughed when she heard him groan as he shut the door.

I shook my head and handed her a plate. "That demon is whipped. I would tell you to throw him a bone, but . . ." I motioned to the bathroom. "I think he's got his own."

Ray finally reappeared from the bathroom a few minutes after Penelope went home to take her own shower and get ready for bed. She'd wanted to wait him out, but after *Supernatural,* she was dozing off on the couch. Part of me thought that working herself too hard to avoid Ray was silly since they were pretty much an item at this point, but the other part of me was glad she wasn't spending too much time with him, especially when he came out of the bathroom bare-chested with a pair of tight, frayed Levi's on, looking every bit like the kind of male that would fuck her, break her heart, and disappear.

"You're wasting your time with that sexy *look at me* thing you've got going on," I said, digging into a pint of Cherry Garcia. "She's gone."

"Is this the part where you threaten me for having designs on your friend?" he asked, sitting in the chair across from me and lacing his fingers across his tanned, muscled abs.

I stuck the spoon into the ice cream and squinted at him. "No, this is the part where I tell you that if you hurt her, I will hunt you to the ends of the earth and make you wish you were dead."

Unfazed, his expression didn't change. "You can cool your jets, Mavis. I don't want to hurt her. I actually really like her. She's prickly and sexy, and sarcastic—all the things I like in a woman."

"She's also human," I pointed out. "A human that Cam and I love very much. I don't want her getting mixed up with any clandestine demon shit you've got going on, on the outside."

"Says the demon that hangs out with her, knowing that she could end up being collateral damage in this whole Exitium Daemonium thing with Severin," he said, a note of accusation in his voice. "Aren't you the least bit concerned that he could use her as leverage to get what he wants?"

"Of course I'm concerned," I retorted, setting the ice cream down on the coffee table a little harder than I intended. "I would never involve her with anything regarding Severin . . . ever. Especially since Cameron's father has always pressured him to take her soul."

"He what?" he demanded, his hands practically strangling the arms of the chair as he sat up straight.

Stunned at the intensity in his voice, I stared at him, wondering what was going through his mind. He'd worked for Severin before. He had to know what kind of sick fuck he could be, and he had to know what he was capable of. Why was this such a shock to him?

"Cam told me that he's been trying to pressure him into stealing Penelope's soul ever since she met him," I reiterated.

"Do you know when the last time Severin saw her with Cam was?"

I shook my head. "Not a clue. I only met him once before our showdown on Mount Sousa."

He nodded and ran his hand through his hair, making it stand up on end. "Do you think Penelope would temporarily move in here with us until after things get resolved between you and Severin?"

I laughed. "Penelope? No. Not unless you do some major convincing. If you haven't noticed, she's pretty fucking independent."

He frowned. "That I have."

"So, what now?" I asked, offering him some of my ice cream. "What do you think we should do?"

He dug out a huge spoonful and shrugged. "Short of hiring a guard armed with some sort of demon-killing artifact to follow her around twenty-four seven, I have no idea. Are you still getting the weird vibes?"

I furrowed my brow. "Not tonight, which is actually kind of strange. The vibrations have been constant while you were gone."

He nodded again, lost in thought as he chewed.

"What are you thinking?" I asked, hoping he wasn't planning something crazy.

"I don't know what to think," he said, getting up and starting to pace as he dug out another spoonful. "If Severin wants her, what can we do? You said he wasn't affected by your demon-killing powers, right?"

"Yeah, he laughed when it didn't work and said, 'Who do you think had the throttle put in your chest,' or something to that effect."

Ray handed the container back to me and continued his pacing. "Will the powers that be in Havenwood Falls force her to leave for her own good?"

"I honestly don't know why they would. This is the safest place in the world. Where could we take her that would be safer than here?"

He stopped suddenly and sat back down, looking completely hopeless. "I can't lose her, Mavis. I love her. We have to do something to keep her safe."

I smiled at his honesty. "I think she might feel the same for you.

Although, seriously, you two have the weirdest way of showing your affection."

"I think that's why I like her so much," he said, a smile playing at his lips. "She doesn't put up with any of my bullshit, and she doesn't fall all over herself trying to impress me like the demon females do."

"I'm thinking a lot of demon females do that, don't they?"

He winked at me, perking up. "More than you'd think. I'm nearly irresistible."

"You and Cam have that in common."

He chuckled. "Yeah, but I've been doing it with only God-given hotness. Cam's magic draws females to him."

"I see modesty is also something you two have in common," I said, rolling my eyes toward the heavens.

Ray smirked, then gave me a wry smile. "Who needs modesty when you look like this?"

# CHAPTER 9

*J* was sleeping when Cameron came home in a blind panic late the next morning. He rushed into the apartment, slinging the door open wide, screamed out my name, then nearly cried in relief when I stumbled sleepily out of the bedroom and met him in the hall.

"What's going on?" I asked, leaning heavily against the wall, when a wave of hostile intent crashed over me.

"Thank God" was all Cam said as he pulled me into his embrace, holding me tight against his body. "I thought . . . I thought he'd gotten to you."

"Who?" I asked, pulling away to look into his worried brown eyes.

"Rayonus," he spat.

Confused, I asked, "Rayonus? What do you mean? He was just here last night."

A look of rage filled his features as what I said sank in. "When was the last time you saw him, Mavis? When?"

I stared at him, shocked. I'd never seen him angry like this before. "I don't know. It couldn't have been later than nine o'clock. He showed up right after Penelope brought dinner."

"Penelope!" he exclaimed, running to the door. "Wait there. Right there. Don't move."

I wrapped my arms around myself, scared of what was coming next. I knew he wouldn't find Penelope there. I knew she would be gone, and from the sound of it, Rayonus had taken her. But why? What was happening?

Cam ran back into the apartment, breathless and forlorn. "She's gone, Mavis," he said, his voice cracking as he grabbed me and buried his face in my hair. "She's gone, and I don't know where to look for her."

"Baby, tell me what's happening," I said, stroking his back and trying to comfort him as best as I could.

"Rayonus," he said when he finally found his voice. "He and my father . . ."

"They were working together," I guessed, knowing the answer before he even said it. "That motherfucker."

He nodded. "I ran into an old acquaintance working at a gas station in Denver. She told me that she'd seen Severin and Rayonus in Grand Junction not a week ago."

"Why didn't she call you to let you know?" I asked with unshed tears in my eyes.

He cupped my face in his hands. "She doesn't know about our situation. If I told her I'm marrying the Exitium Daemonium, we'd have every would-be evil overlord in the world trying to figure out how to get into Havenwood Falls."

I raised my brows. "So, she's a trustworthy old friend."

Cam almost smiled. "Actually, yes. But Mavis, you're the Exitium Daemonium. No one else can know about you. Even abnormally nice demons are still demons. There's always a little evil lurking within us. You can't trust us."

I sighed, in complete disbelief over what was about to come out of my mouth. "Cameron, I know you think that, but in Rayonus's case, I don't think you have anything to worry about. At least, not where Penelope is concerned."

Incredulous, he dropped his hands and stepped away from me. "How could you know that?"

"Because when he was here last night, he kind of freaked out. He told me he loved her and wanted to get her out of town, or at the least, to move in here with us where she could be watched. Now that this has happened, I'm guessing he knew she was about to be used to blackmail us into coming to Severin, and he decided to get her out of town."

"Or my father told him to take her," he argued. "There's no way to know for sure."

"Not until we talk to Ray, no," I said, thinking aloud as I stared at the carpet. "And either way, I'm sure he's doing what he thought was safest for her. He's been loyal to you out of friendship, but he loves her. I have a feeling if it came down to it, he would do anything to keep her from getting hurt, even if that meant he would have to betray us."

"Mavis, you said you were feeling your douche radar when I left yesterday. Did it get worse or better when he was here?"

"Neither. It disappeared."

I looked up to see a glimmer of hope in his eyes. "It disappeared?" he asked.

I shrugged. "Yeah, a few hours after you left."

Cam sighed in relief, closing his eyes. "Mavis, this is good news."

Astonished, I asked, "It is? How?"

"You weren't feeling any negative intent from him," he explained, leading me to the couch to sit. "He didn't set off your radar."

"That's good, I guess, but that still doesn't leave us with any way to find her. Or to kick his ass from here to next Tuesday. Because, right now, I don't give a shit whether his intentions were good. His ass is grass when I get ahold of him. She wouldn't even be in this mess if he didn't come here to try to buddy up to us for your father."

"I know," he said, pulling me into a hug. "And I know you want to kick his ass, but I want you to promise me you'll dial back that demon-killing urge until we know the whole truth, okay?"

I pushed away from him, knowing he was right, but not wanting to listen. I just wanted Penelope back, safe and sound in Havenwood Falls, where she belonged.

"Look," he said, trying to get me to see reason. "Rayonus has a place about an hour and a half from here, up near Montrose. We'll drive up there and see if they're there. If they're not, we'll assume he's joined the dark side, and we'll figure out our next step."

"Don't you think we should call Sheriff Kasun and report this?"

He shook his head. "No, his jurisdiction doesn't go any farther than the county limits. Plus, I just don't want him getting caught in the crosshairs of some demon fight he can't handle."

Taking a deep breath to steel myself, I stood. "Okay, I'll get dressed, and we'll go."

Cam and I drove out of Havenwood Falls in silence, both of us with thoughts weighing heavy on our minds. I so wanted to agree with Cam and think the best of Rayonus. I really did; he had seemed so sincere about his worry for Penelope the night before, but when I thought back to all the lies and deceptive things he'd done, the secrecy he'd always kept himself shrouded in, I didn't know if I believed he could be on our side. I kept thinking back to his words in the outdoors store when he said that not all demons have the capacity for good that Cameron does.

Those words hadn't meant much then, but they were glaringly accurate to me now. As far as I was concerned, I'd never met and would never meet a demon that had the capacity for good Cam did, because they were never human. His humanity—that goodness his mom had given him—was what made him the decent male I wanted to marry, that I wanted to be with for an eternity. Ray had never had that, and he never would.

Cam had been driving for thirty or forty minutes when he bit out a sudden, alarmed curse and said, "I think we're in trouble, darling."

"What is it?" I asked, squinting ahead at the metallic shimmer blocking the road in the distance.

"If I had to take a guess, I'd say it's my father and his cohorts. There are another two cars behind us as well."

"Fuck!" I exclaimed, whipping around in my seat to see that there were, in fact, two dark-windowed black sedans following closely behind us. "What do we do?"

He reached across the console and squeezed my hand. "Protect yourself as best as you can. If we get taken and something happens to me, try to find Penelope. If you can find her, get yourselves out and away however you can."

Fat tears rolled down my cheeks. "Cam, you're scaring me."

He lifted my hand to his mouth, kissed it, then wiggled the engagement ring loose. "Hide this in between the seats. My father will torture me to get you to agree to his wishes. Don't give him any more leverage than he already has."

Nodding woodenly, I quickly grabbed a receipt from the dash, balled the ring up in it, and shoved it between the console and the passenger seat. "Now what?"

He gripped the steering wheel tightly and stared ahead at what we could see were two black SUVs parked across the lanes. "We try to go around them if there's room, or we go through the middle. Is your seatbelt buckled tight?"

I jerked on the shoulder strap, cinching it tighter to my hips. "Yes."

"Then hold on, darling," he said, gunning the accelerator. "I'm bringing us up to ramming speed."

Blowing out a deep breath, I closed my eyes and prayed that we'd make it, prayed that we'd get out of this with our lives, prayed that Penelope was okay, and prayed that I would never get ahold of Ray because I was going to kill him.

"Hold on!" Cam yelled as we slammed into the middle of the SUVs.

The deafening screech of metal against metal drowned out my screams as our SUV plowed through, pushing the two cars to a diagonal position on either side of us. We sped ahead for a few beats, and for a second, I thought we'd made it, but then the front driver's side tire blew, leaving us skidding across the road and into the snow-filled ditch.

"Run!" Cam screamed as soon as our momentum stopped. "Run as fast as you can! I'm right behind you."

Dazed, I threw the seatbelt off me and opened the door, ready to dash up the mountain to the safety of the trees. I knew they'd easily catch up to me if I ran down the highway. I'd only gotten a few steps from the car when electricity, so white-hot it blinded me, shot through my body. I stumbled, falling to my knees, but still tried to crawl to the tree line. In my addled mind, I thought if I could make it to the trees, I'd be safe. If I could make it to the trees, this would be over. And then everything went black.

# CHAPTER 10

*T*he first thing I saw when I woke was blackness. Panicked, I tried to sit up from my prone position on what felt like concrete and was rewarded with a cruel laugh for my trouble.

"Don't even try it," a male voice said. "Severin's not letting you go anywhere."

I feigned ignorance. "Who? I don't understand what's going on."

Cue another annoying laugh. "Sure you don't."

"Stop toying with her, Felix," another voice said. "Severin has been looking for you."

This voice I knew. It was Rayonus. The backstabbing, lying asshole who had betrayed us.

"Mavis?" he inquired, gingerly lifting the blindfold from my eyes.

"Evil henchman," I retorted coldly as I blinked the black-haired demon into focus.

"I deserve that," he said, giving me a significant look that I didn't understand. "You must be pissed that I lied to you."

"Pissed?" I seethed. "Pissed? I don't think 'pissed' really covers it, do you?"

He grimaced and said, "No," but then mouthed out, "Cam is okay."

I glanced around the small eight-by-ten cell I was in. There was nothing in it—not a bed, chair, or toilet—and it smelled like mildew and mold. "Where's Penelope? What did you do with her?"

"I'll answer that if you don't mind," Severin said, walking into the small cell, looking like a model on the cover of a romance novel. "We haven't had a chance to talk for a few months."

Ray bowed. "Yes, Lord Severin."

"Aw . . . is someone having an identity crisis?" I asked, taunting my incubus douchebag soon-to-be father-in-law.

Closing the door behind Rayonus, he hissed, "Shut your mouth, ice demon."

I laughed shrilly. "Or what? You'll tell your mommy on me?"

Severin dragged me from the ground by my hair and squeezed my chin painfully in his grip as he hovered over me. "I said to shut up, Mavis."

Scoffing, I spit in his face. "Go fuck yourself, demon boy."

Chuckling darkly, Severin wiped the spit from his face with his hand and licked it. "Breaking you is going to give me so much pleasure. When I'm done with you—"

"I'm going to ask if you've put it in yet. Yeah, that's sad, Severin. That's not the kind of thing you should tell folks either. Lest they pity your poor impotent ass."

He bared his fangs at me and shoved me away, turning to leave, then, second-guessing his decision, he backhanded me so hard I fell to the floor.

The rough concrete dug painfully into my hands and knees as I landed, and the room spun around me. I scrambled back to my feet, swaying but ready to take him on. "Is that all you got, Severin?"

"No," he said coldly. "But sadly, as much pleasure as it brings me to see you bleeding, I have more important things to attend to." He grinned down at me, his black eyes roaming over my body as he adjusted his growing erection.

"I'm going to kill you, Severin DeSalle," I said, ambling toward him through the pain. "I'm going to kill you and rejoice in the sound of your screams."

His voice was hard and unforgiving as he turned away from me, not even remotely afraid of what I might do. "You do that," he said. "If you think you can."

"I can!" I yelled, slinging an icicle at the door as it closed behind him. "And I will!"

His taunting laugh echoed in the hallway before he called, "Put my son in here with her," to the guard outside the cell. "And make sure he knows the weight of my displeasure with him when you do."

~

Rayonus returned as soon as Severin left. He was carrying a bowl of water, a washcloth, and a worried expression. "You're bleeding, Mavis. You have a bad cut on your cheek."

I reached up to the cheek Severin had just struck and hissed in pain. "You are all going to pay for this," I told him, my voice as frigid and unfeeling as the ice in my veins. "I'm going to kill every single last one of you."

Ray winced, knowing I meant every word. "I know, and I don't blame you," he whispered. "But before you do, let me get you three out of here."

"How?" I asked skeptically, not believing him for a second.

He shook his head. "I don't know, but I will. I promised you once that I didn't mean you any harm. That hasn't changed. I never wanted any of this to happen."

"He has us both. Why doesn't he let Penelope go now?"

He gave me a bitter smile and squeezed out the cloth. "I love her. He knows I'll do anything he says to keep her safe."

I let out a little sob as what little hope I had that Penelope would get out of this alive left me. "Can I see her?"

"Eventually," he told me, his jaw clenching and unclenching in anger as he looked over my wounded hands. "But I'm sure Severin will want to try to get you in line before he rewards you."

Tears sprang into my eyes. "I hate you, Ray."

Dabbing at the drying blood on my cheek, he nodded. "I hate myself."

"Good."

~

For what seemed like an eternity, I waited for Severin to keep his promise of sending Cam to me bloody. I didn't doubt his threats and bitterly regretted antagonizing him into doing it, even though Ray assured me he would heal quickly. I knew he was right—demons did heal incredibly fast—but I still asked him to leave the bowl of water and the cloth just in case I needed it.

Finally, after I'd paced around the four-walled cell a hundred times, I heard the snick of the lock. I ran forward, careful to keep my distance from the actual door, and prayed I'd see Cam walk in on his own two feet.

No such luck.

Cam was battered and bruised on every inch of his body. His dark hair had been torn out in patches. His eyes were so swollen, he couldn't open them. Bloody tears leaked between the lids. But he was alive and mad enough to call out anatomically impossible threats to the goons that brought him in before they left.

I waited until they closed the door to rush to his side. "Cam," I said, whispering so low, I hoped he could hear me.

Mavis," he sighed out, another bloody tear leaking down his face. "Darling, I'm so sorry. If I would have known they were going to ambush us—"

"Shhh," I said, gently wiping his cheeks with the cloth. "It's okay. I'm okay. Penelope's okay, too. Ray said she's in the basement."

"Thank God," he breathed. "Do you know where we're at?"

"No, I think they tased me. The last thing I remember is

running and feeling a searing pain in my chest. I woke up blindfolded in this cell."

He was silent for a moment before he asked, "And my father? Have you seen him?"

"He was here about thirty minutes ago. I'm afraid I might have caused your injuries by smarting off to him. I'm so sorry."

Cameron smiled, though it looked like it pained him. "You? Smart off to someone? Never."

"How can you make jokes right now?" I asked, sniffing and wiping my tears from my cheeks with the back of my hand.

He pushed himself slowly to a sitting position. "This isn't the first time my father has had me beaten. It won't be the last."

"You can't take any more, Cam. If you could see what I'm seeing, you'd understand. It's bad, Cam."

"We're demons," he said, smiling ruefully. "That's the beauty of it to him. It used to take days for me to heal, but now, I can already feel my ribs knitting themselves back together. He'll be able to do this again within the next couple of hours."

Horrified, I asked, "He did this to you before, when you were half human?"

"He's done it a thousand times, Mavis. Why do you think I was so keen to keep stealing souls for him? Angering him wasn't worth the weekly beatings."

I stared at Cam, trying to center my emotions through the rusty smell of his blood, the torrent of vibrations in my chest, and the homicidal urge that shot through me when I focused on his bruised and beaten face. "I'm so sorry you were born into this life," I told him, meaning every word with all my heart. "If I can stop this, if I can snuff him out, I will."

"It could be worse," he said, trying to open his eyes. "If he had demanded that I stay in his entourage of lackeys, this would happen much more regularly, and I would've never met you."

"Well, that may not be exactly true. If we hadn't met on the road that night, he'd probably have me as one of his lackeys by now."

His square jaw hardened as he clenched his teeth against the pain and stood up to take a look at our surroundings. "That will never happen," he said firmly. "I won't let it."

"You may not have a choice, Cam. I mean, seriously, how are we going to get out of here? If I can't fight against him, we're going to need help."

Turning to me, he gathered me into his arms and hugged me tightly. "It may take time," he whispered. "We may have to do things we never thought possible. But Mavis, one day, he will slip up. One day, we'll overtake him. And on that day, you will kill him."

I knew he was right. This was a bad situation, a terrible one, but it wasn't an impossible situation. We were immortal. We could wait Severin out. In time, he would make a mistake, and we would be ready.

"Isn't this sweet," Severin said, walking into the cell. "The two lovebirds are reunited."

Cam and I remained silent as he closed the door behind him and casually leaned against the wall. "What?" he asked. "No biting wit or comments, ice demon? No more threats or spitting in my face? I thought you were going to—what was it—rejoice in the sound of my screams?"

A scathing reply was on the tip of my tongue, but I held it back when Cameron gave my arm a nearly imperceptible squeeze, letting the hatred in my eyes say everything I couldn't.

Severin chuckled. "I thought seeing this embarrassment of an incubus beaten and broken would change your mind. You lesser demons are so fucking predictable."

"Father, allow me to—"

"Quiet!" Severin bellowed. "I've heard quite enough from you two today. As a matter of fact, I like the calm your lover has when she sees you like this. It seems to make that feral attitude she has a bit more docile."

I glared at him, biting my cheek so hard I could taste blood welling into my mouth.

Severin crossed the room to stand in front of me. "You want to hurt me, don't you, you little hellcat? You want to grind me into a spot on the ground like you did your poor grandfather, don't you?"

I didn't answer, but I didn't cower, either. I just stared up at him, memorizing every line on his face, every hair on his head. I wanted to remember it all because when I killed him —and I would —he would be nothing. He would be less than nothing. There would be no way to recognize him when I was done.

Stroking a hand down my cheek, Severin smiled. "I can see the burning desire in you, Mavis. I can practically feel the heat of your anger, the depth of your hatred. I can't help but wonder, if I made you my lover, would you still have that fire behind your eyes or would you cower in fear like the rest of the demons do when they see my cock?"

Disgusted, I sneered at him. "Fuck you, Severin."

The corners of his mouth lifted in a half smile. "Oh, little demon, you think this bastard son of mine has brought you pleasure? You have no idea the pain, the degradation that you would enjoy with me. You would beg me for it. Do anything for it. They all do . . . after a little persuasion."

Severin glanced at his son's defiant face and sneered. "Relinquish her to me, Cameron, and I'll free you and your human friend. Give me my prize, and I will let you walk away from this life."

Cameron shook his head, though he knew the consequences of refusing his father. "No."

Severin's voice was deceptively calm as he asked, "You dare to defy me?"

"She is *my* prize," Cam told him. "My destiny. Taint her with your evil if you will, but she will always be mine."

"Foolish words from a foolish demon," his father retorted, dragging me from his son's arms and throwing me against the wall.

The breath flew from my chest as I hit the concrete, but I righted myself quickly. I would stand and fight him, no matter if it was with my last dying breath. I wouldn't just roll over and let him win.

"When will you both understand that I am lord here?" Severin screamed, his face distorted with unbridled rage. "I make the rules! I care nothing for your sentiments and bravery! You will bend to my will!"

Then like someone flipped a switch, he calmed, turned to me, and gave me a serene smile. "I enjoy seeing that righteous light die in your eyes. I revel in it, just like you will, Exitium Daemonium. Oh, sure, you'll fight me now, but there will come a time very soon that you'll crave the destruction I want, and you'll do anything I ask to get it."

Stalking to where I stood, Severin grabbed my face with both hands and tilted it up. His black eyes swam with a sea of swirling souls, twisting, turning, yearning to break out of their prison. I tried to shrink away from the horror in those eyes, the clear intent in his movements, but he held fast.

"You already know what's to come, don't you? Your power—it can feel them, can't it?" He shook his head in wonder. "You will be magnificent," he said, before brushing his lips against mine.

I stiffened and tried to pull away, but he held me in place, pushing the soul into my mouth until I couldn't breathe. Helplessly, I tried to fight against him, scratching, punching, and kicking anything within my reach until whatever hold he had on me evaporated. I was left standing, cold and shaking, as he swept from the room without another glance.

# CHAPTER 11

hen the shock of what Severin had done wore off, an overwhelming sense of fear, love, hate, betrayal, and anger struck me all at once. Nearly doubling over with the emotions, I asked, "What is this, Cam?"

His voice was even and without emotion as he answered, "Humanity."

I jerked my gaze to his face. "It feels . . . I've never felt like this before. It's so . . . much."

He nodded, understanding exactly how it felt to have a soul. He'd had his own only five and a half short months ago.

"Why did he do this?"

Cameron laughed, but there was no mirth in it, no joy. "I'm an incubus, Mavis. You know what we do."

"But what purpose could it have? What's his game?"

Cam closed his eyes and breathed out slowly as he shook his head. "He wants me to take it. He knows that we won't be able to resist each other."

Confused, I said, "I still don't get it, Cam. Why would he give a demon a soul?"

"To weaken me. Well, to be more precise, to weaken both of us."

"Me, I get. But how would stealing a soul weaken you?"

"It's my soul that he gave you."

My mouth dropped open. "Your soul? But how?"

"My father is well-known for his . . . let's call them talents. He can collect the souls of half demons, but they are no use to the powers that be above him; demons are already creatures of hell, so he saves them and uses them to strengthen himself.

"Then why would he voluntarily give yours to me?" I asked, still not quite understanding.

"With my soul inside of you, you won't have the amount of power you had before, just like I didn't have my full incubus powers. It'll be like before the throttle in your chest broke open. And if I steal it—which, let's face it, I will—these injuries that have healed in minutes might take days to heal. He doesn't like that I'm stronger as a demon. I can't be properly punished like this. I heal too quickly for his tastes."

"So, this is a really bad thing."

"A horrible thing," he agreed. "He knows that if he leaves us in here long enough together, one of us will lose control. You won't be able to resist me, and I won't be able to withstand your soul. Do you remember what it was like the first night we stayed together at that hotel?

I thought back to that night and the cringe-inducing way I'd acted without even realizing I was doing it. "Yes. I believe I tackled you like a 'sexed up cheetah' if I recall correctly.

He smiled at the memory, despite our shitty situation. "That you did."

I shook my head. "Cameron, what are we going to do?"

He pursed his lips. "I think we should have sex . . . eventually."

"But if you take your soul, you'll be defenseless."

"That's true, but you won't. You're the Exitium Daemonium. You're the only one who can kill him. We just need to figure out a way to remove his talisman to make him vulnerable."

"How are we going to do that? We're locked in this cage."

"We won't be in here forever. This is just a temporary cell. He'll have to move us somewhere else. I'm guessing to his mansion in Grand Junction. That's where my father keeps all his prisoners."

With my mind still reeling from all the new emotions, I sank to the floor and wrapped my arms around my knees. "I know you're probably right about his motives, but I'm still worried that he might decide to separate us."

"He won't. He could have given you any number of souls, but he gave you mine. There's only one reason he'd do that."

I shuddered, thinking of all the souls I'd seen in his black eyes. "Why is he like this?"

Cam shed his jacket, handed it to me, then sighed. "Have you ever heard the phrase 'mad with power'?"

An hour or so after my soul transplant, Rayonus woke Cameron and me where we'd curled up together in a corner. We'd tried to stay apart, not wanting to risk the temptation we were already feeling, but without my ice magic, it was bitterly cold in the empty concrete cell, and my teeth chattering was getting bad enough that Cam had worried about me cracking a tooth that might not grow back.

"Severin wants you both moved downstairs with Penelope," he said, to both of our relief. As fiery as her short temper could be and as brave as she was, Penelope would be consumed by terror by now.

"Where are we, Rayonus?" Cam asked his friend quietly. "Where is he keeping us?"

Ray frowned, but said, "In a rented house about fifty miles east of Havenwood Falls."

Cam's hopeful expression fell. "So, it's too far for them to run if we can get them out."

"Do you really think Penelope would be here if I could get her out?" he asked.

"I don't know," I snapped, my swirling emotions getting the better of me. "Would she? You are the reason she's here."

Cam laid a hand on my shoulder to calm me. "That's not helping, Mavis. Don't let anger cloud your judgment."

"I've never had a soul before, Cam. This is a lot harder than you made it look."

Ray stared at us, realizing what we were saying. "Severin gave Mavis a soul?"

"He gave her my soul," Cam explained. "He's buying time and clearly planning on taking out a few of his frustrations on me later."

Ray froze as if the implications of having an incubus locked in a room with his pseudo-girlfriend had just hit him.

Cam sucked in a breath, following his line of thought. "You have my word, Rayonus. I won't touch her."

"It's not you I'm worried about. You know how humans react to you when you're not in Havenwood Falls. I don't think your tattoo will work here."

"Trust me," I told him. "She's going to be too angry at you to think about sex."

"She's right," Cam agreed. "Just go in there and act like your normal charming self. She'll be so pissed that you're acting like that, there's no way she'll think about sex with me."

Ray nodded. "Okay, but Cam?"

"You don't have to worry," Cam promised. "If the urge is too much to bear, I'll fuck my own girlfriend. I know you love her."

"Can you tell her that?" he asked. "I'm pretty sure I don't have a chance in hell with her after all the shit that's happened today, and even if I did, I don't deserve her.

The guard unlocked the cell door a few minutes later, allowing Ray to lead Cam and me down a white-walled hallway, past several closed doors, and down a set of narrow steps to the damp basement. Only lit by a few candles, it was dark and gloomy and smelled like wet dog, but, thankfully, it was warmer than the cell we'd been in and furnished with a room off to the side that apparently had a toilet in it. It would be a lot more comfortable than the concrete floor we'd been sleeping on before.

When Penelope saw us, she jumped to her feet and ran to hug the absolute hell out of me.

"Are you okay?" I asked, looking her over for obvious injuries. Her long brown hair was tangled, and her clothes were disheveled, but otherwise, she didn't look any worse for wear.

"I'm okay," she said, tears in her eyes, "What's going on?"

"I tried to tell her," Ray said. "But once she found out I was connected to Severin, she wouldn't listen to me."

I squinted at him. "Do you really blame her, Ray? You lied to all of us. You're lucky we're not kicking your ass right now."

"Speak for yourself," Penelope said, rearing back and punching Rayonus as hard as she could in the nose.

"Ow!" Ray yelled, holding his broken nose.

"Whoa," I said, grabbing her by the arm and dragging her to the dirty couch. "Calm down. A lot of stuff is going on that you need to know about."

"More important than sweet, sweet vengeance?" she asked, seething with rage.

"For once, yes." I turned back to Ray. "Go, before Severin realizes that you're taking too long. I don't want him to come anywhere near Penelope."

He nodded but didn't move a muscle. "Penny, I'm sorry. I really am. I never wanted any of this to happen."

She stared right through him as he apologized, not once acknowledging that he was speaking to her. She would not be swayed by offers of regret or remorse. She was more pissed than I'd ever seen her. And I'd seen her throw a chair when she didn't realize *Supernatural* was on winter break.

Cam finally spoke up. "Rayonus, she'll be fine. Clearly, she can handle a demon on her own."

Ray took the stairs two at a time, only stopping once to glance back at Penelope, then he shut the door and locked it from the outside.

Penelope shook out her bloody hand and flexed her fingers. "Can someone please fill in the human? I'm starting to get a little cabin fevery in here."

# CHAPTER 12

*W*ith Rayonus gone, Penelope deflated, sinking onto the couch with tears filling her brown eyes until they spilled down her cheeks. "I loved him, Mavis. When he came to my apartment to ask me to blow off work to go to his house in Montrose, I was going to tell him. How could he do this to me—to us? We trusted him."

Cameron sat down in the farthest chair from us and sighed. "You know the kind of demon my father is."

"Yes, but what does that have to do with me? Why would he want Ray to kidnap me?"

"To keep us in line," Cam explained. "What else?"

"What does he mean, 'keep you in line'?" she asked me.

For a moment, I sat there in silence, not knowing what to say. Everything felt so hard and never-ending now that I had a soul. I just wanted to wake up tomorrow and find this was all a terrible dream.

"Mavis?" Cam asked, sounding concerned, though he didn't dare come closer to us.

"I'm fine," I said, wiping my eyes. "I'm just not used to this soul thing. That's all."

"Soul thing?" Penelope asked. "What soul thing? Someone

needs to start at the beginning and tell me what the hell is going on."

Sighing, I sat down next to her. "When Cam got wind of Ray's involvement with his father, he came home. After he realized I was okay, he went to your apartment and found it empty. With no leads on where you might be, the only logical place was Ray's house in Montrose. We thought that he was probably going to try to sneak you out of Havenwood Falls under Severin's nose after we put two and two together."

"Two and two?" she asked.

"I wasn't feeling the weird vibe anymore. It disappeared before you came home with dinner, and after you left, Ray sort of had a breakdown. He told me he loved you and berated me for not taking more steps to keep you safe with the impending deadline coming up."

"So, he was trying to save me, not kidnap me? And he told you he loved me?"

"We think so, and yes, he did say he loved you. He's been helping us a little bit since we've been in here."

She blew out a heavy breath. "Okay, where does the soul thing come in?"

"After Severin's goons made us wreck our car and tased us, we were brought here. I was taken to a cell and Cam was . . ." I searched for a word that wouldn't scare Penelope.

"I was beaten with a lead pipe," Cam supplied, apparently not feeling the need to sugarcoat the situation like I did.

"But you've healed already?" she asked, amazed.

"I've told you before how much faster demons heal than half-demons and humans, yes?"

She nodded and shrugged. "Yeah, I just didn't expect it to be this fast." Frowning, she added, "I knew I should have kicked one of those goons in the nuts."

Cam smirked. "And that is why we're friends. You always know what to say to lighten the mood."

I shook my head at the two. I couldn't believe they were making jokes right now. "Anyway, Severin came in and did the compulsory evil overlord speech. I spat in his stupidly handsome face and got backhanded for my trouble."

"You neglected to tell me that part," Cam admonished.

"You looked like you'd been run over by several cars when you came in," I shot back. "I didn't want to upset you."

"Point taken," he said, holding up his hands in defeat. "Continue, please."

I smiled at him. "Thank you. So, as I was saying, Ray came in after that with a wet cloth to wash the blood from my face, and Cam showed up shortly after. We were alone for a few minutes before Severin made a reappearance and gave another trite, boring attempt at overlord douchebaggery. He kissed me and kind of pushed Cam's soul into my mouth."

Penelope looked from me to Cam. "One, ew to the kiss, and two, why would he do that?"

"I'm an incubus," he said, shrugging. "He knew I wouldn't be able to resist the siren song of a soul, much less my own, and once I have my soul back, I won't heal nearly as fast. He can keep me weak."

"Not to mention," I added, "now that I've got a soul, it's almost just like when my throttle was whole. I can't transform at all, and I'm sensitive to the cold again."

"But what about the demon-killing thing? Does it affect that?"

"I haven't tried that out. I didn't want to hurt Cam or Ray, and Severin still has his amulet or talisman, whatever that is."

"I think he's keeping her weak until he can make other, more permanent, arrangements for us somewhere farther away from Havenwood Falls," Cam added.

Penelope suddenly looked apprehensive. "Cam, does your tattoo still work?"

He pressed his lips together. "No. I'm sorry, Penny. But don't worry. I promise I won't touch you."

She blew out another breath, this one shaky. "What do we do now?"

"We wait," I told her, settling onto the couch and looping my arm into hers. "There's not much else we can do."

"Welp," she said, her voice bright. "Who's up for a game of Three Questions?"

∽

The time we spent waiting on word from Rayonus was some of the scariest but also the most lust-filled moments of my life. After talking for a couple of hours, an exhausted Penelope curled up on the couch and dozed off, leaving Cam and me alone to speak softly to each other while we watched her sleep. I tried to ignore the pull of his incubus power, tried to keep my eyes away from him, but the allure was too great.

"Do you think we can trust Ray?" I asked, trying to take our minds off the elephant in the room. I'd been staring at his full lips with hunger like I'd never felt before.

"I do," he growled, his eyes black with the same hunger I felt. "I just don't know if I can trust myself. You, with a soul, are the most beautiful, most seductive thing I've ever seen."

A slow smile spread across my lips. "Now you know how I felt when we met, incubus."

"I seriously doubt you felt like this, Mavis. The pull to your soul is almost impossible to ignore. As is your incredible body. Knowing exactly how you taste and how you feel while I'm inside of you makes it that much harder."

I moved closer to where he sat, my heart pounding in my ears. "Harder, you say?"

"Mavis," he warned. "I don't think I can control myself if you do this. Please don't make me do something we'll both regret later."

My eyes traveled the length of his body, stopping on the outline of his huge denim-clad erection. "I think having that big cock of yours deep inside of me would make me forget any regrets I might have."

He groaned, shifting his hips. "Mavis, please. It's hard enough without the verbal foreplay."

I bit my lip. "I love it when you say the word *hard*."

"For the love of *Supernatural*, guys!" Penelope exclaimed, sitting up. "Can you keep it in your pants for two seconds, so I can sleep?"

"Sorry," Cam and I said in unison as the bolt on the door was slid back.

"It's just me," Ray said, appearing with a tray of sandwiches and water.

I, for one, couldn't have been happier to see him. After he'd come to my aid in the cell and my initial anger had faded, I didn't really think he would leave us out to dry, but there was the underlying worry that he would, or that he would be found out by Severin and punished accordingly. Even after everything he'd done, I didn't want to see another friend hurt or worse.

After distributing pre-packaged sandwiches and bottles of water, he sat on the third step of the stairs and stared at Penelope, who, of course, refused to glance in his direction. "Is everything going okay down here?" he asked.

Cam nodded and took a swig from his water bottle. "As good as can be expected. Have you figured anything out yet?"

"Actually, I think so."

"What?" I asked, sitting on the edge of the couch to catch every word of his quiet conversation.

"Severin mentioned something about moving you to a 'long-term solution' for your imprisonment later tonight when he didn't think I was listening. I think that if we plan things right, we can escape during that transition. He's already sent most of the demons back to wherever that is to get it ready."

"What about his amulet?" Cam asked. "Mavis can't touch him while he's wearing it."

"You mean this one?" Ray asked, holding up the small charm between his fingers.

Cam jumped up, a triumphant expression on his face as he took the small runed piece of ivory from his friend and pocketed it. "How did you get it?"

Ray smiled winsomely. "I convinced one of his lovers to switch it out while she and another demoness were . . . uh, servicing him."

"How did you talk them into doing that?"

Ray smiled. "Severin may be powerful, but he's also a selfish lover with zero redeemable qualities. The sooner we kill him, the sooner they'll be free to go back to the life they had before he took them as sex slaves. I always told him that his treatment of others and burned bridges within the demon community would come back to bite him in the ass."

"I could kiss you," I told him, getting up to hug him.

He wrapped me in his warm embrace and grinned down at me. "Why don't you save that for Cameron? It'll be a good start to you giving his soul back."

"That it would," Cam said, eyeing me with renewed interest.

"You guys go ahead," he said, nodding his head toward the bathroom. "You may not get another chance. I'll watch Penelope while you're busy, then I'll go secure a car that will get her back to Havenwood Falls while you guys do the deed with Severin."

"Doesn't this seem a little too good to be true?" Penelope asked skeptically. "I mean, we all get kidnapped by one of the most powerful shape-shifting demons in the world and Rayonus Rixa is the one who outsmarts him? Really?"

Ray's smile fell as her words cut into him. "Penny, I know it's hard for you to trust me right now. I've hurt you. I've lied and done terrible things, but I really do love you. Seeing you here in this dank basement, scared and alone, you have no idea what it's done to me. I'll admit, I'm a selfish creature. I've always been selfish, but that stopped today. It's time that I put someone else's wishes and safety ahead of my own, and that someone is you."

Unfazed by a speech that had brought tears to my eyes, Penelope asked, "Okay, if you are who you say you are, what did you put on the top of Mavis and Cam's Christmas tree in December?"

With palpable relief, he smiled and answered, "Your favorite angel, Castiel, of course."

"That's good enough for me," Cam said, taking the water from me to hand it to Penelope. "We'll be right back," he told them, pulling me to the tiny bathroom and slamming the door shut behind us.

I laughed, almost feeling nervous as Cam's eyes roamed over my body. "Like what you see?" I asked.

He smiled, his fangs snagging on his lip. "I don't know where to start."

"Unzipping your pants might be a good place," I suggested, slipping my jeans off my hips. "I'm sure the rest will work itself out."

Making quick work of taking off his clothes, Cam stood naked in his demon form. "How do you want it, Mavis?"

Pulling him down to meet my mouth, I kissed him and murmured against his lips. "I want it with you, the real you, not your demon form."

In the blink of an eye, the Cameron DeSalle I'd met on that lonely highway in Utah was standing in front of me. "Better?"

"I'll be better when you have your cock between my legs," I told him.

Cam threaded his fingers in my hair, kissing me hard before sliding his hands down to cup my ass and pick me up. He groaned loudly as I moved my hand between us to lead him inside of my warmth, and I cried out as I sank down on him, pure, unadulterated pleasure shooting through my body like lightning.

"I love you, Mavis," he said as we moved together, both of us searching, reaching for that one perfect moment of ecstasy.

"I love you," I replied, eyes shut tight as a coil tightened deep within me and the first sweet sensations of orgasm flittered through me, making me tighten around his cock.

"Fuck!" Cam yelled, his eyes flickering between black and brown as he came closer to his own release.

"Take it," I whispered against his mouth, before licking it open and letting him breathe in the soul I'd been given. I cried out, the emotions I'd felt with his humanity amplifying to a crescendo and then stopping suddenly as if we were standing in the eye of a hurricane. I broke away, burying my face into his neck.

Roaring as the human feelings filtered through him, he turned me so that my back was against the wall and pounded into me until I was sore and trembling, my thighs slick. Both of us breathing heavily, we stared at each other, knowing what had just occurred between us was more than sex. It was the return of us—what we'd had before Severin had taken it all away.

"I have to admit," he said, smiling as he broke the silence. "I thought you'd want me in my demon form one last time."

I shook my head and softly kissed his lips. "I wanted the man I fell in love with, Cam. That's all I've ever wanted."

# CHAPTER 13

Once we were cleaned up and dressed, we walked out of the bathroom to meet Ray and Penelope. I was glad to see that they were sitting within a few feet of each other and talking, something I hadn't expected. I knew it would take a long, long time for him to convince her that she should forgive him, but this was definitely a start.

"Are you guys good?" Ray asked.

I held up the water bottle I'd picked up on the way out of the bathroom and froze it solid. "Yep."

"You?" he asked Cam.

Cam nodded, his honey-brown eyes alight with happiness instead of the emotionless black we'd become used to.

He smiled at us. "Good. I'll run upstairs and see where things are. Remember, there are still a few demon guards up there, in and out of the house. I don't want you to try to take them all on, on your own, Mavis. Severin can't escape in the chaos of another battle. He needs to be the first to die."

I nodded, steeling myself for what was to come. "Kill Severin first. Got it."

He turned to Penelope. "Are you ready? I can get you back to Havenwood Falls, then come back to help."

"Wait," Penelope said. "Are you sure we shouldn't stay? What if Severin notices that Mavis doesn't have a soul as soon as he sees her, and strikes first?"

"With what?" Cameron asked. "He can't defeat her. No demon can. The second she lets her power loose—well, you've seen what happens."

"It still sounds risky," she said, worry in her voice.

"I'll be fine," I assured her. "It will help me to know that you're safe and far away from what's going to happen here."

Reluctant to leave us, she hugged me and then Cameron. "Get home safely, guys. I'll be waiting."

Cameron tousled her hair and grinned, something he hadn't done in months. "We will, Penny. Now get out of this shithole and go home. Sam, Dean, and Castiel are waiting for you."

She grinned back at him and followed Rayonus up the stairs. "Love you, guys . . . even though your sex life completely grosses me out."

I laughed, shaking my head as we watched the door close behind them. "It's nice to see her smile again."

"Yes," he agreed. "Maybe now things can get back to normal."

"Or not," I hissed, as the light from the hallway above spilled onto the stairs.

Taking a fighting stance, we readied ourselves for whatever was about to happen and were surprised to see a gray-haired old woman with bright green eyes stroll down the stairs. "Severin wants to see you, Cameron," she said.

"Tell him to come down here himself," I told her. "He's not going anywhere."

She breathed out a very put-upon sigh. "Mavis, don't make this harder than it has to be on yourself. You don't want to piss me off. You can't win in a fight against me. Don't even bother."

I scoffed at the woman's presumption. "Wanna bet? Maybe you should worry about pissing me off."

She looked at Cameron. "Is she serious?"

Cameron looked from the woman to me and tried to relay

something meaningful with his eyes. I just didn't know what that something was.

"Fine," the woman said, lifting her hands to her chest level, palms out. "I did try to warn you."

A little frightened now, I took a step back. "What are you doing?"

"Showing your smart mouth a lesson," she said, as a surge of power filled the room.

Putting my hands over my ears to stop the pressure in my head, I screamed and threw myself at her, only moving my hand away from my ear long enough to wrap one around her wrist and push my magic into her. The familiar pop shot through my chest, but the magic didn't stop the attack. In fact, it only seemed to make it worse.

Falling to my knees, the old woman cackled with laughter. "This will teach you to mess with the likes of me, demon!"

Just when I thought I couldn't take any more of the onslaught, Cam rushed to the other side of the room unnoticed and came back with a folding chair, which he promptly brought down on her head.

The pressure died down instantly, and I sagged to the ground with relief.

Cam was at my side in an instant. "Are you okay, darling? Talk to me. Are you hurt?"

I shook my head, though it made everything in the room seem to spin out of control. "I'm okay."

He held out a hand to help me up, and I took it, glad to have something in the room that wasn't spinning. "Do you need to sit down?"

"No," I said, trying to move away from the unconscious woman. "We need to go. I don't think we should be here when she wakes up."

He glanced down at the woman's bleeding head. "No, definitely not. She will not appreciate the chair to the head."

"What is she?" I asked, intrigued by the green blood matted in her frizzled hair.

Cam shook his head. "Someone very powerful. I don't exactly know what, but she's been in line with my father for as long as I can remember."

I nodded and took a deep breath, careful to navigate the dark stairs as I climbed up with Cameron. We stopped at the top, and Cam peeked out into the hallway. "It's clear," he whispered.

"To the right," I reminded him, stopping to bolt the door behind us. "The other way leads back to the cell."

"Yes, it does, and that's exactly where you're going," said the voice I'd heard Ray say belonged to Felix.

Without thinking or stopping, I shot two spears of ice into the demon, pinning him to the wall through his shoulders. His screams echoed through the house, bringing two more guards running into the hallway.

"Fuck!" Cam yelled, grabbing me and yanking me the other way, back toward the cell we'd come from.

"No!" I said, resisting. "We can't go that way."

"What do you suggest then?" he asked, trying to shove me behind him.

"Move," I yelled, startling him into obeying me. "I've got this!"

Suddenly, in all the commotion and noise, I realized something that had never crossed my mind before. I was the Exitium Daemonium, but I was also an ice demon. I didn't know a ton of demons, but it was safe to say that I'd never met one with dual power. But somehow, I had it. What would happen if I combined my magic? Could I kill demons from afar with my ice?

Summoning my power to the forefront of my mind, I imagined infusing it with the same spears I'd used on Felix, sending them spinning toward both guards running our direction. At first, nothing out of the ordinary seemed to happen, but as the ice stopped its forward motion and sank into the chests of the guards, they stopped and howled with pain before bursting into a fine mist of disintegrated demon.

Cam stared at me, dumbfounded. "Mavis, you can combine your magic?"

I nodded, making my way to Felix, who was still struggling to pry himself off the wall. When he saw me coming, he screamed in earnest, knowing what was happening next. Holding up my hand, I formed a long dagger and pushed my magic through it, bringing it down right into the center of his chest. His screams died instantly as his body shared the same fate as the others.

Cam seemed shaken for a moment, but then he rushed forward, keeping a hand on me as he led the way to the relative safety of outdoors.

We were almost to the front door when Severin walked into the room from what must have been the kitchen. The moment he saw us, he smiled and tsked as if we were naughty children who had snuck into the cookie jar.

"What do we have here?" he asked, a moment before he seemed to realize that the soul he'd given me was gone.

Moving quicker than we expected him to, he pulled a gun from his waistband and aimed it at his son, pulling the trigger twice before turning the gun on me and screaming, "You thought you could escape me? You thought I'd just let you go? I'm never letting you go. You will serve my every need for an eternity!"

Ignoring the gun he aimed at me, I fell down to my knees beside Cameron. I knew Severin wouldn't shoot me. He needed me. He had plans for me.

"Cameron," I said, shaking him when he didn't respond. "Cameron!"

Panic filled me as I saw the two bleeding bullet holes in his chest. He couldn't die like this. Not when we were so close. Not after everything we'd been through over the past six months. This couldn't be happening.

"Baby, please," I wailed, starting CPR. "Please, stay with me. I can't lose you."

"He's dead," Severin said coldly. "As he should be. He only had one job in his worthless life, to serve me, and he couldn't even do that right. He didn't deserve the breath I gave him when I impregnated his bitch of a mother."

Anger, white-hot and raging, filled me as his stinging words registered in my grief-addled brain. Worthless?

Lifting myself to my feet, I turned to Severin, my eyes not really seeing him. "Did you just call the love of my life worthless?"

Severin stepped back but didn't answer.

"Did you?" I screamed, no longer in my right mind.

"You're better off without him," he said, looking over Cameron with a sneer of distaste. "He was never what he could've been, should've been. He wasn't anything. Just a waste of oxygen."

Stunned, I stood there next to the body of the man I loved and stared at his father. I stared at the demon who had tortured him throughout his long life. I stared at the demon who had shot him and taken him away from me.

And then I snapped.

Throwing my arms wide, I shot two long shards of jagged ice into my grip, pushing my magic into every molecule of their makeup, and then I took a menacing step toward him. "I'm going to kill you, Severin. I'm going to see the light fade from your eyes. And I'm going to rejoice in the sound of your screams."

"Try it, ice demon," he said, inviting me forward. "You will rue the day you brought this suffering on yourself."

With a warrior's cry, I rushed forward, stabbing and slashing any part of him that I could reach. I could've done it without getting my hands dirty, but I wanted this. I needed this. It was my right to avenge my mate.

Severin laughed as the ice cut into him, not realizing the severity of his injuries until it was far too late. Finally looking down at himself, he saw his skin falling away in fragments. And then he screamed, and screamed, and screamed.

# EPILOGUE

$\mathcal{I}$ never got to say thank you to Rayonus Rixa.

Sure, it was the demon's fault the three of us had gotten kidnapped, his fault Penelope had been distant since her dramatic return, and his fault Cameron had been shot, but even with all that taken into consideration, I couldn't deny that he'd given us the only opportunity we were likely ever to have to kill Severin DeSalle.

"Are you still pining over Rayonus?" Cam asked, kissing the top of my head before handing me a mug of chai tea.

I sighed and smiled, closing the journal I was writing in and throwing it to the coffee table. Hearing Cam's voice was a balm to my nerves and something I would never take for granted. He'd survived the gunshot wounds, but only just, and only because, underneath the human façade, he had the power of a demon running through his veins. It was fitting that the only thing that saved him was the one thing his father couldn't ever take away from him.

"I just wish he'd come back," I said, accepting the mug with a grateful smile.

Cam sighed and hugged me to his side. "I know, darling. I miss him, too."

For days upon days, after Cam healed, we searched and wondered and worried what had happened to Rayonus, but those days had turned into weeks, and though the hope we'd see him strolling into the apartment uninvited sometime soon was starting to feel like a far-fetched dream, we'd left all his things neatly stowed in the spare bedroom, on the chance that, one day, he'd come back for them . . . and for a devastated Penelope.

A knock at the door set my heart racing, as it always did since the incident. I ran to the door, hoping beyond hope that the black-and-blue-eyed demon would be standing there, giving us his trademark smirk, but just like all the times before, it was Penelope coming over to pass the time.

Tonight, I found her wearing one of Ray's favorite flannel shirts, a pair of leggings, and a weary smile. "Hi," she said. "It's almost time for *Supernatural*. Mind if I watch it over here?"

I pulled her inside and closed the door, happy she was doing something so ordinary. "Sure. Want some chai tea?"

She shrugged. "Sure. I'm probably going to die alone and be eaten by my twelve cats anyway. Why not start drinking old lady drinks now?"

Cam jumped up to make the tea before I had a chance to ask. He understood that Penelope was facing Ray's disappearance like she did any tough situation—with her trademark sarcasm and overreaction—but we were glad to suffer through it for her. We would do anything for her, especially after she'd planned our expedited wedding from top to bottom while I nursed Cam back to health.

"So, are you guys still getting married this weekend?" she asked.

Yes, we are," Cam said, handing her a steaming hot mug of tea. "And yes, you still have to come."

Cam sat back down next to me and squeezed my hand. Regardless of Ray seemingly vanishing into thin air, we weren't willing to wait any longer to be married. We'd been together through the worst months any couple could ever go through. There was no reason to put it off or prolong the engagement. We'd survived, and we had each other, and that was all that mattered.

"What do you think the odds are of me finding a hot demon guy at the reception?" Penelope asked as the front door opened unexpectedly.

I grinned and felt all the air leave the room as the newcomer came into sight. "Oh, I think the odds are pretty good."

~

# ABOUT THE AUTHOR

JD Nelson is a bestselling author of Fantasy Romance and Adult Paranormal Romance. An avid time-waster, JD enjoys watching TV and listening to audiobooks when she really should be writing.

JD loves to hear from her readers. You can contact her through her website, AuthorJDNelson.com, or on Facebook, where she spends an alarming amount of time chatting with her many author and reader friends, much to the dismay of her continually neglected manuscripts.

# ACKNOWLEDGMENTS

I want to send a huge thank you out to the readers that wanted to murder me when I made *Plans Laid Bare* a cliffhanger. Without your restraint, this book would not be possible. XOXO

# STRAY WITH ME

## E.J. FECHENDA

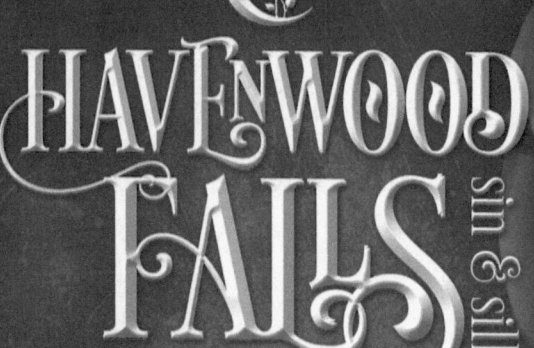

~ A Havenwood Falls Sin & Silk Novella ~

# Havenwood Falls

sin & silk

## Stray with Me

# E.J. Fechenda

# ALSO BY E.J. FECHENDA

**The New Mafia Trilogy**

The Beautiful People

Clean Slate

Endings & Beginnings

Enforcer (a prequel novella)

**The Ghost Stories Trilogy**

End of the Road

Havoc

The Triangle (Coming Soon)

**Havenwood Falls**

Fate, Love & Loyalty

**Havenwood Falls High**

Fata Morgana

**Legends of Havenwood Falls**

Fated Beginnings

*To my Hubba Bubba*

# CHAPTER 1

*H*arlow kept her pace and breathing even. Eyes focused on the road ahead. Sweat dripped down her back as she rounded the bend. Havenwood Falls stretched out before her as she ran down Blackstone Road. Creekwood Estates was to her right. Aspen trees, leaves already turning gold, added to the colorful landscape. Sunlight hit solar panels and twinkled brightly. To the left was the cemetery, and while she couldn't hear them, her sister Taylor said the dead often whispered to her when she passed by the hallowed grounds. Harlow's sister was a medium, though, so she wasn't surprised.

A car that Harlow recognized slowed to stop at the end of Stuart Street. She waved to Amanda George, and the young kindergarten teacher waved back before pulling out to make a left onto Blackstone Road, cutting off a motorcycle. Harlow inhaled sharply when she realized the motorcyclist didn't have time to slow down and would hit the car. Without thinking, Harlow snapped her fingers, and instantaneously, time came to a halt. The car and motorcycle paused, along with a bird flying overhead.

"Shit! You've really done it now," she scolded herself. Resigned to the fact that she had just used her magic in front of a human, she quickly proceeded to manipulate the car, so it completed the turn and was out of the way of the motorcycle. As soon as it was clear, she snapped her fingers, and time resumed.

Hoping Amanda, the human she had just used magic on, didn't notice, Harlow continued her run as if nothing had happened. Unfortunately, the man on the motorcycle did notice and pulled over to the side of the road, directly in front of her. She had heard about Ryker Pride, remembered when he arrived in Havenwood Falls a couple years ago. He was a lion shifter—a rarity in Colorado—and that had created some local gossip. The fact that he was hot and single had added to the gossip among her girlfriends.

Ryker had long, dirty-blond hair that was tangled from the wind. He removed his sunglasses, pinning her in place with smoldering blue-gray eyes. A thick layer of stubble blanketed his square jaw. He wore jeans and a long-sleeved flannel shirt that stretched over massive biceps. But the black leather vest he wore over his shirt revealed who he really was. The Swords of the Infernal Night, or SIN Motorcycle Club, was full of men her grandmother warned her about it. By the way Harlow's body responded just by standing within three feet of the giant piece of man candy, she knew her grandmother was right. This man needed to come with a warning label.

"Nice save back there, Country Club. I owe you one," Ryker said, his voice more like a sultry growl that caused her nipples to harden. When his gaze drifted down her body and he gave her a feral grin, followed by a wink, she knew he noticed. Of course, she was wearing a tight black running shirt over her sports bra and skintight leggings, leaving little to the imagination.

Swallowing hard, she crossed her arms over her chest and firmly met his gaze.

"Country Club?" she asked, narrowing her eyes.

His grin widened. "Just a nickname the boys have come up with. Your pops is some big wig at the club and you work there, right?"

Harlow's eyes narrowed even further. "You sure know a lot

about me for never having met before, and I already have a nickname? What's that all about?"

Sure, Havenwood Falls was a small town and her dad was the Director of Member Services at Creekwood Country Club, so he knew a lot of people, but that crowd generally didn't mix with bikers. Realizing she sounded judgmental, Harlow closed her eyes and took a deep breath to center herself. When she looked at the biker again, he had his hands in the air as if in surrender. He straddled his bike, a monster black and chrome machine that looked almost as dangerous as its rider.

"Hey, it's no big deal. My brothers and I take notice of all the beautiful single females in town. You're one of them."

*Okay, so he's an ass—a hot ass, but an ass. Judgment totally earned,* she thought to herself. Harlow was about ready to tell him off when her phone that was strapped to her right bicep started to ring. She glanced at the screen and saw her grandmother's name. Mathilde Augustine was the matriarch of the family, a leader in the Luna Coven, and she sat on the Court of the Sun and the Moon, which was the governing body of the supernatural community in Havenwood Falls. With a sinking sensation in her stomach, Harlow knew the use of her magic had triggered the wards that surrounded the town. Lately, Harlow's grandmother had been extra everything: nosy, controlling, and protective. Harlow didn't know what was going on, but she had heard whispers about an outside threat.

"Harlow, did you just use a little more magic than usual? Are you okay?" she asked when Harlow answered her phone.

"I'm fine, Grandma."

"Are you sure? Nothing unusual happened?"

"Nope, everything is fine."

"No witnesses?"

"Nope," Harlow lied, and she made eye contact with Ryker, whose eyebrows were raised. Based on his reaction Harlow knew he was able to hear the conversation. Shifters were known for their enhanced senses.

"Okay, dear. I was just worried." Harlow's heart softened, and any annoyance at her grandmother being overbearing vanished. She sounded more like a concerned grandmother than a critical leader. It had been a few months since Harlow got in trouble for using her magic in public, and she was relieved to not be on the receiving end of another lecture—or worse.

"No need to be. I'll see you soon. Bye."

She disconnected the call and reached up to tighten her ponytail, in preparation to start running again.

Ryker's gaze roved over her body before he said, "I can think of some other forms of exercise."

He winked at her and laughed when she rolled her eyes before turning away.

"You wish," she said over her shoulder and began to jog back the way she came.

"Wait!" he called out. "I was just fucking around. Want to go out for drinks or something? I owe you. I'd be a heap of road rash right about now if not for you."

"Nothing happened, okay? You didn't see anything." Harlow waved him off and kept running, knowing it was best to put distance between them.

The next morning, Harlow arrived at Coffee Haven to open. The sun was just beginning to rise, but it didn't hold much promise to beat back the cold. The weather in their box canyon town was unpredictable. A front had blown in overnight, ushering in temperatures low enough to make snow possible. The bell above the door chimed when she pushed it open, and she inhaled the fresh aroma of coffee brewing. The manager, Davis George, looked up from where he was placing a tray of scones in the display case. They said good morning, and Harlow jumped in on her opening chores. Davis became the manager more than a year ago, when he and his wife Amanda, the woman Harlow had stopped time for the day before, moved to town. Harlow and Davis had established a routine. Neither was usually talkative in the morning, so they worked well together. Except that morning, Davis had a story to tell, and it was one that made Harlow cringe.

"Amanda keeps going on and on about an experience she had yesterday. She claims it was divine intervention or something." Davis took off his dark-framed glasses and cleaned the lenses with the bottom of his apron.

"Really?" Harlow asked, wiping flour off the counter and pretending to be intrigued while ignoring the sinking feeling in her stomach.

"Yeah, she said you were there. She saw you running, and she waved at you, and the next minute, she said she almost collided with a motorcycle, but it was like time stopped or slowed down. She could see the stubble on his jaw, she was that close, but somehow, she avoided hitting him. Did you see it?"

Harlow chose her next words carefully. "I did see the close call, but I'd say it was just luck. I didn't see anything out of the ordinary."

"Good. I'll make sure to tell her that. She's been obsessing over it. I'm just glad she and Junior weren't in an accident."

"Same here." Harlow left the conversation at that, convinced she had nipped the situation in the bud.

There was a steady stream of business all day—customers eager to warm up with a hot coffee or cocoa. By closing time, Harlow had forgotten about the conversation. She and Davis left together, Davis locking the door behind them. They walked down the sidewalk, waving at Sedona, the owner of the bookstore next door, as she was in the front window setting up a new display. They walked several blocks, past the medical center, and Harlow split off to head up to her house. She hunched forward against the cold wind and burrowed her face in her scarf to keep her nose from freezing. Dusk was already descending; the days had noticeably begun to grow shorter.

She had just slipped her shoes off and hung up her jacket when her phone rang. It was her grandmother again.

"Grandma, what's up?" She walked down the short hallway into the kitchen.

"Imagine my surprise when Letitia Blackstone called me up just now with an interesting story."

"Okay . . . what story?" Harlow pulled out her rice cooker from the cabinet next to the refrigerator and set it on the counter.

"Amanda George was in an afternoon yoga class and couldn't stop talking about a miracle that happened."

Harlow groaned internally and hung her head. The beauty of living in a small town. There weren't any secrets, and of all people to overhear Amanda, it had to be Letitia Blackstone. She ran Yoga in the Vines at NamaStays Inn. She was also the retired matriarch of the Blackstone family, one of the founding families, like the Augustines. The two families shared a long history, and Letitia and her grandmother were friends. "The way Amanda described time stopping sounded awfully familiar, and it was right around the time the wards picked up a surge of your magic. Do you have anything to tell me?" Gone was the grandmother tone.

After breathing out a sigh, Harlow admitted she had used her magic to prevent an accident.

"You lied to me."

"Not really. I didn't think Amanda had noticed, so there wasn't anything to worry about. I'm sorry, Grandma. If I'd known, I would have wiped her memory, as I've been trained."

There was a long pause, and Harlow chewed on her lip. She hoped her grandmother didn't press further. If she revealed she had been distracted by a hot biker—well, that excuse would not fly.

Her grandmother breathed out a heavy sigh. "I have to report it to the Court, Harlow. It's my duty."

"But—"

"I can't show leniency because you're my granddaughter. It will call my leadership into question. I'm sorry. I came to your defense after the incident at the Dirty Knuckle, and it caused a stir. I'll let you know what they say."

Before Harlow could respond, her grandmother ended the call.

"Ugh!" she growled and tossed her phone onto the counter. The incident her grandmother referred to had happened over three months earlier, and she was still being punished for it—even though all she did was defend her friend, Shayna. Although, in hindsight, sending a guy flying across the bar for sticking his hand up her friend's skirt might have been a bit overkill, but she had zero tolerance for gropey fuckers, and the guy had been warned after he grabbed Harlow's ass earlier that night. Unfortunately for her, there was a room full of witnesses and a room full of cell phones, plus the guy was angry and wanted to press charges against her for assault. Considerable damage control had to be employed, and Harlow was called in front of the Court. Because of her grandmother, she had been dismissed with a stern warning. Somehow, she had a feeling she wasn't going to be so lucky this time.

Two days later, just before eight p.m. on Tuesday, Harlow parked her Mini Cooper in front of City Hall. She turned off the ignition and sat in her car, focusing on getting her breathing under control. Thoughts of her friend Aster ran through her mind. Aster and her sister, Reeve, had both been banished from Havenwood Falls for using their abilities in public. Fear rendered her immobile, her hands gripping the steering wheel tight. Aster and Reeve's situation was different; it was really, really public. Harlow hoped for a slap on the wrist. As much as she hated the suffocating confines of being an Augustine, she didn't want to be forced from where she was born and raised.

With a final deep exhale, she stepped out of her car and strode with false confidence down the walkway that led around back of the building, to the special entrance for the Court of the Sun and the Moon. Minutes later, Harlow sat at one of the two tables that faced the elevated dais where the members of the Court had convened. Addie Beaumont sat off to the side, taking minutes. A large mural depicting all of the supernatural species that resided in town provided a backdrop for the court members.

Elsmed Fairchild, the fae representative, spoke first, breaking the uncomfortable silence. His long silver hair was pulled back, drawing attention to his preternatural features: extremely pointy ears and a long, narrow face. So long his chin seemed to touch his chest. His penetrating icy blue gaze held Harlow captive. "Ms. Augustine. Your grandmother tells us you used a considerable amount of magic in public, in front of a human, is this correct?"

Harlow broke away from his gaze to look at her grandmother, who sat to the right of Elsmed. Her back was straight and hands clasped in front of her. Her expression didn't betray any emotion.

"That's correct. There would have been a terrible accident," Harlow started to plead her case, but was cut off by Lawrence Mills. His sharp voice silenced her.

"This is your second offense, is it not? You received a pass the last time." He cast a severe glance at Harlow's grandmother. Harlow swallowed hard.

"Lawrence, let the girl speak," Sandra Beaumont, Addie's grandmother, said. Mr. Mills huffed and leaned back in his chair, crossing his arms over his chest. "Tell us what happened, Harlow."

Harlow relayed the brief incident, making sure to emphasize that Amanda George hadn't seemed aware that anything unusual had occurred.

"Amanda George, the kindergarten teacher?" Mayor Barbie Stuart spoke up. The mayor was the only human who sat on the Court. It made sense that all species, including humans, had representation. With her height and large build, though, the mayor could have been a supe. Perhaps some giant blood ran in her genes. Add in a sky-high bouffant of cotton-candy-pink hair, and she certainly didn't look like a typical politician.

"Yes, and her child was in the car. When I knew an accident was imminent, I reacted. It was a knee-jerk reaction and not an intentional disregard of the law."

"Hmph," Lawrence huffed again.

"She speaks the truth," Elsmed said, after Harlow felt his presence inside her head probing her thoughts. A sensation she had experienced once before and would never get used to—like the tip of a feather was being dragged across her brain.

"Sounds like your granddaughter needs better control over her reactions, Mathilde," Lawrence said to Harlow's grandmother. "And a reminder of the Luna Coven's role: to use magic to cover up mishaps, especially when a human is exposed—not to create a problem."

"Harlow does understand the coven's role. Remember when she covered up after Paisley Underwood healed that human in public? However, I agree she needs to work on her impulsiveness. The coven will address that. I will see to it."

Harlow ground her molars together to keep her mouth shut. Her grandmother, a high priestess of the Luna Coven, had been trying to pull her into coven business more and more. Harlow preferred to stay on the periphery and do her own thing, but her mishap had just given her grandmother leverage.

"The younger generations have zero respect anymore and lack discipline. I propose we start implementing harsher punishments, or they're going to continue to disregard the law. An example must be made! We have more pressing issues at hand, and if people can't follow the law, then I say we be done with them!" Lawrence glowered from under his bushy eyebrows. He opened his mouth to say something else but he was interrupted.

"You mean my generation, Lawrence?" Michaela Petran chided and rolled her eyes. "Because of these issues you mention, we need every capable witch, which Harlow very much is. I propose she does receive further training, though. I believe that would make everyone happy, Lawrence?" The moroi vampire dipped her head in deference to the elder frost dragon shifter. Harlow silently cheered, thankful for Michaela's support. She was also curious about the issues they were referring to that would require every capable witch. What exactly was going on?

"I propose the three-strike rule should apply. One more incident will be the third strike and grounds for banishment," Roman Bishop added in a bored tone. He straightened the sleeves of his suit jacket and brushed at the fabric as if it were covered in dust. Harlow couldn't see any imperfection, and that was Roman, always perfectly dressed and exuding confidence.

"That seems reasonable. Shall we put it to a vote?" Elsmed motioned. There were murmurs of agreement, and when he called for everyone in favor to say aye, Harlow waited, scarcely breathing, for the Court to determine her fate.

A sigh of relief rushed out of her lungs when all but one member voted in favor. She wasn't surprised Lawrence Mills opposed. She'd heard he was a stickler for the rules and old school. Before she could leave, Harlow had to agree to training, and Mathilde would oversee her progress. Another term of the agreement was that if Harlow used her magic in the presence of a human again, without ensuring memories were altered to cover up the incident, she could face immediate banishment.

After that, she was free to go, and she left quickly, rushing up the stairs, pushing open the door, and stepping out into the night. The cool, fresh air was a jarring transition from the oppressive Court's chambers, and she paused to take a few deep breaths. When she reached the end of the walkway and started to approach her car, she was surprised to see someone waiting for her. Ryker sat astride his bike, which was parked next to her Mini. He was leaning forward, his arms resting on tall handlebars with his large hands draping over top. He was facing her, and she felt the weight of his gaze. She faltered and came to a stop in front of her car. He was parked on the left, and she'd have to pass him to get to the driver's side door.

"What are you doing here?" she asked.

"I happened to be driving by and saw you walking in. Does this have anything to do with the other day? Are you good?"

"Oh." Surprised at his concern, she let her guard down and relaxed. Her shoulders seemed to melt away from her ears, and she didn't realize how tense she had been. "I'm okay. Thanks for checking in."

At that moment she heard her grandmother approaching, recognizing her voice by the almost Southern drawl. Harlow looked over her shoulder to see her grandmother walking with Lawrence Mills. Wanting to avoid her, Harlow rushed over to her door. Just as she had her hand on the handle, her grandmother called out.

"Harlow, I need to speak with you!"

"Fuck," she muttered under her breath, and dipped her head forward, causing a cascade of dark waves to shield her face.

"You can hop on the back of my bike and escape," a deep voice growled from behind her. Harlow let out a sigh. Releasing the door handle, she turned to face Ryker.

"Tempting, but my grandmother kind of has me by the balls right now. I need to hear her out."

Ryker chuckled and shook his head. "Quite the mouth you have there, Country Club." He smirked.

"Sorry, did I offend the big bad biker? I didn't realize you were so sensitive."

Another chuckle rumbled from his barrel chest. "Not at all. I like it."

A throat being cleared interrupted their banter, and Harlow stifled a groan as she looked over at her grandmother who was standing at the curb's edge, eyes darting between her and Ryker. She pursed her lips.

"Harlow, I need to speak to you. Alone." Mathilde directed this toward Ryker, dismissing him with a single word.

"Whatever," Ryker growled and fired up his bike. He backed out of the spot and dipped his head in Harlow's direction. "See ya 'round, Country Club," he called before roaring off, the rumble of his pipes vibrating through her.

Harlow watched him go, enjoying the way his arm muscles bunched as he controlled his motorcycle, instantly regretting that she didn't take him up on the offer of escaping with him.

"Really, Harlow, a SIN member? Since when did you start associating with them? I don't approve and don't think your father will, either."

"Grandma, I don't hang out with SIN. I just met that guy when I saved his ass."

"Well, good. You're an Augustine, and we don't socialize with thugs and outlaws."

Harlow shook her head and pressed her lips together to keep from smirking. Roman Bishop and his brothers had a legendary reputation of conducting business that wasn't exactly on the up and up, and yet Roman sat on the Court. The fact that he was also from one of the town's founding families, wore fancy suits, and lived in Havenwood Heights helped people see past any indiscretions.

"What did you need to talk to me about?" she asked, eager to salvage the rest of her night.

"Are you scheduled to work at the country club Saturday night?"

"No. I'm working during the day at Coffee Haven. Shayna and I are going to grab drinks somewhere after her shift at the medical center. Why?"

"Cancel. Saturday you start your lessons with me, and I'm having a dinner party after. Your attendance is mandatory." Her grandmother spun and started to walk away while Harlow stood there with her mouth hanging open in disbelief. She felt like she was twelve again and being reprimanded. "Be at my house by four and bring something nice to change into. Don't be late!" Her grandmother called over her shoulder and waved her hand in the air, causing the giant moonstone ring she always wore to flash. Whether it was night or day, the ring seemed to attract any light. Mathilde's long skirt billowed as she walked down the sidewalk.

"Unbelievable. I'm a grown ass witch and don't need lessons," Harlow muttered to herself as she slid into her car and turned on the engine, cranking the heat.

The next day Harlow wasn't working at either of her jobs, and she started the morning off with a latte and some retail therapy.

Harlow breathed in deep, inhaling the familiar, tantalizing smells of fresh coffee and baked pastries. There was always good energy in Coffee Haven, and that's why she liked working there. Strategically placed crystals, live plants, and colorful artwork on the walls, from local artists, kept the atmosphere positive. Her boss,

Willow Fairchild, was behind the marble counter. Willow's long silvery-blond hair—similar to her great-grandfather Elsmed's hair and a common fae trait—was pulled back in a ponytail, and her black apron was dusted with flour. She was mixing batter in a large red bowl.

"Hey, what are you doing here on your day off?" she asked.

"I need my fix," Harlow said with a grin and walked around behind the counter to make herself a latte, expertly working the espresso machine. Right before she steamed the milk, she added a drop of vanilla in to sweeten it a little. As soon as it was ready, Harlow took a sip, and even though she almost scalded her tongue, she groaned with pleasure.

"Wow. Just one sip and your mood shifted. Your love for coffee is real," Willow joked, as she poured the batter she had been mixing into muffin tins. Willow was an empath and could pick up moods and energy a person was emitting. "Rough day?"

"You could say that."

"Want to talk about it?"

Harlow looked around the shop at the few customers seated at tables throughout. It was between the early morning and lunch rushes, so quieter than usual. Leaning in closer to Willow and keeping her voice down, she filled her boss in on everything that had happened and recounted her meeting with the Court. She hadn't said anything to Willow earlier, or to anyone else, because she didn't want anyone to worry—or fight her battles for her. Willow would have gone to Elsmed.

"Davis told me about Amanda's experience, but it sounds like she's already moved on. Wait, back up. Who is Ryker?"

"He's the biker Amanda would have hit."

"He made an impression on you," Willow said with a sly smile and a wink, her turquoise blue eyes sparkling. The timer buzzed on the oven. She put oven mitts on before pulling a tray of steaming hot muffins out and setting it on the counter to cool.

"Not really. He's kind of an ass. A real bro type. All muscle and cockiness."

Willow snorted and shook her head as she untied her apron and tossed it in the hamper under the counter. "Your words don't match with what I'm sensing. Your aura lights up like a fireworks display whenever you mention him. You're definitely attracted to him."

"Pft. I am not," Harlow sputtered. Visions of Ryker's muscular body filled her mind, causing a flush to wash over her.

"Uh huh. Sure!" Willow teased. "You can't fool me. I say go for it. Didn't you just tell me last week that you needed to end your dry streak? Bad boys have an appeal. Go scratch that itch, girl!"

Harlow was still laughing at her boss when she left Coffee Haven and went next door to check out Callie's Consignments. If she had to suffer through one of her grandmother's hoity toity dinner parties, she was going to splurge on a new outfit for the occasion. Stepping inside the boutique was like stepping back in time. Callie specialized in vintage. One wall was lined with heavily beaded gowns that sparkled like jewels in the sun pouring in from the large storefront window. Classic denim and leather items that were just as trendy now as they were in the fifties caught her attention, particularly a leather vest that reminded her of a biker who was occupying too much space in her thoughts. She lifted the hanger off the rack and subtly brought the vest to her nose, taking a deep sniff. The rich oily scent seemed almost exotic and forbidden to her, but there wasn't anything special about it—it was just a leather vest.

"Did you just smell that?" Callie asked from directly behind Harlow, making her jump. She had been so fixated she hadn't heard the store owner approach.

"I like the smell of leather," she responded, a little defensively.

"Your newfound love of leather smell doesn't have anything to do with Ryker, does it? I saw you two talking last night." Callie gestured with her head in the direction of City Hall, her long dark brown hair shifting with the movement.

"You know Ryker?"

Callie shrugged. "I know of him. I think he's delivered packages to Ronan. I didn't realize you were friends with him?"

The question hung in the air unanswered as Harlow processed the information. Callie and Ronan were an on-again, off-again couple and had lately been on-again. Ronan Bishop was one of Roman's younger brothers, and Harlow had heard through the coven grapevine that if you needed to procure something through untraceable channels, Ronan was the guy you went to. She shouldn't have been surprised that Ryker and Ronan knew each other, but she was, and a little disappointed.

"I don't know him. We just met the other day. Anyway, I'm here about an outfit." Harlow changed the subject, and soon she and Callie were going through the racks. When she left the store over an hour later, she had a ruby-red dress in one hand and a pair of black leather boots with four-inch spiked heels in the other. They were an impulse buy after she imagined riding on the back of Ryker's bike, her arms wrapped around his barrel chest and her thighs pressed against his.

It wasn't going to happen. It couldn't. Her grandmother would have a stroke. But the idea of breaking free of her familial obligations, of having a fling with a bad boy was appealing—not that she'd ever act on it, especially since she now had to be on her best behavior. At least with the boots she could fantasize.

# CHAPTER 2

On Saturday, Harlow arrived at her grandparents' house located in Creekwood Estates. She pulled her car into the detached three-car garage. There was space since her grandparents owned two vehicles: a Subaru hatchback and her grandfather's baby, a vintage Bentley. Their house was large for Creekwood Estates but small in comparison to the Augustine manor in Havenwood Heights, where they used to live. Harlow's uncle Dominic lived in the manor now with his family.

She grabbed her bag and dress that was on a hanger. The front door opened on its own as she approached, and she warily stepped inside, listening to her intuition that her grandmother was going to test her from the start, and she was right. As soon as she stepped in the door, a baseball went whizzing by, and Harlow stepped back just in time to avoid being pegged in the head. It hit the wall to her left with a thud and rolled to a stop on the marble floor.

"Grandma, what the hell?"

"Testing your reaction, dear. You said it's a knee-jerk reaction to use your magic to stop time but you didn't use it just now to protect yourself. Why is that?"

Harlow set her bag down in the foyer and draped her dress across her arm. "I don't know. I reflexively took a step back."

"I have a theory. Come." Her grandmother turned and gestured for Harlow to follow down the hallway past the dining room to the office. The hallway was wide, and the walls were covered with family portraits and a few landscape paintings of the untamed wilderness, out of which the founding families carved Havenwood Falls. Harlow's sneakers squeaked on the hardwood floors that shone like polished amber.

Her grandfather's presence was strong in the office. His spicy cologne seemed to have been absorbed into the very walls along with faint traces of cigar smoke. Mathilde had recently redecorated, painted the navy walls a creamy white, which lightened the room considerably, but she had kept two large brown leather chairs, which faced the fireplace. The wall behind the heavy walnut desk was lined with built-in bookshelves. The family grimoire was kept in a glass case to protect the brittle pages. Harlow's grandmother crossed the room, and after pushing the sleeves of her heather-gray tunic up to her elbows, she opened the glass case to lift out the grimoire. This book had been in the Augustine family for generations and contained all sorts of spells, incantations, and enchantments. It also served as a genealogical guide. Far more in-depth than a family tree, it contained a written history of each witch's abilities.

"Did you know your great-great-aunt Lucille was able to control time, too?" her grandmother asked as she set the leather-bound grimoire down on the desk and pointed at a page full of flowing handwriting that had begun to fade. "Not only could she stop time, but she could rewind it by a few minutes. Enough to reverse if someone was killed or injured."

"No, I didn't know that." Harlow walked around the desk to stand next to her grandmother and look at the book. There was a note scribbled in the margins next to the name Lucille Augustine.

*Reversed time enough so Harvey and Eloise could escape the house fire. Slept for twelve hours straight after.*

On the other side of the page, there was another note. Here the handwriting was harder to read as the letters were cramped together near the binding.

*Charles was dead, then I changed time, and he was whole again, as if his death didn't happen, except he was altered. Death should remain final.*

This last sentence was underlined, and a chill traveled down Harlow's spine as she noted the warning. There was a general rule with magic that one didn't mess with death and try to restore life. Necromancy was considered dark magic. Apparently, altering time to change the outcome of someone's fate bordered on immoral.

"Who is Charles?" Harlow asked.

"He was Aunt Lucille's husband. You will find, dear, that when you love someone, you will do anything to save them. That's not necessarily a good thing, as in this case. Sadly, Charles and Lucille's romance ended in tragedy. As her note suggests, all didn't go well when she reversed time, which brings me to my theory." Mathilde closed the grimoire with a thud and placed the tome back in its case. "You used your magic to lessen the impact of Paisley using her abilities in public last year. More recently, you used your magic to protect Shayna and then you used it to keep Amanda George from hitting that biker. I threw a baseball at your head, and yet you didn't use your magic to protect yourself."

"Yeah, so?" Harlow tilted her head and regarded her grandmother while waiting for her to make her point.

"My point is, I think when someone you know is in danger, it serves as a trigger for your magic. This is what we'll work on. Teaching yourself to slow down and evaluate before immediately stopping time. The incident with Paisley was an appropriate use to protect our people and our town's secrets, but I don't think it was calculated as such, was it?"

"Not exactly," Harlow admitted, knowing it had been another knee-jerk reaction. She just hadn't been reprimanded for it that time, because her actions served the Court.

Mathilde nodded. "We're also going to explore your abilities. I've been wanting to see what you're capable of for a long time. It's only fair to the coven to know what magic we have to call upon if necessary. Now"—Mathilde started walking toward the door—"it's time to get ready for dinner. Feel free to use the guest suite at the top of the stairs."

Stifling a groan, Harlow followed her grandmother out of the office and down the hall. When Mathilde peeled off in the direction of the kitchen, Harlow kept going. Retrieving her bag and dress from where she had left them by the front door, she climbed the sweeping staircase to the second floor and found the door to the guest suite open. Thick carpet absorbed her footsteps as she crossed the room to a king bed covered in a multitude of throw pillows. A restored leather steamer trunk was at the foot of the bed, and Harlow laid her dress across the top before setting her bag on the floor, slipping off her sneakers, and climbing onto the bed.

"Goddess, give me strength to get through another one of Grandma's dinner parties," she said to the canopy that stretched above her. She lay there for a few minutes, enjoying the silence and being off her feet. After working and standing most of the day, she was tired. Her eyes had started to drift closed when the sounds of voices and car doors closing outside caught her attention. Getting up, she walked over to the window and parted the curtain. The driveway was directly below the guest suite, and she recognized her dad's BMW. She caught a glimpse of the top of her parents' heads before they walked up the front steps and disappeared inside.

Harlow quickly changed into her dress, which was a scarlet red and made from the softest silk. The dress had spaghetti straps and was flowy, but not so flowy that it hid her curves. The hem stopped a few inches above her knees, showcasing her muscular calves. She went into the bathroom to finish getting ready. Her hair had been held back in a loose ponytail. Pulling the elastic off set her long dark waves free. She ran her fingers through her hair to set any tangles straight, then brushed her teeth and touched up her makeup. Right before she left to go downstairs, Harlow put on a pair of black strappy heels. A final glance in the mirror on the antique wardrobe was met with satisfaction, not that she expected to meet anyone new at a coven dinner party.

As she descended the stairs, the buzz of numerous conversations grew louder. She followed the noise to what her grandmother still referred to as the parlor. Her aunt Ronya and cousin Gianna were sitting next to each other on the settee, deep in conversation. Her father was holding court over by the bar with her grandfather, flanked by her uncle Dominic and Martin Parker. Each had a glass of amber liquid in their hands, which she assumed was Warded Whiskey, her father's favorite. Harlow spotted Curtis Parker, who was standing somewhat in the corner with his grandmother, Patty Parker. Based on the blank look on his face, Harlow guessed he was bored and needed an interruption.

"Hey, Curtis, long time no see," she said, sidling up beside him and slipping her arm through his. They had grown up together and graduated from Sun and Moon Academy the same year. Since he had started to help out managing Parker's Perfect Placement Agency, the family business his grandparents had founded, it seemed like the only time she saw him was when he came into Coffee Haven.

"Harlow, dear. Don't you look lovely!" Patty Parker said. "Curtis, don't you think she looks lovely?" Patty's smile was a little too big as she stared down her grandson.

Curtis turned his head to look at Harlow, and his brown eyes scanned her body from head to toe. "You look great. That's a fabulous color red. Where did you get the dress?"

"Callie's."

"Of course. I could spend all day in that store. She has amazing things."

Patty beamed at them and patted Curtis on the arm. "I'll let you two catch up," she said before walking away.

"That was weird," they said at the same time, which prompted Harlow to laugh.

"This whole thing is. It's all my family, except for yours."

"I think they're up to something—look."

Harlow followed Curtis's gaze and saw his grandmother and her grandmother talking to each other, occasionally glancing in their direction. The way they leaned in toward each other made them look like two thieves plotting.

"Well, that can't be good."

"You're right. Drink?"

"Goddess, yes!"

They made their way across the room to the bar, where Harlow's father looked at them in surprise. "Sweet pea, what are you doing here?"

"Grandma didn't tell you I was coming?"

"No. Well, she may have, and I might have forgotten or not listened." He winked and took a sip of whiskey. "So, why are you here?"

Harlow sighed and gratefully accepted the gin and tonic that Curtis handed her. "I'm Grandma's latest project. Haven't you heard?"

"I did and wish I had heard about your hearing with the Court from you. Why didn't you say anything?"

"What hearing?" Curtis asked. He was leaning against the bar, the small of his back at the height of the counter. Harlow filled him in on how she had used her magic on a human and as a result had been added to the Court's version of a watch list. Curtis laughed and shook his head. "Can't leave you unsupervised for one minute, can I?" he teased.

Just then her grandmother announced to the room that dinner was ready.

"Where's Mom?" Harlow asked her dad, realizing she wasn't in the room. "I saw you two arrive. And where's Taylor?"

"Oh, right." He sighed. "Your mom's out on the patio. I'll go get her. And your sister is visiting Paisley at school this weekend."

Harlow tipped her glass and drained her cocktail while watching her dad leave. She should have known her mom would have made herself scarce. She and Harlow's grandmother got along as well as two feral cats stuck in a crate together.

"Tonight is going to be so much fun," she muttered and set her empty glass down on the bar.

"Shall we?" Curtis placed his hand on the small of her back and guided her forward.

They followed the rest of the guests into the formal dining room across the hall. A huge candelabra took up the center of the table, and twelve white taper candles flickered as people moved around the table looking for their seats. Harlow found her nameplate and discovered she would be sitting between her grandmother, who was at one end of the table, and Curtis. Curtis's grandmother, Patty, sat on his other side. Curtis held the high-backed chair out for her, and she dropped down onto the upholstered cushion.

"Always the gentleman, aren't you, my boy?" Patty beamed at Curtis before leaning forward to get Harlow's attention. "He's quite the catch, isn't he?"

"Gram, what are you doing?"

"What? I can't compliment my grandson in front of a beautiful woman?" As if offended, Patty sniffed and turned her head, chin first, to talk to Gianna, who had just taken the seat next to her.

Harlow's parents appeared in the high-arched entranceway to the dining room. The only remaining open seats were across from Harlow and Curtis. Spotting the chairs, they quickly made their way over.

"Hi, Mom," Harlow said with a smile. "You look amazing."

Her mom smiled radiantly in response to the compliment. Wearing a dove gray wrap dress that accentuated her thin waist and with her dark hair twisted into a chignon, Aimi Augustine looked young enough to be Harlow's older sister, not mother. Her skin was smooth and wrinkle-free. Prominent cheekbones helped to keep her skin taut.

"Thank you, honey. You look lovely, too. I was surprised when your dad told me you were here. We didn't see your car in the driveway."

"I parked in the garage."

The small talk continued like that until her grandmother stood up and tapped a spoon against her wineglass to get everyone's attention.

"Thank you all for coming tonight. It's important for families to stick together and stay connected. We're stronger and more united when we care about each other and are involved in each other's lives, which is why I asked you all here. This past year has brought some challenges, and I fear our town is going to be tested even more in the coming months."

This statement prompted side conversations to erupt around the table. Whatever Mathilde knew, she didn't elaborate on. Perhaps it was Court business, and she revealed as much as she was able to. Mathilde paused and smiled nervously at Harlow and Curtis. She licked her lips before casting a glance at Patty. Clearing her throat to get everyone's attention again, she continued.

"It's essential, more than ever, to close ranks and look out for each other. Each generation tends to drift further away. My grandson, Gallad, is the exception, and his alliance with the witch hunters, through his girlfriend Macy Blackstone, is one that will benefit us. It was less than two hundred years ago when marriages were arranged with alliances like this in mind. Bloodlines and the coven were strengthened as a result. In fact, Del and I are an example of such a successful arrangement." Mathilde smiled down the length of the table to where Harlow's grandfather sat at the other end.

Harlow looked around the room and saw similar confused expressions mirroring her own. What was her grandmother rattling on about?

"Patty and I, being the matriarchs of our families, think that the future of our families and the coven will benefit from such an arrangement. While this may seem archaic and unfair, we all have to make sacrifices for the greater good. We've decided Curtis and Harlow are a good match, and we shall celebrate their marriage in the near future. Isn't that exciting?" Mathilde raised her wineglass in the air to make a toast. "Join me in celebrating this happy news."

The room grew eerily quiet, as if Harlow had stopped time, but she hadn't. The words registered, the announcement took root, and Harlow reacted.

"What?" She shoved away from the table and jumped to her feet, her mouth hanging open in shock.

"Mother, what are you doing?" her father yelled. Looking over at him, she noticed his face had gone bright red. Curtis was in an equal state and yelling at his grandmother while his grandfather, Martin, shook his head in disappointment.

"Grandma, this isn't the 1800s. You can't just marry me off like a piece of property!" Harlow had found her voice and lit into Mathilde. "This is ridiculous, and it's not happening."

"Exactly. How dare you go around us and make decisions about our daughter like this?" Aimi chimed in. "Have you lost your mind?"

"Like my son did when he married you?" Mathilde fired back, and all of the color drained from Aimi's face.

Harlow's hands itched, and she wanted to slap her grandmother for saying that to her mom. Comments like that weren't new. Ever since Harlow could remember, her mom and grandmother didn't get along. Apparently, her grandmother expected her son to marry a witch, but when he left for college, he fell in love with a Japanese exchange student. Her mom wasn't a witch, but she wasn't completely human either. Aimi was a descendant of a long line of itako—blind women who were spirit mediums. While Aimi wasn't blind, she communicated with spirits, an ability she passed on to Harlow's little sister, Taylor.

"Oh, not this again!" Harlow's dad came to her mom's defense, and the shouting match escalated. Harlow glanced over at Curtis to see him looking equally pissed off. His grandmother was crying, and Martin had his arm around her shoulders.

"I'm out," Harlow said to Curtis. "You?"

He nodded, and Harlow, placing her hand on his arm, whispered a spell. Everyone, except for her and Curtis, froze. The room went from DEFCON 1 to complete silence. They rushed out of the dining room and headed for the front door.

"Wait, I need to grab my shit!" Harlow gestured for Curtis to stay and ran as fast as her high heels allowed, up the stairs to the guest bedroom. She tossed her makeup bag in her duffel and zipped it closed. She stuck her cell phone in the back pocket of her handbag and swung that over her shoulder. Curtis was holding the door open when she came back downstairs.

As soon as the door closed behind them, Harlow took a deep breath of the crisp night air.

"Where to next?" she asked.

"Anywhere but here. Drinks?"

"Goddess, yes! Where?"

"I know a place. I'll follow you back to your house, and we'll take my car."

Within seconds, Harlow had punched the garage door code into the panel on the side of the garage. Her bags preceded her into the car and landed on the passenger seat. She backed out and as she drove past the front of her grandmother's house, she released the spell. Her cell phone started ringing before she reached the main entrance to Creekwood Estates. She ignored it. She'd had enough of family for the night.

Pulling into the short driveway next to her house, Harlow parked her car, and Curtis pulled in behind her. The headlights from his Tahoe illuminated the inside of her Mini. With keys in hand, she walked up the small set of steps that led to the porch. Curtis held the screen door open for her while she unlocked the front door and stepped inside her dark house. With a snap of her fingers, she turned on the lamp next to the sofa in her cozy living room. She lived in a two-bedroom bungalow that was just the right size for her. A fenced-in backyard provided a safe area, reinforced with wards, of course, for her familiar, Mamoru, who hopped down the narrow hallway from the kitchen to greet her. Mamoru meant "protector" in Japanese, and he was a beautiful snowshoe hare. While he wasn't a vicious rabbit out of *Monty Python and the Holy Grail*, he thumped a warning whenever he felt a threat to Harlow was near.

"Hi, sweet Mamoru," Harlow cooed, bending over to scoop up the white ball of fur after taking her heels off. She scratched him behind his ears as she walked toward her bedroom. "I'm going to go change," she called over her shoulder.

Curtis had taken off his shoes, too, adhering to the Japanese tradition Harlow had learned from her mom. He draped his suit jacket on the back of the loveseat before sitting down. He stretched his legs out, propping his feet up on the coffee table. "No need to change. What you have on is perfect for where we're going."

"And where is that?" Harlow reappeared and set Mamoru down next to Curtis. She tossed her hair over her shoulder and crossed her arms, waiting impatiently for her friend, who was acting very mysterious.

Looking up at her, he grinned, flashing a brilliant display of perfect teeth. "Have you ever been to Silk?"

Her nose scrunched up as if she smelled something awful. "The sex club? Uh, no!" She snagged a plush decorative pillow and chucked it at Curtis, who caught it with ease.

"It's not a sex club. Well, maybe it is, but it's a regular nightclub, too. Silk is exclusive, but I can get us in."

"Oh, really?" Harlow arched an eyebrow.

"Yeah, I know a guy."

She burst out laughing. "Let me guess, some guy you're fucking."

"Harlow, I am shocked you think of me in that way." Curtis pressed a hand against his chest as if she had wounded his heart. "You're not wrong." He winked and grinned again. "Although fucking is so crass. We're part-time lovers."

Harlow held a hand out in front her. "Do not start singing that Stevie Wonder song!" she warned, and Curtis snorted, startling Mamoru, who hopped down off the sofa and thumped his hind feet indignantly against the hardwood floor before settling into his little bed near the fireplace.

"Can I invite Shayna? We were supposed to go out tonight before Grandma summoned me to her dinner party."

"Of course. I'll text my friend and let him know."

Harlow walked over to the small table by her front door and next to the coatrack. She had tossed her handbag on the table when she came in. Retrieving her cell phone, she saw the notification light blinking. When she unlocked her screen, she discovered she had over thirty text messages and five missed calls. All were from her parents except from her grandmother, who'd left a voicemail. She had no desire to hear that message anytime soon. Ignoring all of the messages, she cleared her notifications so her phone would stop blinking and texted Shayna.

**Harlow: Hey girl, still up for drinks but at Silk? Curtis has an in.**

She brought her phone with her back to her bedroom, where she eyed the black leather boots she had purchased at Callie's. The weather had turned cooler in the past week and had officially become boot weather.

Harlow went into the bathroom. Her bungalow was small, and the only bathroom was in the hall right outside her bedroom. While she was touching up her eye makeup, adding a smoky effect to enhance the almond shape of her eyes, her phone buzzed. She glanced down at where it was on the sink vanity with trepidation until she saw it was Shayna texting her back.

Shayna was her best friend who, like Harlow, worked two jobs. Between their schedules, they barely saw each other.

**Shayna: That's so cool. I can't go. 😢 ER is cray tonight. Working a double.**

**Harlow: That sucks! I need to go out. Grandma's party was a shitshow.**

**Shayna: Uh oh. What happened?**

**Harlow: Nothing except an ARRANGED MARRIAGE BETWEEN ME AND CURTIS!!**

**Shayna: WHAT?!**

**Harlow: It's so not happening. We need to talk. Are you free tomorrow?**

**Shayna: Yes. Lunch at Sakura?**

### Harlow: OMG Yes!

They made arrangements to meet at noon, and Harlow finished getting ready. Grabbing her boots, she joined Curtis in the living room. Sitting on the edge of the sofa, she put the boots on. They stopped right above her knees and hugged her calves like a second skin, with crisscross leather laces that ran up the back. The heels were at least four inches and the toes pointy. Not the most comfortable, but as Harlow looked in the mirror above the table by her front door, she loved what she saw. There was a glimpse of toned thigh between where the boots ended and her dress began. The black leather and red silk boldly complemented each other. It was an edgier look, and she loved it. She fluffed her hair, which hung in long, thick waves to the middle of her back.

Curtis whistled. "Girl, you're looking for trouble in that outfit. Those boots are fierce!"

"You like?" She twirled once and ended with a hand on her cocked hip.

"If I wasn't gay, I'd be trying to get in your panties," Curtis said, with a flirtatious wink that made her giggle. He stood up and put his shoes and suit jacket on, pulling the keys to his car out of one of his pants pockets. "Are we picking up Shayna?"

Harlow shook her head. "She's working at the medical center tonight."

Shayna worked admissions in the emergency department and had helped get Harlow's sister a similar position as receptionist at the main desk.

They drove down her street to Main Street and made a right. Main Street turned into County Road 13. Trees lined the sides, and Harlow occasionally caught the glimpse of a shifter or some wild animal as the light reflected off its eyes.

"So what do you think got into our grandmothers?" Harlow asked, turning down the volume on the radio.

"Honestly, I don't know. Gram is convinced that I can choose to not be gay, and she thinks it's a phase. But an arranged marriage? That's a whole new level of crazy."

"Right?" Harlow twisted in her seat to face Curtis. "How archaic is that? And Grandma was so blasé about it, like she thought I'd just fall in line. No offense, but I'm not marrying you."

Curtis snorted and laughed. "You're such a mean witch!"

She swatted his leg before flipping him off.

A few seconds later, Curtis pulled into a parking lot nearly hidden behind the trees. The lot was almost full, but he found a spot big enough for his Tahoe and parked. Harlow stepped down, grateful she was wearing boots. Had she still been wearing her strappy heels, her toes would have frozen. She grabbed a black wool knit wrap that she had brought along as an afterthought and was glad she did as a cold wind ripped through the trees.

Adjacent to the parking lot was a gondola lift station for the gondolas that ran up the side of Miles Mountain. A large man in a black suit stood outside the station like a sentry, checking the IDs of a man and woman. As Harlow drew closer, she noticed he had an earpiece.

Tugging her wrap tighter around her shoulders, Harlow stepped up to the guard, following Curtis's lead.

"Driver's licenses."

Heeding his request, they handed their IDs over. After he looked at each one to verify they were legal, he nodded at them and stepped to the side, letting them pass through to inside the station, where there was yet another guard manning the lift.

From the outside, the gondola looked like standard issue: metal on the bottom half and all windows for the top half. On the inside, it was anything but standard. The windows were blacked out, and each wall was lined with a plush bench. Soft lighting created a dreamy vibe. The man and the woman who had gone in right before them were the only other people in the car. They were too busy kissing to notice they had company. Harlow and Curtis chose a bench as far away as possible and waited. The wait wasn't very long before the door clanged shut and the gondola jerked as it began its ascent up the mountain.

Harlow couldn't help but watch the couple as their kissing

progressed to a level ten PDA. The woman, wearing a black dress much shorter than Harlow's, so basically a shirt, was pressed against her lover with one leg thrown over his lap. He was gripping her ass tight. She rocked against him, her left hand buried in his hair as they kissed. Harlow watched, fascinated, as the man's hand slipped underneath the woman's dress. A gasp and a moan later made Harlow flush, and she looked away while adjusting her skirt so it covered more of her thighs, which she had pressed together, hoping to relieve her sudden arousal.

It seemed like the gondola was going at a snail's pace, and Harlow was glad when it finally came to a stop. There was a loud clank, and a vibration shuddered through the lift when it was locked into place at the station. The couple managed to separate and left with their arms around each other.

"If this ride had been any longer, they'd have had to send in a clean-up crew. Those two were really into each other," Harlow commented with a laugh.

"Yeah, no shit. There was no shame in their game." Curtis fanned his face with a hand. "It was kind of hot."

A narrow passageway lit by white twinkle lights led to a huge metal door that was blanketed with protective runes and glyphs. Mounted above the door was a neon sign that displayed one word: *Silk*. They had finally arrived.

Two bouncers stood on each side of the door. They wore sunglasses even though it was nighttime. Harlow only knew of one species who did this: hellhounds. Flames of hellfire burned in their eyes, and making eye contact could be fatal.

After verifying their identification again, one of the bouncers grabbed the door handle. As soon as the door opened, the heavy electronic drum and bass beat of house music poured forth.

Silk wasn't an ordinary nightclub and sure beat out anything the Haven Saloon or the Dirty Knuckle had to offer. Stepping through the door was like stepping through a portal to a new world. Silk's hellhound owner, Melaina Savage, added a little bit of underworld flavor to the décor of the club, which was a series of connected caves.

"Each room has its own theme. Here is the main nightclub." Curtis shouted his explanation over the music. "There are various levels. We can stay here or go to the supernatural room. Your choice."

"Let's stay here," she shouted back. Instinctually her hips swayed with the beat as they walked to a crowded bar for drinks. With gin and tonic in hand, Harlow grabbed Curtis and started pulling him toward the dance floor when she came to a sudden stop. Curtis practically knocked her over, and some of her drink spilled onto her hand. Straight ahead, watching over the dance floor, was Ryker. He stood at an angle, so she could see his profile. His hair was pulled back in a man bun and the scruff he was sporting earlier in the week had been shaved off. A glimpse of a tattoo peeked up above the collar of his black dress shirt, which was tucked into black jeans. The chain from his wallet caught the light and drew her attention to his ass. Damn.

"Who is tall, dark, and dangerous that you're eye fucking?" Curtis said in her ear, snapping her out of her daze. She wouldn't be surprised if she had drool hanging off her lip.

"That's the guy I stopped Amanda from hitting the other day."

"Damn, girl. He stops traffic for sure."

Harlow laughed at her friend and took a deep breath to get her wits about her. "Come on."

She grabbed Curtis's hand again, and they continued on to the dance floor.

"Who knew my fiancée was so bossy," Curtis said just as they passed Ryker. Harlow didn't see her friend wink at the biker.

"We're not getting married!" she yelled over her shoulder. "But we are dancing!"

Curtis was a great dancer, and they moved together to the music. He was safe. Harlow didn't have to worry about him getting aroused and grinding an erection into her like some guys did at clubs. She didn't have to worry about Curtis slipping something into her drink. She could just let go and have fun, forgetting about her grandmother's ridiculous expectations.

As Harlow danced, she couldn't stop looking at Ryker. Between his stance and hulking figure, he reminded her of a gargoyle watching over the sea of people. He wasn't watching everyone, though. His gaze was fixed on her. The longer he watched her, the more it turned her on. Her movements became more seductive and suggestive. A slow roll of her hips, an arch of her back. All for him. Harlow imagined Ryker dancing with her, his big hands moving over her body, cupping her breasts from behind before running a hand up her thigh and under her dress. He'd slide her panties to the side or rip them off completely, and slip a finger inside her. Harlow closed her eyes and bit her lip, imagining losing control. Hands on her hips gripped hard enough to stop her movements, and she glanced over her shoulder to see Curtis. His eyes were narrowed into slits, and he was frowning. Her gaze darted over to Ryker, and she saw he was still watching her, his nostrils flared. He flicked a tongue across his bottom lip, his mouth curled up in a knowing smirk. Oh goddess, he probably smelled her arousal. Was he like Elsmed—could he read her thoughts?

"Harlow, what was that?" Curtis asked before dropping his hands from her hips and taking a step back, putting space between them.

"What was what?"

"You were practically dry humping me."

"Sorry. I must have been caught up in the music." She tipped her glass up and drew an ice cube into her mouth. The back of her neck was sweaty, her hair damp, and arousal pulsed through her body like an electrical charge. "I need some air."

"Well, we're in a cave so that's kind of hard. Come on, let's take a break." She followed Curtis through the crowd of people packed onto the dance floor, and she hid her face behind her hair, avoiding looking at Ryker when they walked by. She could have sworn she heard a low growl. The sound elicited a wave of goose bumps and caused her nipples to harden. It took every ounce of willpower to keep moving past him.

Curtis found two seats at the bar and ordered another round of drinks. After looking at Harlow, he ordered her a glass of water too. He peeled his suit jacket off and rolled up the sleeves of his dress shirt, revealing a tattoo on the inside of his forearm. It was the triple moon symbol, a circle with a half-moon on either side facing away, like reverse parentheses. The symbol was an ancient one that represented the three phases of the moon: waxing crescent, full, and waning crescent. It was also commonly believed to represent the triple goddess: maiden, mother, and crone. Curtis had added his own flair by incorporating rainbow colors into the simple design.

"Are you ready for some real talk?" Curtis asked, as soon as the bartender had set their drinks down and walked away.

"Maybe."

"You need to get laid. You broke up with what's his face douche canoe back in March, and it's been drier than the Sahara for you ever since. I think that biker dude is the perfect opportunity. Have one night of ridiculously sinful, dirty sex."

Harlow scowled around the straw at the mention of her ex-boyfriend. Fortunately, he didn't live in Havenwood Falls anymore, so she didn't have to see his lying, cheating face. She finished taking a sip before responding. "You know I don't do one-night stands."

"Bah." Curtis waved her off. "You've been trying to be a good little Augustine for far too long. It's time to live a little. Oh!" His face lit up like he just won the lottery. "Even better. Don't make it a one-night stand. Go on a few dates with him and take him for a spin. It's time to get back on the horse. If you know what I mean?" He wiggled his eyebrows.

"You're being fucking ridiculous." She said this with a laugh, though, entertained by her friend's antics. "Why would I do this?"

"Well, for one, he's hot and you have an itch that needs to be scratched. Two, I see the way he looks at you and you look at him —smolder, baby. The attraction is mutual, so it's not like you're going in for dental surgery or anything. Three, and the best of all, is that it would piss your grandmother off. Teach Mathilde to try to control who you marry. An Augustine dating a member of SIN? Harlow, honey, you'll be the talk of the town."

It had to have been the alcohol clouding her brain, because Harlow was actually considering it. Curtis's plan had merit, and he was right about all three points. But could she go through with it and use Ryker like that? She adjusted herself on the stool and crossed her legs. The sight of her boots reminded her of the reason why she bought them in the first place: her fantasy about riding behind Ryker on his bike and being pressed up close against him, his hips cradled between her thighs.

"Fuck it. Okay, let's do this. How do I do this?"

Curtis actually squealed and tapped his hands against the bar like a drum. "Another round," he yelled down to the bartender who was at the opposite end, and pointed at their empty glasses. "Oh, and shots—Death by Sex!"

This got a few catcalls and laughs from everyone else at the bar —a few looks, too.

Harlow groaned and shook her head. "I hope I don't regret this, Parker!"

Two hours later, Harlow had lost count of how many drinks Curtis had ordered. She had also lost sensation in a lot of places and was feeling blissfully numb. Curtis's phone lit up from where it was set on the bar. He snatched it up and grinned.

"Part-time lover has finally arrived, and he's waiting for me in his kink room," he announced.

"His wh-what?" she sputtered, unsure she heard him correctly.

"You heard me. I'm not sure how long we'll be. If you don't hear from me, are you good to call Luber for a ride or someone else?" He tilted his head in Ryker's direction and stood up, placing a hundred-dollar bill on the bar. "Tell me how Operation Get Some goes."

He winked at her and before she could say or do anything, he disappeared into the crowd.

A half hour later, Harlow finished the drink she had been nursing. She hadn't heard from Curtis, so she sent him a text.

Minutes later, the text showed as unable to deliver. After several attempts, she gave up, silently cursing the shitty cell service in town. She was about ready to call Luber when Ryker appeared next to her. With his elbows on the bar, he leaned forward when the bartender approached.

"Hey, Crusher, whatcha want?" he asked.

"Bourbon. Make it a double." His voice rumbled and resonated through Harlow. She pretended to ignore he was so close to her while hyperaware of his presence. How could she not be? He was huge, easily a foot taller than her, and his muscles bulged, testing the very fabric of his shirt. His scent swirled around her. It reminded her of cedar and winter air when it was laden with snow and wood smoke. She could sense him looking at her, so she slowly turned her head to return the stare. Up close and with his hair pulled away from his face, his gorgeous dark blue eyes, ringed with thick dark eyelashes, were on full display. His nose was slightly crooked, like it had been broken before and didn't heal properly. Being clean shaven revealed his square jawline and the true thickness of his neck. "Where's your fiancé, Country Club? He's been gone a long time."

"Who? Oh, you mean Curtis? He's not my fiancé. Well, my grandmother wanted him to be, but he's gay and I'm not into him that way. At all. My grandmother can be a little overbearing. You know how family can be. Am I right?" *Oh, sweet Jesus, I'm babbling!* Harlow cringed internally at the verbal vomit she just threw up. *Damn the booze!*

"Don't know about the family part, but I am glad to hear he's not your fiancé. Any man who would leave you alone this long, looking as good as you do, doesn't deserve you."

"Oh. Thank you." Harlow smiled and sat up straighter, preening at his compliment.

"Can I get you another drink?"

"Actually, I was going to call Luber. Curtis was my ride, but I don't think he's coming back. He was meeting someone in a kink room? I don't even want to know what goes on there." She shuddered, and Ryker laughed.

"He'll probably be a while. Tell you what, have a drink with me, and I'll take you home. I owe you, since you saved my ass."

Harlow regarded him. This was the moment she could initiate Operation Get Some. He'd take her home, and she'd invite him inside, in more ways than one. Before she could talk herself out of saying yes, she agreed. Ryker smiled and ordered her a gin and tonic.

"How did you know that's what I was drinking?" she asked, surprised.

Ryker pointed at his nose. "I'm a lion shifter and have an enhanced sense of smell. I could smell the quinine in the tonic water and juniper gives gin a distinct scent."

"Wow! Impressive. Now, let's back things up. The bartender called you Crusher. What's that all about?"

After taking a long pull of bourbon, Ryker turned toward Harlow, keeping one elbow on the bar. "That's my road name for the club."

"Why? Do you crush a lot of hearts?" she teased.

He paused and regarded her before answering. "More like bones."

Silence hung in the air between them as she processed that information. Based on his size alone, she imagined breaking bones came easy. He could probably snap her arm like a twig. She didn't get any warning vibes from him, though. He came across as more protective. Like he would hurt anyone who tried to harm her.

"That's honest."

He shrugged. "The punishment usually fits the crime."

They finished their drinks, and when Harlow stood up, she swayed and almost fell over.

"Whoa, easy there, Country Club. I got you." Ryker wrapped his arm around her waist and waved to the bartender. The crowd parted for him as he guided them to the entrance. A bouncer nodded at Ryker and opened the door.

A gust of arctic wind blasted them as soon as they stepped outside, and Harlow shivered, her wrap providing little warmth. Inside, the club was almost tropical from the number of sweaty bodies. Ryker seemed unfazed by the change in temperature. He noticed her shivering and drew her closer to his side.

"One of the perks of being a lion shifter," he whispered in her ear. "I run at a hotter temperature. Stick close to me, and I'll keep you warm."

Ryker wasn't lying. He radiated warmth, and she wrapped her arms around his waist, clinging to him like a barnacle.

"Mmm . . . you are warm. And you smell good." She inhaled his winter forest scent deeply and then froze, horrified at what she had just done. She buried her face, out of sheer mortification, in his chest, which rumbled when he laughed.

The gondola to take them down to the parking lot was packed, and they had to stand. Ryker kept her steady—she might as well have been holding onto a steel beam. He was as unaffected by the swaying of the gondola as he was the temperature. Harlow focused on keeping her mouth shut before the alcohol made her say anything else remotely idiotic, like how she wanted to climb him like a tree.

The gondola docked, and they filed out with the other passengers. Ryker kept his arm around Harlow's shoulders as they walked across the parking lot to the back corner on the left, where he stopped next to his bike. It was a Harley Davidson, and the black paint almost blended in with the night.

"Have you ever ridden a motorcycle before?" he asked her.

"No."

He nodded and bent over to unlatch a bag on the back. He pulled out a helmet and hoodie. "Put these on."

Harlow set her wrap down on the narrow back seat and pulled the hoodie on. She was practically swimming in it, and it covered more than her dress did, but it was warm and smelled like Ryker. She wondered if he'd let her keep it. Next, she put the helmet on and struggled with the buckle. Ryker chuckled and stepped in front of her, taking the two straps into his hands. She tilted her head up toward him so he wouldn't have to bend over as far. Even in her high heels, the height difference was significant. Ryker gently brushed some stray hairs aside and free of the strap running underneath her chin. His hands were rough on her skin, but she liked the sensation and leaned into his touch. She watched his face as he made some final adjustments, noticing when his gaze drifted to her lips.

Just when she thought he was going to kiss her, Ryker stepped away and pulled his leather vest out of the compartment on the other side. He stuffed her wrap in and latched the compartment closed. He straddled his bike and gestured for Harlow to climb on board. She walked around to the left side of the bike as directed and followed his instructions, placing her left foot on a peg and using his shoulders for support, then swinging her right leg over to the other side. The leather was cold against her ass, and her teeth immediately started chattering.

"Scooch forward closer to me. I'll keep you warm. It's going to get colder once we start moving."

"Well, winter is coming." It was a popular line from one of her favorite shows, and if the opportunity presented itself to use it, she took full advantage.

"You watch *Game of Thrones*?" he asked, turning to look at her over his shoulder.

"Yes. Do you?"

"It's one of my favorite shows."

"Me too." The idea that they had something in common helped Harlow to relax. Their attraction to each other was obvious, but knowing there could be more than just lust didn't make her plan to use Ryker seem as shallow. She wouldn't have to pretend so hard.

"Okay, so hold onto me and lean with me when I go around corners and curves. I can't have you moving around back there, as it's harder to steer the bike. Got it?"

"Got it."

Using his body, Ryker centered the bike and raised the

kickstand with his left foot. With just that little movement, Harlow moved closer, squeezing her legs around his body. Leaning forward, she wrapped her arms around his waist, pressing her boobs against his back patch.

He turned the key and fired up the engine, which made her entire body vibrate. *Thank Goddess I don't have to pee*, she thought.

Then they were off, and Harlow squealed, gripping Ryker tighter. Closing her eyes, she buried her face in his back. After a few minutes, she relaxed and opened her eyes, sitting up a little straighter to look around. The wind rushed past her face, reminding her of downhill skiing. The mountain air always smelled the freshest when she was flying downhill at a ridiculous speed. Here, the air combined with Ryker's scent, and she wished she could bottle it. Free of the confines of a car, the entire universe stretched out before her. Gobsmacked, she tilted her head back to take in the expanse of stars. They were in a waxing gibbous moon period, and the almost full orb seemed to hover over the town, making snowcapped peaks glow against the dark night sky. The natural beauty of Havenwood Falls never ceased to amaze her, but with it on display like this, while pressed against a man who made her pulse race, Harlow was left breathless. Ryker draped his arm over her left leg and began to lightly caress her calf, which she barely felt through her boot, but it was enough to know he was touching her in such a way. Between that subtle touch and the vibration of the bike, Harlow thought her panties were going to melt right off. If it was possible to spontaneously combust from sensory overload, she was rapidly approaching that point.

Before she knew it, Ryker was pulling up in front of her house. He cut the engine, restoring quiet to her neighborhood.

"Wait, how do you know where I live?" she asked, realizing she had never told him.

"I asked around about you."

"You did? Stalk much?"

This caused Ryker to laugh as he helped her to dismount. "I'm a lion. It's what I do."

"Fair point, stalker," she said with a wink and handed him his helmet.

She was still unsteady on her feet, a combination of the motorcycle ride and the alcohol. Ryker walked her to her door. Before she unlocked it, she turned and stepped closer to him—so close she could feel the warmth radiating off of his body.

"Do you want to come inside?" she asked, looking up at him and drawing her lower lip in between her teeth, trying to look as seductive as possible.

Ryker placed his hands on her hips and leaned forward so his forehead was pressed against hers. Reaching up, she threaded her fingers through his hair. With a tilt of her head, his mouth was on hers. What had been simmering embers exploded into scorching flames, and Harlow moaned, parting her lips, opening up to Ryker. His tongue slipped inside and was even hotter than his hands that were moving up her back as he pulled her into an embrace. He tasted of bourbon, and she couldn't get enough. Suddenly, Harlow was against the door, and Ryker's hands were under her dress, cupping her bare ass, tilting her so she rubbed against his hardness. Wrapping her legs around his waist brought him closer, and she gasped with pleasure. And just like in her fantasy on the dance floor, one of Ryker's fingers moved underneath her soaked lace panties and slid inside her.

"Oh!" she cried out against his lips, and holding onto his shoulders, she rode his hand as he inserted another finger, filling her. Pressure kept building, and she cried out again when he brushed against her clit, sending her over the edge. An electric wave of warmth washed over her body, and she clung to Ryker with shaking arms and legs. Her face was buried in the crook of his neck, her breathing erratic as she came down from her peak. Ryker removed his fingers, and she slowly unwrapped her legs from his waist. Leaning against her door, grateful for a steady surface to support her, Harlow looked up at Ryker. "Shall we take this inside?"

He brought his fingers to his mouth and she watched as he slowly sucked the two that had been inside her clean, like he was savoring her flavor. It was quite possibly the most erotic thing Harlow had ever seen.

"No, that was a taste of what's to come. You're still drunk. When I have you—and I will have you—I want you to be sober so you remember everything. Feel everything," he said with a growl, and placing a hand at the curve of her waist, he pulled Harlow forward, capturing her mouth with his. This time it wasn't bourbon she tasted, but her own essence. Ryker sucked on her bottom lip and released it with a pop. "See you soon, Country Club," he said, before walking away and leaving her a trembling hot mess of hormones on the front porch.

*Good Goddess, I am so out of my league.*

# CHAPTER 3

The next morning, Harlow woke with a pounding headache and hazy memories of the night before. Her cheeks burned with mortification when she remembered what had transpired on her front porch for all the neighbors to see. With the porch light on, she might as well have been on a stage. But her lips still ached from their kiss, a delicious ache and a reminder of Ryker's promise. In the bright light of day, her plans for Operation Get Some seemed foolish, but now that she had a taste, she was bound and determined to follow through. Ryker appeared to be a willing and very much able partner.

Rolling from her side to her back, she stretched her legs, wiggling her toes underneath her white down comforter. Her feet were a little sore from breaking in her new boots. *So worth it*, she thought, smiling and replaying the previous night over in her mind.

A chime rang from somewhere in the house. Recognizing the sound as a low battery notification for her phone, Harlow climbed out of bed. Her hardwood floors were cold, and the house held a chill that meant her heat would need to be turned on soon. Once the mountains were capped with snow, it didn't take long for the rest of the box canyon to catch up. She stopped in the bathroom before going in search of her phone. It was in her clutch handbag on the small table by the front door.

Mamoru was nowhere to be found, so Harlow peeked her head out the back kitchen window and saw his white fluff. He had found a patch of sunlight and was chewing on some grass. Harlow put a cup of rabbit food in his bowl and got him some fresh water. After plugging her phone in to charge, Harlow set about making a tonic to cure her hangover.

She set a tea infuser down next to the stove and turned on her copper teakettle. Her herb cabinet was to the right of the stove, and she pulled out chamomile and turmeric. A pinch of each went into the infuser. From her refrigerator, she grabbed fresh ginger and a sprig of mint. A few shavings of ginger and two leaves of mint went into the infuser before she snapped it closed and dropped it in her favorite mug. It had a picture of Tyrion from *Game of Thrones* and said *I drink and I know things*. She had a wineglass to match. The teakettle started to whistle and steam billowed out the spout. She poured boiling water into her mug and breathed in the aroma as the herbs steeped. Just before she removed the infuser, she whispered an incantation that caused the water in her mug to come to a rapid boil. Almost as quickly as the bubbles erupted, they dissipated. Her cure was ready.

Sitting at the bistro table by the back window, Harlow took a few sips of her tea and immediately felt better. Her head stopped pounding, and the queasiness went away.

"Blessed be," she sighed.

A different kind of headache began to form when she started going through all of the missed messages from her family.

First, they were sorry, then they were concerned because she wasn't responding, and then they started taking a different tone. The one voicemail from her grandmother telling her she was being selfish and that every Augustine has made sacrifices for the greater good really pissed her off. She fired off a group text that included her grandmother and her parents.

**Harlow: No need to be concerned. I'm safe. Not happy about**

what happened. **I'll marry who I love when I meet the right person.**

The responses started immediately, and Harlow felt a stab of guilt. They probably were genuinely worried about her.

**Mom: I agree with you, honey. Call me.**

**Dad: Glad you're safe, sweet pea.**

**G-Ma: We'll talk.**

Having checked in, Harlow left her phone to finish charging. Walking into her bedroom, she snapped her fingers, and her bed started to make itself à la Mary Poppins. She pointed at her closet and selected a pair of black leggings and an emerald-green long-sleeved T-shirt. They floated through the air and landed on her bed. Fortunately, she wasn't restricted from using a little bit of magic in her own home. Crossing the room to her dresser, she picked out underwear and a bra.

After taking a quick shower and blow-drying her hair, she got dressed. As she was getting ready to leave to meet Shayna, she went to grab her fleece pullover from the coatrack when she spotted Ryker's hoodie. Being surrounded by his scent was too much to resist, so she pulled it on and slipped out the door.

Sakura Buffet was located two blocks from her house, so she walked, enjoying the crisp fall day. Halloween decorations were on full display, and she chuckled at the human houses because their ideas of witches, vampires, and ghosts were way off. Most of the humans in Havenwood Falls had no idea they lived among the real deal.

Harlow spotted Shayna sitting in one of the booths by the window when she first stepped inside the restaurant. She was bent over a menu, her brown hair partially hiding her face. Several of the tables in the dining area were already full, even though Sakura had just opened. Sometimes, like at Coffee Haven, there was a line waiting for the doors to open.

Shayna looked up when Harlow approached, and her eyebrows rose. She paused with her glass of water halfway to her mouth.

"What are you wearing?" she asked. "Biker chick is a new look for you."

Harlow looked down at the black hoodie. She hadn't really paid attention, and it was dark when she received it. A ghost of Uncle Sam riding a motorcycle with a ghost of a buffalo running along beside him was screen-printed on the front, along with a logo for the 77th Annual Sturgis Bike Week. "Oh, this? There's a story behind this."

She sat down across from her friend.

"I hope it's a good one. I need a break from work talk and school talk. Midterms have fried my brain." In addition to working part time at the medical center and at Burger Bar, Shayna was taking online college courses.

Over plates piled high with fried rice, General Tso's chicken, tempura, and beef and broccoli, Harlow filled Shayna in on the past twenty-four hours. She had to edit the supernatural parts out since Shayna was human and had no idea Harlow was a descendant of a long line of witches.

Shayna threw her head back and laughed out loud when Harlow told her about Operation Get Some. Several diners looked over in their direction after her outburst. "So after Curtis left me at Silk, Ryker gave me a ride home and loaned me this sweatshirt."

"And that's it?" Shayna asked, frowning with disappointment.

"No, there's more." Harlow leaned forward and gestured for Shayna to as well. "We kissed, and then he finger-banged me on my front porch," she whispered.

Shayna's mouth dropped open.

"What?" She laughed and shook her head, her brown eyes twinkling with amusement. "You go, Harlow! That's way more exciting than my Saturday night. I swear, the week leading up to the full moon makes people nuts. The ER is always busiest this time of the month. Ugh, and you know how I don't like all that gross medical shit? Well, this guy came in, dripping blood all over the floor, and I swear he was holding his arm on. I almost lost it right there." Shayna pressed a hand against her stomach and shuddered.

"I bet." Harlow often wondered why her friend, whose stomach went queasy at the sight of blood, worked at the medical center.

They chatted some more and finished eating lunch.

"So are you going to go out with him again to follow through with this plan Curtis cooked up?" Shayna asked as they were getting ready to leave.

"My hormones might go on strike if I don't."

Three days later her hormones were on strike. Harlow's dreams had been hijacked by Ryker, and she'd taken to sleeping in his hoodie so she could be surrounded by his scent. The damn biker had given her a taste, and now that's all her body craved. He hadn't called, but they had never exchanged numbers. As Harlow was closing down Coffee Haven for the day, she contemplated going next door to Callie's to see if she could get Ryker's number from Ronan.

Harlow gathered up the trash and went out the side door to the alley. When she was lifting up the lid for the dumpster, she heard a motorcycle. The rumble of the pipes echoed off the brick walls. She tossed the trash bag in and when she turned to go back inside, saw the source of the noise. Ryker sat on his bike at the end of the alley with the engine idling, which he turned off when Harlow approached.

"I was just thinking about you," she said, scanning him from head to toe. Damn, he was hot, she thought. His dark jeans hugged muscular thighs, and despite the cold, he wore a white T-shirt underneath his leather vest. The late-day sunlight filtered through the trees that lined Town Square Park and made the tattoos on his arms appear brighter. His hair was wild and free, a true lion's mane. Ryker took his sunglasses off and set them on top of the windblown tangles. They made eye contact, and her breath stuttered.

"Oh yeah, what kind of thoughts were you having?" He raised an eyebrow and licked his lips as he looked her over. The slow, predatory perusal of her body made Harlow's mouth go dry and her panties damp. It also made her feel sexy as hell even though she was wearing jeans and a sweater, which was covered by a black Coffee Haven apron. Not exactly the sexiest attire.

"Uh, um, I have your hoodie still and didn't have your number?" Harlow had never been more appreciative of her Japanese heritage than that moment, because her olive skin didn't blush easily.

"I have your sweater scarf thing. How about we arrange a trade . . . over dinner?"

"I'd like that." Harlow stepped closer and ran her hand along his bike's handlebars, which were taller than what she was used to seeing.

"Those are ape hangers," Ryker explained. "They work better with my height than the standard issue."

"Oh. I don't know anything about bikes."

"I know. I like that about you. So, dinner. What's your schedule like—are you free Friday night?"

He tugged on Harlow's apron strings and pulled her closer until she was straddling his thigh. It took all her willpower to not sink down and grind. She placed a hand on his chest to keep herself from falling against him, but when he wrapped an arm around her waist, she slid her hand up and around the back of his neck, underneath his thick hair. With Ryker sitting down, their height was almost even. He angled his head just right, an invitation she accepted by placing her lips on his. Just like before, it was as if electricity were coursing through her veins, a pleasant buzz that caused her nipples to harden. Ryker's tongue teased along the seam of her lips, and she opened for him. Their kiss deepened, and Harlow's legs became weak. She sank down on Ryker's thigh and moaned in his mouth when the seam of her jeans pressed against her sensitive clit.

"Harlow Augustine!" The shout was as effective as being doused by freezing water from the falls in the middle of January. Harlow broke off the kiss, turning around to see her grandmother standing less than five feet away.

"Fuck," Harlow muttered. Her legs were unsteady when she climbed off of Ryker's thigh. "I have to go."

"I guess so, and it's a damn shame." Ryker flashed a lopsided grin. "We didn't finalize dinner. Are you free Friday?"

Harlow ran through her schedule in her head. She had to work Saturday night at the Country Club, as they were having a Halloween party for the members. Friday night was free. "I'm available."

"Good. I'll pick you up at seven o'clock." He put his sunglasses back on, fired up his bike, and pulled out onto Main Street.

Harlow watched him leave before turning to face her grandmother, her arms crossed in front of her chest. "We can talk out here, or you can come inside. I have to finish closing."

"I'd prefer a more private setting instead of sharing out here for everyone to witness." Mathilde gestured at the dozen or so people walking around the Main Street businesses. Not one of them was paying any attention to Harlow and her grandmother.

"It was just a kiss, Grandma," Harlow said, walking down the alley toward the side entrance. She heard her grandmother's heels as she followed behind.

"You were practically on top of him. Certainly not ladylike behavior. And with a man like that. He's not good enough for you."

Pausing with her hand on the doorknob, Harlow closed her eyes and took a deep breath. *Goddess, give me strength.* They stepped inside, and Harlow locked the door before walking back behind the counter to unload the dishwasher, which had finished its cycle while she was outside. "We're getting to know each other, and he's a nice guy—respectful even. Besides, have you looked at him?" She fanned herself, laying it on thick.

Based on the scowl, her grandmother was not amused, but Harlow was—Operation Get Some was already having its intended effect.

"Curtis is respectful."

"Curtis is gay, or did his grandmother leave that part out when you were negotiating our marriage?"

Her grandmother pursed her lips and lowered her eyes—actually looking contrite.

"Yes, that was a misunderstanding. Your father and uncle let me have it after you left. I want to apologize for springing that on you." She pulled out a chair and sank wearily down. "Being a high priestess is exhausting sometimes. I want you more involved, Harlow. You've never shown an interest in the coven, not like Gallad or your sister. You have skills and can be an asset. Most importantly, I want you protected, and I need to know you can protect yourself. What happened to Sedona—" She trailed off, and they both looked at the patch in the wall that connected Coffee Haven to Sedona's store, Shelf Indulgence.

Sedona was attacked, and a hole was blown through the wall. Fortunately, the store suffered more damage than Sedona—well, physical damage at least. Harlow suspected the empathic witch was haunted by memories. Sedona was like Harlow and on the fringe of coven life, resisting her aunt's influence.

"There are threats of more attacks to come." This statement hung heavy in the air, and Harlow looked at her grandmother—really looked at her. Mathilde Augustine was well over one hundred years old but usually looked a youthful sixty. Her hair was now threaded more heavily with silver. It was pinned up in a loose bun, so her face was in full view, revealing bags under her eyes, and there was a sagginess around her jawline that hadn't been there before.

"Grandma . . ." Harlow sat down across from her grandmother and captured her hand, which was cold and the skin felt papery thin.

"I won't fight you on the marriage, Harlow. I should have known you would react that way. You've always been an advocate for free will."

"Thank you. I thought you had lost it. 'It's time to put grandma in a home,' ran through my mind," she teased, and Mathilde chuckled.

"I have at least a hundred more years in me, missy." She sighed and sat up straighter. "But I won't budge on the training sessions.

Those are Court ordered. Besides, I'd feel better knowing you are practiced in defense."

"Agreed. That's a decent compromise."

"Suppose you won't be willing to compromise some more and not associate with that biker?"

"Not a chance." Harlow stood up. "Can I make you a coffee to go—a Witch's Brew with that energy tincture you like?"

"That would be lovely, dear. I'm glad we talked and cleared the air."

"Me too, Grandma." Harlow leaned over and kissed her grandmother's cheek before going behind the counter to make her coffee.

They made plans for Harlow to start training every Sunday afternoon and Wednesday evening. Mathilde left a few minutes later, and Harlow finished closing up. She brought the bank bag, which contained all of the cash and credit card receipts, to Willow's office. When she opened the top drawer, a pink pacifier rolled toward the front, and Harlow smiled, discovering a treasure trove of baby items like a pair of mismatched socks, one pastel green and the other white, both with ruffle cuffs. There was a teething ring and a unicorn plushy. Willow's office was always super organized before she became a mom. Now there were piles of paper on the desk and a basket of toys in the corner that had spilled over onto the floor. A strong longing to be a mother, to carry a child in her womb, hit Harlow out of nowhere. The emotion was so powerful it practically knocked the wind out of her, and she sat down hard in the desk chair.

*What the hell was that?* Spooked, Harlow shoved the bank bag on top of the baby items, shut the drawer, and quickly left.

# CHAPTER 4

"*Y*ou should, like, totally wear this one." Harlow's sister, Taylor, held up a black V-neck cashmere sweater from where she was standing in the walk-in closet. "Wear this with your dark denim jeans and those kick-ass boots, which I'm going to be borrowing. Soon."

"Over my cold dead body you're borrowing these. I'll never see them again."

"Won't be the first witch sister in history to die over a pair of shoes."

Harlow rolled her eyes. Her sister never got tired of making *Wizard of Oz* jokes, which was one of their favorite movies they watched together—next to *Practical Magic*. Taylor was over helping Harlow get ready for her date with Ryker. She was anxious to meet the bad boy who had their grandmother in a state.

Taking her sister's advice, she put on the dark denim jeans and black sweater. The cashmere was soft and warm. The sweater hugged her curves, and the V-neck dipped low enough to be sexy but not inappropriate. Her favorite bra pushed up the girls and showcased them just right.

Harlow wore her hair down. The soft waves cascaded down her back. She did her makeup, accentuating the slight slant of her eye with eyeliner. She was sitting on the sofa, counting down the minutes, when there was a knock on the front door. Taylor, who was next to her texting on her phone, jumped up and raced to the door. Harlow walked up behind her as Taylor was letting Ryker in. He was so tall he had to duck to clear the doorframe. In his hands he carried a giant potted mum the color of red wine.

"Whoa," Taylor said, staring up at Ryker, apparently rendered speechless. He did look good. His long hair was combed out and smooth. A dusting of stubble lined his square jaw. He wore a black-and-gray plaid flannel shirt, the top buttons undone to accommodate his thick neck.

"Ryker, come in. This is my sister, Taylor. Is that for me?" She pointed at the plant.

"It is. I didn't know what flowers you like, and they match the trim on your house—thought the mums would look nice on your porch." He shrugged and handed her the flowers.

"That's very thoughtful. Thank you." Standing on tiptoe, she kissed his cheek.

"Did you ride your bike here? Can I see it?" Taylor asked, hands clasped in front of her like she was just shy of begging.

"No, I drove my Bronco. It's supposed to get below freezing tonight, and it can get really cold for passengers not used to riding."

"Plus, it will keep Harlow's hair from turning into a disaster," Taylor added with a grin, and Ryker laughed.

"She's gorgeous no matter what. She could be bald and will still be beautiful."

Taylor rolled her eyes, which caused Ryker to laugh some more. Harlow waved her hand and whispered a spell. Suddenly a gust of wind appeared out of nowhere and swirled around Taylor, whipping her hair, which was long like Harlow's but straighter with red highlights, into chaos.

"Hey!" she cried. "I'm going out too, you know!" With an annoyed huff, Taylor stomped down the hall to the bathroom.

"Well, that was fun," Harlow said, turning her attention back to Ryker. "Want the grand tour?"

"Sure." She pointed at Ryker's boots and explained her house rule of leaving shoes at the door. She set the mums on the coffee table and out of Mamoru's reach while Ryker took his boots off.

Hyperaware of Ryker at her back, Harlow showed him around her bungalow. She pointed to the guest bedroom to the right of the front door and across the hall from the living room. In between the guest bedroom and her bedroom was the bathroom. When they walked by, Taylor was combing her fingers through her hair. Across from the bathroom were stairs that led to the second floor.

"My meditation room is up here. Since the ceiling slopes, it wasn't really a good spot for a bedroom," she explained as they climbed the stairs. Ryker couldn't stand up straight except at the center of the room. Skylights were on each side, providing glimpses of stars. A yoga mat, blocks, and a bolster were stacked in a cubicle in the left corner. White candles, large and small, covered almost every available surface. Along the right wall there was a beanbag chair next to a bookshelf so loaded with books, the shelves were bowed. A desk was in front of the wide window that overlooked the street and Cook's Corner Park. Bundles of sage and a collection of crystals were scattered across the top. The only light was from the overhead ceiling fan, and it was a low wattage bulb. The dim lighting added warmth to the toffee-colored walls.

"Wow. It's really peaceful up here," Ryker commented. He stood with his head back and eyes closed, breathing in the positive energy.

"This is where I come to recharge."

She led him back downstairs and showed him the kitchen. With butter-yellow walls and whitewashed cabinets, this was one of her favorite rooms. Ryker examined the shelf of cookbooks on the wall next to the stove.

"Do you like to cook?" he asked.

"I do. I hope to open run my own food truck one day. Give Tacos for Daze some competition."

"Oh yeah? What kind of food?"

"Japanese fusion. You know, traditional noodle dishes with different influences. Dishes like that."

"My sister is an amazing cook." Taylor appeared in the arched entryway, her hair tamed. "I'm heading out now to meet Paisley at Burger Bar."

"Oh, she's home?" Harlow asked.

"Yeah, for the weekend."

"Tell her I said hi and that I miss working with her."

"I will." Taylor turned to face Ryker. "It was nice meeting you."

"Same here. Do you want us to drop you off on our way out?"

"Nah. It's a quick walk. Thanks, though!" She was already walking toward the front door, her voice echoing off the walls.

A strange thwap sound came from the back of the house, and Harlow watched with amusement as Mamoru came in from the backyard through the pet door and froze. His nose twitched rapidly as he sniffed the air, detecting the new presence, and Ryker did the same thing. He looked down at the hare, and the hare looked at him. They regarded each other for a few minutes. Harlow waited for her familiar to raise the alarm if he felt any kind of threat coming from Ryker. When he didn't start thumping his hind legs and instead hopped over to sniff Ryker's feet, she relaxed. Her familiar would let her know if danger was near.

"That's Mamoru. He's not a snack," she teased. When she said that, a growl from Ryker's stomach rumbled low and deep like thunder. "I mean it."

"I won't eat your pet," he assured her. "I am hungry, though. Ready to go?"

"Oh, he's not a pet. He's my familiar." Harlow tried to keep the annoyance from her tone. Mamoru had taken offense, though, as he turned around and pooped directly in front of Ryker's feet.

"What the fuck?"

Harlow burst out laughing. "He told you!"

She continued to laugh as she walked down the hall to the bathroom, returning with a wad of toilet paper to clean up the mess.

Minutes later, Ryker was holding the passenger door to his Bronco open. It was all black and the older blockier style. Harlow scrambled inside as gracefully as possible. The inside of the cab was pure, unadulterated, concentrated Ryker, and she breathed in deep, stifling a moan just as he opened the driver's side door and effortlessly hopped in.

He took her to Fallview Tavern, a restaurant with a fantastic view of the cascading waterfalls the town was named after. The water contained mystical properties that called to supernaturals, and Harlow felt the magic humming through her veins as they drew closer. The Luna Coven had several circles located near the falls.

As far as first dates went, this was one of the better ones Harlow had been on. Ryker held doors open for her, he assisted her with her chair, and their conversation flowed naturally. They were tucked away in an alcove, an intimate setting away from the noise of the bar and heavy foot traffic areas like the kitchen and bathrooms—and away from prying ears. She learned that in addition to working at Silk, he also worked for McCabe & Sons Construction as a laborer when needed and made deliveries for CDI. Ryker was also surprisingly open with her about his past.

"I'm not big on secrets, and I'm one to tell people like it is. With me, what you see is what you get. My brothers in the MC, they are my family. I don't have any blood family—that I'm aware of. You see, my mom abandoned me when I was two, and I was raised in the system down in Tucson. That wasn't an easy life, being a kid who's bigger than every other kid his age and has a temper."

"I can't imagine it's easy for anyone." Harlow cut into her pork chop and took a bite, waiting for Ryker to continue.

"You're right—it's pretty shitty. I got out when I was sixteen."

"You were adopted?"

"No." Ryker paused and looked past Harlow's shoulder. Emotions flickered in his blue eyes as if he was watching his memories play out on a movie screen.

"What happened?" Harlow asked. Whatever the memories were, she could tell they troubled him.

Ryker leaned forward and reached for Harlow's hand that was resting on the table near her wine glass. He clasped her hand in his, dwarfing hers. Warmth seeped into her bones, which practically turned to liquid just from the simple contact. His touch wasn't sensual this time. He was reaching out to her for strength and comfort, like she was his anchor and he didn't want to be carried away by his memories.

"I shifted for the first time and freaked the fuck out. I had no idea I was a lion shifter."

"Oh, my goddess! That had to have been terrifying. Where were you when you shifted?"

Ryker got quiet and started to pull away, but Harlow wouldn't let him. She needed to know more about this mysterious man.

"I had cut school that day and thought I had gotten away with it, until I got home to my latest temporary home and Bob, my foster 'dad' was there to greet me. We fought. It was bad. I was bigger than him, meaner, and had so much anger just boiling in my blood. Our fights had never been physical, only shouting matches. That day was different. Bob shoved me. Placed his hands right here." Ryker tapped at his chest with his free hand. "Next thing I knew, pain went ripping through my body. Joints and bones made the most horrible cracking sound, like a bunch of branches being broken all at once. Then I was on all fours, and instead of shouting, I was roaring. Bob became ghost white, and he turned to run. I bet you know what instinct that triggered?"

By this point of the story, Harlow was gripping Ryker's hand tight.

"Holy shit! He became the prey. Did you kill him?" She whispered this question and looked around covertly to make sure no one was walking by and overheard.

"No. Came real fucking close, though. I don't remember the attack so much. But I remember the hot gush of his blood filling my mouth, and the taste made me feel complete. I'd never fit in anywhere and had always been this angry misfit. It wasn't until my shift that something clicked into place. For the first time, opposing forces had become one."

"What did you do?"

"I ran and kept running—mainly fueled by fear that I was going to be arrested or put down like a rabid dog. My emotions were all over the place, so much so that I couldn't figure out how to shift back. I was forced to head into the mountains. I stumbled upon a small supernatural community in the Superstition Mountains outside of Phoenix. They saw me for what I was. I mean, African lions aren't native to Arizona. Anyway, a wolf shifter taught me how to return to my human form. He lent me clothes, too. The community offered to let me stay, and I did for a while. Long enough to learn about what I was and how to control my shift. I moved on after a few months, picking up odd jobs here and there, eventually making my way to Colorado."

"Wow! I can't even imagine. Ever since I was little, I've known I'm a witch. My family history has been drilled into me—it still is."

"Yeah, I know. A couple of my brothers are shocked you agreed to go out with me. Your family might as well be Havenwood Falls royalty. Does that make you a princess?" Ryker smirked and let go of her hand but not before gently squeezing it first. He picked up his fork and continued eating his steak that was bigger than his plate.

Harlow rolled her eyes and reached for her glass of pinot grigio. "I'm definitely not a princess."

Ryker paused to finish chewing, regarding Harlow from across the table. A candle in the middle cast shadows and light across his face. "No. You're much more."

Warmth spread out from within when he said that, and it wasn't from the wine. *You're much more, too.* She wanted to tell him, but that admission would definitely move things beyond "just a fling" territory, and Harlow felt like she was dangling on the edge of a precipice already—dangerously close to falling.

The ride back to her house after dinner was quiet—full of unspoken expectation. Ryker held her hand, steering confidently with one hand. Harlow was relaxed. The glass of wine at dinner had taken the edge off any nerves, but she wasn't drunk like the last time Ryker had taken her home. She wondered if he would accept her invitation to come inside. When Ryker parked behind her car in the driveway and turned off the engine, she twisted in her seat to face him, only to find he was facing her. Their hands were still linked, and he gently ran his thumb along the side of her hand.

"Thank you for dinner," she said, breaking the silence. "Do you want—"

Before she could finish inviting him inside, Ryker leaned forward and at the same time tugged on her hand, drawing her closer to him on the bench seat. Then his mouth was on hers, and she let him in. Their tongues moved against each other in a slow dance. Traces of dessert, a slice of devil's food cake they had shared, sweetened his kiss, and she nibbled on his bottom lip, which apparently flipped a switch. With a growl that sounded more like a purr, Ryker lifted Harlow onto his lap.

"Oh!" she cried out in surprise. "Oh." She gave him a knowing smile once she sank down onto the bulge being barely contained by his jeans. Ryker held her hips in place and ground against her center.

"Do you like that?" His voice was husky, and he thrust again.

"Yes," she gasped and leaned forward to kiss him.

Rolling her hips in a slow grind against his erection, fingers threaded through his thick hair, Harlow immersed herself in the moment. Ryker's hands slid underneath her sweater and moved up her back. Rough callouses against her bare skin made her shiver, and her nipples hardened, the lace of her bra rubbing against the tight points, adding an extra sensation. His hands moved around to the front and cupped her breasts. Arching her back, she pressed further into his touch, encouraging him to squeeze harder. He did, right before he started to lift her sweater. Breaking the kiss, she raised her arms, and he stripped the sweater completely off, unclasping her bra in seconds. Cold air hit her nipples, and when Ryker sucked one into his hot mouth, she almost came on the spot. Her fingers were still buried in his hair, and she held him close to her breasts, begging him to suck harder. With each tug on her nipple, she cried out for more.

Ryker released her nipple and made his way up to her neck, kissing and nipping the entire way. Every time he playfully bit down on her skin, it made her clit tingle, and she ground down on him, enjoying the way he twitched and throbbed beneath her.

Reaching down between them, she ran her hand along his length before unbuttoning his jeans. Just as she was lowering the zipper, his phone started to ring.

"I'm not answering that," he groaned in her ear when she dipped her hand into his pants and wrapped it around his dick. As soon as his phone stopped ringing, it started up again. "Fuck!"

Harlow started stroking him and looked up to see he had his head tilted back. His eyes were closed, and his chest was rising and falling rapidly.

Whoever was trying to reach him called again.

"I'm sorry, babe." Ryker peered down at her. His eyes had changed from blue to gold, and they almost glowed in the dark. "I don't want you to stop, but I need to see who's calling."

Harlow removed her hand and scooted back on his lap so he had room to reach for his phone, which was in the ashtray. This was the old school type that dropped down from beneath the dash.

Ryker frowned when he looked at the phone and immediately dialed someone. Holding the phone up to his ear, he traced lazy circles around her nipples with his other hand.

"What's up?" Ryker frowned again, and his hand slid down her side, coming to a stop on her hip. "I'm on it and right around the corner, so I'll be there fast."

"What's going on?" Harlow asked when he ended the call. She started to climb off his lap, but he stopped her.

"Some of my brothers got in a fight at the Haven Saloon and need an assist." He cupped her breasts, rolling her nipples between his fingers. "I hate to leave when things were just getting interesting."

Harlow leaned into his hands, melting at his touch. He pulled her into a hug, and her sensitive tips brushed against his shirt. He nuzzled her neck, placing soft kisses right below her ear. Harlow slowly sat up, bracing herself on his broad shoulders.

"You have to go," she said and put her sweater on sans bra, which she grabbed when she climbed off his lap. When she went to open the passenger door, she noticed all of the windows were fogged up.

"I'll be seeing you again, Country Club. We have unfinished business," Ryker said right before she shut the door. This made her smile, and she skipped up her porch steps.

∾

The next morning, Harlow strolled into Coffee Haven in a dreamlike state. The bliss from her date had yet to wear off. Willow noticed immediately and gave her a knowing smile, her turquoise eyes twinkling.

"Oh my, you are on a totally different planet right now, aren't you?"

Harlow tied an apron around her waist and pulled her hair back in a ponytail. "Something like that." She winked.

The bell above the door chimed, signaling the arrival of the first customers of the day. Biddie Half-Moon held the door open for her best friend, Irene Beckett, who was pushing a walker in front of her. They were an odd pairing. Biddie was a retired actress who had been married seven times, and Irene was a retired teacher who had only been married once. They had one thing in common, though: gossip.

"We'll catch up later," Willow said and turned to greet Irene and Biddie as they approached the counter. Irene completely ignored Willow and zeroed in on Harlow.

"How was your date last night, dear?"

"Uh, it was fine, Ms. Beckett. How did you know?"

"It's all the talk in your neighborhood, dear. A word of advice from an elder: when getting intimate, it's best to do those things behind closed doors."

Biddie Half-Moon nodded in agreement with her busybody

friend and added, "Imagine how shocked I was when I was taking Chester for his last walk before bedtime and saw you in that Bronco."

Harlow's mouth hung open in shock, then embarrassment took over. "Oh my goddess!" She pulled the bottom half of her apron up to cover her face. Willow laughing at the situation didn't help. At all.

"I have to say it made me sentimental. Made me long for the days when my tits were perky. Enjoy them while they last!" Biddie chuckled and went to join Irene at a table near the window. This was one of their favorite spots because it gave the town gossips a great view of Main Street and happenings on the square. Those two didn't miss a thing, apparently.

"Did Biddie just say tits?" a stunned Harlow asked Willow, and they both burst into laughter.

The day only got weirder from there. When Harlow showed up at the Creekwood Country Club to work the Halloween party, her dad called her into his office. His office was almost as big as her house. A L-shaped desk faced the door, and to the left was a seating area consisting of a brown suede sofa, coffee table, and two high-backed chairs in a bold pattern of greens and blues. Floor-to-ceiling windows looked out onto the golf course, which was slowly becoming shrouded in darkness as the sun set. She walked in to find her dad standing by one of these windows, his back to her. He was wearing a voluminous white shirt, black pants, and black leather boots that stopped just below his knee.

"You needed to see me, Dad?"

He turned at the sound of her voice, and that's when she saw his eye patch and a sword strapped to his leg. He was dressed as a pirate. With his salt and pepper goatee, he looked the part.

"Shut the door please, sweet pea."

She did as he asked, bracing herself for whatever conversation they were about to have. Whenever he asked her to close the door, it usually meant she was either in trouble or about to be on the receiving end of a lecture. He crossed the room and sat in one of the chairs, so Harlow chose the chair next to him. He didn't waste any time getting to the point.

"Your grandmother called me this morning and gave me an earful about you. Apparently, you're dating a member of the SIN MC? Is this true?"

"We went on *a* date."

He stood up and walked over to the sideboard where a small selection of bourbons and whiskeys were lined up. He poured himself a glass and took a long sip. "I don't agree with your grandmother on arranged marriages. That shit with Curtis was just plain idiocy. But a biker? SIN isn't a group of angels. I know you know that."

"I know, but—"

"Let me finish." He sat down next to her again. "Your grandmother does have a point about marrying one of our kind."

"Who's talking about marrying Ryker? I went on one date with him. Besides, we should be able to marry who we want. You did. Mom isn't a witch, and you're happy, right?"

Her dad didn't say anything and took another drink. He leaned forward and set his glass on the table before running a hand through his dark hair that was threaded with gray. "I love your mother, but part of me marrying her was an act of rebellion. I know my mom can be overbearing, and keeping the Augustine line strong is important. She was on me like she is on you. I don't regret marrying your mom and having you and your sister, but I regret how hard it has been for your mom. Not being accepted by your grandmother has taken its toll on her, especially since her family is in Japan. Not being a witch hasn't been easy for her either. She feels excluded."

There was a knock on the door.

"Valerio, the members are beginning to arrive," someone called from the other side. Her dad stood up, signaling an end to the conversation.

"Dad, I hear you and don't worry. I'm having some fun. Besides,

Ryker is a nice guy. You should know that I wouldn't tolerate anything else."

"I know, sweet pea." He bent over and kissed her cheek before walking over to the door.

"Hey, Dad?" He stopped and looked over at her. "Can you wear the pirate costume every time we have a serious talk? I kept imagining you telling me to walk the plank." She grinned at him, and he was shaking his head and chuckling when he left.

That certainly wasn't the last of her hearing from family members. The next day she arrived at her grandparents' house for a training session. Her grandfather answered the door and gave her a hug.

"She's on the warpath. Be prepared," he whispered in her ear before they separated. "I want you to know, even though your grandmother and I started out as an arranged marriage, I didn't agree with how she went about everything with Curtis. Times have changed. Kids these days are much more independent."

"Thanks, Grandpa. Where is she?"

"The office. Good luck." He sauntered off in the direction of the living room with a book tucked under his arm while Harlow went to find her grandmother.

As soon as she walked into the office, a vase came flying at her, and she froze time. Her grandmother was next to the desk, arm still in the air post-throw. Harlow grabbed hold of the vase and then started time again.

Her grandmother clucked her tongue in disappointment. "You reacted without thinking. What would have been a better approach?"

"Other than getting hit in the head with a vase?" Harlow crossed the room and set the vase down on the table. With her hands on her hips, she squared off with her grandmother. "What if that had hit me?"

"Psshht." Mathilde waved her hand dismissively. "I would patch you up with a healing spell or tincture. An alternative response to this situation is to freeze the object or redirect it. Redirecting is better because it's less obvious to human eyes. However, if there are humans around, the best choice is to not react at all and take the hit. Learning not to respond, like not sending a man flying across a crowded bar, is what we're going to be working on today. After the lesson, we're going to talk about your recent date and behavior that is very unbecoming of an Augustine."

*Goddess, give me strength.*

# CHAPTER 5

*M*ore than a week had passed since Ryker had taken Harlow out, and she hadn't heard from him. Then again, they hadn't exchanged phone numbers. His hoodie still hung on her coat rack, and he still had her wrap. They had been too wrapped up in each other to even think about the swap, which was the impetus for Ryker asking her out. He was never far from her thoughts. It was more than just the sex-filled dreams that had her thinking about him, but the man himself.

Ryker had shared a lot with her over dinner. He had overcome many obstacles in life. Her initial impression of him had been that he was hot but an ass. The few interactions she had with him since then changed her mind. The time they spent learning about each other also caused her to think twice about using him. If they ever went out again, she'd have to decide to end things or to go all in. Both options terrified her.

"When did things get so complicated?" she asked Shayna when they caught up over a wine tasting at Soothing Sips, a business owned by the Blackstone family, who also owned Stone Falls Winery. Brock Blackstone brought over two flights, and he couldn't keep his eyes off of Shayna. *Interesting. Once I get my shit together maybe I can do some matchmaking of my own.*

"Do you actually have feelings for Ryker?"

Harlow sighed and sipped the red blend. "I do, but I haven't heard from him, and we're so different. Maybe it's not meant to be."

"Bullshit." Shayna fished around in her bag and pulled out her cell phone.

"Who are you texting?"

"Curtis."

"Why?"

"He can get anyone's number, and I just asked him to track down Ryker's. If you like this guy, and I know you do, then you call him. Don't wait for him to call you. We're modern women, and that's how we roll."

So that's how Harlow ended up going out with Ryker two weeks later. He had been out of town on club business, which was why he hadn't contacted her. He had been planning to get in touch when he got back. She beat him to it.

Their second date was the complete opposite of their first.

"I'm showing you my world tonight, Country Club," Ryker announced when he met her in the parking lot of the SIN clubhouse. She parked next to a row of motorcycles, careful to leave plenty of space. They were having a party, and from the sounds of things, it was already in full swing. "Some pointers before we go in. Stay by me so the guys know you're mine. They don't know you and might mistake you for a club bunny."

"A what?"

"Club bunnies are chicks that hang out around the MC with aspirations to become a member's old lady. They'll literally do anything, fuck anyone to earn that title. You are nothing like them."

"Okay." Harlow swallowed hard, processing that information. "There will be skanks. Got it."

"You're going to see some crazy shit. Sex out in the open, women running around half naked, and a lot of booze. This clubhouse is way different than the country club."

"Says you. You haven't been to the Christmas party."

Ryker cocked his head and looked at her with his eyes slightly narrowed, like he was trying to figure out if she was serious. She kept a straight face and let him ponder.

"Finally, if at any time you want to leave, say the word. These parties can get out of hand. I need to keep an eye on the prospects and on you. Just watch your back, especially wearing that dress. You look incredible, by the way."

Harlow wore a leather jacket over a formfitting black V-neck dress with red suede ankle boots. The V was too deep to wear a bra, and with the way Ryker's nostrils flared when he zeroed in on her breasts, she knew he noticed. He pulled her into his arms and kissed her. He tasted of mint toothpaste, and he hadn't shaved in a few days. His stubble had already grown past the rough, bristly stage.

"Oh, and one other thing," he said, threading his fingers through hers as they started walking toward the entrance to the clubhouse. "This place is warded. If you need to use your magic, you can without getting in trouble with the Court."

"Good to know."

Ryker held the door open for her, and she stepped into chaos. His hand on the small of her back added the little bit of reassurance she needed to move forward. He hadn't been lying. The party was the living definition of debauchery. Five Finger Death Punch blasted from speakers mounted in all corners of the room, which was an open area somewhat larger than a spacious living room. A haze of cigarette and pot smoke clouded the air, making her eyes burn. The smells of sweat, sex, and booze were also part of the mix. In the center of the room was a pool table that, aside from the bar, was the hub of activity. Bikers wearing their leather cuts indicating they were members of SIN filled the room, which reminded Harlow of a tavern. The hardwood floors were beat to hell, and neon signs for various beers decorated the walls. A few sofas were scattered throughout. A SIN member sat on one of the sofas, with a woman on her knees in front of him, sucking his dick for everyone to see. In fact, a few men watched. Around the pool table there were several high-top tables with red-cushioned, metal-back chairs. Ryker guided her toward one that was unoccupied, stopping to bro hug several guys along the way.

"Do you want a drink?" he asked as soon as she was seated.

"Sure."

"Beer or hard stuff? We don't have wine."

"That's fine. Can I get a gin and tonic?"

He nodded and headed toward the bar. Harlow observed that everyone moved out of his way. She also noticed a couple women glaring at her. They could have been twins. They looked like they spent too much time in a tanning bed and lived on diet pills, basically leathery and skinny like pieces of beef jerky. She was willing to bet money that they were club bunnies. *Back off, bunnies. He's mine.*

Ryker returned with her drink and a bourbon for him. He wasn't alone.

"Harlow, this is Savage, my VP." He introduced her to a man she knew of but had never officially met. Savage had long dark hair that turned lighter at the ends, and he was just as big as Ryker. He wore sunglasses, so it was hard to get a read on him.

"Savage, this is my girl, Harlow."

Savage's face may not have moved much to betray his reaction, but she saw his eyebrows rise above his sunglasses.

"You're Luna Coven," he stated.

"That's right."

He nodded once. "What you see here, stays here. Got it?"

"I understand."

"Good." With that he clapped Ryker on the shoulder and left. A couple more of Ryker's brothers stopped by the table, and he introduced her to them. There was Monte or "Axle" and "Trapper" or Hunter; they went by both. Hunter had a woman with him who was new to town. Izzie was her name, and she moved with the fluid grace of a dancer. The prospect, which was how Ryker referred to him, she knew as Kai because he had graduated high school the same year as Taylor and Paisley. He came into Coffee Haven often.

That night, as part of his prospect duties, he was in charge of refilling their drinks and bussing tables.

"He looks up to you," Harlow commented after Kai left to get them another round. "I can tell he wants to please you. It's not out of fear but respect."

Ryker flashed a lopsided grin. "Yeah, the kid has potential. Like me, he spent some time homeless and on the streets. Unlike me, he was adopted, but apparently it wasn't a good situation. We both found a family here with the MC. If I do right by him, he'll do right for the club. I still like to scare the piss out of him every once in a while. Keeps the young ones from getting too cocky."

As the night wore on, inhibitions ceased to exist. Harlow took it all in. Women straddled bikers, letting them do whatever they wanted to their naked bodies. Some of the women played with each other, putting on a show. Harlow stiffened when the beef jerky twins approached Ryker, pressing against him, one on each side. Insecurities surfaced when she was reminded of how easily her ex had strayed. *This is just a fling. He's not your boyfriend*, she reminded herself. She did feel some satisfaction when Ryker shooed them away like they were flies trying to land on his food. His focus remained solely on Harlow, and as things escalated around them, his hand moved farther up her thigh, slipping under her dress. She uncrossed her legs, and his eyes flashed gold at the subtle invitation.

Leaning forward, he whispered huskily in her ear over the deafening music, his breath hot against her neck, "Do you want to see my room?"

Harlow nodded, and they stood at the same time. Holding her hand, Ryker led them across the room to a hallway lined with doors. About halfway down, he stopped and opened one. Flicking on a light, he tugged her inside and closed the door, pressing Harlow against it. Cupping her cheeks with his big hands, Ryker captured her lips in a searing kiss.

They moved away from the door, and Harlow peeled Ryker's vest off. Right before it hit the floor, he caught it and hung it on a hook on the back of the door.

"Gotta respect the patch," he explained. Harlow had no idea what he meant, her focus on getting him naked. Next, she tugged at the bottom of his black T-shirt and slowly lifted it up, revealing rock hard abs and several scars. She skimmed his bare skin as she lifted the shirt higher. He had a tattoo of a lion's face covering his right pec, the lion's mane transitioning into flames that connected with the ink on his shoulder—a giant skull. His shirt landed on the floor.

With a flick of her fingers, Harlow paused time. Ryker stood before her, frozen. He was shirtless, every defined muscle on display. The man was usually in constant motion and to observe him this way was a rare treat. She dragged her index finger across his chest and down his sculpted abdomen, following the trail of golden-brown hair that disappeared below the waist of his jeans. His skin was tan and covered with tattoos and scars. His body told a story. He was a fighter, a survivor.

She slipped the top of her dress off her shoulders and down her arms. The soft fabric caressed her skin as the dress slid down her body and pooled at her feet. She wasn't wearing a bra, only black lace panties, and these too were cast aside on the floor. Crossing Ryker's room, she tossed the comforter down to the foot of the bed, and she climbed in, lying down on her back right in the middle. The sheets smelled of him, and she moaned when she breathed in his scent.

She snapped her fingers, time resumed, and she watched with amusement as Ryker blinked in confusion when he noticed her clothes on the floor where he last saw her standing. Her giggle gave away her location, and he spun around, his long hair moving with him. Once he saw her there, bare to him, it was like time had frozen still again—only briefly. It took just a few seconds for Ryker to kick off his boots, remove his jeans, and pounce.

Pinned underneath him, she opened her legs wider to cradle his hips. Ryker was already hard and ready, his erection pressed against her, heavy, warm, and throbbing. She moaned, arching so her breasts pressed even closer to his chest. It would have been so easy to have him slide right into her, notching them together, but she didn't want to move that fast. She wanted to savor this night. His eyes changed from stormy blue to gold, and he stared down her at like the master predator he was and she was his prey. *Fuck, that's hot,* she thought, and wrapped her arms around his back, pulling him closer. He growled and burrowed his head into her hair at the crook of her neck. His lips were urgent on her skin, his tongue rough as he sucked, licked, and kissed in that sensitive area. She shuddered and moaned at the sensation. She wanted to writhe, but his body weight limited her movement. She was at his mercy. He licked and sucked his way down to her breasts, drawing a nipple into his mouth. Teeth grazed the sensitive bud, and she cried out. He chuckled, the vibration adding an extra layer of sensation. Harlow's nails dug into his back, and she threw her head back against the pillow with a gasp.

Ryker continued his journey, nipping and sucking at the taut skin on her stomach. Her hands slid into his thick hair as he went lower, his breath hot against her mound. That was the only warning before he was devouring her, lifting her up to meet his mouth. With her hands buried in his hair, she held him there as he sucked her clit and dipped his tongue in deep. His beard scraped against her inner thighs, the burn on her sensitive skin an unexpected turn-on. Nerves were firing little electrical pulses that started in her toes and surged up to where Ryker was owning her pussy. His rough tongue against her clit caused her to twitch and howl. It was like their roles were reversed; Ryker was the one casting a spell and she was turning into a wild animal.

An orgasm surged forth, and Harlow exploded into Ryker's mouth, her nipples almost painful points as her whole body was consumed by desire. Breathless, panting, and boneless, Harlow's arms fell to her sides, releasing their hold on the magnificent man. Ryker grinned at her from between her legs, his eyes still gold, like shimmering jewels. He crawled back up her body, slowly, like he was stalking her and daring her to move. She wasn't going anywhere. His cock bobbed between them, the tip brushing along her thigh, leaving a glistening trail. He was huge, and she wasn't surprised. Everything about Ryker was big—from his towering height and bodybuilder physique to his personality. His presence filled any room, and she couldn't wait for him to fill her.

"I need you," she pleaded, moving a hand to wrap around his length. Now it was his turn to groan. His eyelids fluttered closed as she stroked him. His arms trembled, and she marveled at the fact that she could make this mountain of a man weak from her touch.

"You have me," Ryker growled, then captured her lips with his. The kiss was fierce and hungry. Harlow tasted her juices on his tongue, smelled her essence clinging to his facial hair, and this stoked the flames burning in her blood. Ryker moved so fast, suddenly he was on his back and sliding a condom on before he reached for her, effortlessly lifting her and settling her so she was straddling him. Harlow lowered herself down, taking him inside her slowly as he stretched her wide. It had been a while for her, and once fully seated on him she didn't move, giving her body a chance to adjust. They both moaned with pleasure, and their gazes locked on each other. Ryker's hands trailed down her body, pausing at the curve of her waist before settling on her hips. Holding her in place, he thrust up and slid in even deeper. Harlow gasped and placed a hand on his chest to steady herself before beginning to move, rocking her hips to meet Ryker's subtle thrusts. Electricity hummed and built between them like an approaching storm.

"Oh, my goddess!" she cried out, as it felt like he was growing even bigger and harder as she rode him. Ryker cupped her breasts and tweaked her nipples, increasing the delicious pressure building deep inside. She threw her head back, her long hair tickling the skin on her back. Everything was so sensitive. Ryker's thrusts increased in intensity, and his hands slid back down her sides to hold onto her hips. His grip was tight as he anchored her in place and drove in deeper. Spots danced in her vision as another orgasm washed over her. Reaching behind her, Harlow cupped his balls and squeezed.

"Oh fuck, baby!" Ryker growled, and with a final thrust, he started pulsing inside her as he came. She collapsed on top of him, felt his heart beating against her cheek. Wrapping his arms around her, he held her close, and they stayed joined together until their breathing returned to normal. As weak as a kitten, she managed to climb off of Ryker and lay down next to him. He removed the condom and tossed it in the Denver Broncos trash can next to his bed. With a contented growl, he pulled her into his arms and curled up behind her. From this view she examined his bedroom. In addition to the leather chair, he had an unfinished dresser on the wall between the door and his closet. Another door was propped open, and she saw the edge of a sink vanity and tile floor. He had a few framed posters on the wall. All of motorcycles.

"It's not much," Ryker said, playing with her hair and placing kisses along her shoulder. "But it's the most I've had that I can call my own."

They stayed there in a sated haze. Ryker emitted so much body heat that her bare skin was comfortably warm. His arm was draped over her hip, and his hand was so large that it spanned her abdomen.

"I can't wait until you're swollen with our child," Ryker whispered, pressing his hand against her flat stomach.

His announcement cut through the haze.

"What did you say?" Harlow sat up and pushed free of his embrace. His eyes, now back to their gray blue, narrowed at her reaction.

"You're mine, Harlow Augustine. You're it. I don't want anyone else. I want you. I want to make babies with you and build a home. It may be an unconventional life, but it will be a great life."

He was dead serious, and she felt more exposed than just being naked in his bed. Yes, his unconventional life was what drew her to him. The constraints of being an Augustine were a burden. Expectations were everything, and she was supposed to follow a path plotted out for her. A path she didn't want to follow. Ryker was offering her an alternative, but his declaration was so sudden and unexpected, and way too much, too soon.

"I can't do this," she choked out and scrambled off the bed, narrowly escaping his hand as he reached for her. Flicking her fingers, she froze time again and gathered up her clothes. Once dressed, she crossed to the door and opened it. Before leaving the room, she turned back to look at Ryker. His face bore an expression of hurt and desperation. She almost stopped, unable to bear the guilt knowing she was responsible for that look. He was beautiful and so soft underneath that hard exterior. She swallowed hard as she took in his scars again. A tear spilled down her cheek at the realization that her leaving like this was probably going to break him even more.

Fighting the urge to go back and crawl into the warmth of his arms, to tether herself to him forever, Harlow took a deep, steadying breath and walked out the door. The chaos of the clubhouse was on pause and eerily silent. Monte was leaning over the pool table, his cue poised to shoot a ball into a pocket, while several other patched members stood around watching, unblinking. A club bunny was straddling a man's lap where he was sitting on a sofa near the jukebox. Her tank top was pulled down, and his face was buried in her breasts, his hands gripping her ass. Kai was behind the bar pouring a shot, the liquid frozen in an amber arc that extended from the bottle to the shot glass.

Stepping outside, Harlow carried the spell with her, the coverage and duration of which was beginning to wear on her, so she hurried past the men standing outside by the row of parked motorcycles. They could have been mannequins on display at a Harley dealership. One patched member was frozen in the middle of lighting a cigarette. The flame from his lighter didn't even flicker, and his face was illuminated in its glow.

As soon as Harlow was in her car, she released her spell and sound rushed forth. As she was driving away, she heard Ryker roar. It echoed through the commercial neighborhood, sending birds scattering from the treetops.

~

A week later, Harlow was at work at Coffee Haven and on her third latte with an extra dose of energy tincture, but her ass was still dragging. She hadn't slept much the past few days. Guilt over how she left things with Ryker had her feeling anxious and unsettled.

"I'm such an asshole," she said with a sigh, setting her coffee down to retrieve a tray of scones out of the oven. The morning rush was over, and it was just her and Davis in the shop.

"Okay there?" Davis responded with a lift of an eyebrow. Sensing her mood, he had been giving her a wide berth. Smart man.

The thunder of pipes was unmistakable, and as the roar grew loader, Harlow suspected their destination and braced herself for Ryker's appearance. She'd left his numerous texts and phone calls unanswered, so she fully expected him to walk in the door. She was surprised when Monte walked in, followed by Hunter. They were both wearing jeans and black long-sleeved shirts under their leather vests. While there still wasn't snow on the ground, it was cold enough for it, but these bikers seemed impervious to the weather. Davis moved to stand beside Harlow, tension radiating off of him, and she noticed his hand hovered near a bread knife as if anticipating violence.

"Monte, Hunter," Harlow greeted the SIN brothers. "Can I interest you in a scone? They're fresh out of the oven."

"We need to talk," Hunter growled. "Somewhere private." He eyeballed Davis, who had angled himself so he was partially blocking her.

"Fine." Harlow turned to Davis. "Can I take my break now?"

"Are you going to be okay?" he asked, casting a nervous glance at the two men.

"Yeah, I'm good." Harlow walked out from behind the long marble counter. Hunter followed her through the shop, his heavy boots thudding against the hardwood floors. Monte hung back, and she heard him ordering a scone from Davis. They walked past Willow's office and exited through the rear door that led to the back alley. Harlow turned to face Hunter, crossing her arms over her chest.

"If this is about Ryker, it's none of your business," she spat, because she was disappointed and annoyed that the man wasn't here to confront her himself. Ryker didn't strike her as a cowardly lion.

"Crusher and I prospected together. We got patched together. He's my brother and this is absolutely my business, princess."

"Princess? My name's Harlow. Don't belittle me with some cutesy nickname. And whatever is going on between me and Ryker is between me and Ryker."

Hunter slammed his fist into the brick wall, causing Harlow to flinch, but she didn't back down. "I warned him, you know? You're an Augustine, basically fucking royalty in this town, and I told him he was stupid for even thinking about anything beyond a quick fuck with you. I told him that once you got over your little rebellion and had your taste of slumming it, you'd be gone. Thanks for proving me right."

"It's not like that . . . it's . . . complicated," Harlow stammered, taken aback at how fierce he was being.

"Crusher told me what happened, what he said to you right before you bolted. Bitchy witch move, by the way. Do you know how much it means for a shifter?"

"How much what means?"

"That wasn't just pillow talk or a guy telling a chick what he thinks she wants to hear. A shifter doesn't go around declaring he wants to make babies with just anyone. He wants to mate with you. He's chosen you, princess. Why? I don't fucking know, but if you're who my brother wants, I'll do whatever is in my power to make it happen."

"What are you going to do—force me to be with him? I'm not going to be forced into anything." Harlow was immediately reminded of her grandmother.

"Fuck no. Jesus, between Crusher and myself I've had my hands full with relationship issues. Just talk to him before he rips someone's head off."

"I'll think about it. Is he really that upset?"

Hunter snorted and shook his head. "You have no idea. Just talk to him."

They went back inside, and Harlow noticed Davis scanning her as if checking for bodily harm. She smiled at him as a way to let him know she was fine. It was adorable really. Davis was human and had no idea how well she could defend herself. Monte was sitting at a table, his long legs stretched out before him. There were some black scuff marks on the floor from his boots. He had a pumpkin spiced latte in a cardboard to-go cup and was stuffing a blueberry scone in his face.

"Bro," he said to Hunter. "You gotta get one of these, man. They're fucking delicious."

As soon as they left, Harlow fished her phone out of her bag that she kept in Willow's office and texted Ryker.

**Harlow: I'm sorry. Can we talk? My place tonight at 7? I'll make dinner.**

**Ryker: Yeah. I'll be there.**

She put her phone down and exhaled. At least he responded, and Hunter was right. Ryker deserved an explanation.

That night she was in her kitchen, putting the finishing touches on a batch of yakisoba, when she heard the familiar sound of a motorcycle. Her heart started to race, and she took a few calming breaths. She ran her hands through her hair and smoothed her sweater as she walked to the front door, opening it before Ryker could knock. Harlow let out a gasp when she saw him.

He looked like hell. His hair was unkempt, and his eyes were bloodshot. His stubble had grown out and was approaching a full beard. The facial hair didn't hide his split bottom lip. He eyed her warily when he stepped past her and into her house. He was cold, distant, and she didn't blame him. She had done that. Where he had been so open, he was now closed off. She hated it.

He remembered to take off his boots, and afterward, he followed her into the kitchen. She offered him bourbon, having bought a bottle of his favorite brand. He nodded and looked around as she poured him a glass. Her bedroom was right off the kitchen, and the door was open. He peered inside, and she noticed his nostrils flaring as he sniffed the air.

"So there isn't someone else?" he asked, taking the drink from her hand.

"What? No. I'm not seeing anyone else."

He nodded. "I didn't smell anyone here except you . . . and your familiar."

Ryker glanced down, and Harlow followed suit. Mamoru was sniffing Ryker's feet again.

She served up bowls of yakisoba, piling an extra helping onto Ryker's, and brought them over to the bistro table that was near the window with a view of her backyard.

Ryker moved the chopsticks to the side and picked up a fork, shoveling a forkful of noodles into his mouth. He growled in approval and took another bite. "So why?"

"Why what?" Harlow asked.

"Why did you fucking run?"

With a sigh, Harlow set her chopsticks down and dabbed at the corner of her mouth with a napkin. "I like you, Ryker. But when you started talking about babies and settling down . . . I freaked out. I'm not ready for that. We're still getting to know each other. I have a lot going on right now and don't even know if I want a serious relationship. My last one ended badly."

"Your ex cheated on you?" Harlow nodded and looked down at her bowl. "Monte reminded me that you're not a shifter and wouldn't get the mating instinct. I didn't want to listen. It wouldn't be the first time someone I care about has left me."

"Ouch." Harlow winced at the reference to Ryker's mother abandoning him. "I deserve that, and I'm sorry."

Ryker shrugged and picked up his glass, draining the rest of the bourbon in two gulps. He set the glass down on the table, and when he looked at her, his irises were ringed with gold. "I don't date. I can't tell you the last time I had a girlfriend. I avoid getting close because . . . well, you know my history. Getting close means getting burned."

"Trust me, I know, and I've been there."

He scratched at his beard and regarded her from across the table. "I'm willing to give you time and space. For you." Harlow started to smile, and she sat up straighter until he said, "Just know that you're it for me. I know it and my animal knows it."

"Now see, you say shit like that, and it makes me freak out. You gotta dial it back, dude."

He scowled, but then she saw his lips quirk up. "Dude?" He laughed and shook his head. "I'll try to tone it down, but only expect honesty from me. I tell it like it is."

"Honesty is good." She reached across the table and tucked her hand in his, giving it a squeeze. "I'll be honest with you, too."

After they finished eating, Ryker had to leave. He was needed at the clubhouse. That's when he told her that club business was one thing he couldn't talk to her about, unless he had permission.

"Why?" she asked, her eyes narrowing with suspicion.

"That's just how it is, out of respect to the brotherhood." Ryker stood up from where he had been tying his boots. When he saw her standing with her arms crossed over her chest and giving him the stink eye, he chuckled.

"Come here, Country Club."

Closing the space between them, he cupped her face with his hands and gently ran a thumb along her bottom lip. She uncrossed her arms and stepped closer, her gaze not wavering from his. She ran her hands underneath his vest, enjoying the flex of his muscles and the heat coming off his body. Tilting her head, she licked her lips, drawing Ryker's attention. His eyes, more gold than blue, stared hungrily at her mouth before capturing it with a kiss. His mouth moved over hers slowly, his beard surprisingly soft where it brushed against her skin. Suddenly he broke off the kiss and rested his forehead against hers. She noticed he was panting.

"I want to take you against this wall or bend you over your couch, baby. I want to fill you, mark you as mine right here and right now," he growled. His hands that were still cupping her cheeks trembled, letting her know how much he was holding back. "If we don't stop now, I won't be able to stop. I want you to be sure about us. When you're ready, you let me know."

Ryker placed a kiss on her forehead and stepped away, opening the front door. His boots thudded as he crossed the porch, and Harlow watched his retreat, her lips still tingling from their kiss.

*This is for the best, right?*

# CHAPTER 6

TWO MONTHS LATER

*T*he bell above the door chimed, and Harlow looked over to see a petite woman walking through, her face hidden by a giant bouquet of red and white roses. The bouquet was set down on the counter, and Willow's mom appeared from behind, wearing a huge smile. Her cheeks were extra rosy from the cold, a bloom of color against her porcelain skin.

Harlow rolled her eyes. "Let me guess, Ryker sent these?"

Reagan Fairchild, Willow's mom, co-owned Fairy Tale Florists, and she usually had an employee handle deliveries, but she took any opportunity to drop in at Coffee Haven to see her daughter and grab a cup of coffee. Ryker had been giving her plenty of opportunities over the past two months. Once a week he ordered flowers to be delivered to Harlow. Willow's mom couldn't get enough of the big biker's romantic side.

"He sure did." Reagan handed her a small envelope. "Oh, Harlow, you should see him. He has no idea what to do, and the flowers sometimes make him sneeze. It's adorable. He's smart, though, and figured out to leave the bouquet choice up to us."

Harlow chuckled, picturing Ryker, all six feet five inches of him in his leathers, surrounded by flowers. Picking up a bread knife, she sliced the top of the envelope open and pulled out the card.

*These petals are as soft as your skin. Their fragrance is not nearly as sweet as your scent. My heart races thinking of you. I miss you. Happy Valentine's Day.*

*Yours, Ryker*

A flush washed over her body when she read his intimate message written in his cramped handwriting. She'd had no idea that a romantic was hiding beneath the rough exterior. True to his word, Ryker had slowed things down. He had been busy with his three jobs and club business. She had been busy straight through the holidays. Despite their schedules, Ryker found time to woo her while still giving her space. In addition to the weekly flowers, she had come home one day to find a stuffed lion on her porch with a sweet note attached. That lion had been in her bed ever since. She fell asleep hugging it to her chest, and she would dream of Ryker, dreams so vivid she woke up disappointed to find herself alone. Other gifts he left for her showed how much he had been paying attention during their brief time together: white sage candles for her meditation room, a cookbook with fusion recipes, her favorite tea, and her favorite lotion from Madame Tahini's Potions, Lotions, and Palm Readings.

"Harlow, I'm not one to meddle, but this guy has it bad for you. While I enjoy the business, when are you going to put him out of his lovesick misery?" Reagan asked.

"He isn't lovesick."

"Honey, I can feel him pining away, and I'm not even empathic like my daughter. Speaking of, is Willow in her office?"

"No, she ran to the bank."

"Oh, I'll go catch up with her. Don't let that poor boy wait too long," she said before leaving, holding the door open for Shayna, who whistled when she saw the bouquet.

"Damn, girl, he's not giving up, is he? I agree with Willow's mom."

Harlow groaned and set about making her friend a latte. "Not you too. You know I'm not ready."

"Bullshit. You're scared of getting hurt again and of what your family thinks. You need to do you, Harlow. You only live once."

"You did not just YOLO me," Harlow teased when she handed Shayna her coffee.

"I sure as hell did!" Shayna winked at her before taking a sip. She closed her eyes and sighed. "God, I needed this. Listen, I gotta get back to the medical center, but we're not done talking about this."

Shayna left, and Harlow was surprisingly alone in Coffee Haven. Taking advantage of the rare lull, she sat down at one of the tables by the window. Harlow read Ryker's card again, then she thought about what Shayna said. Her friend knew her too well. She stood up and walked to the back of the shop where she kept her bag in Willow's office. Pulling out her phone, she texted Ryker.

**Harlow: Thank you for the roses. They're beautiful. I miss you too.**

She immediately followed up with a second text:

**Harlow: I'm ready.**

Harlow slipped the phone into the back pocket of her jeans and went back up to the counter to start closing down. She was washing one of the coffee urns when her phone buzzed. She couldn't dry her hand fast enough and left a streak of moisture on the screen when she unlocked it. Ryker had texted her back.

**Ryker: Thank fuck! I've been goin out of my mind. Do you have plans tonight?**

At first, she wanted to tease him and tell him she had a Valentine's date, but she didn't. He had been patient long enough. Instead she replied:

**Harlow: Hopefully I do now?**

It didn't take long to make plans. He would bring takeout and meet her at her house. She didn't want a fancy night out. Most places in town would be booked anyway. She had no desire to go to the Cupids and Cuties party at Whisper Falls Inn, either. All

Harlow wanted was to see Ryker. Now that she had made up her mind, she wondered why she had waited so long.

Harlow had just stepped out of the shower when the doorbell rang. Not wanting Ryker to stand outside in the cold, she slipped on her robe and went to answer the door. There he stood on the porch, larger than ever and holding a pizza from Napoli's. They stared at each other, not saying anything at first. Harlow didn't know what to say, suddenly feeling shy. Would jumping his bones right away be appropriate? He certainly was more appealing than the pizza. Dark denim jeans hugged his thighs and hung on his hips. He wore a Harley Davidson hoodie underneath his cut. His beard was shorter and more groomed than the last time she saw him. His hair was pulled back and way too tame.

"Hi," she managed to say and stepped backwards, making room for Ryker to come inside. He set the pizza down on the small table by her coat rack. It balanced precariously on her keys but didn't slide off onto the floor. In one swift movement, she was swept up in his arms, and Ryker was kissing her. He nipped at her bottom lip, and his hands slid down her back to grab her ass, pressing her against him. Her silk robe clung to her damp skin, and his touch was so hot she imagined steam would rise from her body. The material was thin, and she wasn't wearing anything underneath, which meant she felt everything. The pizza was long forgotten. They were both too hungry for each other.

Ryker set Harlow down and took a step back, tugging on the sash that held her robe closed. The knot loosened and her robe parted. His golden eyes flashed as he took in her naked body, and he licked his lips, nostrils flaring as he breathed her scent in, looking every bit the lion. He traced a finger from her neck down, swirling around a nipple until it tightened into a hard point. She swayed into his touch as he continued past her stomach at a leisurely, teasing pace. She let out a sigh when his finger finally slipped between her folds.

"Fuck, babe, you're already so wet," he growled as he stroked her clit, his calloused thumb running over the sensitive bud. "I can't wait. We'll go nice and slow next time."

Ryker backed Harlow up until she was against the sofa and then he spun her around and bent her over, lifting her robe up until it pooled on her back. The air was cool on her ass but not for long. Ryker's jeans hit the floor, she heard the tear of a condom wrapper, and then he was pushing inside her with a grunt. She gasped at the fullness and how warm he was as he slid in deep. Having her bent over this way gave him all the control. He wrapped her ponytail around his hand, simultaneously holding her in place and pulling her closer to where they were joined. He fucked her hard and fast, and she met his every thrust, until she came apart with a cry and her legs threatened to stop supporting her. Sensing this, Ryker wrapped an arm around her waist, and raising her up higher, he continued moving. She felt every ridge as he slid in and out, pushing deeper every time. Tightening around him, increasing the sensation, did them both in, and when Ryker released, his pulses triggered another orgasm. Harlow collapsed face first into her sofa, Ryker draped over her, panting hot air onto the back of her neck. They stayed like that for a few minutes, catching their breath.

Later that night they were lying in bed, clothes discarded on the floor. Harlow was curled up next to Ryker, her head resting on his chest. She traced his lion tattoo with her finger, her eyelids growing heavy.

"I have to go to Denver," Ryker said, breaking the silence and bringing Harlow back from the brink of sleep. "There's a supernatural fight club where I used to be one of the elite fighters before I moved to Havenwood Falls. There's somebody I need to talk to there . . . club business."

"When do you have to go?" Harlow asked, looking up at him. Ryker had been open about his past. This information about him fighting in some supernatural fight club was new but not surprising. The fact that he was an elite fighter didn't surprise her either. If he had claim to a pride, he for sure would be the alpha.

"As soon as possible. Would you be able to go with me? We can make a getaway out of it—hotel, room service, and no one bothering us." Ryker's hands began to roam, small strokes along her spine until he was squeezing her ass, pressing her body closer to his. They were already naked, and just that small touch . . .

# CHAPTER 7

Two days later, they were in Denver. The location for the fights that Saturday night was an abandoned warehouse on the edge of the city—away from prying eyes. Sections of the roof were missing, which meant there were patches of snow covering parts of the cracked concrete floor. Ryker had told Harlow that Fuzzbert, the troll who ran the fights, preferred locations that accommodated avian creatures, like dragons. Sometimes a fight would be held in an alley in the city. With enough glamours in place, passersby wouldn't notice anything amiss.

They arrived early in hopes of talking to Fuzzbert ahead of the fights. Following Ryker's suggestion, Harlow hung back and let Ryker do the talking. He and the troll had a history. She was fascinated by the crowd that was beginning to gather—a cross section of supernaturals placing bets on the first match, which was a vampire versus an Unseelie fae.

"My grandmother and the Court would stroke out if something like this was held in Havenwood Falls," she said.

"We have fight nights at the clubhouse. I'm pretty sure the Court's aware. The Bishops and even Addie have fought before."

"Are you serious?" Harlow looked up at him in disbelief, and Ryker shrugged.

"What? They don't have that at the country club?" he teased, and she smacked his arm.

Fuzzbert was hard to miss. A seven-foot troll with a wart-covered nose the size of an eggplant stood out, even in the crowd that contained ogres and a griffin. Ryker finally got Fuzzbert's undivided attention, so Harlow stopped people-watching to listen.

"Stray! What are you doing here? It's been a while. Are you here to fight? I'm sure I can get you a match." Fuzzbert's voice was huskier than a smoker's with a sore throat.

"Nah, those days are over. I'm actually here on club business." He gestured at his cut. "I'm checking in with other supernatural communities in Colorado to see if anyone's seen this woman." Ryker held out a picture. "Have you seen her before?"

Fuzzbert's bulbous eyes narrowed. "Nah. Can she fight?"

"Yeah. She's a known associate of the Collector. Does that name ring a bell?"

"Not that I know of."

Ryker handed him the picture. He had written his phone number on the back. "Call me if you see this woman, okay? And keep your distance from her—she's dangerous."

Fuzzbert stared at the paper in Ryker's hand and didn't take it. "Whatever it is, I don't want to be involved. Every troll for himself, you know what I mean?"

"I get it. If you change your mind, I'll make it worth your while. Me and my girl are going to hang and watch for a bit. She's never been and is curious." Ryker started to walk away when Fuzzbert called after him.

"There is someone here you'll want to talk to—he'll be fighting the winner of this match."

"Is this about the woman?"

"No. You. He's been looking for you. Claims he's your brother. I don't know. He looks like you and fights like you, too. Not as fierce, but he's young and learning. Reminds me so much of you that I've taken to calling him Stray Jr."

Harlow noticed the tension in Ryker's stance and saw he was clenching his fists. "I don't have a brother."

"Hey, that's what this guy's been saying. Might be worth your while to stick around and find out."

Ryker joined Harlow and clasped her hand, holding it tighter than usual.

"Are you okay?" she asked.

"I guess it's possible that I have a brother. I don't know what happened to my mom after she abandoned me."

On their first date, Ryker told her how he never researched his mom after he was out of foster care. She had abandoned him, and he didn't want to chase her if she didn't want him.

"And if this man is your brother?"

Ryker licked his lips and looked down at her, hope lighting up his eyes. "Then he's my brother, and we have a lot of catching up to do."

The vampire won the first match. He managed to pin the fae down and latched onto a vein, slowly draining him dry in front of a stunned audience. The Unseelie had been favored to win. After the match, the vampire was juiced and moving faster than ever. Fae blood was like an amphetamine to vamps. He raced around the center of the warehouse in a blur as Fuzzbert called Stray Jr. in to fight.

"Why Stray?" Harlow asked Ryker, who snorted in response.

"Fuzzbert has a sense of humor. I'm a lion, so a cat, and I was homeless—no family."

"Oh, a stray cat. I get it. That's really not that funny."

"No." Ryker's focus was pulled to the center of the warehouse, where a lion stood poised to fight. Harlow had only seen Ryker in his lion form once. He had shifted for her in the clubhouse right before they left for Denver, and he was glorious. The lion getting ready to fight was leaner, and his mane wasn't as resplendent. The vampire drew first blood. He moved so fast that it was impossible to see when he struck. One minute the lion was crouched, ready to pounce, and the next minute, he had a gaping bite wound on his left shoulder.

"The vamp is juiced and has an unfair advantage. Fuzzbert should never have allowed this fight," Ryker growled, his eyes flashing gold and nostrils flaring as he struggled to contain his cat.

He paced in front of Harlow, anxiously watching the fight. The lion was watching his opponent though, and as if counting down in his head how long it took from the moment the vampire disappeared to the time it struck last time, the lion was ready. Swiping with a paw the size of a baseball mitt, he hit the vampire, slashing deep cuts in its chest. Blood sprayed out across the concrete floor, and the crowd cheered. While the vampire's wounds closed almost immediately, the lion's wound was still bleeding. A sluggish flow, but fresh blood nonetheless, which served as a beacon for vampires. As Harlow looked around the crowd, she saw several vamps with their fangs dropped, eyeing the lion hungrily.

The two fighters circled each other, each waiting to make the next move. Harlow started chewing on the corner of her fingernail from the anticipation. When the vampire disappeared again, her heart jumped in her throat. He reappeared on the back of the lion, his fangs embedded deep in the lion's neck. The lion bucked and roared, trying to shake the parasite loose, but the vampire held on like he was a professional bull rider.

"Roll!" Ryker bellowed. "Roll, god damn it!"

The lion must have heard him, because he did just that. He rolled, and his weight caused the vampire to loosen his hold enough that when the lion was back on all four paws, he could shake him off. Stray Jr. was weak, though, and stumbled slightly. The vampire had managed to drain a lot of blood.

Harlow couldn't bear to watch anymore. Ryker was right—the vampire had an unfair advantage. She couldn't imagine what Ryker was experiencing. This could be his brother, and he was watching him growing weaker by the minute.

Then it was over. The vampire practically flew through the air, landing with such impact on the lion that his front legs collapsed under him. The vampire struck like a cobra and buried his fangs in deep. The lion struggled to regain his footing but was too weak. Within seconds, his eyes closed, and the magnificent animal slumped as the last of his life was drained from him. The crowd roared and cheered. Harlow and Ryker were completely silent as they watched the lion transform back to human. A naked man covered in blood lay on the concrete. Even from where they were standing, Harlow could see the resemblance, and horror washed over her. Then Ryker was running, yelling at the trolls who had come to clear the body away.

Harlow was right behind him and helped to push people aside as Ryker sunk to his knees beside the dead man. She glanced down at his face and gasped. It was like looking at a younger version of Ryker. The jaw wasn't as square, and his hair darker, but there was no denying the resemblance.

"Oh, my goddess." She joined Ryker and reached for him, but he angrily pulled away.

Fuzzbert had arrived to see what all the commotion was, and Ryker rounded on him. "You should have called the fight, Fuzz! You know that was a dirty play."

The troll laughed his smoker's laugh. "Stray, you know the rules of Supernatural Fight Club. No weapons, only abilities. The vamp used his abilities to his advantage."

"What was his real name?" Ryker growled. "At least give me that."

"I don't know it. Maybe someone else does?" Fuzzbert asked the small crowd that had gathered around them.

An older man stepped forward. He was holding a plastic shopping bag. "This is the boy's. He checked this in before the fight."

He handed the bag to Ryker, and Harlow peered inside when he opened it. There was a pair of jeans that were frayed at the ankles, a blue hoodie, a pair of black Converse, and on top, a wallet. Grabbing the wallet, Ryker opened it and pulled out a driver's license.

"Holy fuck."

He fell to his knees. Harlow looked over his shoulder and saw an Arizona license, but the name made her throat thick with emotion: Orion Pride. The look of devastation on Ryker's face was too much to bear. How cruel was fate to deliver a blood brother to him, only to snatch him away before they had a chance to know each other? She would do anything to take that pain from him. If only she could turn back time.

That's when it hit her. She could turn back time. Her grandmother had warned her against it, but why would Harlow be given the power if she wasn't meant to use it? She could help Ryker. Give him the family he'd always wanted. She loved him and would give him the world. *Oh, my goddess, I love him!*

Thinking back to the spell she saw written in the family grimoire, Harlow recited the verse in her head repeatedly before speaking the words out loud. First, she waved her hand then whispered the spell to stop time. Everything came to a complete halt. In the silence, she concentrated on the spell. She had to concentrate to go far back enough to prevent death from happening again.

With her arms raised in the air, she closed her eyes and tilted her head back, calling her words out for the universe to hear. Wind began to howl, and her hair lifted up. It was like she was caught in the middle of a tornado, and she was seeing images of the recent events whipping by. When she saw the part where Ryker and Fuzzbert were talking, she stopped.

"I mote it done. Blessed be," she said and sound erupted around her as everything around her resumed. Sweat dripped down the back of her neck, and a wave a dizziness almost caused her to fall over. Struggling to get her wits about her, Harlow focused on the conversation Ryker was having with Fuzzbert.

"There is someone here you'll want to talk to—he'll be fighting the winner of this match."

"Is this about the woman?"

"No. You. He's been looking for you. Claims he's your brother. I don't know. He looks like you and fights like you, too. Not as fierce, but he's young and learning. Reminds me so much of you that I've taken to calling him Stray Jr."

Now Harlow had to act fast to keep the match with Ryker's little brother from happening. She frantically looked around for some ideas. The area they were in was deserted. Nothing surrounded the abandoned warehouse except for several cars in the parking lot, Ryker's Bronco included. *Think, Harlow, think!* She muttered to herself, panic beginning to set in as she was running out of time. The vampire and fae fight had already begun. Then inspiration struck. Calling upon her elemental magic, she borrowed fire when someone used a lighter to light their cigarette. By the time the flame hit one of the cars in the parking lot, it was a fireball. She sent another, and a second car caught fire. Chaos ensued as supes scattered to check on their vehicles. The fight stopped, and Fuzzbert's shouts were falling on deaf ears.

Ryker started to run toward his Bronco, but Harlow stopped him. "I'll go. You find Stray Jr. Now's your chance to find out if he's really your brother."

She was practically swaying on her feet, the amount of magic Harlow had used taking its toll. She felt like she could curl up on the ground and sleep for days. She staggered across the uneven parking lot, each step requiring all the energy she had left. Harlow made it to the Bronco and sat down heavily on the back bumper. She looked up and saw Ryker walking toward her, grinning and with his brother by his side. She knew it was worth it.

"Harlow, meet Orion. My brother." Ryker beamed with joy, and Harlow felt the sting of tears in her eyes at seeing that joy.

"Nice to meet you," she said. Seeing them standing side by side, there was no doubt they were brothers. Orion was a little shorter, and his eyes were hazel ringed with gold. Those were the only major differences. "Let's get out of here. You guys have some serious catching up to do."

"Do you have a car here?" Ryker asked Orion.

"Nah, I ran here. Haven't been able to afford a car just yet."

"Good. Ride with us, and we can talk."

Harlow climbed into the back, giving the brothers the front seat. She practically collapsed and stretched out on the bench. She closed her eyes and half drifted in and out of sleep as she listened to them talking.

She learned that the brothers shared the same mother but had different fathers. Both were unknown, and the half-brothers had their mother's surname. Jeanine Pride died in April 2015 when Orion was sixteen. From there, he was placed in foster care. When he was released on his eighteenth birthday, he was handed an envelope from his mom that revealed he had an older half-brother named Ryker whom she had abandoned. Inside the envelope was a child's shirt sealed in a plastic bag to preserve Ryker's scent. With just a name and a scent, Orion was able to track his brother to Denver.

"How long have you been looking for me?" Ryker asked.

"A little over a year. I turned nineteen in November."

"Jesus, man. I'm glad we found each other."

"Me too."

Harlow fell asleep after that. The murmur of male voices lulled her to sleep. She woke up when they arrived back at the hotel.

"Orion's going to stay with us. We have the sofa that pulls out to a bed in the room."

"Of course." Her eyes drifted closed again. She didn't have the energy to keep them open.

"Babe, are you okay?" Ryker's voice was close to her ear, and she realized he was carrying her.

"So tired," she managed to say, and that's the last thing she remembered. When she woke the next morning, she was still wearing her jeans and sweater from the day before. Ryker was sprawled out beside her in his boxer briefs. Light snoring from across the room caught her attention, and she looked over to see Orion sprawled out on the sofa bed, his feet hanging off the end. He was in boxers and a ratty Metallica T-shirt that she recognized as Ryker's.

"Hey, are you feeling better?"

Harlow turned her head to find Ryker's blue gaze fixed on her. He was lying on his side facing her, one hand tucked underneath his pillow.

"I'm good. Just needed sleep." She hated not telling him the truth. They had made a promise to be honest with each other and not keep secrets. But no one could know what she did. Bringing Orion back crossed so many lines—ethical and natural.

# CHAPTER 8

$O$rion returned to Havenwood Falls with them. Ryker had called ahead to let Liam Peters, the president of SIN, know, and he was going to make arrangements for Orion to be vetted by the Court. After a string of recent attacks on the town, the Court had issued a lockdown of sorts. All new supes entering the wards needed to be cleared by Elsmed Fairchild. His ability to read minds expedited the process. Harlow made sure to stay far away during that interview. She didn't need Elsmed poking around in her brain and discovering what happened.

Fortunately, Orion passed with flying colors. Harlow offered her guest room to him, and he moved in. He traveled light and came to town with only one duffel bag. Clothes, his birth certificate, and a few pictures were all he owned. Everything was going great. Orion was settling in, and he and Ryker quickly formed a bond. Then Taylor came over.

Harlow thought that with Taylor and Orion being the same age, Taylor could show Orion around and introduce him to other supes their age.

"Are you sure you didn't bring me to heaven, Harlow? Because your sister is an angel." Orion flirted shamelessly with her sister, and Taylor took it in stride by rolling her eyes.

"I can introduce you to an angel, if you want. But he's a dude."

Chuckling at her sister's spicy response, Harlow left them in the living room and went to the kitchen for a glass of water.

"There's something wrong," Taylor said from right behind her. Harlow jumped and almost dropped her glass.

"What's wrong?"

"Not what—who. Orion, there's something wrong with him," Taylor whispered, looking over her shoulder to make sure he hadn't followed her in. "Can we go upstairs and talk? You know you can do the soundproofing spell."

After setting her glass on the counter, Harlow followed Taylor upstairs to her meditation room. Harlow recited a soundproofing spell so their conversation couldn't be heard outside of the room.

"Taylor, what is going on?"

"You know how I can see spirits and talk to the dead? Well, I can see death on Orion. He's been dead before. Darkness clings to him."

"Shit." Harlow sunk down to the floor and cradled her head in her hands. Laughter echoed up the stairs from below. Even their laugh was the same, and since Orion had showed up, Ryker was laughing a lot more. His happiness made her heart full.

"Harlow, what do you know?"

*Charles was dead then I changed time, and he was whole again, as if his death didn't happen, except he was altered. Death should remain final.* Harlow remembered the warning from her great-great-aunt Lucille's notes—a warning she chose to ignore.

"If I tell you, you have to sister swear that you won't repeat any of this to anyone. Do you swear?"

"I swear." Taylor sat down cross-legged on the floor, and Harlow told her sister everything.

"Holy shit," Taylor said when Harlow finished. "So you don't know what happened to Charles for Lucille to issue such a warning?"

"I don't. All Grandma said was that their romance ended in tragedy."

"So we have no idea what Orion might become." Taylor chewed on her lip and tapped her finger against her leg, things she did whenever she was deep in thought. "Tell you what. I'll keep an eye on the darkness that's attached to Orion. If it gets worse, we'll figure out what to do. In the meantime, he's staying here, so you can watch him. Look for any strange behaviors."

"Thanks, Tay." Harlow hugged her sister, holding on to her longer than usual.

∼

Life resumed, and by mid-March, nothing unusual had happened. Orion was even considering prospecting for the MC. Harlow began to sleep a little easier. Surely if something was going to happen, it would have happened already.

The night of the full moon and first day of spring, Harlow and Ryker had the house to themselves. Orion had gone out hunting with Kai Reynolds. The two teens had hit it off, and Ryker trusted Kai to not let anything happen to his brother.

The spring equinox coinciding with a supermoon affected all of the supernaturals differently. Where Orion was drawn to hunt, Ryker wanted to fuck, and so did Harlow. She felt twitchy and antsy. The moment they were alone, Ryker scooped Harlow up and carried her into her bedroom. The few seconds it took for him to set her on the bed gave her enough time to cast a spell that caused their clothes to disappear from their bodies and reappear on the floor.

"That's a handy trick," Ryker said, before covering her with his body and kissing her deeply. Harlow wrapped her legs around his hips, crossing her ankles right above his ass to hold him in place as he slid inside and filled her. Ryker hovered over her, muscles rippling as he rocked his hips forward in deep, steady thrusts. He stared down at her, and she stared back, unable to look away from the intensity of his glowing gold eyes. Shifting to support his weight on one arm, he cupped her breast. The heat of his palm seeped into her skin, a slow sensual burn that accelerated when he rolled her nipple between calloused fingers. This sent a straight shock to where their bodies were joined.

"Oh my goddess, yes!" Harlow closed her eyes and cried out, pressing her head back into the pile of pillows. Her hips rose to meet his—in an attempt to ease or increase the pressure, she didn't know. All she knew was that she was so close to the edge, but Ryker controlled the pace, and he was taking his time. Harlow opened up her eyes and was getting ready to beg for release when she noticed the intensity of his gaze had shifted. He looked upon her almost reverently.

"Do you know how much I love you?" he asked.

"As much as I love you," she responded. This was the first time she let him know her true feelings for him. Her family was going to have to get used to Ryker being around, because she wasn't giving him up for anything. She had already moved time for him.

"Oh, baby, say it again," he begged and thrust into her, making her moan.

"I love you!"

He smiled down at her before devouring her lips. They moved together, making love to each other, and ended up a tangle of limbs. Their bliss was interrupted by Ryker's cell phone. He groaned and rolled over to grab his phone out of his jeans pocket.

"Prospect, what's going on?" Ryker sat up, and Harlow couldn't help but admire the way his abs tightened with each movement. "What do you mean—wait, slow down." The change of tone caused Harlow to look at Ryker, who was on the move again. He stood up and started pulling his jeans on. "I'll be right there. No. Don't tell anyone else."

"Babe, what happened?" Harlow got up too and started getting dressed.

"Apparently Orion snapped and attacked someone."

"What?" She rushed out of the bedroom, following Ryker as he tugged on his boots and grabbed his keys from the table by the front door.

"I don't know. Kai said he was fine one minute and the next he was completely out of control."

Harlow froze mid-step, realizing this was her fault. This was that moment she had been dreading. Her magic had consequences, and someone was hurt because of it. More people were going to be hurt when they found out what she did.

"Let's go to him," she said. She'd tell him later. She'd confess even if it meant losing him. Even if it meant losing everything.

# CHAPTER 9

*N*ot knowing what they were walking into, Ryker grabbed a change of clothes and a pair of boots from Orion's room while Harlow gathered up extra blankets and a few bottles of water. They dressed for the cold night, packed up the Bronco, and drove out of town. Kai and Orion had gone past the wards to go hunting, and Kai was waiting for them at a gas station located on the outskirts of Eldredge, a small town less than an hour north of Havenwood Falls and near the Ridgway Reservoir. The reservoir was a popular water source for wildlife. Perfect hunting grounds for a lion and a vampire. Hunting beyond the wards added a bit of a rush, too. The risk of getting caught heightened the experience.

They pulled into the gas station, parking in a dark corner, just out of reach of the lights from the pumps. Kai seemed to melt out of the shadows. Wearing all black and with his dark hair, his pale face appeared first. He climbed into the back seat and gave Ryker directions.

"I'm sorry, Crusher. He was beyond reason and so strong. Tossed me against a tree, and I thought he broke my fucking back." Harlow twisted around to look at Kai, and he definitely wasn't his usual put-together self. There were a few leaves in his dark hair, and his jacket sleeve was almost torn off. "I ran until I got cell service and called you."

"You did good, prospect." Ryker concentrated on the road, turning onto a narrow dirt road that had more ruts than smooth sections. Harlow was glad they were in the Bronco. Had they taken her Mini, they would have broken an axle a mile back.

"Stop here," Kai barked from the back, and Ryker slammed on the brakes. They stopped behind a pickup truck that had a missing tailgate and bumper sticker declaring the owner loved the Second Amendment. "This truck belongs to the guy Orion killed. I recognize his scent."

"How far of a hike is it in to get to the scene?" Ryker asked, getting out of the truck and beginning to strip off his clothes, placing them on the driver's seat. He was sniffing the air, his nostrils flaring.

"Not far. About a mile through the trees that way." Kai pointed to the west.

"What the fuck is someone doing out here alone? It's not like this is ideal camping weather, and it's not hunting season."

"The guy looked like a hunter. Maybe he was a poacher?" Kai suggested. This caused Ryker to growl.

"Babe, do you want hang back here? Kai and I can handle this." Ryker's eyes flickered gold. His lion was close to the surface.

"Not a chance." Harlow tightened her ponytail, secured the hood of her parka, and pulled on a pair of ski gloves. She grabbed the bag that contained the blankets, water, and clothes, slinging it over her shoulder.

"I'm not talking you out of this, am I?"

"Nope."

Ryker shook his head and muttered something about stubborn-ass witches before shifting. Harlow winced, as it sounded like his muscles were tearing as his body morphed into his majestic beast. Seconds later, a lion stood in the clearing. It had started to flurry, and snowflakes collected on his golden-brown mane and immediately evaporated. He chuffed, raised his head into the air, and sniffed before running into the woods. His big paws barely made a sound.

Kai lifted the bag off of Harlow's shoulders and secured it on his.

"Ready to run?" he asked. "Crusher is on a mission."

"Let's go."

Kai could have run a lot faster, but he kept even with Harlow, and she suspected he provided protection as part of his prospect duties. She wasn't a slouch and had been running her entire life. A mile run through the woods was nothing. Ryker's tracks were easy to follow in the snow, and it didn't take long for them to reach the campsite.

"Oh, my goddess." Harlow bent over and gasped like someone had punched her in the stomach. The pizza from Napoli's she had eaten for dinner threatened to come back up as she took in the scene before her.

The man was dead. There was no surviving the devastation that had happened to his body. Parts were missing. His left arm had been completely ripped off and lay in a puddle of bloody slush several feet away. Entrails spilled out from where his stomach had been slashed open. The man's right leg smoldered in what remained of the campfire he had been huddled around. Harlow's stomach turned again when she realized it wasn't barbecue she had smelled. Sure enough, a hunting rifle was propped against his cooler. He hadn't had a chance to reach for it.

Bloody paw prints, slightly smaller than Ryker's, were everywhere. But Orion was nowhere to be found.

"Go find him," Harlow told Ryker. "I've got this. It's my mess, and I should be the one to clean it up."

Ryker tilted his head and narrowed his gold ringed eyes. Harlow knew he would have questions once he was back in his human form, and she'd answer them honestly.

"What does that mean?" Kai asked.

Harlow shook her head. "Long story. Stand back. I'm going to work my magic."

Just as Harlow raised her hands in the air to clean up evidence that would link the animal attack to an African lion, which would surely raise questions with the game warden, Kai shouted at her to look out. She spun around to see a lion charging at her, Ryker right on his tail. Orion's maw was soaked in blood, and his eyes were bottomless dark pools. He pounced, and Harlow fell backward, bracing herself for his crushing weight, but then her magic responded. Orion froze midair, his razor-sharp, two-inch-long canines inches from her face. Her magic had risen in self-defense, like from muscle memory.

Ryker slid to a stop beside her, the muscles along his side rippling under his fur as he breathed heavily. He nuzzled against her chest, bumping her with his nose, checking her for injuries. She buried her hands in his mane and told him she was okay. She stood up to show him she was unscathed. He chuffed and bumped her again, forcing her to move.

"You want me out of the way?" she asked, and he dipped his head, which she assumed meant yes. She stood off the side, and Kai positioned himself in front of her as Ryker stood in front of his brother, ready to face off.

"Should I release him?" she called across the clearing, and Ryker chuffed. She did, and the two lions clashed. Their roars echoed into the night, raising the hair on her arms. Ryker managed to get his teeth into Orion's neck and brought him to the ground, where he thrashed, clawing at Ryker with all four paws, but Ryker held on, forcing his brother to submit.

Minutes later, Orion was back in his human form, and his naked body was curled up in a fetal position. He was covered in blood and trembling. Kai rushed forward and draped a blanket over him. Ryker shifted back and crouched next to Orion.

"Bro, what happened?" Ryker asked his little brother.

"I—I don't know. The urge to kill just came over me. I've never hurt a human before and that . . ." Orion stared at the macabre scene of his creation and started to sob. "Holy fuck, Harlow!"

He frantically looked around and sobbed with relief when he saw her unharmed and in one piece.

Ryker helped his brother to his feet and handed him the change of clothes before wrapping a blanket around himself.

"You guys stay here and don't move," Harlow told them and walked around the crime scene. She found the tracks Kai and Orion had left behind when they first came upon the campsite. She envisioned the snow ahead of her as pristine and sent a ripple of magic out that erased the prints. She backtracked, erasing her own prints as she went. She moved around the campsite, cleaning up so there was only one set of tracks, and they were damaged enough that it would be hard to determine what type of animal was responsible. A few strands from a lion's mane vanished into the air with a snap of her fingers. Satisfied, she met up with the men, who watched her work with solemn expressions. They were all quiet as they made their way back to the Bronco. Harlow brought up the rear, erasing any evidence of their journey. She continued to do this once they were driving in reverse, bouncing over the ruts. The only tire tracks left in the partially frozen mud belonged to the hunter's truck.

Orion was sleeping on the backseat, covered in blankets. Harlow sat up front in the middle, sandwiched between Ryker and Kai.

"What did you mean back there when you said that was your mess?" Ryker asked, and Harlow closed her eyes, unable to look at him. "Baby, is there something you're not telling me?"

She swallowed hard and clenched her fists on her lap. "I think I know what's wrong with Orion."

The inside of the Bronco became deathly quiet except for the soft snores coming from the backseat.

"Babe?" Ryker prompted, placing his hand on her left fist and unfurling it to lace his fingers with hers. "Talk to me."

Taking a deep breath, she squeezed his hand and told him everything. How Orion had died and she brought him back for Ryker because she loved him. She wanted him to know his brother after he had lost so much already. By the time she finished telling him, she was damn near hysterical because Ryker hadn't said a single word. He didn't have to. She could tell by the way he wrenched his hand away from hers and his jaw clenched that he was pissed.

The sky was beginning to lighten to the east, illuminating the craggy outline of Mount Sousa, when Ryker pulled up in front of Harlow's house. He didn't turn the ignition off or make any movements to get out of the car. Kai did, so Harlow could get out. He climbed back in, and before Kai shut the door, Ryker finally broke his angry silence.

"That was a big fucking secret to keep. What happened to being honest with each other?" He looked at her with such disgust that it took her breath away. Then he was driving off, and she had a horrible feeling that he was never coming back.

# CHAPTER 10

The front door clicked softly closed behind her, and she leaned against it. Her entire body ached with exhaustion, and her eyes felt sticky from crying and lack of sleep. Unable to go any further, Harlow slid down the door and sat on the floor, her legs splayed out before her. Snow dripped off her boots, collecting in small puddles under her heels.

Sensing her distress, Mamoru appeared in the hallway. His nose twitched as he hopped toward Harlow and up onto her lap. She scooped him up and cradled him close. She had used a lot of magic that night, and just holding Mamoru, she started to recharge. He was her personal Energizer Bunny.

Eventually she pried herself off the floor, hung her parka up, and took off her wet boots. After putting on pajamas and making a cup of chamomile tea, she picked Mamoru up and brought him upstairs with her to her meditation area. She set her mug down on the table and set Mamoru on the floor before lighting a candle. Concentrating on that single flame, she mentally directed it to light the other candles around the room. One by one, they ignited, casting the room in soft light.

Harlow lay down on a yoga mat and draped a blanket over her

legs. She stretched out on her back in savasana pose, arms extended out from her body with her palms facing the ceiling. Focusing on deeply inhaling and exhaling to fall into a meditative state wasn't working. Images of the man smoldering in the fire kept flashing through her mind, the smell buried in her nose. She struggled to push past the vivid memories, and eventually exhaustion won out. Harlow fell into a fitful sleep.

She was jerked awake when the front door slammed shut, rattling the house.

"Harlow, are you here?" her sister called out.

"Upstairs."

Soft footsteps sounded on the stairs, and seconds later, Taylor appeared. Her dark hair was pulled back in a ponytail, and she wore jeans with an old Sun and Moon Academy shirt. Taylor's eyebrows rose when she saw her sister on the floor with Mamoru tucked into the crook of her arm.

"I knew something was wrong," she said. "When you didn't show for lunch and weren't answering your phone, I just knew. What happened?"

Taylor sat down cross-legged on the floor next to her sister.

"Oh, shit. I forgot we were supposed to meet at Burger Bar today. Is it noon already?" Harlow looked around, disoriented and squinting to block the sun streaming in from the skylights.

"It's almost one. What, are you hungover or something?"

"No. Nothing like that." With a sigh, Harlow sat up, pulling the blanket over her lap. "I really screwed up."

"Harlow, I swear to goddess, will you just spit it out already? You're freaking me out!"

"Orion killed a man last night. Ripped an innocent human to shreds. And it's all my fault."

Taylor's mouth hung partly open, and her eyebrows had practically disappeared into her hairline. "Are you serious right now?"

"I wish I wasn't. According to Kai Reynolds, Orion just

snapped. I witnessed it. Orion tried to attack me. There was zero recognition in his eyes."

"Holy shit!"

"I told Ryker how I had reversed time to stop Orion from dying and how I think that's why he's not in control."

"And?"

Harlow rolled onto her back and sighed. "It didn't go well. What a disaster, and that poor man!" Tears spilled over and ran down the sides of her face into her hair. "I need to fix this, but I can't. A man is dead because of me, and the man I love can't even look at me."

Taylor stretched out next to her sister, and they lay side by side staring at the ceiling. Through the skylights it looked like a beautiful spring day. The sky was a clear blue, and the room was bathed in sunlight.

"Do you think there's information in the grimoire that will tell us how to help Orion, at least?" Taylor asked.

"Grandma keeps that guarded like it's the crown jewels. I don't know the spell to open the case. Do you?"

Taylor shook her head. "I think Gallad does."

"Well, he can't know what's going on."

Out of suggestions, Taylor stood up and forced Harlow to stand too, declaring she was starving. They went downstairs, and Harlow let Mamoru outside in the backyard where he immediately disappeared, his white fur blending in with the snow. Taylor helped herself and made a sandwich while Harlow made a cup of coffee. Her sister tried to cheer her up, but Harlow wasn't ready. Her emotions were too raw.

Soon after, Taylor left, and Harlow was alone again. She sat at the table, staring blankly at the backyard. The house was eerily quiet. She had become so used to having Ryker or Orion there, and without their big presences, her house was empty. Ryker was supposed to be a quick fling, but he had quickly assimilated into her life. His Harley Davidson coffee mug was in the dish drain, and his muscle-building protein shake mix was on top of the refrigerator. He liked to make one before he worked out at Get Buffed!, a gym owned by Oscar Vega, the sergeant at arms for SIN. Harlow hoped he would calm down, and they could find a way to see past her fuckup. She longed to reach out to him but decided to give him some time to cool off.

After a night spent tossing and turning, haunted by nightmares featuring the man Orion killed, Harlow woke up before her alarm went off. She managed to get a decent Wi-Fi signal and used her phone to search for any news on a body being discovered. Either he hadn't been found yet, or it hadn't hit the news. Harlow finished getting ready for work and walked to Coffee Haven, thinking fresh air was just what she needed to clear her head and reduce the puffiness around her eyes. Turns out that crying for almost twenty-four hours is hell on the face.

It was only her and Davis opening that morning. Davis had become an expert in sensing her mood, which made her wonder if he was slightly empathic like Willow, and he left her alone. They had worked together long enough to establish a rhythm. Around midmorning, Willow showed up, and she zeroed right in on Harlow.

"Can I see you in my office?" she asked her. Harlow followed the petite blonde to the back of the shop and into the small office. Willow shut the door. She didn't waste any time. "Holy fairies, girl! You're like a tornado of emotion. I felt it before I even stepped inside the shop. I'm surprised Sedona hasn't been over here to check on you. What is going on?" Willow set her bag down on her desk on top of a stack of paperwork.

"I didn't realize. I thought I was suppressing."

"More like broadcasting. Are you going to tell me what's wrong?"

"Ryker and I are having some issues." Harlow looked down at the tops of her black boots, at the walls, at the pile of toys in the corner—everywhere but Willow's eyes. She knew the sensitive fae would be able to read more if they made eye contact. Willow sat on the edge of her desk, and Harlow felt her boss surveying her.

"It's more than that. You're spilling over with guilt, hurt, and fear, but I can also sense you're not ready to tell me. Is there anything I can do to help?"

Tears welled up in Harlow's eyes, and she blinked them away. Swallowing hard over the lump that had formed in her throat, she shook her head no. "I wish there was something. This is my burden to bear."

"Well, I can give you the rest of the day off. Paid. Go get a pedicure at VIP Nails or take a yoga class. Take care of you, okay? Davis and I can handle things here."

Harlow sniffed and wiped a stray tear off her cheek. "Thank you."

With that, she grabbed her coat and bag from the rack on the back of the office door and went out the side door into the alley. She didn't want customers to see her upset. Especially Irene Beckett and Biddie Half-Moon, who were holding court in the front of the shop.

Instead of dropping in for a pedicure or taking a yoga class, Harlow walked home, and as she approached her house, she was surprised to see Ryker's Bronco parked in her driveway. He was just coming down the steps from the porch, and he stopped when he saw her walking toward him. His hair was pulled back at the nape of his neck, revealing his face and making the shadows under his eyes more visible. A plain black duffel bag was over his shoulder.

"I was grabbing Orion's things," he explained.

Harlow shivered and crossed her arms over her stomach, like she was hugging her belly; his demeanor was so cold. "How is he?"

"He's fine right now and will stay at the clubhouse so we can keep an eye on him."

Harlow nodded and looked down at her foot as she kicked at a section of ice on the walkway. Steeling herself, she took a deep breath and looked back up, meeting his stormy blue gaze. "And how are you?"

He started to reach for her but pulled back. "I'm still mad at you. I understand why you did it. I just . . ." He trailed off and looked at her, softness seeping into his gaze. "I need some time. I need to figure out how to fix Orion. The little shit has been in my life for a little over a month, and I can't imagine him not in my life. Even though he's fucked up right now, he's here because of you."

"I'm going to find a way to fix him," Harlow promised, before Ryker walked away and got into his Bronco.

# CHAPTER 11

It was the middle of April when the hunter's body, or what was left of it, was found. The elements and animals had apparently feasted on him. Harlow came across the news story during what had become her morning ritual of scouring the internet while having her first of many cups of coffee. She basically lived on coffee anymore, since sleep all but evaded her. Guilt haunted her like a specter. Now she knew the man's name. Knew he was a retired plumber who lived alone after his wife died. He was a grandfather. Because of her, this devoted family man was gone.

It was Sunday, and she was due at her grandparents' for more training. She went through the motions on autopilot: get dressed, feed Mamoru, brush teeth. She arrived at ten o'clock on the nose, and her grandfather opened the door. He frowned as he took in her appearance. Harlow knew she had lost more weight and didn't have much more to lose. Her leggings were loose, and she could count her ribs through her skin.

"Surely your broken heart must be on the mend soon? You're young and will find love again," he said as he hugged her, placing a kiss on her cheek before stepping away.

Everyone thought Harlow was falling apart because of what they assumed was her breakup with Ryker. Very few knew what ate away at her from within. Now she understood Lady Macbeth being driven mad by the spot of blood on her hand. That stain never washed clean. Harlow had practiced magic she was warned against using and was paying the price.

Ryker hadn't disappeared from her life. They talked several times a week. He occasionally spent the night, and she savored those moments wrapped in his arms. They hadn't made love since that night and that was okay. She didn't deserve what he offered. Each night he stayed with her, someone with the MC kept watch over Orion. When Orion went hunting, he went with a group. The area was scouted and secured so no innocents could be harmed. He was getting worse, though.

"It's almost like he's two different people," Ryker had told her two nights earlier. He spooned her from behind and spilled his frustrations out, his breath tickling the hair by her ear. "One hour he's fine, and the next he doesn't know who I am and he's like a fucking feral beast."

Her heart broke all over again when she heard the pain in his voice.

"I'm so sorry." She rolled over in his arms to face him. "Will you ever forgive me?"

"Shhh, baby." Ryker kissed her forehead. "That's already done. You just need to forgive yourself."

That conversation resonated in her head as she walked down the hallway to the office where her grandmother was waiting. Harlow knew the only way to relieve herself of the guilt and to even begin to forgive herself—she needed to come clean.

"Good morning, Grandma," Harlow greeted her grandmother, who was sitting at the desk writing something down.

The doorbell rang, and Mathilde looked up, a confused expression on her face. "If you're here, who is that, I wonder?"

"I called a family meeting," Harlow answered.

"You did— What for?"

"You'll find out. We're gathering in the living room."

Mathilde rose from the chair and followed Harlow down the

hall. As they drew closer, the murmur of voices became louder. Seated around the living room were Harlow's parents, sister, grandfather, and one non-family member: Ryker. He looked extremely odd, wearing his leather cut while sitting on a floral chair.

"What is he doing here?" her grandmother hissed from behind.

"Wait and see." Harlow remained standing while everyone else sat. She paced in front of them, wringing her hands together.

"In February, when Ryker and I went to Denver, I did something bad," Harlow began and didn't stop until she told them everything. When she finally finished, the only sound in the room was the creak of the chair as Ryker got up. He crossed the room and pulled her into a hug.

"It's because of him. He asked you to use your magic to save his brother! He's pulling you away from your family and making you do these things." Her grandmother stood up and pointed a finger at Ryker.

"That is not true!" Harlow straightened her spine, wiped tears from her cheeks, and squared off with her grandmother. "He didn't know—not until the night Orion killed the man. I am responsible. I made the decision. Yes, it was impulsive, but it was done out of love. I love Ryker and only wanted to lessen his pain."

At her admission, Ryker reached for her hand, and she held on tight. "This isn't about whether you think Ryker is good for me or not. He was angry at first, but he's been more than understanding. I'm struggling under the burden, and I asked you here for your help as family." Harlow looked at her grandmother. "Not as high priestess of the Luna Coven or as a member of the Court. But if you can't separate the two, and I need to be punished? So be it."

Ryker growled at that and pulled her against his side protectively.

Harlow's mom rose from where she had been sitting on the loveseat and crossed the room to stand in front of Harlow. "I'll do everything within my power to help you. I wish you came to us sooner."

"Yes, sweet pea, you're our daughter." Her father joined them, and he nodded at Ryker. "I can tell by the way you look at her that you love Harlow."

"I do. I don't have much, but she makes me want a better life—with her by my side."

"Mathilde, are you going to help our granddaughter or what?" Del's voice held a commanding tone. "Or are you going to continue to let her fade away before our eyes?"

"Fine. Only because this death and your use of magic happened outside of the wards, beyond the Court's jurisdiction. However, this Orion is unpredictable and still poses a threat to our town. He needs to be dealt with immediately."

Ryker tensed. Harlow felt his muscles stiffen, and a low growl rumbled deep in his chest.

"What do you mean, 'dealt with'?" he asked.

"That attitude won't win you any favors with me, young man," Mathilde snapped back at him. "Bring your brother here and we'll assess him."

Taylor spoke up then. She'd been quiet the entire time. "There's a darkness within him. Like death never left him."

"You knew about this?" Mathilde's voice raised an octave with shock. She looked between her two granddaughters with narrowed eyes, as if seeking out any more deception.

"I did," Taylor admitted softly. "I didn't want Harlow to get in trouble. I don't want to lose her. The Court can be harsh with its judgments, and she's already on probation."

Harlow moved away from Ryker and pulled her sister into a hug. Taylor gripped her back tightly, and they held each other for a long time.

"It's a good thing your sister and I have a connection to the dead," Harlow's mom spoke up. "Ryker, please bring Orion here. I won't let any harm come to him." At that statement, Aimi glared at her mother-in-law. "Isn't that right, Mathilde?"

Clearly outnumbered, Harlow's grandmother finally nodded in agreement. "Bring the boy here."

An hour later, Ryker arrived with Orion. Harlow was shocked at his appearance. She hadn't seen him since that fateful night, and he too had lost weight. His face was more angular, his cheekbones more pronounced. They stood out like sharp points above a scruffy beard. Whatever battle was raging within was taking a toll.

"Orion," Harlow cried out and rushed to hug him, but Ryker held a hand up to stop her. He had a firm grip on Orion's upper arm.

"Don't. He's hanging on by a thread."

Without any advance warning, Harlow thought out her intentions and snapped her fingers, freezing Orion in place. "Hurry. Now's the time to do this."

The urgency in her tone was unmistakable, and everyone jumped into action.

Harlow's mom and sister approached Orion's still form. He stared ahead, unblinking. He reminded Harlow of a figurine from Madame Tussauds wax museum. She had visited the one in Las Vegas a few years ago when her dad was attending a golf course managers' conference. Mathilde retrieved the grimoire from the office and flipped through the fragile pages as quickly as possible. Harlow's dad and grandfather recited incantations while pouring a circle of salt around Orion.

Her mom explained that most likely Orion was stuck between both realms: the living and the dead. Each side struggled for dominance. She and Taylor were going to attempt to connect with the dead half and try to get it to release its hold. If not, an exorcism of sorts would have to be performed. The salt circle ensured that if they had to go that route, whatever energy escaped would be contained.

Following Aimi's instructions, Taylor placed a palm against Orion's left temple and Aimi placed her hand on the other side. Since they weren't blind like itakos of Japanese legend, they closed their eyes and began, their lips moving as they whispered, calling to the dead. Harlow and Ryker stood close by, hand in hand, anxiously watching and ready to react. Minutes ticked by, the grandfather clock documenting each passing second the only sound in the room. Mathilde had stopped researching and stood by, watching in fascination.

A dark mist began to seep out of Orion. It swirled around him like fog. Tendrils reached out and caressed Taylor's cheek, only to recoil back. The same happened when tendrils brushed against her mom's face. If it was seeking another host, the two itakos were incompatible. Taylor swayed slightly, but her mom clasped her hand. They stood a united force, drawing strength from each other, their combined chant growing louder as they expelled the darkness from Orion, who still stood unmoving and unblinking, as if he was already dead.

Suddenly the mist was free of Orion. Untethered, it hovered in the air like a storm cloud, roiling and angry, seeking escape but hitting invisible boundaries. The salt circle held, forming a protective dome. While it couldn't escape, magic could penetrate from the outside, and Mathilde stepped forward, her arms raised like she was conducting an orchestra. "I banish thee from this realm. You are not welcome here and are uninvited. Go back from whence you came. I mote it be!"

A rushing wind swirled around the room, knocking over picture frames and candles from surfaces. The coffee table was upended as the wind gathered speed. Mathilde's hair escaped the confines of her bun and blew around her face in a frenzy. She directed the wind, and it rushed forth, colliding with the mist.

Then it was gone.

Calm was restored, and no traces of the mist remained.

The spell on Orion released, he started to fall. Harlow's sister and mom grabbed his arms and steadied him. Blinking several times, Orion looked around the room in confusion at the upended furniture and items on the floor.

"What the fuck happened?" he asked his brother.

Whatever storm had resided in Orion's eyes was now gone. Ryker laughed and crossed the room, pulling his brother into a big bear hug, actually lifting him off the ground.

The joy was contagious, and Harlow felt a release. She was still burdened by the death of an innocent man, but at least Orion was back. His life wasn't forfeited either.

Harlow grinned when she noticed her grandmother nod approvingly at Ryker as he proceeded to clean up the items that had been tossed. She smiled even more when her grandmother applauded her mom and they left the room together.

"I'm proud of you, sweet pea. In fact, I'm proud of all my girls." Her dad gave her a hug and kissed the top of her head. "Are you hungry? I think it's time for lunch."

At the mention of food, Harlow's stomach growled. Her appetite, suppressed by all of the stress and anxiety, had come surging back. "I could eat a horse!"

"I actually have. Not my favorite. I think it's an acquired taste," Ryker joked as he set the last picture frame upright.

Her father laughed and clapped Ryker on the back.

"I bet you have lots of stories," he said before he left, heading for the kitchen.

"Your family is pretty cool. You know that, right?" Ryker came up behind Harlow and wrapped his arms around her.

"Yeah, they're not perfect, but they're mine." Placing her hands over his, she leaned back against him. He rested his head on top of hers, and she melted into his embrace.

"I need to thank you." His voice vibrated against the back of her head. She turned in his arms so she could peer up at him, and he placed his hands on her hips.

"What for?"

"For saving my brother. Not once, but twice."

He leaned forward and captured her mouth in a kiss that almost incinerated her panties. He pulled her hips against his and growled in his throat as he deepened the kiss, his tongue teasing her lips before slipping between them. If they weren't standing in the middle of her grandparents' living room, she would have encouraged him to do more than kiss. A cough from behind broke through their lust, and Ryker lifted his head. His eyes were gold as he looked at her. She was warm from head to toe, and her lips felt swollen. Slowly they separated to see Orion grinning at them.

"Geez, get a room, you two.

Ryker flipped his brother off, and Harlow laughed at them as they continued to hassle each other on their way to the dining room. Her grandmother had conjured up a feast of epic proportions. A prime rib and a roast turkey sat simmering in their juices. Mashed potatoes, roasted vegetables, and fresh-baked rolls rounded out the feast. Her grandfather poured bourbon and wine for guests; even Taylor had a glass of red wine in front of her.

"Wow, how did you cook this so fast?" Orion asked, his eyes hungrily taking in the food.

"Magic, son," Harlow's grandfather replied with a wink.

Her family didn't publicly announce their acceptance of Ryker, but their actions said it all. Somewhere along the way, they must have seen her love for the lion shifter wasn't fleeting and his affection for her was real. Ryker had been considered a stray at one point, but as he told her father about his plans to build a house, that he was working so many jobs to save up money for land, she knew he was serious about putting down roots. She reached under the table and squeezed his thigh as he accepted another slice of prime rib from her grandmother.

"What?" He leaned over and nuzzled her neck, whispering the one-word question in her ear.

"Does the offer still stand?"

"What offer?"

"You, me, babies, a life together?"

His eyes flashed gold, and his fork dropped with a clatter onto his plate.

"Fuck yeah it does," Ryker growled, and the vibration raced along every nerve ending in her body. Turning her head, she met his lips, kissing him, sealing the promise. What started out as a one-night stand was going to be forever.

∼

We hope you enjoyed this story in the Havenwood Falls world featuring a variety of supernatural creatures. Havenwood Falls is a collaborative effort by multiple authors.

E.J.'s other books in the Havenwood Falls universe:

*Fate, Love & Loyalty* (Havenwood Falls)
*Fata Morgana* (Havenwood Falls High)
*Fated Beginnings* (Legends of Havenwood Falls)
*Sun & Moon Academy Book One: Fall Semester* (Sun & Moon Academy)
*Sun & Moon Academy Book Two: Spring Semester* (Sun & Moon Academy)

You may also enjoy these Sin & Silk books:

*Shift of Fate* by Victoria Escobar
*Damned Allure* by Justine Winter
*Savage Salvation* by Kristie Cook

Stay up to date at www.HavenwoodFalls.com

# ABOUT THE AUTHOR

E.J. Fechenda has lived in Philadelphia and Phoenix, and now calls Portland, Maine, home. She is the Amazon bestselling author of the New Mafia Trilogy and in addition to working on the Ghost Stories Trilogy, she's a contributing author for the Havenwood Falls series. She has a degree in Journalism from Temple University, and her short stories have been published in *Suspense Magazine* and several anthologies.

You can find her on the internet here:
Facebook: https://www.facebook.com/EJFechendaAuthor
Twitter @ebusjaneus (https://twitter.com/ebusjaneus)
Tumblr: http://ejfechenda.tumblr.com/
Bookbub: https://www.bookbub.com/authors/e-j-fechenda

# ACKNOWLEDGMENTS

There are so many people to acknowledge, especially the authors and readers who have made Havenwood Falls grow since the series launched in 2017. A huge shout-out to Kristie Cook for everything she does behind the scenes. Kristie, it's an honor to be a part of this journey with you. Thank you to fellow HWF authors who let me use their characters:

Amy Hale for the use of Kai Reynolds and Lawrence Mills.

C.J. Pinard for the use of Shayna Collins.

Randi Cooley Wilson for the use of Roman Bishop, Callie Montgomery, Irene Beckett, and Biddie Half-Moon.

Nadirah Foxx for the use of Monte and Hunter.

Amy Miles for the use of Fuzzbert and the Denver supernatural fight club.

Morgan Wylie for your beta reading and guidance on developing Mathilde Augustine as well as the use of a few other Augustines and Brock Blackstone.

My husband (Steve a.k.a. Bubba) deserves props for picking up the slack around the house when I lock myself away to write. He's also a great sounding board for ideas and providing insight into the biker world.

Finally, I need to thank my mom and dad for raising me to pursue my dreams and for their constant support. Just skip over the sex scenes, okay?

# AN EXCERPT

## *Chase the Flames* (A Havenwood Falls Sin & Silk Novella) by Desiree Lafawn

**He came for his mate. She can't fathom the idea of it. But the gods' will always wins.**

Chevy Walker didn't come to Havenwood Falls to spread his wings or find a safe haven. No, he followed his natural instinct and the scent of his mate. He's got the bloodline, the power, and the money to make men and women fall at his feet, so why can't he bring one willful woman to heel? Chevy can play the nice guy. He hasn't broken the rules once—but even nice guys have their limits.

Hannah likes men, but not well enough to give up her freedom. Not like her ancestor, River, who had her power locked away in an amulet by a dusty old vampire. Hannah has her life in order and control of the heat and flames. She might not know the origins of her power, but she knows her future, and it does not include a cocky, controlling stranger—no matter that his voice gives her chills or how delicious he smells.

But Chevy's lineage could be the key to filling in the blank spaces in Hannah's history. She can choose to accept him as her mate willingly, or she can allow the madness to consume her until there's nothing left of either of them but a spark. For that seems to be the will of the gods.

# CHASE THE FLAMES

## BY DESIREE LAFAWN

I'd never witnessed a bar fight before. As someone in my position, I've had my share of struggles. I've fought for power, position, and authority. I've fought for my freedom in an oppressive establishment, but I'd never even seen a bar fight. Until now.

I'd also never seen a woman that small throw a punch hard enough to knock a guy twice her size clean off his feet. He went from towering over her as she sat in a chair, talking quietly with her young, curlyhaired companion, to flying through the air about eight feet away. It happened so fast, I might have missed the entire exchange if I hadn't already been staring at her. For reasons unrelated to her fight.

If the caterpillar from *Alice in Wonderland* reincarnated as a hippy, I was surely looking right at him. I'd been in Havenwood Falls for two days, and while the owner of the Haven Saloon wasn't the weirdest person I'd met so far, he certainly was one of the most interesting. Bent Brent—I couldn't get a read on him. Human for sure, but there was no way he didn't know that half his clientele was of the supernatural variety. Not when he had a shelf behind the bar, so low I almost couldn't see it, of bottles with labels that didn't have a damn thing to do with human consumption.

It couldn't be just the circle of smoke that wafted around his head that made him so mellow he didn't blink at the shocking violence happening right in front of him. That home roll clamped between his teeth might have been a special blend, but there wasn't a sticky on this earth that could make a man that relaxed. No, Bent Brent had the laid-back air of a man who had *seen some things*.

He didn't even quirk an eyebrow at the five-foot-nothing redhead who just sent a six-foot two-hundred-fifty-pound meat pinwheel somersaulting across the bar.

"You probably want to move over a hair." I barely heard the words as the barkeep mumbled them around the smoke still tucked between his lips.

The big guy landed right next to me, and if I'd been any slower, I would have taken a boot to the kneecaps as he sprawled haphazardly on his back, legs folded up against the bar wall and one arm flung over his face.

"Damnit, Hannah I wasn't ready." For a man who just had his innards reorganized, he sure had record recovery time. He was already on his feet and lumbering back to the table before I had time to blink.

"I wasn't aware there was a time frame I was supposed to operate in." The voice rang out merrily from across the room. Light, and maybe just the tiniest bit musical, if I wanted to admit my bias. "You said take my best shot. I took it." She walked toward where the man stood, mere feet from me, and patted the bigger man on the arm as she passed him. He flinched, but grinned good-naturedly.

"You're too little to hit so hard."

"I work out." She smiled back at him and laughed, making her way to my side of the room.

She reached the bar then, and the beast inside me, the one I shared my soul with, raised his head and eyed her hungrily. She was the one we were looking for. The one we came all the way here to find. This slip of a woman with fiery orange anime hair and a mean right hook was my mate.

I'd been following the pull for a few hundred miles. I would know her anywhere. That's the power of the mate bond. Genetics. Or at least that was what I'd found out, after a lifetime of thinking it was just heresy.

The mate bond existed, and every lie the elders of my caste had told me fell at our feet. They raised us to think we weren't like other shifters. No, our lineage was special; our sacred blood fragile. The elders paired us off to make sure we did everything in our power to perpetuate the continuation of our species.

At least that was the doctrine.

But I knew the truth now. And someday the rest of them would too, but before I could blow the conspiracy of the elders of my kind wide open, I had to come back with proof. Ranting like a lunatic and railing against the system about the medication we took to "stabilize our fragile blood and moody beasts" would not convince anyone to stop taking the meds. No. I had to find and bring them proof, and the only way to do that was to make an example out of myself. The only way to do that was to leave the family.

If it weren't for my best friend Baz, next in line for an elder position, I never would have made it. But here I was, clean from a lifetime of suppression drugs and feeling the pull of the mate bond for the first time in my life. It dragged me all the way across several states and up a mountainside. A feeling so strong I couldn't ignore it —neither could my beast. Dreams of smoke and ashes plagued me every night, but not nightmares. No, these dreams were filled with scents and sounds so pleasing I thought I would go crazy trying to find their source.

And then at the bottom of the mountain I'd caught her scent. The scent of my mate.

There was one for me, and she was right there in front of me. Everything I'd suffered in my thirty-some years of existence had led me right to this point. The lies, the grand plan, the breaking away to find out the truth—it all led up to this moment.

She was perfect.

"BB, can I get a . . ." Her words trailed off, and it was in that moment I knew. I didn't even have to see her sniff the air to tell the exact second she caught my scent. I wondered what I smelled like to her? I knew what she smelled like to me. Burning wood. Campfire. Fall leaves.

Sex.

That was there too, the underlying intent. When two mates found each other, the result could be explosive at first, as the desire to connect became overpowering. At least that's what I'd read. I'd been suppressed by the system of lies I was raised in, so I didn't have much time to process the information. But my rock-hard response had me believing that small bit of lore I'd uncovered before I'd made the move. Before I'd started my hunt.

I needed to touch her.

I also needed to not be a creep about it.

"What smells so good?" I didn't know who she was asking, but she was looking right at me, the dark pupils in her amber eyes expanding and contracting. Target acquired; I was in her sights. "Hello." She licked her lips, and my blood sang in response.

I'd done all of the research I could do with the limited resources available, but every bit of information I found pointed to how overwhelming and absolute the instant attraction and pull would be. I was prepared to exert iron control over my emotions and physical desires while I navigated the treacherous path of my mission. It didn't occur to me she would be just as affected as I was.

She touched my arm and I knew I would follow her anywhere.

"I'm Hannah. You're new here. What's your name? Where are you staying?" Those amber eyes studied me, and a light flickered there, a candle burning, nothing more.

That was a lot of questions to answer for someone who wasn't even looking me in the eye. I wondered if she expected my dick to answer, because her gaze moved down to my zipper and stuck there. If she didn't knock it off, I would give her something to look at, all right.

"I'm Chevy Walker, I'm from Arizona, and I'm staying at Whisper Falls Inn." Was she at the bar with anyone? Would she introduce me to them? What was her next move? Her hand was still on my arm, and I swear I could feel her heartbeat through her fingers and the fabric of my shirt—through the air even.

"The inn? That's close. Walking-distance close. That's good. Let's go there." And she turned toward the door, her hand still on my arm, steering me toward the exit with no other option but to follow her. Because I *had* to follow her. I inhaled her scent deep into my lungs and imprinted her on my body. The beast inside me did the same. This whole trip—this whole mission—was for her. It couldn't be this easy.

But it was that easy.

No one followed us out of the bar. No one raised an eyebrow at either of us as we left. I'd only been in Havenwood Falls for two days, and barring the sweet old ladies I met on my way into town, it seemed like a real *mind your own damn business* type of place.

But even a place where everyone minded their own probably wouldn't look the other way regarding two people boning in the street. Which is what *almost happened.* As soon as the old-fashioned batwing bar doors closed behind us, she was on me, hands grabbing, lips teasing. She went for my ear first, and I barely had time to catch her before she crawled up my body and stayed there, legs wrapped around my waist.

She weighed nothing.

She felt amazing.

For someone so slim and lithe, her curves were as soft as I thought they would be, and her small teeth nibbling on my earlobe froze the breath in my lungs. I had to lock my legs to keep from stumbling. The urgent need to possess her punched through me; I'd felt nothing so strong in my life. The books did not cover this kind of need. If I didn't strengthen my willpower, I would nail her in the street, and by the sounds coming out of her throat and the way her fingers dug into the flesh of my arms, Hannah would accept it willingly. The only other option was to hurry—or come in my pants like a first-timer.

I didn't have the heart or the willpower to push her away from me, so I did the next best thing I could think of. "Can you run?"

She grinned like a lunatic.

Turns out, she could.

There was no one at the inn, not in the hallways and not working the desk. Or at least it seemed that way as we escaped to the room, but most likely we were too wrapped up in each other to notice any innocent bystanders. I don't even remember taking the stairs, but I remember the sound of her small gasping breaths. Would she make the same sounds as we mated? I couldn't wait to find out. We made it, after an eternity of keeping our hands to ourselves, and I shut the door to the suite I rented, the lock clicking in place with a sinful finality.

Finally. I could touch her. Peel back the layers of clothing and savor with touch and taste the skin laid bare. There wasn't a spot of visible flesh I didn't want to bite, and some I couldn't see that I wanted to put my mouth on.

I don't know why I thought I would be in control.

She went straight for my pants. And by went straight for them, I mean she ripped them right down the seam on one side and tore them off. Hannah was *strong*, and a lesser man would have been terrified at the ferocity with which she disrobed me.

But I was not a lesser man, and there was nothing about Hannah I couldn't handle.

I appreciated her little gasp of happy surprise though, when she saw I went commando. Underwear was too restricting, and the less I had to remove before shifting the better. But she didn't know that. She knew none of it yet.

*She will.* My beast huffed in agreement.

"Hannah, slow down."

Her busy hands stopped briefly, and she uttered a small grunt of impatience. "Why?"

*Why?* I didn't know why. I couldn't shake off the lust-filled haze long enough to think of a single good reason she shouldn't do exactly what she wanted to me. But while I was fumbling for the words for what I was feeling, she dropped to her knees and slid her warm, moist mouth over the tip of my cock, stopping time completely.

"Hannah. Stop." I was as firm as possible, which was difficult with her mouth wrapped around my shaft and her hand cupping my balls. "Woman. Please."

Her only answer was to close her mouth and swallow, the muscles of her throat working to send me to the brink of destruction. In the space of a few mind-blowing seconds of pleasure, I realized two things: Hannah was a woman used to doing whatever she wanted whenever she wanted, as was obvious by her refusal to get off her knees and spit out my dick; and I was so turned on by the thought of taming her, I almost let her get away with it.

But I couldn't. Establishing dominance early was important for me and my beast. It was our nature to be alpha, and giving up the reins of control during sex was not acceptable—at least not the first time. Once we got to know our mate a little better, there would be plenty of time for experimenting, but right now she needed to stop or I was going to come, and Hannah would have made the first power move. Reaching down, I fisted my hands in her wild hair and tugged—not hard enough to sting, just enough to get her attention.

"Hannah, stop." I repeated my earlier order.

I don't know if she planned on obeying, but I broke her concentration enough for her to let go of me, and I hauled her back to her feet, spinning us both around, and pressing her back against the door so hard, she gasped with pleasure.

*Oh? So Hannah likes to be handled a little bit.* I squirreled the information away for future enjoyment.

"I'm the alpha here." I emphasized my point by gripping her hands and holding them above her head, my other hand resting lightly against her throat.

"Oh yes." The words were the barest of whispers. I bet she didn't even know she said them.

"I'm going to fuck you, Hannah, and you're going to look me in the eye while I do it." The scent of her arousal intensified—my filthy words pleased her. She wiggled against me but I didn't pull away—didn't allow her an inch of room. There was no way she didn't want me to pin her down, not with her eyes closed and that peaceful fucking smile on her face. Screw it. I'd held back for long enough. There was no one here to see or interrupt us. The beast inside me demanded I finish what the mate bond started. She was right there; no need to wait any longer. Hannah reared back against my restraining hands not because she didn't want me touching her, but because she wanted to hang on to that role of being in control.

*Not today.* Not right now. She had to submit; my beast wouldn't allow anything else. We were just animals, after all.

"Tell me what you want me to do to you, Hannah. Tell me every dirty thing going on in that mind, right now." Still holding her hands immobile, I blazed a wet trail with my tongue from her ear to her collarbone, pausing at intervals to suck the flesh of her neck, bringing the blood to the surface. Leaving hickeys was juvenile. Maybe. But I would mark her as mine for anyone to see and to hell with the consequences. She was *my* mate. *Mine.* She wriggled, and I bit her firmly on the shoulder, wrangling a shriek of pleasure from her lips.

Hannah liked it rough. Excellent.

Purchase *Chase the Flames* where books are sold.